PRINCIPLES
OF
CLINICAL RESEARCH

Edited By

Dr. R. B. GHOOI

Professor,
Drug Discovery and Clinical Research
Symbiosis School of Biomedical Sciences,
Lavale.
Pune - 412 115, India

NIRALI PRAKASHAN

N1651

PRINCIPLES OF CLINICAL RESEARCH   ISBN: 978-93-82448-39-6

First Edition : **January, 2013**

© : **Author**

Published By :

NIRALI PRAKASHAN
Abhyudaya Pragati, 1312, Shivaji Nagar,
Off J.M. Road, PUNE – 411005
Tel - (020) 25512336/37/39, Fax - (020) 25511379
Email : niralipune@pragationline.com

DISTRIBUTION CENTRES

PUNE

Nirali Prakashan
119, Budhwar Peth, Jogeshwari Mandir Lane
Pune 411002, Maharashtra
Tel : (020) 2445 2044, 66022708
Fax : (020) 2445 1538
Email : bookorder@pragationline.com

MUMBAI

Nirali Prakashan
385, S.V.P. Road, Rasdhara Co-op. Hsg. Society Ltd.,
Girgaum, Mumbai 400004, Maharashtra
Tel : (022) 2385 6339 / 2386 9976,
Fax : (022) 2386 9976
Email : niralimumbai@pragationline.com

DISTRIBUTION BRANCHES

NAGPUR

Pratibha Book Distributors
Above Maratha Mandir, Shop No. 3, First Floor,
Rani Jhanshi Square, Sitabuldi, Nagpur 440012,
Maharashtra, Tel : (0712) 254 7129

BENGALURU

Pragati Book House
House No. 1, Sanjeevappa Lane, Avenue Road Cross,
Opp. Rice Church, Bengaluru – 560002.
Tel : (080) 64513344, 64513355,
Mob : 9880582331, 9845021552
Email:bharatsavla@yahoo.com

JALGAON

Nirali Prakashan
34, V. V. Golani Market, Navi Peth, Jalgaon 425001,
Maharashtra, Tel : (0257) 222 0395
Mob : 94234 91860

KOLHAPUR

Nirali Prakashan
New Mahadvar Road,
Kedar Plaza, 1st Floor Opp. IDBI Bank
Kolhapur 416 012, Maharashtra. Mob : 9855046155

CHENNAI
Pragati Books
9/1, Montieth Road, Behind Taas Mahal, Egmore,
Chennai 600008 Tamil Nadu, Tel : (044) 6518 3535,
Mob : 94440 01782 / 98450 21552 / 98805 82331
Email : bharatsavla@yahoo.com

RETAIL OUTLETS
PUNE

Pragati Book Centre
157, Budhwar Peth, Opp. Ratan Talkies,
Pune 411002, Maharashtra
Tel : (020) 2445 8887 / 6602 2707, Fax : (020) 2445 8887

Pragati Book Centre
Amber Chamber, 28/A, Budhwar Peth,
Appa Balwant Chowk, Pune : 411002, Maharashtra,
Tel : (020) 20240335 / 66281669
Email : pbcpune@pragationline.com

Pragati Book Centre
676/B, Budhwar Peth, Opp. Jogeshwari Mandir,
Pune 411002, Maharashtra
Tel : (020) 6601 7784 / 6602 0855

Pragati Book Centre
917/22, Sai Complex, F.C. Road, Opp. Hotel Roopali,
Shivajinagar, Pune 411004, Maharashtra
Tel : (020) 2566 3372 / 6602 2728

PBC Book Sellers & Stationers
152, Budhwar Peth, Pune 411002, Maharashtra
Tel : (020) 2445 2254 / 6609 2463

MUMBAI
Pragati Book Corner
Indira Niwas, 111 - A, Bhavani Shankar Road, Dadar (W), Mumbai 400028, Maharashtra
Tel : (022) 2422 3526 / 6662 5254
Email : pbcmumbai@pragationline.com

www.pragationline.com   info@pragationline.com

PREFACE

The clinical research industry in India is maturing, after a 40 year long hiatus. India is emerging out of the shadows, so far as new drug development is concerned. The needs of the industry in terms of personnel, training and resources are therefore rising. Clinical research is now a part of the syllabi at a number of courses at both bachelor's and master's levels. Many students are now choosing this as a career, and hence there will be a need for teachers too. There is also an urgent need for a textbook of clinical research for the use of students and professionals alike.

The best option in this milieu, would be a book where the expertise of a number of people is pooled, giving the readers the advantage of learning and experience of people from academics and the industry. The present book is our first step in this direction. In this book we have authors from the pharmaceutical and CRO industry, research institutes and educational institutes. With a multi author book one hopes to have continuity, when authors from the present lot retire, they will be replaced by younger people and hopefully the book will continue to be published for years to come.

When one looks back at clinical research over the last three decades, it is changes that have come about, that strike us the most. There were no CROs, CRAs or co-ordinators to help in clinical trials. Most studies involved only one of two individuals, the sponsor, the Medical Advisor and the investigator. The industry looked on clinical research with an indulgent eye, at times as an unavoidable expenditure. The scenario has changed considerably. The industry realizes the importance of clinical research, and the marketing colleagues don't look at us, to provide favourable data for their promotional material.

The pharmaceutical industry based overseas initially was wary about studies conducted in India. From the sheer volume of work that is flowing in, one feels that their confidence is rising. As more and more studies are initiated in the country, new issues are cropping up. The regulators in India are tackling each issue as it emerges and the industry reacts with either a sense of relief or disappointment. There is still need for more understanding among the different stakeholders in research.

This book will hopefully provide students with the much needed Indian perspective of clinical research. It is hoped that more and more professionals from this field will contribute to future editions to make this book a comprehensive source of information.

Dr. R. B. Ghooi

Professor,
Drug Discovery and Clinical Research
Symbiosis School of Biomedical Sciences,
Lavale.
Pune - 412 115, India

CONTENTS

***

Chapter ... 1

ORIENTATION TO DRUG RESEARCH

"Advances in medicine and agriculture have saved vastly more lives than have been lost in all the wars in history."
Carl Sagan

NOMENCLATURE AND STANDARDS FOR DRUGS

Introduction

In order to meet the multiple objectives of conformity, standardization, esoteric values of manufactures, research and replication and quality assurance, drugs are classified into various groups.

Objectives

1. To discuss the accepted approach to drug classification.
2. To distinguish between the various drug names; chemical, generic and trade.
3. To identify the reason for the preference of generic names of drugs over their chemical and trade names.

Drug Nomenclature/Naming of Drugs

This is a system of classification of drugs. The three name classifications of drugs are: the Chemical/Molecular/Scientific name, the Generic or Non-Proprietary name, and the Brand or Trade or Proprietary name.

Chemical names; convenient components for laboratory inventions and replication; assures quality, Image provided by courtesy of commons-commons.wikimedia.org

- **Chemical Name:** It depicts the chemical/molecular structure of the drug in terms of atoms and molecules accompanied by a diagram of the chemical structure. They are long and can be clumsy and are useful to only a select few, technically-qualified personnel. For example, acetyl-p-amino-phenol is the chemical name for Paracetamol and the image above gives the structure of Vitamin C.

- **Non-Proprietary/Generic/Approved Name:** This is the abbreviated and approved name of the drug. It is the official medical name assigned by the producer in collaboration with the Food and Drugs Board and the Nomenclature Committee. Since they have the same chemical structure, generic names may be used by any interested organisation irrespective of the manufacturer and also helps to avoid the dilemma of naming the drug. A generic drug name is not capitalized; for example, aluminum hydroxide.

- **Proprietary/Trade/Brand Name:** These are names given to the drug by the manufacturing and marketing company. They are copyrighted terms selected by a manufacturer to designate a particular product. Copyright laws prevent any other person or entity from using the name, and other laws prevent pharmacists from substituting chemically-identical products for the trade name article. In most cases, one drug could have many trade/brand names e.g. Acetaminophen has about 30 trade names. Some of them are Tylenol, Paramol, Panadol, Calpol etc.

DEFINITIONS IN PHARMACOLOGY

1. **Absorption:** The movement of drug particles from the GI tract to body fluids.
2. **Active absorption:** Requires a carrier, an enzyme or a protein to move the drug against a concentration gradient.
3. **Adverse reactions:** More severe than side effects, always undesirable.
4. **Agonists:** Drugs that produce a response.
5. **Antagonists:** Drugs that block a response.
6. **Bioavailability:** (Subcategory of absorption) the percentage of a drug that reaches systemic circulation.
7. **Disintegration:** The breakdown of a tablet into smaller particles.
8. **Dissolution:** The dissolving of smaller particles in the GI fluid prior to absorption.
9. **Distribution:** The process by which a drug becomes available to body fluids and body tissue.
10. **Duration of action:** The length of time the drug has a pharmacologic effect.
11. **First-pass effect:** The process in which a drug passes to the liver first.
12. **Half-life:** The time it takes for one-half of the drug concentration to be eliminated; a drug goes through several half-lives before 90% of the drug is eliminated.
13. **Loading dose:** Large initial dose given to achieve a rapid minimum effective concentration in the plasma.
14. **Onset:** The time it takes to reach the minimum effective concentration (MEC) after a drug is administered.
15. **Passive absorption:** Occurs mostly by diffusion.

16. **Peak action:** The point at which a drug reaches it's highest blood or plasma concentration.

17. **Peak drug level:** The highest plasma concentration of a drug at a specific time.

18. **Pharmaceutics:** The first phase of drug action.

19. **Pharmacodynamic phase:** The study of drug concentration and it's effects on the body.

20. **Pharmacogenetics:** The effect of a drug action that varies from a predicted drug response because of genetic factors or hereditary influence.

21. **Pharmacokinetic:** The process of drug movement to achieve drug action.

22. **Pinocytosis:** The process by which cells carry a drug across the cell membrane by engulfing the particles.

23. **Protein-binding effect:** The portion of a drug that is bound is inactive because it is not available to the receptors.

24. **Side-effects:** Physiological effects unrelated to desired drug effects.

25. **Therapeutic range:** Drug concentration in plasma should be between the minimum effective concentration in the plasma and the minimum toxic concentration.

26. **Trough level:** The lowest plasma concentration of a drug. The trough level measures the rate at which a drug is eliminated; levels are drawn immediately before the next dose of a drug is given.

ABSORPTION, DISTRIBUTION, METABOLISM AND EXCRETION OF DRUGS

The four processes involved when a drug is taken are absorption, distribution, metabolism and elimination or excretion (ADME).

Pharmacokinetics is the way the body reacts to the drug once it is administered. It is the measure of the rate (kinetics) of absorption, distribution, metabolism and excretion (ADME). All the four processes involve drug movement across membranes. To be able to cross the membranes, it is necessary that the drugs should be able to dissolve directly into the lipid bi-layer of the membrane; hence lipid-soluble drugs cross directly whereas drugs that are polar do not.

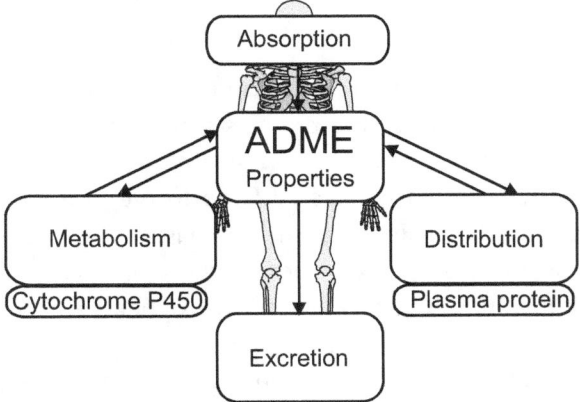

Fig. 1.1: The Interplay between Absorption, Distribution, Metabolism and Excretion (ADME)

(a) Absorption

Absorption is the movement of a drug from it's site of administration into the blood. Most drugs are absorbed by passive absorption but some drugs need carrier-mediated transport. Small molecules diffuse more rapidly than larger molecules. Lipid-soluble non-ionized drugs are absorbed faster. Absorption is affected by blood flow, pain, stress etc.

Acidic drugs such as aspirin will be better absorbed in the stomach whereas a basic drug like morphine will be absorbed better in the intestine. Most of the absorption of the drug takes place in the small intestine since the surface area of the stomach is much smaller than that of the intestine. Most of the drugs are absorbed in the small intestine as the amount of time the drugs spend in the stomach is less and also the surface area of the stomach is small. If a basic drug is taken after a meal, the activity of the drug can be reduced whereas if an acidic drug is taken after a meal the action of the drug can be noticed much more quickly, owing to the gastric absorption.

Even a drug like lipophilic to be absorbed in the intestine, some portion of it needs to be dissolved in the intestinal juices which are aqueous. There are some substances that are partly soluble in water and it is these that will be absorbed followed by an equivalent amount from the undissolved portion. Thus complete absorption takes place in this manner. There are bile salts present in the intestine which aid in salvation of the drug and their resultant absorption. Drugs that are amphipathic have no problem in getting absorbed. There are some drugs that are completely insoluble in water. Such drugs float as globules in the intestine but the bile salts emulsify these into small enough particles such that absorption can take place. e.g. vitamins. Some of the drugs are similar to compounds found in the body e.g. thyroxine and such drugs can be absorbed into the system by active transport.

When drugs are injected into the muscle, subcutaneous layer absorption still has to take place but it is less dependent on the chemical nature of the drugs since the drugs are absorbed into the circulatory system through the small pores in the capillary walls.

(b) Distribution

Distribution is the movement of drugs throughout the body. Determined by the blood flow to the tissues, it is ability of the drug to enter the vasculature system and the ability of the drug to enter the cell if required.

Plasma Protein Binding

The blood stream has the ability to transport relatively insoluble substances. These substances are transferred by binding to the proteins which have a very amphipathic structure. The hydrophilic group renders the protein soluble in water and the lipophilic compounds are attracted to the lipophilic group and are loosely bound to the protein molecule hence protein-bound. Most of the drugs which travel in the plasma are partly in solution and partly bound to the plasma protein. The bound drug is inactive whereas the unbound drug is active. The ratio of bound to the unbound drug varies. Binding is reversible. Generally, acidic drugs bind to albumin and basic drugs to α_1-acid glycoprotein. Diseased state can adversely impact the effectiveness of the drug. Globin levels in the body increase with age; a factor that should be taken into account when treating an elderly person with a basic drug.

The protein bound drug is in equilibrium with the free drug. That means that once the free drug enters the target tissue, the protein bound drug will be released to maintain equilibrium. There can be problems if two drugs bind at the same site of the protein and are administered together. e.g. warfarin and asprin. Asprin displaces warfarin from its bound protein as a result of which there are elevated levels of warfarin in the unbound state which may lead to warfarin toxicity.

Tissue Distribution

After absorption, most drugs are distributed in the blood to the body tissue where they have their effect. The degree to which the drug is likely to accumulate in the tissue is dependent on the lipophilicity and local blood flow to the tissue. Highly perfused organs receive most of the drugs.

The Role of the Liver in Drug Distribution

After the drug is absorbed by the GI tract, it is taken up by the part of the bloodstream called hepatic portal system. Most of the drugs are absorbed into this system except for the lipids which are absorbed into the lymphatic system and then delivered into the blood by the thoracic duct into the superior vena cava.

The hepatic portal system is designed to take digested foodstuff into the liver where it is processed. In some cases, it is stored before being distributed and it is possible that this may also happen to the drug which would then be metabolized before reaching the rest of the body. Such drugs that are metabolized by the liver are said to have a high hepatic first pass. Due to this reason, drugs with a very high hepatic first pass cannot be given orally.

The Blood–Brain Barrier (BBB)

The capillaries in the CNS are different as they have pores which are sealed by the connective tissue therefore only small molecules can cross the blood brain barrier and similar substances that can cross over have to be very lipophilic in nature. The blood-brain barrier (BBB) is the protective mechanism of the CNS and is not present everywhere in the brain. This is sometimes useful as it avoids some drugs from crossing the CNS and causing deleterious effects e.g. neuromuscular blocking agents. Sometimes the blood brain barrier also allows the transport of drugs resulting in unwanted effect e.g. antihistamines cross the BBB and result in drowsiness. To prevent this from happening, antihistamines that are manufactured these days are not so lipophilic in nature.

(c) Metabolism or Biotransformation

It is the process of transformation of a drug within the body to make it more hydrophilic so that it can be excreted by the kidneys. This is necessary as drugs and chemicals are foreign substances in our body. If the drug continues to be in the lipohilic state and is going to be filtered by the glomerulus, it will be reabsorbed and will remain in the body for prolonged periods. Hence metabolism deals with making the drug more hydrophilic such that it can be excreted from the body. In some cases, the metabolites can be more active than the drug itself e.g. anxiolytic benzodiazepines.

Some enzymes are highly specific and will breakdown only those compounds that they recognize e.g. glucose dehydrogenase. But there are also some enzymes such as pepsin which are not specific and breakdown most soluble proteins into smaller polypeptides or amino acids. These and many other proteolytic enzymes attack the peptide bond that joins the amino acids to make proteins, and in this way break down the protein.

Two types of enzymes are involved in metabolism:

Phase I Metabolism

These enzymes chemically modify the drug by processes such as oxidation, reduction and hydrolysis or by the removal and addition of an active group.

Phase II Metabolism

These include the conjugation of a drug or a phase I metabolite with a polar group to render it possible for excretion. e.g. sulphates and glucuronide

The deconjugation of drug by bacterial enzymes is called the enterohepatic cycle. Sometimes this deconjugation can lead to increased levels of drugs in the body. But sometimes due to treatment with antibiotics, there may be less or no deconjugation as a result of which there will be less drug in the body.

Principal sites of metabolism are Liver and Kidney and once the drug is rendered hydrophilic they can be easily excreted by the bile and urine without significant re-absorption.

Enzyme Induction

There are some drugs that can lead to an increase in the production of enzymes and speed up the metabolism of the drug due to which a higher dose of the drug is required to achieve therapeutic effect.

Enzyme Inhibition

Some drugs ,result in the inhibition of certain enzymes and as a result there is an accumulation of the drug in the body which may lead to drug toxicity. This is also a form of drug – drug interaction.

(d) Excretion

Excretion is the removal of substance from the body. Some drugs are either excreted unchanged while some are excreted as metabolites in urine or bile. Drugs may also leave the body by natural routes such as tears, sweat, breath and saliva. Patients with kidney or liver problem can have elevated levels of drug in the system and it may be necessary to monitor the dose of the drug appropriately since a high dose in the blood may lead to drug toxicity.

Drug Dosage and Drug levels – Basic Definitions

- *Half life:* Half life of a drug is the time for the drug to decrease to half of its concentration.
- *Minimum effective concentration:* Below which there will be no therapeutic effect.
- *Maximum safe concentration:* Above which there will be a toxic effect. The larger the therapeutic index, the safer the drug.
- *Bioavailability:* It describes the amount of drug available to the body to produce a therapeutic effect.
- *Onset of action:* It is the time taken by the drug to reach minimum effective concentration after being administered.
- *Peak Action:* Occurs when the drug reaches it's highest blood or plasma concentration
- *Duration of action:* Is the length of time the drug has a pharmacological action.

MECHANISMS OF DRUG ACTION

Drug Classification

Drugs can be classified according to various criteria including chemical structure or pharmacological action. The preferred classification is the latter one which may be divided into main groups as follows:

(a) **Chemotherapeutic agents:** Used to cure infectious diseases and cancer. (Sulfa drugs, Antibiotics).

(b) **Pharmacodynamic agents:** Used in non-infectious diseases (Cholinergic, Adrenergic, Hallucinogenic, Sedatives).

(c) Miscellaneous agents (Narcotic Analgesics, Local Anesthetics).

Drug Names

Drugs have three or more names including a: chemical name, brand or trade name, and generic or common name. The chemical name is assigned according to rules of nomenclature of chemical compounds. The brand name is always capitalized and is selected by the manufacturer. The generic name refers to a common established name irrespective of it's manufacturer.

In most cases, a drug bearing a generic name is equivalent to the same drug with a brand name. However, this equivalency is not always true. Although drugs are chemically equivalent, different manufacturing processes may cause differences in pharmacological action. Several differences may be: crystal size or form, isomers, crystal hydration, purity-(type and number of impurities), vehicles, binders, coatings, dissolution rate, and storage stability.

Introduction to Drug Action

Definition:

A very broad definition of a drug would include "all chemicals other than food that affect living processes." If the effect helps the body, the drug is a medicine. However, if a drug causes a harmful effect on the body, the drug is a poison. The same chemical can be a medicine and a poison depending on conditions of use and the person using it.

Another definition would be "medicinal agents used for diagnosis, prevention, treatment of symptoms, and cure of diseases." Contraceptives would be outside of this definition unless pregnancy were considered a disease.

Disease Classification

A disease is a condition of impaired health resulting from a disturbance in the structure or function of the body. Diseases may be classified into the following major categories:

1. **Infections** caused by viruses, ricketsia, bacteria, fungi, protozoa and worms.
2. **Allergic diseases** caused by antigens and foreign substances.
3. **Metabolic disorders** caused by defects in the body's ability to carry out normal reactions - these may be hereditary, deficiency, and congenital defects.
4. **Cancer.**
5. **Toxic diseases** caused by poisons.
6. **Psychosomatic and mental diseases.**

Chemotherapy, broadly defined, means the treatment of any disease by chemicals including infectious and non-infectious diseases. The original definition applied only to drugs which were used in the treatment of infectious diseases. The proper term for the treatment of non-infectious diseases is pharmacodynamics.

Mode of Drug Action

It is important to distinguish between actions of drugs and their effects. Actions of drugs are the biochemical physiological mechanisms by which the chemical produces a response in living organisms. The effect is the observable consequence of a drug action. For example, the action of penicillin is to interfere with cell wall synthesis in bacteria and the effect is the death of the bacteria.

One major problem of pharmacology is that no drug produces a single effect. The primary effect is the desired therapeutic effect. Secondary effects are all other effects beside the desired effect which may be either beneficial or harmful. **Drugs are chosen to exploit differences between normal metabolic processes and any abnormalities which may be present.** Since the differences may not be very great, drugs may be non-specific in action and alter normal functions as well as the undesirable ones. This leads to undesirable side-effects.

The biological effects observed after a drug has been administered are the result of an interaction between that chemical and some part of the organism. Mechanisms of drug action can be viewed from different perspectives, namely, the site of action and the general nature of the drug-cell interaction.

1.   Killing Foreign Organisms:

Chemotherapeutic agents act by killing or weakening foreign organisms such as bacteria, worms, viruses. The main principle of action is selective toxicity, i.e. the drug must be more toxic to the parasite than to the host.

2.   Stimulation and Depression:

Drugs act by stimulating or depressing normal physiological functions. Stimulation increases the rate of activity while depression reduces it's rate.

Sites of Drug Action

1.   Enzyme Inhibition:

Drugs act within the cell by modifying normal biochemical reactions. Enzyme inhibition may be reversible or non-reversible; competitive or non-competitive. Antimetabolites may be used which mimic natural metabolites. Gene functions may be suppressed.

2.   Drug-Receptor Interaction:

Drugs act on the cell membrane by physical and/or chemical interactions. This is usually through specific drug receptor sites located on the membrane. A receptor is the specific chemical constituent of the cell with which a drug interacts to produce it's pharmacological effects. Some receptor sites have been identified with specific parts of proteins and nucleic acids. In most cases, the chemical nature of the receptor site remains obscure.

3. Non-specific Interactions:

Drugs act exclusively by physical means outside of cells. These sites include external surfaces of skin and gastrointestinal tract. Drugs also act outside of cell membranes by chemical interactions. Neutralization of stomach acid by antacids is a good example.

ADVERSE EFFECTS OF DRUGS

Classification

ADRs may be classified by e.g. cause and severity.

Cause

- **Type A:** Augmented pharmacologic effects - dose dependent and predictable.

Intolerance, Side Effects

- **Type B:** Bizarre effects (or idiosyncratic) - dose independent and unpredictable.
- **Type C:** Chronic effects.
- **Type D:** Delayed effects.
- **Type E:** End-of-treatment effects.
- **Type F:** Failure of therapy.
- **Type G:** Genetic reactions.

Types A and B were proposed in the 1970s, and the other types were proposed subsequently when the first two proved insufficient to classify ADRs.

Seriousness and Severity

The American Food and Drug Administration defines a serious adverse event as one when the patient outcome is one of the following:

- Death.
- Life-threatening.
- Hospitalization (initial or prolonged).
- Disability - significant, persistent, or permanent change, impairment, damage or disruption in the patient's body function/structure, physical activities or quality of life.
- Congenital anomaly.
- Requires intervention to prevent permanent impairment or damage.

Severity is a point on an arbitrary scale of intensity of the adverse event in question. The terms "severe" and "serious" when applied to adverse events are technically very different. They are easily confused but can not be used interchangeably, require care in usage.

A headache is severe, if it causes intense pain. There are scales like "visual analog scale" that help us assess the severity. On the other hand, a headache is not usually serious (but may be in case of subarachnoid haemorrhage, subdural bleed, even a migraine may temporarily fit the criteria), unless it also satisfies the criteria for seriousness listed above.

Overall Drug Risk

While no official scale exists yet to communicate overall drug risk, the iGuard Drug Risk Rating System is a five-colour rating scale similar to the Homeland Security Advisory System:

- Red (high risk),
- Orange (elevated risk),
- Yellow (guarded risk),
- Blue (general risk),
- Green (low risk).

Location

Adverse effects may be local, i.e. limited to a certain location, or systemic, where a medication has caused adverse effects throughout the systemic circulation.

For instance, some ocular antihypertensives cause systemic effects, although they are administered locally as eye drops, since a fraction escapes to the systemic circulation.

Mechanisms

As research better explains the biochemistry of drug use, fewer ADRs are Type B and more are Type A. Common mechanisms are:

- Abnormal pharmacokinetics due to genetic factors, comorbid disease states.
- Synergistic effects between a drug or a disease, two drugs.
- **Abnormal Pharmacokinetics**.

Comorbid disease states.

Various diseases, especially those that cause renal or hepatic insufficiency, may alter drug metabolism. Resources are available that report changes in a drug's metabolism due to disease states.

- **Genetic factors**

Abnormal drug metabolism may be due to inherited factors of either Phase I oxidation or Phase II conjugation. Pharmacogenomics is the study of the inherited basis for abnormal drug reactions.

Phase I reactions

Inheriting abnormal alleles of cytochrome P450 can alter drug metabolism. Tables are available to check for drug interactions due to P450 interactions.

Inheriting abnormal butyrylcholinesterase (pseudocholinesterase) may affect metabolism of drugs such as succinylcholine.

Phase II reactions

Inheriting abnormal N-acetyltransferase which conjugated some drugs to facilitate excretion may affect the metabolism of drugs such as isoniazid, hydralazine, and procainamide.

Inheriting abnormal thiopurine S-methyltransferase may affect the metabolism of the thiopurine drugs mercaptopurine and azathioprine.

Interactions with other drugs

The risk of drug interactions is increased with polypharmacy.

- **Protein binding**

These interactions are usually transient and mild until a new steady state is achieved. These are mainly for drugs without much first-pass liver metabolism. The principal plasma proteins for drug binding are:

1. Albumin
2. α_1-acid glycoprotein
3. Lipoproteins

Some drug interactions with warfarin are due to changes in protein binding.

- **Cytochrome P450**

Patients have abnormal metabolism by cytochrome P450 due to either inheriting abnormal alleles or due to drug interactions. Tables are available to check for drug interactions due to P450 interactions.

- **Synergistic Effects**

An example of synergism is two drugs that both prolong the QT interval.

Assessing causality

Causality assessment is used to determine the likelihood of a drug causing a suspected ADR. There are a number of different methods used to judge causation, including the Naranjo algorithm, the Venulet algorithm and the WHO causality term assessment criteria. Each have pros and cons associated with their use and most require some level of expert judgement to apply. An ADR should not be labelled as 'certain' unless the ADR abates with a challenge-dechallenge-rechallenge protocol (stopping and starting the agent in question). The chronology of the onset of the suspected ADR is important, as another substance or factor may be implicated as a cause; co-prescribed medications and underlying psychiatric conditions may be factors in the ADR. A simple scale is available at http://annals.org/cgi/content/full/140/10/795.

Assigning causality to a specific agent often proves difficult, unless the event is found during a clinical study or large databases are used. Both methods have difficulties and can be fraught with error. Some ADRs may be missed even in clinical studies. Psychiatric ADRs are often missed as they are clubbed together in questionnaires used to assess the population.

Monitoring bodies

Many countries have official bodies that monitor drug safety and reactions. On an international level, the WHO runs the Uppsala Monitoring Centre, and the European Union runs the European Medicines Agency (EMEA). In the United States, the Food and Drug Administration (FDA) is responsible for monitoring post-marketing studies.

Examples of adverse effects associated with specific medications are as follows.

- Abortion, miscarriage or uterine hemorrhage misoprostol (Cytotec), a labor-inducing drug (this is a case where the adverse effect has been used legally and illegally for performing abortions).

- Addiction.

    Many sedatives and analgesics such as diazepam, morphine, etc.
- Birth defects

    Thalidomide and Accutane.
- Bleeding of the intestine

    Aspirin therapy
- Cardiovascular disease

    COX-2 inhibitors (i.e. Vioxx)
- Deafness and kidney failure

    Gentamicin (an antibiotic)

DRUG INTERACTIONS

What Is Drug Interaction?

Drug interactions occur when one drug interacts with another drug that you are taking or when your medications interact with what you eat or drink. Drug interactions can change the way medications act in your body. Drug interactions can make your medications less effective or they can cause unexpected and potentially dangerous side effects.

Your risk of having a drug interaction increases with the number of prescription and over-the-counter medications that you use. Moreover, the type of medications you take, your age, diet, disease, and overall health can all affect your risk. The elderly are at greater risk for drug interactions than younger adults since a larger proportion of seniors take prescription medications or over-the-counter products.

There are three important types of drug interactions:

(i) Drug-drug interactions occur when two or more drugs interact with each other. Interactions may occur with prescription drugs, over-the-counter drugs, vitamins, and alternative medications such as supplements and herbal products.

Some examples of drug-drug interactions include:

- Mixing a prescription sedative to help you sleep with an over-the-counter antihistamine for allergies can cause daytime drowsiness and make driving or operating machinery dangerous.
- Combining aspirin with a prescription blood thinner such as Plavix (clopidogrel) can cause excessive bleeding.
- Some over-the-counter antacids interfere with the absorption of antibiotics into the bloodstream. Certain medications used to treat fungal infections can cause serious side-effects when combined with cholesterol-lowering medications such as Lipitor (atorvastatin).
- The herbal supplement ginkgo bilboa can cause bleeding if taken with aspirin.

(ii) Drug-food interactions occur when a drug interacts with something you eat or drink.

Some examples of drug-food interactions include:

- Dairy products such as milk, yogurt and cheese can interfere with the absorption of antibiotics into the bloodstream.
- More than 50 prescription drugs are affected by grapefruit juice. Grapefruit juice inhibits an enzyme in the intestine that normally breaks down certain drugs and hence allows more of a medication to enter the blood stream.
- Vegetables containing vitamin K, such as broccoli, kale and spinach, can decrease the effectiveness of drugs, such as Coumadin (warfarin), given to prevent blood clotting.
- Mixing alcohol with some drugs is particularly dangerous. Alcohol interacts with most antidepressants and with other drugs that affect the brain. The combination can cause fatigue, dizziness, and slow reactions. A small amount of beer, wine, or liquor can increase your risk of stomach bleeding or liver damage when mixed with over-the-counter anti-inflammatory drugs and medications used to treat pain and fever. These drugs include aspirin, ibuprofen, and acetaminophen.

Drug-condition interactions may occur when a medication interacts with an existing health condition.

Some examples of drug-condition interactions include:

- Decongestants, such as pseudoephedrine found in many cough and cold preparations, can increase blood pressure and may be dangerous for people with hypertension.
- Beta blockers such as Toprol XL (metoprolol) and Tenormin (atenolol), used to treat high blood pressure and certain types of heart disease can worsen the symptoms of asthma and COPD.
- Diuretics, such as Hydrodiuril (hydrochlorothiazide), can increase blood sugar in people with diabetes.

What Can I Do to Help Prevent Drug Interactions?

- Before starting any new prescription drug or over-the-counter drug, talk to your primary healthcare provider or pharmacist. Make sure that they are aware of any vitamins or supplements that you take.
- Make sure to read the patient information handout given to you at the pharmacy. If you are not given an information sheet, ask your pharmacist for one.
- Check the labels of your medications for any warnings and look for the "Drug Interaction Precaution". Read these warnings carefully.
- Make a list of all your prescription medications and over-the-counter products, including drugs, vitamins, and supplements. Review this list with all healthcare providers and your pharmacist.
- If possible, use one pharmacy for all your prescription medications and over-the-counter products. This way your pharmacist has a record of all your prescription drugs and can advise you about drug interactions and side effects.

Where Can I Find Information About Drug Interactions for My Medications?

Drugs A to Z: This drug guide has in depth information about several thousand prescription and over-the-counter medications. Each drug profile in the guide has a page with information about drug interactions.

U.S. Food and Drug Administration (FDA): The FDA is responsible for monitoring drug interactions and side effects, and assuring that drugs sold in the United States are safe. The FDA website has useful information about drug safety issues.

DRUG USE IN SPECIAL POPULATION

Introduction

Special Population have Special Needs and Unique Obstacles to Treatment

Special populations are defined as groups whose needs may not be fully addressed by traditional addiction service providers. These include certain segments of our society based on age, ethnicity, gender, and geography.

Certain biological, psychological, and social factors can put any individual, regardless of age, gender, or ethnicity, at risk for addiction. These 'at-risk' population have special challenges that can complicate treatment efforts.

Special population may also be defined by groups who feel they may not comfortably or safely access and use the standard resources offered in typical addiction, prevention and treatment. Groups that fit into this category are typically employed in certain occupations such as armed forces, law enforcement, law, and medicine.

The Rationale for Customized Treatment for Special Population

Treatment programming has been designed for special population, which assumes that retaining clients in treatment may be facilitated by recognizing shared characteristics attracting, motivating. However, little scientific research is available to prove that outcomes from programmes designed for special populations are any better than their generic counterparts.

TYPES OF SPECIAL POPULATION

STRUCTURAL SPECIAL POPULATION

Structural characteristics are those that define a population by a fixed characteristic (i.e. gender, race, or ethnicity) or a developmental characteristic (age).

A. **Age-Related Special Population**

    A.1. Adolescents

    A.2. Adults (adult children of alcoholics)

    A.3. Seniors

B. **Ethnic- or Race-Specific Special Population**

    B.1. Aboriginals

    B.2. Blacks

    B.3. Hispanics

C. Gender-Specific Special Population

C.1 Women

C.2 Men

FUNCTIONAL SPECIAL POPULATION

Functional characteristics are those social, clinical or legal conditions which are shared by a certain group (co-existing mental illness, being incarcerated, having a similar occupation, etc.).

D. Occupation-Specific Special Population

D.1 Military

- Active duty

- Veterans

D.2 Law enforcement

D.3 Lawyers

D.4 Medical professionals

E. Geography-Based Special Population

E.1 Rural and frontier

E.2 Inner cities

F. At-Risk Special Population

F.1 Biological Risk Factors

F.1.1 Pregnant mothers

F.1.2 Injection drug users

F.1.3 Chronic pain

F.2 Psychological Risk Factors

F.2.1 Psychiatric disorders (dual diagnosis)

F.3 Social Risk Factors

F.3.1 Homeless

F.3.2 Prostitutes

F.3.3 Gay, lesbian, bisexual, transgender (GLBT)

F.3.4 Offenders

PHARMACOGENOMICS

Pharmacogenomics: Predicting which drugs will work and which won't.

Introduction

Pharmacogenomics is the study of how drugs are metabolized in the body and the variations in the genes that produce the metabolizing enzymes. By studying the genes that produce the specific enzymes that metabolize a drug to be prescribed, a doctor may decide to raise or lower the dose, or even switch over to a different drug. The decision about which drug to prescribe may also be influenced by other drugs the patient is taking, in order to avoid drug-drug interactions.

Currently, doctors typically prescribe one of several appropriate drugs for their patients. They prescribe a "standard" dose based on factors such as weight, sex, and age, and then adjust the dose over time, depending on whether the patient's condition is responding to the medication and whether the patient is experiencing unpleasant or dangerous side effects. The concentrations of some drugs are monitored with blood tests and the dosages increased or decreased to maintain the drug level in an established "therapeutic" range. Follow-up of such processes is called Therapeutic Drug Monitoring. If the drug is not effective in treating or controlling the patient's condition, then the patient is given a different drug and the process is started again.

Instead, pharmacogenomics offers physicians the opportunity to individualize drug therapy for patients based on their genetic make-up. For certain drugs, pharmacogenomics is already helping physicians pre-determine dosages to have a better chance of achieving the desired therapeutic effect while also simultaneously reducing the likelihood of adverse effects

Benefits of Pharmacogenomic Testing

As with other types of genetic testing, pharmacogenomic tests usually require only a small sample, such as blood or a scraping from inside the cheek. Results would let the physician predict whether someone will respond positively to drug therapy within hours rather than in the days or weeks it might take with the trial-and-error method and with substantially less risk to the patient. In the end, these tests may give doctors invaluable information about their patients not otherwise available to them.

Patient's Ability to Metabolize Drugs

Testing patients prior to initiating drug therapy to determine their ability to metabolize different classes of drugs is a key emerging area of investigation. Such metabolic information could prove useful to both the doctor and patient when choosing current and future drug therapies and drug doses.

There are many types of enzymes in the liver that metabolize medications. Genetic variations in these enzymes that affect metabolic rate are relatively common, but the prevalence of the variations differs significantly by ethnic background. Some of these enzymes include:

- The Cytochrome P450 family
- N-acetyltransferase
- Thiopurine methyltransferase (TPMT)
- UDP-glucuronosyltransferase

The Cytochrome P450 family: Some of the most studied enzymes are the members of the Cytochrome P450 (CYP) family of about 50 liver enzymes. These enzymes metabolize more than 30 classes of drugs, including antidepressants, antiepileptics and cardiovascular drugs. Patients can be separated into poor, normal and ultra-rapid metabolizers of drugs by the CYP enzymes. These classifications are due to variations in the associated CYP gene. When a poor metabolizer of a particular drug is given a standard dose of that drug, he will process the drug more slowly, resulting in increased levels of the drug in his bloodstream, the potential for side effects, and an increased risk of toxicity. For an ultra-rapid metabolizer, the same dose may be ineffective as the drug is processed too rapidly to have its full effect. Dosages of these drugs must be altered to accommodate the rate of metabolism. The CYP family is important as it affects the metabolism of a significant percentage of available drugs and because a significant proportion of the population are poor or ultra-rapid metabolizers.

N-acetyltransferase: This is a liver enzyme that activates some drugs and deactivates others. Some patients can acetylate (a type of metabolic change) drugs slowly while other patients acetylate drugs quickly. Those who are slow acetylators may experience toxicity when taking drugs such as procainamide, isoniazid, hydralazine, and sulfonamides. Those who are fast acetylators may not respond to isoniazid or hydralazine. About 40 to 70% of Caucasians and African-Americans are considered slow acetylators.

Thiopurine methyltransferase (TPMT): This enzyme metabolizes the immune suppressant azathioprine and other thiopurine medications such as 6-mercaptopurine and 6-thioguanine (used to treat children with acute lymphocytic leukemia and also used to treat autoimmune diseases). Each copy of the TPMT gene will produce some TPMT enzyme. This leads to three different groups of enzyme activity levels (low/low, low/high, and high/high or deficient, intermediate, and normal). About 1 in 300 Caucasians and African-Americans are TPMT- deficient. If these patients are given a standard drug dose, they may suffer severe hematopoietic (red blood cell producing) toxicity. Many are able to achieve the desired therapeutic effect from a dose that is one tenth of the "normal" dose.

UDP-glucuronosyltransferase: This enzyme is involved in the metabolism of the chemotherapy drug irinotecan, which is used in the treatment of metastatic colorectal cancer. Variations in the gene that code for this enzyme can influence the patient's ability to break down the major active metabolite. The inability to break the metabolite down can lead to increased levels of it in the blood and a higher risk of side effects, which include reduced white blood cell count and severe diarrhoea.

Age-related Genetic Variations

Some researchers are looking at changes in genetic variation over time to help evaluate how age may affect genetic response to drug therapy.

Interpreting Pharmacogenomic Tests

Pharmacogenomic test results can be difficult to interpret. There are limitations to interpretation because enzymes involved in drug metabolism arise from multiple genes which is a very complex process often. The test results are predictions based on information about the specific genetic variations, information about the associated diseases, adverse drug reactions, patient outcomes that have been gathered during studies and clinical trials. In many cases, the predictions will be very accurate, but it is difficult to accurately predict the outcome on the individual patient and neither do they incorporate or make allowances for other factors in a patient's life related to the disease condition or the individual that may also affect their response to treatment. This is one of the reasons why the results are intended to be used in conjunction with other relevant clinical findings.

Some currently available pharmacogenomic tests include:

- A DNA microarray that tests for 29 CYP2D6 genetic variants and 2 for the CYP2C19. It is meant to aid in individualizing treatment selection and dosing for drugs metabolized through these genes. It helps predict poor, intermediate, extensive, or ultra-rapid metabolizers.

- A test that detects variations in the UGT1A1 gene, which produces the enzyme UDP-glucuronosyltransferase. The enzyme is active in the metabolism of drugs such as irinotecan, a drug used in metastatic colorectal cancer treatment. The test is used to identify patients who may be at increased risk of adverse reaction to the drug. The gene that the test detects has been shown to be an effective genetic marker for predicting irinotecan-induced toxicity.

- Tests that detect genetic variants of the CYP2C9 and VKORC1 (vitamin K epoxide reductase) enzymes. These enzymes are involved in the efficacy of warfarin as an anticoagulant. Warfarin is used to prevent dangerous blood clots from forming in the blood vessels of certain patients, but it can significantly increase the risk of bleeding into the head or gastrointestinal tract. These tests identify patients who have genetic variations and so need a reduced dose of warfarin to avoid bleeding episodes. In November 2005, an FDA advisory committee voted in favour of changing Warfarin's label to reflect the fact that pharmacogenomic information can be useful in deciding a patient's individual dose.

Questions and Concerns

Pharmacogenomic tests are promising but there are questions and concerns about their utility, use, interpretation, ability to predict actual drug response, their effect on patient outcome, and the potential for the results of testing to be used to discriminate against the patient or to prevent them from access to treatment.

Should other family members be tested?

This is a question to discuss with your doctor and your family members. It may be useful in some cases while in others it may only be relevant if you are going to be taking the same drug or a drug in the same class. Pharmacogenomic test results are useful information for a family member to keep in mind. However, talk to their own doctor about as it adds to the family's medical history.

How can I tell when a pharmacogenomic test becomes truly clinically useful?

Things to consider include:

- Has the test been approved by the FDA? For what use? Are there major organizations, such as the American Medical Association, recommending and guiding it's use?

- How many participants were included in the studies that evaluated and support its use? What population(s) were evaluated (children with leukemia, postmenopausal women, people in a specific geographical area and/or of a specific ethnic background, patients who had a previous adverse drug reaction, etc.)?

- Are there major organizations who do not recommend the test's use? What are they saying?
- Will major health insurance companies and government programmes like Medicare pay for the test? Under what circumstances? Do they mandate the use of the test prior to approving drug treatment?
- Are physicians and laboratory personnel adequately trained to perform and interpret the test results?

When the answers to most of these questions have been answered satisfactorily, the test is likely to be considered clinically useful for specific situations.

How does a patient and his or her doctor decide whether a test is right for them?

Patients and doctors should consider the condition that the patient has, their history of drug-related side-effects and/or adverse drug reactions, the drug therapies that are available, and the uses the test is intended for. Pharmacogenomic tests are not meant to stand-alone but are meant to be used in conjunction with the patient's other clinical findings. Does the doctor understand how to interpret and utilize the results? How is he expecting the results to affect the patient's current and future treatment? Doctors and patients should both understand why they are performing the test.

How are drug discovery, development, and marketing affected by pharmacogenomics?

In the past, drug companies have focused primarily on blockbuster drugs – drugs that could be marketed to a large portion of the general population. Each of these drugs took hundreds of millions of dollars and years of research and clinical testing before it was cleared by the FDA and released in the market. For every blockbuster, there were numerous drugs that were orphaned (shelved) during the development process. Some of these drugs were only effective for a small percentage of those enrolled in clinical trials; others had too many associated side effects and complications.

Each of the blockbusters released was also associated with rare but sometimes serious complications. Some of which were not evident during clinical trials but emergedonly with long-term use. When a large number of people begin taking these medications, even a tiny percentage of rare complications could become a significant number of affected patients. In some cases, these blockbusters had to be removed from the market and/or their benefits versus their risks weighed carefully by the patients taking them and the doctors prescribing them.

With pharmacogenomics, the process of new drug development could be concluded in a couple of ways. This has been possible due to two reasons. Firstly, the human genome project and advances in the mapping and collecting of specific types of genetic variations (called Single Nucleotide Polymorphisms (SNPs), haplotypes, and microsatellites) have made it potentially easier for drug companies to identify genes of interest (those in which genetic variation is strongly associated with an identifiable disease) and targets of interest (the functioning of specific enzymes, proteins, or receptors that can be used as drug targets to block, inhibit, replace, or enhance the action of the target and have an effect on the condition).

And second, it can make it easier to identify the population most likely to benefit from the drug being developed. The results of phase I and phase II clinical trials (performed for safety and effectiveness) can be evaluated to determine common factors in patients who responded versus those who did not or who had significant side-effects. Some of the orphaned (shelved) drugs could be able to be re-evaluated and re-targeted at those most likely to respond. In the future, it may become possible to simultaneously develop drugs and as well the tests used to determine their likely beneficiaries.

DRUG TOLERANCE AND ADDICTION

Drug tolerance

Drug tolerance is basically the body's ability to adapt to the presence of a drug.

The magnitude of the body's response to a particular drug depends on two factors:

* Concentration of the drug at it's its site of action.
* Sensitivity of the target site to the drug.

The sensitivity of the target cells is governed by genetic factors and adaptive changes by the body. Adaptive changes occur in response to repeated exposure to a particular drug. The result is usually a loss of sensitivity to the drug. This decreased response is called tolerance.

Tolerance may also be defined as a state of progressively-decreased responsiveness to a drug as a result of which a larger dose of the drug is needed to achieve the effect originally obtained by a smaller dose.

Types of Tolerance

Repeated use of a drug usually enables the body to develop tolerance to it's effects. Tolerance occurs with all drugs, but it can occur slowly or rapidly, and last for a longer or shorter time, depending on the type of drug. Tolerance to opiates can take weeks or even months to evolve and then equally long to resolve, while tolerance to hallucinogens occurs within a day but is resolved within a week.

Tolerance to a drug takes place in several ways such as the following:

Dispositional Tolerance:

The body speeds up the metabolism of the drug in order to eliminate it. This is usually accomplished by an increase in the production of enzymes in the liver that break down the drug. One way of testing the burden of drugs in the body is by measuring these enzymes-if they are high, the body is suffering from the drug effects.

Pharmacologic Tolerance:

With repeated use, the brain's neurons become less sensitive to the effects of the drug and may even produce an antidote or antagonist to the drug. Most neurons react to the overwhelming presence of a neurotransmitter like drug by downgrading the receptors for it. With opioids, the brain can actually produce an opioid antagonist, cholecystoknin, to counteract it's effects. This type of tolerance is very frustrating to drug users, who require increasingly higher doses to achieve the same effect.

Behavioural Tolerance:

The brain learns to compensate for the effects of the drug by using parts of the brain that are not affected. This is how chronic alcohol and marijuana users manage to function quite well despite levels of intoxication that would incapacitate people who are less-accustomed to the drug.

Reverse Tolerance:

A drug user may actually become more sensitive to a drug when that drug destroys brain tissue. The excessive sensitivity may alter the overall drug experience to make it less enjoyable. MDMA is an example of a drug that often becomes very disagreeable with extensive use.

Acute Tolerance:

Also known as tachyphylaxis, this is the almost immediate tolerance to the effect of a drug as the body adapts to it. For example, a single dose of most hallucinogens causes a reduced effect if the drug is taken again, and even if a different type of hallucinogen is taken. For LSD-25, Psilocybin, and other hallucinogens, it may take a week to regain full sensitivity to the drug.

Select Tolerance:

The body develops tolerance to different aspects of the drug at different rates. For example, mental tolerance may proceed rapidly, so that the user wants a higher dose, but if physical tolerance has not caught up the user may take a fatal overdose. This has often happened with barbiturates.

Inverse Tolerance:

Repeated use of some drugs can suddenly cause an increased sensitivity to it, as the brain anticipates and enhances its effects. For example, long-term marijuana or cocaine users often become more sensitive to the drug, and even a fake look-alike drug may give them the drug effect, this is known as the Placebo Effect.

Addiction

Addiction is a difficult word to define since it can be used in various ways. The World Health Organization (WHO) has provided the following definition: "A behavioural pattern of drug use, characterized by overwhelming involvement with the use of a drug (compulsive use), the securing of the supply, and a high tendency to relapse after withdrawal. Addiction is viewed as an extreme on a continuum of drug use patterns. It refers, in a quantitative rather an a qualitative sense, to the degree to which drug use pervades the total life activity of the user, and to the range of circumstances in which drug use controls his/her behaviour."

Addiction refers to dependent patterns of drug self-administration without making a distinction between physical or psychological dependence. Moral weakness is often implied by the term addiction.

The WHO has suggested that the term "addiction" be replaced with the term "drug dependence." It is not possible to identify with precision the point where compulsive use should be considered addiction.

The term addiction cannot be used interchangeably with physical dependence since one can be physically dependent on drugs without being addicted and, in some cases, addicted without being physically dependent.

Self-administration of drugs depends upon a number of factors. These include:

- The properties of the drug itself.
- The route of administration.
- The size of the individual dose.
- The amouht of work required to obtain a dose.
- The presence of other drugs.
- Previous experience with other drugs.

With continuous access, animals show patterns of self-administration that are strikingly similar to those exhibited by human users of the same drug. Scientific studies have shown that pre-existing mental and behavioural disorders are not a prerequisite for drug use and that drugs themselves are powerful reinforcers, even in the absence of phys cal dependence.

PHARMACOEPIDEMIOLOGY

Pharmacoepidemiology is the study of the use and effects of drugs on large groups of people.

To accomplish this study, pharmacoepidemiology borrows from both pharmacology and epidemiology. Thus, pharmacoepidemiology is the bridge between both pharmacology and epidemiology. Pharmacology is the study of the effect of drugs and clinical pharmacology is the study of effect of drugs on clinical humans. Part of the task of clinical pharmacology is to provide a risk benefit assessment by effects of drugs in patients:

- Doing the studies needed to provide an estimate of the probability of beneficial effects on populations,
- Or assessing the probability of adverse effects on populations.

Other parameters relating to drug use may benefit epidemiological methodology. Pharmacoepidemiology then can also be defined as the transparent application of epidemiological methods through pharmacological treatment of conditions to better understand the conditions to be treated.

Epidemiology is defined as the study of the distribution and resulting determinants of diseases on populations. Epidemiological studies can be divided into two main types:

1. Descriptive epidemiology describes disease and/or exposure and may consist of calculating rates, e.g., incidence and prevalence. Such descriptive studies do not at this time use health control groups and can only generate hypotheses, but not test them. Studies of drug use would generally fall under descriptive studies.

2. Analytic epidemiology includes two types of studies: observational studies, such as case-control and cohort studies, and experimental studies which include clinical trials or randomized clinical trials. The analytic studies compare an exposed group with a controlled group and usually designed as an hypothesis testing by studies.

Pharmacoepidemiology benefits from the methodology developed in general epidemiology and may further develop them for applications of methodology unique to needs of pharmacoepidemiology. There are also some areas that are altogether unique to pharmacoepidemiology, e.g., pharmacovigilance. Pharmacovigilance is a type of continual monitoring of unwanted effects and other safety-related aspects of drugs that are already placed in currently growing integrating markets. In practice, pharmacovigilance refers almost exclusively to spontaneous reporting systems which allow health care professionals and others to report adverse drug reactions to the central agency. The central agency combines reports from many sources to produce a more informative profile for drug products than could be done based on reports from one or fewer health care professionals.

REFERENCES

1. Goodman & Gilman's The Pharmacological Basis of Therapeutics by. Joel Griffith Hardman, Lee E. Limbird, Alfred G. Gilman. 10th Ed.

2. Rang & Dale's Pharmacology by. Humphrey Rang, Maureen Dale, James Ritter, Rod Flower. 6th Ed.

3. PK/DB – Database for Pharmacokinetic Properties – IFSC/USP (URL=http://miro.ifsc.usp.br/pkdb/) accessed – April 09, 2011.

4. http://www.drugs-forum.com/forum/showthread.php?t=16382#ixzz1ZW8QXVMq

5. Executive summary of disease management of drug hypersensitivity: a practice parameter. Joint Task Force on Practice Parameters, the American Academy of Allergy, Asthma and Immunology, and the Joint Council of Allergy, Asthma and Immunology. Ann Allergy Asthma Immunol 1999; 83:665-700.

6. deShazo RD, Kemp S. F. Allergic reactions to drugs and biologic agents. JAMA 1997; 278:1895-906.

7. Anderson J. A., Adkinson N. F. Jr. Allergic reactions to drugs and biologic agents. JAMA 1987; 258:2891-9.

8. Hertl M, Merk H. F. Lymphocyte activation in cutaneous drug reactions. J. Invest Dermatol 1995; 105 (1 suppl):95S-8S.

9. Yawalkar N, Egli F, Hari Y, Nievergelt H, Braathen LR, Pichler WJ. Infiltration of cytotoxic T cells in drug-induced cutaneous eruptions. Clin Exp Allergy 2000; 30:847-55.

10. Bocquet H, Bagot M, Roujeau J. C. Drug-induced pseudolymphoma and drug hypersensitivity syndrome (Drug Rash with Eosinophilia and Systemic Symptoms: DRESS). Semin Cutan Med Surg. 1996; 15:250-7.

11. Pramatarov KD. Drug-induced lupus erythematosus. Clin Dermatol 1998; 16:367-77.

12. Ditto AM. Drug allergy. In: Grammer L.C., Greenberger P.A., eds. Patterson's Allergic diseases. 6th ed. Philadelphia: Lippincott Williams & Wilkins, 2002:295.

13. Jick H. Adverse drug reactions: the magnitude of the problem. J. Allergy Clin Immunol 1984; 74:555-7.

14. Lazarou J., Pomeranz B.H., Corey P.N. Incidence of adverse drug reactions in hospitalized patients: a meta-analysis of prospective studies. JAMA 1998; 279:1200-5.

15. Einarson TR. Drug-related hospital admissions. Ann Pharmacother 1993; 27:832-40.

16. Barranco P., Lopez-Serrano M.C. General and epidemiological aspects of allergic drug reactions. Clin Exp Allergy 1998; 28 (suppl 4):61-2.

17. Wastila L.J., Lasagna L, The History of Zidivudine (AZT) J. Clin Res Pharmacoepidemiol 1990; 4:25-37.

18. Peck C.C.. Postmarketing drug dosage changes.Pharmacoepidemiol Drug saf.2003; 12:425-6.

19. Temple R. J. Defining dosage changes.Pharmacoepidemiol Drug saf 2003; 12:151-2.

20. Mckenzie M.W., Marchall G.L., Netzloff M.L., Cluff L.E.: Adverse drug reactions leading to hospitalization in children. J. Pediatr 1976;89 :487-90.

21. May F.E., Stewart RB,Cluff L.E. Drug interactions and multiple drug administration.Clin. Pharmacol Ther 1977; 22:322-8.

22. Stewart R.B., Forgnone M., May F.E., Forbes J., Cluff L.E.. Epidemiology of acute drug interactions: patient characteristics, drugs, and medical complications. Clin.Toxicol 1974;7:513-30.

Chapter ... 2

RESEARCH METHODOLOGY

Research is formalized curiosity. It is poking and prying with a purpose.   **Zora Neale Hurston**

NEW DRUG DEVELOPMENT

New Drug Development (NDD) is a continuous process, and the need for new drugs never ceases. Of the various diseases man suffers; very few can be cured by drugs. Most of the diseases can only be kept in check, and only those due to infection, infestation or a few cancers are really curable. Despite the great advances in medicine, there are no therapeutic options for a large number of diseases.

New drugs are required for a number of reasons, such as:

1. Diseases for which there are no drugs

Autoimmune diseases, degenerative disorders, diseases with poorly-defined pathology are among the many for which there are no treatments. These take a heavy toll of human life and often make life of the patient miserable.

2. Emerging diseases

The past few decades have seen the emergence of AIDS and it's attendant complications. A very significant part of the drug development effort is directed towards the control of this disease. Tuberculosis, which had almost been controlled with antibiotics, has now mutated into a Multi Drug Resistant (MDR) form which does not respond to conventional antibiotics and needs new drugs.

3. Need for safe and efficacious drugs

Our therapeutic armamentarium has both safe and effective drugs. Unfortunately, many of the safe drugs are not efficacious and those that are efficacious are not safe. This problem is most prominent in the treatment of cancers and viral diseases. Anti-cancer drugs are capable of controlling most forms of cancers, but while eliminating cancerous cells they also kill normal healthy cells. We need drugs that have the efficacy and at the same time are safe.

4. Economical drugs

The high cost of drugs is adversely impacting the finances of patients. Having drugs that are beyond the reach of the patients is like having no drugs at all. What we need is drugs that people easily can afford.

The number of new drugs entering the market annually has dropped slightly in the last few years; yet between 20 and 30 new drugs approved annually. The USFDA grades new products entering the market as:

1 = new molecular entity

2 = new ester, new salt

3 = new dosage form

4 = new combination

5 = new formulation or new manufacture

Table 2.1: Number of NCE approved in the US

Year	Drugs Approved	Year	Drugs Approved
1990	23	2001	24
1991	30	2002	17
1992	26	2003	21
1993	25	2004	31
1994	22	2005	18
1995	28	2006	17
1996	53	2007	18
1997	39	2008	25
1998	30	2009	26
1999	35	2010	15
2000	27		

Many reasons have been put forward for the overall drop in the number of new drugs developed. One of the most logical reasons could be mergers and acquisitions that the pharmaceutical industry has seen in the last two decades. A hypothesis that explains this is the "low-hanging fruit" hypothesis. The fruit hanging on the lowest branches gets picked first, and as time progresses, it becomes more and more difficult to pick fruit that could have happened with new drug development. The drugs easy to develop have been already developed, now it is more difficult to develop new drugs.

Drug development is also a very expensive activity, and the cost of developing a single drug reached $ 803 million in 2003. For 2009, the cost has been put at $ 1.7 billion; both these figures have been challenged as being highly inflated. While it would be virtually impossible and meaningless to calculate the average cost of drug development, t is clearly an expensive exercise. Yet the industry follows this activity so assiduously, because at the end it is profitable for it.

Conventional method of drug development involved the synthesis of thousands of chemicals, and testing them for biological activity. Many chemicals have biological activity and those with a therapeutic potential are selected for further studies. Estimates from different sources suggest that only a handful out of the tens of thousands of such compounds had potential. Each of these is subjected to a battery of pharmacological tests, and those emerging successful taken for the next round of testing.

Biological testing begins with studying their toxicity, and compounds are tested at doses 5 to 10 times below their toxic doses. Those showing no activity at this dose are eliminated from the testing program. This eliminates a large number of toxic compounds even if they are biologically active, and selects those with an acceptable therapeutic index.

These compounds are subjected to *in-vitro* and *in vivo* tests to unveil their spectrum of activity and understand the mechanism of their action.

The newer approaches to drug development involve the use of drug design, usually computer-aided. The real targets of drug action are macromolecules which are in the form of receptors, enzymes and often ion channels. Many of the macromolecules have been isolated and their three dimensional structures established. Using computers, one searches for drug molecules with the right shape, size and atomic configuration that would fit the macromolecule. Only those molecules that are likely to fit the target are then synthesized. This approach reduces the number of molecules that need to be synthesized at the start of the drug development program.

Instead of conventional screening in animals, a high throughput screening protocol is employed to search for molecules with the desired biological activity.

High Throughput Screening

High-Throughput Screening (HTS) is a method of scientific experimentation especially used in drug discovery. Using robotics, data processing and control software and sensitive detectors, HTS allows screening of millions of chemicals on biological macromolecules like enzymes. Through this process, one can rapidly identify active compounds which modulate a particular biomolecular pathway. The results of these experiments provide starting points for drug design and for understanding the interaction or role of a particular biochemical process in biology.

The key labware or testing vessel of HTS is the microtiter plate: a small container, usually disposable and made of plastic that features a grid of small, open divots called wells. Modern microplates for HTS generally have either 384, 1536, or 3456 wells. These are all multiples of 96, reflecting the original 96-well microplate with 8 x 12 9mm spaced wells. The wells are coated with target macromolecules, and for the test, substrates and plates are incubated at required conditions of temperature, pH etc. so that the enzyme substrate reaction takes place leading to the formation of the products. Test chemicals are added to check their effect on the reaction, i.e. to find out whether they inhibit the enzymes or not. The progress of the reaction or it's inhibition is studied using a variety of techniques, which track either the reactants or the products.

The reaction may be tracked by measuring the concentration of the substrates, (which decreases as the reaction proceeds) or that of the product (which increases as the reaction proceeds). This measurement is done by using UV or visible range of radiation, with the condition that either the substrate or the product (but not both) absorb the set wavelength.

Depending on the results of this first assay, one can perform follow up assays within the same screen by "cherry-picking" liquid from the source wells that gave interesting results (known as "hits") into new assay plates, and then re-running the experiment to collect further data on this narrowed set, confirming and refining observations.

Enzyme + Substrate → Product

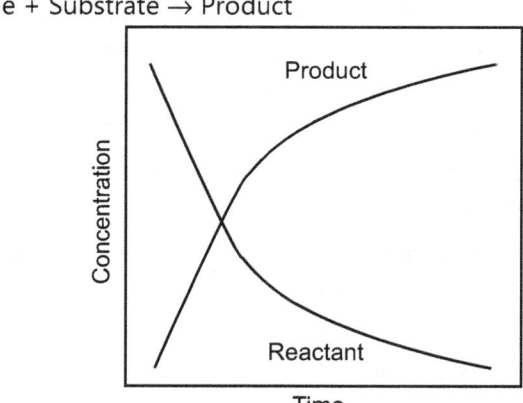

Fig. 2.1: Concentration of Reactants and Product with Time

Automation is an important element in HTS's usefulness. Typically, an integrated robot system consisting of one or more robots transports assay-microplates from station to station for sample and reagent addition, mixing, incubation, and finally readout or detection. An HTS system can usually prepare, incubate, and analyze many plates simultaneously, further speeding the data-collection process. HTS robots currently exist which can test up to 100,000 compounds per day. The term uHTS or ultra high throughput screening refers to screening in excess of 100,000 compounds per day.

In March 2010, a new process demonstrated an HTS process allowing 1,000 times faster screening (100 million reactions in 10 hours) at 1 millionth the cost (using 10^{-7} times the reagent volume) than conventional techniques using drop-based microfluidics. Drops of fluid separated by oil replace microplate wells and allow analysis and hit sorting while reagents are flowing through channels. A silicon sheet of lenses has been developed that can be placed over microfluidic arrays to allow the fluorescence measurement of 64 different output channels simultaneously with a single camera. This process can analyze 200,000 drops per second.

These being technology issues, the scientific issues are more interesting. In an HTS system, one could test the effect of numerous chemicals on a single enzyme system, or one could test a single chemical against numerous enzyme systems. The latter is more complex, since different enzymes have different substrates and hence could require different environments for reaction and different detection systems.

It is therefore more common to test a large number of chemicals on a single enzyme system, at different concentration levels. Thus, one could build dose response curves for a number of active compounds at the same time, so as to select the best candidate drug.

Target enzymes commonly used and their correlation with biological effects are as shown below, in the table below:

Table 2.2: Target enzymes for different categories of drugs

Sr. No.	Enzyme	Activity
1.	Cyclooxygenase II	Anti-inflammatory
2.	HMG CoA	Anti-cholesteremic
3.	Mono amine oxidase	Depression
4.	DNA dependent RNA synthetase	Anti-neoplastic
5.	Choline esterase	Myasthenia
6.	Angiotensin converting enzyme	Hypertension
7.	Dihydrofolate reductase	Antibacterial
8.	DNA Polymerase	Anti-neoplastic
9.	DNA Gyrase	Antibacterial
10.	Viral reverse transcriptase	Anti – viral

, It is possible to narrow down the number of synthetic or natural compounds that go into animal screening using an HTS system. HTS screening today is far cheaper than animal screening and if we eliminate those compounds that are not likely to have a biological activity by using HTS, drug discovery process becomes more economical.

The equipment and expertise required for each domain is so vast that very few laboratories are able to undertake testing of drugs of all types; hence most laboratories concentrate on a few domains. HTS helps select the best among the available compounds which can be put through a vigorous animal screening program.

It is now possible to isolate receptors and ion channels and drugs can be tested against them for accessing their activity. With the inclusion of these macromolecules, the scope of HTS in drug screening has been widened and the system has become more useful and important.

Animal Screening

Use of animals for drug testing has been in progress since a long time., In the first century A.D., Galen studied animals to understand human physiology and probably tested drugs on them. A definite reference to animal studies was made by Avicenna, an Arab physician who lived in the 10th century, in his Canon of Avicenna stating that new drugs should be tested on humans since testing on horses or lions may not give results that are similar to those on humans.

Regular use of animals in drug testing began in the 19th century and reached present levels in the 20th century. Supporters of the use of animals in experiments, argue that virtually every medical achievement in the 20th century relied on the use of animals in some way, and even sophisticated computers have been unable to model interactions between molecules, cells, tissues, organs, organisms, and the environment, making animal research necessary in many areas.

Opponents of animal studies question their legitimacy, arguing that it is cruel, poor scientific practice, poorly regulated, that medical progress is being held back by misleading animal models, that some of the tests are outdated, that it cannot reliably predict effects in humans, that the costs outweigh the benefits, or that animals have an intrinsic right not to be used for experimentation. Yet, the overall opinion is in favor of use of animals for initial studies on new drugs.

Animals serve as a bridge between laboratory and human studies, helping to screen out noxious chemicals from entering human studies. Animal studies provide us with early signals of drug toxicity and give an indication of efficacy in humans. Additionally, they give us an idea of the doses at which efficacy and toxicity may be noted. They also help us in predicting adverse drug reactions that may be observed in humans.

Scientists working with laboratory animals are not callous in their treatment of animals, and there are codes for the ethical use of animals. Most scientist use the three 'R' technique for animal usage, meaning thereby 'Refine, Reduce the use of animals, and Replace them with non-living systems.

When animals are used, three types of experiments are conducted, *in vitro*, *in vivo* and *ex vivo*.

In vitro experiments:

In vitro virtually means in glass (vitreum – Glass Latin), this type of research aims at describing the effects of a drug on a subset of an organism's constituent parts. It tends to focus on organs, tissues, cells, cellular components, proteins, and/or biomolecules. *In vitro* research is better suited than in vivo research for deducing biological mechanisms of action. With fewer variables and perceptually amplified reactions to subtle causes, results are generally more discernible.

In vivo experiments: (Latin –within the living) In vivo experiments is experimentation using a whole, living organism as opposed to a partial or dead organism. Animal testing and clinical trials are two forms of *in vivo* research. *In vivo* testing is often employed over *in vitro* because it is better suited for observing the overall effects of an experiment on a living subject. This is often described by the maxim *in vivo veritas*.

Ex vivo (Latin: out of the living) experiments are those which takes place outside an organism. In science, *ex vivo* refers to experimentation or measurements done in or on tissue in an artificial environment outside the organism with the minimum alteration of natural conditions. *Ex vivo* conditions allow experimentation under more controlled conditions than possible in the intact organism, at the expense of altering the "natural" environment.

A primary advantage of using *ex vivo* tissues is the ability to perform tests or measurements that would otherwise not be possible or ethical in living subjects. Tissues may be removed in many ways, including in part, as whole organs, or as larger organ systems.

It is generally accepted that *in vivo* experiments give us an overall picture of what the drug does to the system, while *in vitro* experiments help us understand why the drug produces effects which it does. In most screening programs *in vitro* and *in vivo* studies begin simultaneously, though a particular order of testing is followed.

The first studies are on acute toxicity and they help us establish the $LD_{50,}$ or the dose that kills 50% of the test animals. This test conducted on mice establishes the upper dose level at which efficacy of the drug will be tested. It is common to use $1/5^{th}$ to $1/10^{th}$ of the LD_{50} dose for testing of efficacy in animals. If the drug does not have a beneficial effect at a dose which is just 20% the toxic dose, the drug is considered as too toxic for further development. It is for this reason that the toxic dose is first established.

Animal toxicity is generally extended to include acute, sub-chronic or chronic toxicity and special studies. For most compounds all these studies are mandatory and only for a few selected compounds chronic or special studies may not be required. Anesthetic agents are a suitable example. These agents are not expected to be used repeatedly for any patient, and only a rather unlucky patient may have to be anesthetized more than once or twice, hence chronic toxicity studies may not be very relevant for such agents. Another class of agents is those intended to be used for Benign Prostatic Hyperplasia (BPH). These agents are rarely used in younger patients and never on females; hence studies on pregnant and lactating animals are irrelevant for these agents as are studies in pediatric age groups.

Safety studies are usually studied in more than one species, often using one rodent and one nonrodent species. Studies in more than one species can give a wider picture of the overall toxicity of the drug candidate since a single specie may not reveal all facets of toxicity.

Next, using proper models, the efficacy of the drug is established on it's own, and in comparison with standard drugs that are already available. Use of standard drugs is a great advantage since their advantages and disadvantages are known, hence one can find out whether the new drug is more efficacious and safer than the older drugs or not. While addressing the issue of efficacy, both the potency and intrinsic activity are measured. By potency, we mean the dosage at which equal effects are produced and intrinsic activity tells us the maximal effect produced by the drugs. The relation of potency and efficacy is graphically shown in Fig. 2.

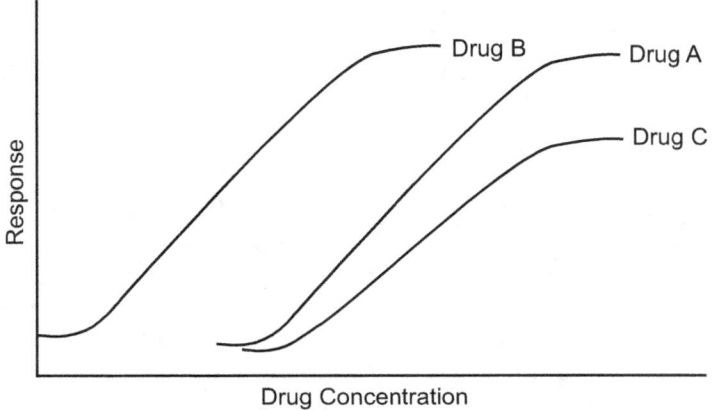

Fig. 2.2: Dose Response Relation Between Drugs

The figure shows the comparison of three drugs A, B and C each used in a graded concentration of a particular biological system. Drug A and Drug C produce biological effects in the same dose range, though the maximal effect produced by Drug C is lower than the maximal effect produced by Drug A. Drug B on the contrary produces a maximal effect equal to that of

Drug A but does so at a significantly lower dose. In this example Drug B is both more potent and has higher intrinsic activity than Drug A, Drug C has lower intrinsic activity than drug A, but its potency is comparable.

Such dose response curves can be built for any biological activity of drugs and is usually expressed as % response as a function of drug concentration. It is also usual to express drug concentration on a logarithmic scale, since the dose response curves tend to demonstrate a linear relation between the response and the concentration when the concentration is plotted logarithmically. In addition to biological activity, such curves can be built for toxicity or adverse events too.

In vitro models are available for testing some activities, while for others *in vivo* or *ex vivo* models may need to be used. Some drugs do not produce measurable effects on healthy animals and hence models of disease may have to be developed and used for the testing of such drugs. It is beyond the scope of this book to discuss in details each of the animals tests which are used for testing new drugs. Table 3 gives a list of tests which are used for the evaluation of antiasthmatics.

It is clear that all models do not simulate the human disease, and some models may be closer to the human disease than others. This is very germane for complex diseases like asthma. Bronchoconstriction can be produced by a variety of agents which have nothing to do with asthma, hence models like Konzett and Rossler are not very good at predicting human efficacy, but chopped lunch anaphylaxis, in which mediators are released by an antigen antibody reaction are better predictors of human efficacy.

Table 2.3: Animals models for the study of antiasthmatic drugs

Sr. No.	Experimental Technique	Activity studied
1.	Guinea Pig Tracheal Chain	Bronchodilator effects
2.	Konzett and Rossler's Technique	Bronchodilator effects
3.	48/80 induced foot pad oedema	Inhibition of histamine release
4.	Passive Cutaneous anaphylaxis	Inhibition of allergic mediator release
5.	Rat Peritoneal Anaphylaxis	Inhibition of allergic mediator release
6.	Chopped lung anaphylaxis	Inhibition of allergic mediator release
7.	Dale Schultz Phenomenon	Inhibition of allergic contractile response

Animal studies are important for yet another reason; we need to know the effects of new drugs on systems other than the target system. Thus, while the drug in development may be an anti-diabetic one, one cannot ignore it's effects on the cardiovascular, respiratory or the nervous system. Studies in animals reveal the total pharmacological profile of the drug.

A large number of diseases have been replicated in animals, and disease models have been created. Some animal models resemble human diseases more closely than others, yet all of these play a role in new drug development. In the case of antiasthmatic drug testing, we have a large number of animal models, including those enlisted in table 3. However, none of these really mimic the human disease. If known antiasthmatic drugs are tested in these models, the results obtained do not tally with clinical efficacy of the drugs. This observation made over two decades ago brought to fore the deficiencies of using animal models in drug testing.

In general, the results of safety testing done on animals correlate well with human safety, but in efficacy studies the correlation is poor. Different authors have given correlation coefficients for safety and efficacy between animal and human studies, however there may not be a universally applicable correlation, each value varying with the quality of the model and response of the animal species used.

Acute and Chronic Toxicity Studies

Animal safety studies are carried out over different periods of time, using single or repeat doses. Each of these studies reveals a particular aspect of the drug's toxicity and as a consequence, its safety. It is reiterated that there is no parameter for the safety of a drug, and the absence of toxicity is the measure of safety. Both safety and toxicity are the two ends of a continuum, and safety is established as an absence of toxicity. This is best depicted in Fig. 2.3.

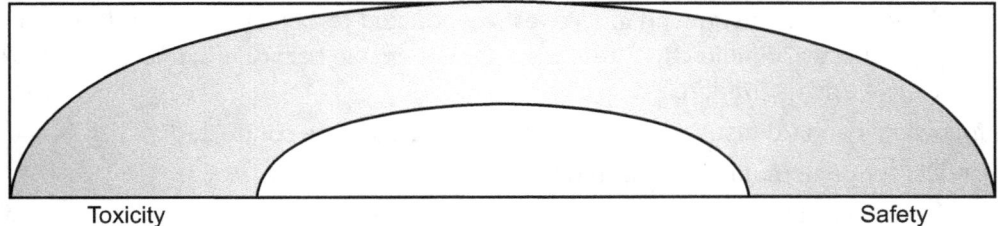

Toxicity   Safety

Fig. 2.3: The Safety Toxicity Continuum

The toxicity studies to be conducted for a drug depends upon it's intended clinical usage. As noted earlier, a drug meant for Benign Prostatic Hyperplasia is never going to be used in women, hence studies to evaluate it's safety in pregnancy and lactation are not required. Animal toxicity studies need not be long drawn out if the drug is not intended for long-term use in humans. The Appendix III of Schedule Y (to the Drugs and Cosmetics Rules 1945) gives details of animal toxicity requirements for different types of drugs, as shown in Table 4.

Table 2.4: Long-term toxicity study requirements for different types of drugs

Route of Administration	Intended duration of administration	Long term Study Requirement
Oral, parenteral or transdermal	Single or multiple doses for < 1 week	2 species 2 weeks
	> 1 week but < 2 weeks	2 species 4 weeks
	> 2 weeks but < 4 weeks	2 species 12 weeks
	> 4 weeks	2 species 24 weeks
Inhalation	< 2 weeks	2 species 1 month, 3 Hours/day
	> 2 weeks but < 4 weeks	2 species 12 weeks, 6 Hours/day
	> 4 weeks	2 species 24 weeks, 6 Hours/day

In acute and chronic studies, the gross health of animals is monitored throughout the period of dosing. Some animals are sacrificed mid-way in the study and their blood and organs are studied for signs of pathology. In all animals, urine is continually checked for any biochemical changes that could result from drug administration.

In addition to acute and chronic studies in animals, special studies are now carried out to rule out carcinogenic, mutagenic and teratogenic potential along with effects on reproduction in the perinatal period. Brief details of these tests, as required by the Indian Laws are given below:

Genotoxicity

Genotoxic compounds are presumed to be trans-species carcinogens, implying a hazard to humans. Such compounds need not be subjected to long-term carcinogenicity studies. However, if such a drug is intended to be administered for chronic illnesses or otherwise over a long period of time - a chronic toxicity study (up to one year) may be necessary to detect early tumorigenic effects.

Genotoxicity tests are *in vitro* and *in vivo* tests conducted to detect compounds which induce genetic damage directly or indirectly. These tests should enable hazard identification with respect to damage to DNA and its fixation.

The following standard test battery is generally expected to be conducted:

(i)   A test for gene mutation in bacteria.

(ii)   An *in vitro* test with cytogenetic evaluation of chromosomal damage with mammalian cells or an *in vitro* mouse lymphoma tk assay.

(iii)   An *in vivo* test for chromosomal damage using rodent hematopoietic cells.

Carcinogenicity

Carcinogenicity studies should be performed for all drugs that are expected to be clinically used for more than 6 months as well as for drugs used frequently in an intermittent manner in the treatment of chronic or recurrent conditions. Carcinogenicity studies are also to be performed for drugs if there is concern about their carcinogenic potential emanating from previous demonstration of carcinogenic potential in the product class that is considered relevant to humans or where structure-activity relationship suggests carcinogenic risk or when there is evidence of preneoplastic lesions in repeated dose toxicity studies or when long-term tissue retention of parent compound or metabolite(s) results in local tissue reactions or other pathophysiological responses.

Carcinogenicity studies should be done in a rodent species (preferably rat). Mice may be employed only with proper scientific justification. The selected strain of animals should not have a very high or very low incidence of spontaneous tumors.

Observations should include macroscopic changes observed at autopsy and detailed histopathology of organs and tissues. Additional tests for carcinogenicity (short-term bioassays, neonatal mouse assay or tests employing transgenic animals) may also be done depending on their applicability on a case to case basis.

Male Fertility Study

One rodent species (preferably rat) should be used. Dose selection should be done from the results of the previous 14 or 28-day toxicity study in rats. Three dose groups, the highest one showing minimal toxicity in systemic studies, and a control group should be taken. Each group should consist of 6 adult male animals. Animals should be treated with the test substance by the intended route of clinical use for minimum 28 days and maximum 70 days before they are paired with female animals of proven fertility in a ratio of 1 : 2 for mating.

Drug treatment of the male animals should continue during pairing. Pairing should be continued till the detection of vaginal plug or 10 days, whichever is earlier. Females getting thus pregnant should be examined for their fertility index after day 13 of gestation. All the male animals should be sacrificed at the end of the study. Weights of each testis and epididymis should be separately recorded. Sperms from one epididymis should be examined for their motility and morphology. The other epididymis and both testes should be examined for their histology.

Female Reproduction and Developmental Toxicity Studies

These studies need to be carried out for all drugs proposed to be studied or used in women of child-bearing age. Segment I, II and III studies (see below) are to be performed in albino mice or rats, and segment II study should include albino rabbits also as a second test species.

On the occasion, when the test article is not compatible with the rabbit (e.g. antibiotics which are effective against gram positive, anaerobic organisms and protozoas), the Segment II data in the mouse may be substituted.

Female Fertility Study (Segment I): The study should be done in one rodent species (rat preferred). The drug should be administered to both males and females, beginning with a sufficient number of days (28 days in males and 14 days in females) before mating. Drug treatment should continue during mating and, subsequently, during the gestation period. Three graded doses should be used, the highest dose (usually the MTD obtained from previous systemic toxicity studies) should not affect general health of the parent animals. At least 15 males and 15 females should be used per dose group. Control and the treated groups should be of similar size. The route of administration should be the same as intended for therapeutic use.

Dams should be allowed to litter and their medication should be continued till the weaning of pups. Observations on body weight, food intake, clinical signs of intoxication, mating behaviour, progress of gestation/ parturition periods, length of gestation, parturition, post-partum health and gross pathology (and histopathology of affected organs) of dams should be recorded. The pups from both treated and control groups should be observed for general signs of intoxication, sex-wise distribution in different treatment groups, body weight, growth parameters, survival, gross examination, and autopsy. Histopathology of affected organs should be done.

Teratogenicity Study (Segment II): One rodent (preferably rat) and one non-rodent (rabbit) species are to be used. The drug should be administered throughout the period of organogenesis, using three dose levels as described for segment I. The highest dose should cause minimum maternal toxicity and the lowest one should be proportional to the proposed dose for clinical use in humans or a multiple of it. The route of administration should be the same as intended for human therapeutic use.

The control and the treated groups should consist of at least 20 pregnant rats (or mice) and 12 rabbits, on each dose level. All foetuses should to be subjected to gross examination, one of the foetuses should be examined for skeletal abnormalities and the other half for visceral abnormalities. Observation parameters should include: (Dams) signs of intoxication, effect on body weight, effect on food intake, examination of uterus, ovaries and uterine contents, number of corpora lutea, implantation sites, resorptions (if any); and for the foetuses, the total number, gender, body length, weight and gross/ visceral/ skeletal abnormalities, if any.

Perinatal Study (Segment III): This study is specially recommended if the drug is to be given to pregnant or nursing mothers for long periods or where there are indications of possible adverse effects on foetal development. One rodent species (preferably rat) is needed. Dosing at levels comparable to multiples of human dose should be done by the intended clinical route. At least 4 groups (including control), each consisting of 15 dams should be used. The drug should be administered throughout the last trimester of pregnancy (from day 15 of gestation) and then the dose that causes low foetal loss should be continued throughout lactation and weaning. Dams should then be sacrificed and examined as described below.

One male and one female from each litter of F_1 generation (total 15 males and 15 females in each group) should be selected at weaning and treated with vehicle or test substance (at the dose levels described above) throughout their periods of growth to sexual maturity, pairing, gestation, parturition and lactation. Mating performance and fertility of F_1 generation should thus be evaluated to obtain the F_2 generation whose growth parameters should be monitored till weaning.

Animals should be sacrificed at the end of the study and the observation parameters should include (Dams) body weight, food intake, general signs of intoxication, progress of gestation/ parturition periods and gross pathology (if any); and for pups, the clinical signs, sex-wise distribution in dose groups, body weight, growth parameters, gross examination, survival and autopsy (if needed) and where necessary, histopathology.

Bias and Randomization

In the 18th century, Charles Lind showed the importance of controls in clinical trials. Since then a control group is almost always included in trials. If one is to have more than one group in a trial, there comes the issue of allocation of subjects to each group. Both during allocation and during all further activities, bias plays an important role. Bias is the conscious or unconscious leaning of the experimenters' opinion in either direction. This bias leads to inequitable distribution of subjects, unequal care, non-uniform observations, recording and reporting of results.

Bias plays a role, and that too a negative role on the fairness of a trial. Some of the bias are recognized while others are not. It is essential to study all possible types of bias that may creep in a trial and attempt in reduce if not eliminate them altogether. Some of the commonly reported types of bias are discussed below:

1. Allocation Bias

Researchers too, are human, and they have all human faults and follies. After assessment of a subject as eligible for the trial, there often springs an idea in the mind of the investigator that this subject would do well in one particular arm of the trial and not in the other. The cause of this may be put down to a quirky path in the human thought process. Sometimes the attitude, the looks the presentation of the subject instigates the investigator's bias. In order to reduce this bias, one must adopt a procedure of randomization, so that allocation of the subjects in different arms of the trial is not controlled by the PI but is really random.

There are many methods to randomize, both static and dynamic, each of which will be discussed briefly.

Static Methods: In these methods, the randomization is pre-determined. This could be by the means of randomization tables, generation of random numbers, or a method that is chosen before the recruitment begins. Thus one may decide to allot a registration number to every patient, based on their order of reporting to the clinic. All subjects with even numbers could be allocated to one arm while those with odd numbers to another arm.

Drawing straws is an age old method, but for those more interested in cricket, flipping a coin could decide the arm to which the patient goes. Generally in static methods, the method of allocation remains constant through out the recruitment process. A word of caution though; sometimes when allocation is truly random, the patients in different arms of the trial may not be similar to each other, in truth there may be high variance with respect to patient demographics. There is a tradeoff between randomization and variance.

Dynamic Methods: The method of randomization changes during the recruitment process, depending upon the covariates of the patient population or on their response to the treatments. In covariate adaptive design, midway in the recruitment the subjects allotted to the different arms of the trial are examined to check if the variables of the subjects are statistically similar, if they are not, the method of randomization tweaked to achieve similarity.

In response to adaptive designs, 'play the winner' methods are used, so that more subjects are allotted to the arm in which the success rate is higher. A detailed analysis of adaptive designs and adherence to research ethics is discussed in various publications of Rosenberger [5]. The role of randomization is to reduce and if possible to eliminate allocation bias in trials, but it does not reduce other forms of bias.

2. Patient Bias

Patients visit the doctor for treatment of the illness they suffer from. The patients on the active drug (or new drug) would mostly have a different perception about the treatment, than those on the Placebo or standard therapy. Patients on Placebo would certainly be dissatisfied with the trial procedures, if they knew that they were on a Placebo . They would feel neglected and as a consequence generally do worse than patients who know they are on an active or newer drug. This is the basis of patient bias, and the method to reduce or eliminate it is blinding the trial. A trial in which the subjects are unaware what they are being treated with is known as a blind trial, more specifically a single blind trial.

3. Investigator or Observer Bias

Investigators and their staff tend to pay more attention towards those patients who are allocated to the active drug or the test drug. Very often, this attention is at the cost of patients on placebos or standard therapy. Investigators and their staff are often biased towards the new therapy (in some cases could be biased against the new therapy, too). To eliminate this bias, trials are often double blinded, thus neither the patients nor the investigator and their staff know which patient is receiving what therapy.

Some authors use the term triple-blinding when other people involved in the trial, such as laboratory personnel or data managers are also blind. However double blind means that both the patient and the investigators are blind, and investigators include all personnel on the investigative team.

Quite often, the trial drug and the standard therapy have different physical forms and double blinding becomes difficult. Let us say that the test drug is an injectable while the standard drug is a tablet. , Blinding becomes difficult in such a situation. A way out is to use a double dummy technique, in which there is a dummy injection and a dummy tablet. Patients of one arm receive the active tablet and the dummy injection, while those on the other arm receive a dummy injection and the active tablet. This ensures that the patients and the investigators do not know the exact medication which a particular patient is receiving in the trial.

There are other types of bias that confound clinical research, however they have little to do with the methodology of clinical trials and will not be touched upon here. If adequate care is taken to reduce the allocation, patient and investigator bias, one can conduct a fair trial which would give credible results.

Initiation of Human Studies

Ignorance about when human studies can be initiated is one of the most common causes of fear of clinical research, both among patients and physicians. A clinical trial is initiated only when:

1. Animal studies of efficacy and safety are completed, and animal study data have helped finalization of the first dose in humans.
2. The Regulatory authority has issued written permission for the trial after approving the protocol, the ICF, the IB and other documents.
3. The Institutional Review Board has issued a written approval for the trial.
4. The drug is expected to have reasonably higher safety or efficacy in the market than it's existing competitors.

The last point is probably very important. The overall cost of clinical studies of one drug has been put at around $400 million.[1] Unless sponsors expect to recover the cost of development from the sales of the drug, they would not sink $400 in clinical studies.

As stated, the decision to conduct clinical trials is taken only after animal safety and efficacy data are in hand. The sponsors review the data very carefully before taking a decision to go for clinical studies. As of today, the legal implications of taking a bad drug to trials are so severe, that it is surprising that new drugs go to trial at all. Hence, the first level of review of animal data is at the sponsor's level.

Regulatory authorities represent the second level of animal data review. The regulators are alive to risks of allowing bad drugs for trials, and they are very critical while examining animal data. The authorities usually take help of organizations like the Indian Council for Medical Research before granting approval for trials. The Drugs Controller General (India) has an exhaustive list of documents required to be submitted for review before granting permission for Phase I trials. Further, as a policy, drugs discovered abroad are not permitted to enter Phase I trials in India. Requirements for submission for permission for clinical trials are given in Appendix I of Schedule Y to the Drugs and Cosmetics Rules 1945.

After the decision to conduct trial is taken by the sponsor, comes the preparation of the protocol. This document is the master document according to which the trial would be conducted. Obviously, this is prepared by a team which comprises domain experts, pharmacologists, statisticians, medical writers etc. The protocol is usually scrutinized by investigators who have experience with trial of similar compounds and often by those who are shortlisted to conduct the trial. The finalization of the protocol is followed by the preparation of less complicated documents such as the IB, ICF, PIS, etc.

The complete documents of the proposed trial, along with the names and CVs of potential investigators, are next forwarded to the Regulators for their permission. In the US and UK, there is time limit for the regulators to respond to the application by a sponsor, but in India there isn't. If the regulators agree with the proposal made by the sponsor, permission to conduct the trial is granted; if not the reasons for withholding the permission are given, and the sponsors may have to rework the proposal.

In addition to the permission of the Regulators, the trials may be initiated only when the written permission is granted by the IRB/IEC. The constitution and function of these bodies is detailed in the next chapter. This body also examines the trial documents both from the ethical and the scientific angle. Some investigators may question the examination of the trial documents from a scientific angle, yet the IRB/IEC has the right and duty to do so, since any research protocol that is not scientifically valid is also unethical. In India, it is common for either body granting approval while stating that the trial may begin only on receiving written approval from the other.

In some countries, the processing IRB/IEC of the proposal by the IRB/IEC may begin only after the regulators have given approval for the trial. However, in India, parallel approval to IRB/IEC and the regulators is permissible, hence reducing the time for trial initiation.

Phases of the clinical trials

Classically, clinical trials have been described as Phase I, II, III or IV, but recently Phase 0 has been added to these types. Each phase has it's own objectives, it's distinct methodology and associated risks and advantages, yet many of these aspects may overlap..

Phase 0 trials are the recent addition and these are conducted to ensure that the drug candidate is 'drugable', meaning that it has the potential to be made into a drug. In this phase, a very small amount of the drug is administered to human volunteers and the drug tracked all over the volunteer's system. Doses hundred times lower than clinical doses are used, often less than 100 mcg are administered. Obviously, the technology is needed to detect and quantify the drug in body fluids. Alternately, radio-labeling of the drug should be feasible to detect low levels of the drug in the body. The principal objective is to ensure that the drug reaches the required sites and not elsewhere.

Phase I trials are primarily safety trials and the objective is to check whether the drug is safe enough to be taken up for further studies. Since safety of a drug cannot be measured but is inferred by lack of toxicity, the investigators need to watch the subjects very carefully for any sign of toxicity, which often may be just a change in laboratory values. This phase is conducted on healthy subjects; healthy meaning those without disorders that might alter or interact with the drug. Only when the potential drug has significant toxicity (like anti-cancer agents) are actual patients used in place of healthy subjects. This phase is conducted in specialized centers where monitoring of various body functions is possible.

In addition to collecting safety data, the investigators collect any efficacy data that is available and may conduct bioavailability studies. Such studies can also include dose escalation, when the starting dose is way below the clinical dose and gradual increase of dose is achieved even beyond the clinical dose. Repeat dose studies are also undertaken, if the drug is one which is expected to be used in such a fashion.

Phase II trials are meant to explore the therapeutic effects of the candidate drug in humans. Since a large number of drugs show no effects in healthy volunteers, this phase is carried out on patients suffering from the target disease. By the time the drug reaches this phase, it's safety has been established in humans, hence Phase II studies are generally safer than Phase I studies. While this phase mainly explores efficacy, safety observations continue to be made. In this phase too, studies may include repeat doses and escalating doses.

The choice of patients is very critical to the success of this phase. In animal studies, inbred strains of animals are used. These animals are genetically similar to each other and hence inter-individual differences are minimal. Among humans, there is a great heterogeneity of genetic material, hence inter-individual variance is high. In order to reduce the difference in results, the patients chosen are within a narrow range of characteristics so that variance is kept at a minimum. Thus, the patients chosen are within a narrow band of age, weight, disease severity, making the group as homogenous as possible.

Phase III studies are the most critical studies that establish the marketability of the new drug. There are many designs that could be used for these studies, prospective, randomized, comparative, double blinded studies have maximal scientific and regulatory acceptability. Placebo controlled studies are no longer ethically acceptable, barring a few select conditions.

This phase should compare the new drug with the best available therapy in the market (this is also required by the DOH). The use of the most effective alternative therapy available as a comparator, is of advantage to the sponsor too, since the results will reveal how well the new drug compares with it. In other words, the results will reveal how the sponsor should position the product and gain market advantage.

In this phase, the type of patients chosen should mirror those who present themselves for treatments in hospitals or clinics. In short, the chosen patients should represent the end-users of the drug. Randomization of patients between the different arms of the trial is essential to prevent allocation bias, and double blinding essential for avoiding observation bias.

In addition to confirming the therapeutic potential of the new drug, this phase compares it with the best available treatment for the target disorder. Being larger in size than Phase II studies, there are better chances of capturing less common side effects, though rare ones may still remain undetected. The sample size used for this phase depends upon the advice of the statistician and based on expected usage of the drug. Regulatory authorities may demand inclusion of a large number of subjects for a trial of drugs that are expected to be widely used, such as oral contraceptives or simple analgesics.

Clinical Trial Designs

Clinical trials are of many types and there are many design that could be used to plan them. These designs could also be classified in a variety of ways, such as open or blinded, comparative or non comparative, prospective or retrospective etc. The main two types of clinical trials are observational and analytical.

In an Observational trial, the aim is to study the relationship between a characteristic and event without manipulating the conditions under which it is studied.

In an experimental study, the researchers control the condition under which the study is performed.

Snapshot and longitudinal studies

Snapshot studies differ from longitudinal studies in their duration and the number of observations recorded. A snapshot study aims to discover the relation between two variables at one time, whereas a longitudinal study tracks the relations over a period of time.

As an example, one may consider the relation between say gender and height, in a particular population. The investigator measures the height of the subjects at one time and draws conclusions. In a longitudinal study, the investigator may pick a number of toddlers of both sexes and follow their growth over many years recording their height every time. Obviously, the longitudinal study gives us more information than a snap shot study. However, , it takes longer time and certainly more effort and money to conduct it.

Comparative and non-comparative trials

Most studies are comparative, either comparing the drug with a standard drug or a placebo. Non-comparative studies are not acceptable in most cases. Comparison with placebo is also considered unethical, except when (a) there is no standard therapy for the disorder under study or (b) when the disorder is so mild that use of placebo does not harm the subjects. While using a standard for comparison, it is best to use the best available treatment for the disorder under study. Thus, if one were to study a new 'statin' then the obvious comparator would be atorvastatin or rosuvastatin, but not lovastatin.

Open or blinded trials

Blinded trials (double blind) have the highest scientific and regulatory acceptance, yet in some conditions trials cannot be double blinded. For example, the STICH trial which was recently completed. In this trial, the efficacy and mortality in patients with heart failure following MI was studied in three arms. The first arm received usual medical therapy, the second received by-pass graft in addition to routine medical therapy, while the third arm underwent surgical ventricular reconstruction along with medial therapy. In such a trial, double-blinding is impossible, since the surgical procedure involved makes the distinction between the arms clear.

Blinding could be single-blind, where only the subjects are unaware of the treatment they are receiving; this does reduce the psychological bias of the subjects but is still open to observer bias. In double-blind trials, observer bias is considerably reduced, though at times the physicians involved may be able to guess what a particular patient was receiving. Triple blinding ensures that the bias of the other members of the investigating team, including statisticians and data analysts, is reduced.

Prospective and retrospective trials

In a trial, an investigator may look ahead or behind in time, which are prospective or retrospective trials. In prospective trials, the investigator administers a drug or device and watches for the change in specific parameters over time. In retrospective trials, the investigator identifies subjects in which there has been a particular incident or effect and goes into the history of the subject to find if there was an exposure to a particular drug or device.

If one were to study the co-relation between the use of a particular brand of shampoo and baldness, one could do a prospective trial, in which subjects with a full head of hair are given the shampoo and they are followed up for a number of years, till they become bald or otherwise. In a retrospective trial, bald subjects are selected and the investigator goes into the history of the subject whether he was exposed to the particular brand of shampoo or not.

The advantage of the retrospective trial in case of the shampoo is that the results are obtained in a short time, while a prospective trial may go on for years before any result becomes available. Obviously, a retrospective trial cannot be performed for a shampoo which has just entered the market.

In such a trial, controls would also be useful. For the prospective trial, another shampoo could be the control, while for a retrospective study men with a full head of hair will serve as the control. Prospective trials are more tedious and often very expensive, but they are not affected by recall bias which strongly affects retrospective trials. For this reason, prospective trials have a higher scientific and regulatory acceptance compared to retrospective ones.

Parallel and crossover trials

A crossover trial is yet another innovative method to conduct a trial even when the subjects available do not come up to the number statistically required. In a parallel study, the subjects are randomized to two or more arms of the trial and followed till the end of the trial. In a cross over trial, the treatments of the subjects are switched midway so that each subject receives both drugs during the study period, thus each subject serves as his own control. Cross-over trials need a lesser number of subjects since each subject receives both the test drug and the standard, and the number of subjects receiving each treatment is also equal.

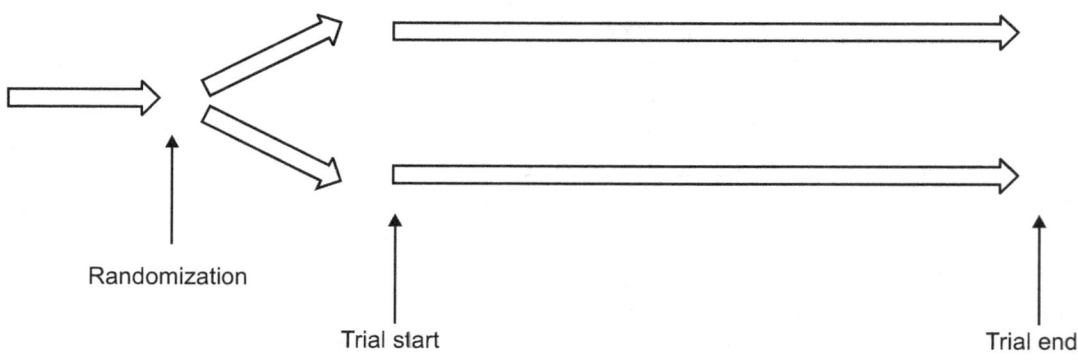

Fig. 2.4: Parallel Trial

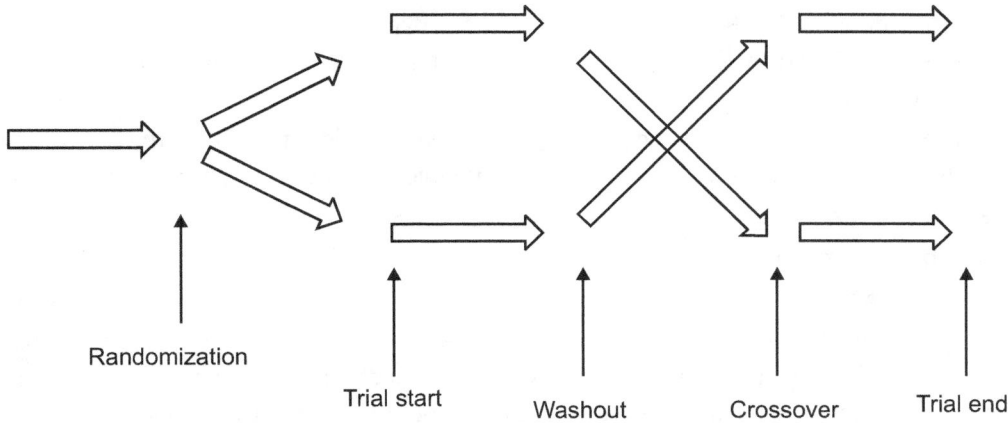

Fig. 2.5: Crossover Trial

The choice of the trial design is very crucial to the success of the trial, and it could either make or mar the prospects of a new drug. This choice has to be made keeping in mind the regulatory requirements and the available resources in terms of subjects, time and money.

Post marketing safety studies

Safety of the drug continues to be studied, right from phase I to long after the drug has been marketed. A drug with an acceptable risk benefit profile, in say 1970 may become unacceptable in 1990 just because safer drugs have entered the market. Very often adverse effects of drugs are seen only when a very large number of patients have been exposed to it, hence safety studies continue after the marketing of the drug.

During trials, high risk patients are usually avoided, thus a 95 year old patient will almost never be included in the trial, but the same patient would be treated with the drug after it is marketed. Post marketing studies therefore reveal more adverse effects than those are seen in the trials. The rule of the thumb is that for an adverse event which has a frequency 1 in 1000, 3000 exposures are required to capture the adverse effect.

In the past, Phase IV trials were in vogue, in which a large number of physicians were chosen as investigators and they conducted a small study of around 10 subjects each. The reports were collected and compiled and submitted to the regulatory authorities. However, these studies added little to existing knowledge on the drug.

Now, Periodic Safety Update Reports are required by the regulators. These reports are compiled by sponsors on the basis of spontaneous reporting of adverse events by physicians. PSURs need to be submitted to the Regulators at specified periodicity as shown in Table 2.5.

Table 2.5: Periodicity of PSUR

	India	US	ICH Region
Initial	6 monthly for first two years	Quarterly for first three years	
	Annually for the next two years	Annually	

The disadvantage of PSURs is under-reporting of adverse events by practicing physicians. In some countries, PSURs and the pharmacovigilance system works excellently while it is still being tested in our country.

All pharmaceuticals carry a risk, but this risk needs to be identified and managed. The FDA recommends as the deployment of risk management which composes of three parts namely;

1. Risk identification
2. Risk quantification
3. Risk minimization

Pharmacovigilance, the branch concerned with pharmaceutical risk, is a programme that must be put in place before clinical trials on a new drug and must continue to operate even after the drug has been marketed if we are to assure our next generations of better and safer drugs.

REFERENCES

1. DiMassi, JA, Hansen, RW, Grabowski, HG. The price of innovation: new estimates of drug development costs. Journal of Health Economics, 2003, 22:151–185.

2. Collier, R. Drug development cost estimates hard to swallow Canadian Medical Association Journal.2009, 180(3): 279–280.

3. Asmild M., Oswald N Krzywkowsk KM, et al Upscaling and Automation of Electrophysiology: Toward High Throughput Screening in Ion Channel Drug Discovery. Receptors and Channels, 2003, 9 (1) 49-58.

4. Church MK, Gradidge CF The activity of sodium cromoglycate analogues in human lung in vitro: a comparison with rat passive cutaneous anaphylaxis and clinical efficacy. Br J Pharmacol. 1980; 70(2):307-11.

5. Rosenberger WF., New Directions in Adaptive Designs, Statistical Sceince, 1996, 11(2): 137-148.

Chapter ... 3

CLINICAL RESEARCH ETHICS

> *"Ethics is not definable, is not implementable, because it is not conscious; it involves not only our thinking, but also our feeling."*
> **Valdemar W. Setzer**

HISTORY OF HUMAN EXPERIMENTATION

The beginning of medicine is more of a conjecture than history. Early man is known to have lived in clans, in which the men hunted together, while the women tended to children and managed the 'home'. It is obvious that injuries to the men which occurred during hunting or due to attacks by animals were tended to by one or more members of the clan, who became the doctors.

Although there is no record to establish when plants were first used for medicinal purposes (herbalism), the use of plants as healing agents is an ancient practice. Over time through emulation of the behavior of fauna, a medicinal knowledge base developed and was passed down the generations. As tribal culture specialized, specific castes, Shamans and apothecaries performed the 'niche occupation' of healing.

A realistic description of clan life has been given in *The Clan of the Cave Bear*, a historical fiction novel by Jean M. Auel about prehistoric times, set somewhat before the extinction of the Neanderthal race after 600,000 years as a species, and at least 10-15,000 years after 'Homo sapiens' remains are documented and dated in Europe as a viable second human species.

The story is of a 5-year old Cro-Magnon girl who is suddenly orphaned and left homeless by an earthquake that destroys her family's camp. She is lost and wanders aimlessly, naked, unable to feed herself, for several days. She is found by a group of Neanderthal people, the "Clan", whose cave was destroyed in the earthquake and is searching for a new home. The medicine woman of the group, Iza, discovers the girl and asks permission from the head of the Clan, to help her, even though she is clearly a daughter of a different clan.

The scenario described comes closest to what probably happened and speaks of the importance of the Medicine man (in this case woman) in the clan life, and matches the one described by Desmond Morris in his seminal work, *'The Naked Ape'*. Early medicine was not guided by any prior knowledge, but was more of trial and error, in fact, most medical practice was medical research.

Since long, human societies have medical beliefs that provide explanations for birth, death, and disease. Throughout history, illness has been attributed to witchcraft, demons, adverse astral influence, or the will of the gods. These ideas still retain some power, with faith-healing and shrines still used in some places, although the rise of scientific medicine over the past millennium has altered or replaced mysticism in most cases.

Ancient Egypt developed a large, varied and fruitful medical tradition. Although medicine dealt with the supernatural, it eventually developed a practical use in the fields of anatomy, public health, and clinical diagnostics. The information in the Edwin Smith Papyrus may date to a time as early as 3000 B.C. The earliest known surgery in Egypt was performed in Egypt around 2750 B.C. Though advances were made in medicine during this period, there is little evidence to suggest that animals were used for research. In fact, all research was done on human subjects and patients.

One of the earliest clinical trial on humans is reported in the Old Testament (Daniel 1:11-16). This was conducted in the prison of the King Nebuchadnezzar, where Daniel is imprisoned. It is believed that Daniel said to the guard: "Please test your servants for ten days: Give us nothing but vegetables to eat and water to drink. Then compare our appearance with that of the young men who eat the royal food, and treat your servants in accordance with what you see." At the end of ten days they looked healthier and better nourished than any of the young men who were fed meat and wine. Daniel has been dated variously but 600 BCE is a date which is agreed upon by many.

The Egyptian Queen Cleopatra (69-30 B.C.) is known to have tested medicines and poisons on her slaves. She also believed that male and female foetuses developed at different rates and to prove her point, she got her slaves impregnated. Then she killed her slaves at different stages of their pregnancy to observe the growth of the foetus, but she left no records of her results. It is recorded that she took adequate care to ensure that conception dates were carefully recorded and products of earlier conception were not present when the experiment began.

In the third and fourth centuries BCE, Aristotle and Erasistratus were among the first to perform experiments on living animals. Galen, a physician in second-century Rome, dissected pigs and goats, and is known as the "father of vivisection." The use of animals for medical research including testing of drugs was opposed to by Avicenna (also known as Ibn Sinna), an Arab physician who lived in the 10th Century in Bukhara. One of his most famous works, *The Canon of Medicine* was a standard medical text at many universities till as late as 1650. While commenting on studies on new drugs Avicenna wrote:

"The experimentation must be done with the human body, for testing a drug on a lion or a horse might not prove anything about its effect on man".

The earliest clinical trial using controls was conducted by James Lind, a ship's doctor in England. During the circumnavigation by Commodore Anson, 380 of the 510 sailors perished due to scurvy prompting Lind to take up a study on treatments for the disease. The trial is described in his own words as follows:

"On the 20th of May 1747, I selected twelve patients in the scurvy, on board the Salisbury at sea. Their cases were as similar as I could have them. They all in general had putrid gums, the spots and lassitude, with weakness of the knees. They lay together in one place, being a proper apartment for the sick in the fore-hold; and had one diet common to all, viz. water gruel sweetened with sugar in the morning; fresh mutton-broth often times for dinner; at other times light puddings, boiled biscuit

with sugar, etc., and for supper, barley and raisins, rice and currants, sago and wine or the like. Two were ordered each a quart of cyder a day. Two others took twenty-five drops of elixir vitriol three times a day ... Two others two spoonfuls of vinegar three times a day ... Two of the worst patients were put on a course who took two spoonfuls of vinegar three times a day ... Two of the worst patients were put on a course of sea-water ... Two others had each two oranges and one lemon given them every day ... The two remaining patients, took ... an electary recommended by a hospital surgeon ... The consequence was, that the most sudden and visible good effects were perceived from the use of oranges and lemons; one of those who had taken them, being at the end of six days fit for duty ... The other was the best recovered of any in his condition; and ... was appointed to attend the rest of the sick. Next to the oranges, I thought the cyder had the best effects ..."

During the trial, all the participants were given a standard diet, and the results meticulously recorded. Lind however failed to mention how the selection was done, were the sailors asked for consent, or did they volunteer. Keeping with the rule of the Royal Navy in force then, Lind probably did not consider these as important.

Throughout history, the use of human beings for research was rampant. In a very large number of cases, the research benefited the subjects and they were not forced to participate. In many instances, slaves and prisoners were used to satisfy the scientific curiosity of researchers, and often the researchers believed that they were doing good for the subjects.

Though protected by the Third Geneva Convention (1929), use of prisoners for research has continued, and probably continues even today. With the abolition of slavery worldwide, there are no slaves for use in medical research.

With slaves being no longer available, and prisoners being protected, medical researchers have had to do with volunteers. Human beings would volunteer for research only when they knew that they would be protected. Other pressures on researchers ensured that the subjects of research would be well-treated and their rights and well- being protected.

In some parts of the world, abuse of human rights and humans continues unabated, but in most parts this has been only sporadic. In countries like Rwanda , Ethiopia, Sierra Leone, large scale violation of human rights is the rule rather than the exception, while elsewhere it is an exception.

Medical research today includes new drug research as a separate entity which uses animals and humans in tandem. All initial studies on new drugs are conducted on animals till the safety and efficacy of the drug is established. Once this has been done, and the drug is considered worthy of further investigations, human studies begin.

Human subjects of today are protected from abuse, and there are a number of systems that ensure their well-being. The first of these is the ethical attitude of the investigator and the investigational team. Secondly, we have the codes of research according to which research can be conducted. Third is the oversight provided by the Ethics Committees (or Institutional Review Boards).

The main tool to ensure that all participation is voluntary is the Informed Consent Form. This document informs the subjects of their rights and gives all information that is required by them to take an educated decision. An external influence that ensures the ethical treatment of human subjects in research is that of the media. This powerful lobby is often over-enthusiastic in condemning the work of scientists, but on the whole it has played a constructive role in protecting subjects.

Oaths and Codes

A majority of humans behave in a socially acceptable way, for others, society makes rules. Thus while an individual has legal rights, there are also legal duties to be carried out. However there are issues which are not strictly legally enforceable, yet desirable, for these, we have moral duties. Ethics is itself a branch of philosophy that addresses questions about morality—that is, concepts such as good and bad, noble and ignoble, right and wrong, justice and virtue etc.

Possibly, the oldest law code is the one given in the Bible, the Ten Commandments. The era of these commandments is unknown since the Bible has not been dated scientifically. The Ten Commandments, or Decalogue, is a list of religious and moral imperatives that, according to the Hebrew Bible, were spoken by God (referred to in several names) to the people of Israel from the mountain referred to as Mount Sinai, and later authored by God and given to Moses in the form of two stone tablets. They are recognized as a moral foundation in Judaism, Christianity and Islam. However they do not speak of medicine or medical practice.

The next written (or carved) code of laws was that of Hammurabi believed to have been prepared around 1750 B.C. Para 215 to 224 speaks of the practice of medicine, payments for the same and punishments for botched-up treatments. The code extensively dealt with many types of crimes, some which are not even covered by criminal codes, and prescribed penalties for them. Maiming or death was a rather common punishment while for physicians chopping off their hands was most common. If this was indeed the practice then, combined with the skills available, there must have been a large number of handless physicians in Babylon at that time.

Around 700 B.C. was the zenith of Indian medicine and a code was evolved for medical practitioners. This oath of initiation contains a number of pointers for good medical practice that are in vogue even today. Physicians of the period were supposed to take this oath before commencing their career, and it included maintaining confidentiality of all information that came to the knowledge of the physician. The physician was also required to treat women (or examine them) only when the latter were accompanied by their husbands or guardians - a precaution taken by most physicians even today.

Within a few centuries, Greek medicine gave us the Hippocratic Oath, a code of medical practice for physicians. This Oath was certainly not written by Hippocrates only, but by some contemporary writers as well, and it appears the work of at least two physicians, one of whom may have probably been Hippocrates. Although mostly of historic and traditional value, the Oath is considered a rite of passage for practitioners of medicine in some countries, although nowadays the modernized version of the text varies among the countries.

A number of oaths were developed in the United States, each with slightly varying language but with a common theme. These prescribed the best medical practices but did not make any specific recommendation for medical research. These fell by the wayside while the Hippocratic Oath continued to be the one most commonly used.

In the year 1900, the Prussian government published the first code for medical research, known as the Berlin Code, which was in the form of a directive issued by the Minister for Educational, Religious and Medical Affairs. The highly controversial experiments conducted by Albert Neisser (1855-1916), were the reason for the minister to issue these directives. The term 'innovative therapy' was used to refer to drug treatments or therapies under development and the directive stated that trials of such treatment could be studied in humans only if:

1. The subject was not a minor or otherwise incompetent to volunteer.
2. The subject gave an informed consent to the study.
3. Consent was given after by a proper explanation of the possible negative effects of intervention.

The concept of informed consent was first introduced in the Berlin Code in 1900, and not in the Nuremberg Code as is widely believed.

In 1929, disaster struck Germany when live tuberculosis bacilli was administered to children in place of the BCG vaccine. Of the 76 children injected, 68 died due to tuberculosis, an enquiry was ordered and the scientists responsible were prosecuted and jailed. The Government of the day (known as the Weimar Republic Government) issued the Guidelines for Human Experimentation (1931).

The guidelines of 1931 were based on the Berlin Code 1900, and each point in the code was expanded and elaborated, in addition to new conditions that were introduced. In these guidelines too, the word research was not used. The terminology used was 'innovative therapy', which is to be read as research. Important issues addressed by these guidelines included the following:

1. A differentiation was made between therapeutic and non-therapeutic interventions.
2. Research must be justified and performed according to ethical principles of medical practice.
3. An assessment of risks and benefits should be made before commencing the research and human studies to be preceded by animal studies.
4. Subjects must have given unambiguous consent, with relevant information being provided to them.
5. Care to be exercised if subjects are below the age of 18.
6. Exploitation of subjects' hardships to be avoided.
7. Extreme caution to be exercised when using live microorganism.
8. Physicians to take complete responsibility of research.
9. Investigators to submit a report on all aspects of the research project, including a statement of consent of subjects.
10. Publication of results to ensure confidentiality of subjects and protect their dignity.
11. Further conditions include:
    (a) Prohibition of research where consent has not been obtained.
    (b) Avoid human experiments if animal research can provide required data.
    (c) Subjects below 18 years of age not to be used if there is danger to their life.
    (d) Experiments in dying subjects are not allowed.

12. Physicians are allowed to use innovative therapy, if they are convinced that existing methods are unlikely to succeed.

13. Continuous training to ensure that physicians are updated on research methodology.

Shortly after issuing these guidelines, the government fell and the *National sozialistische Deutsche Arbeiterpartei* (National Socialist German Workers' Party, NSDAP), abbreviated as Nazi Party, came to power. The Guidelines of 1931 were never officially repealed, and they remained on the statute, though they were ignored and forgotten.

After World War II, doctors and administrators responsible for unethical and inhuman experiments on prisoners and other unwanted populations in Germany were brought to trial in Nuremberg. Officially known as United States of America v. Karl Brandt, et al.), this trial was the first of 12 trials for war crimes that the United States authorities held. These trials were held before U.S. military courts, with 20 of the 23 defendants being medical doctors and all were accused of having been involved in Nazi human experimentation.

During the trial, the prosecution led by Brig. Gen. Telford Taylor, made no reference to the Guidelines for Human Experimentation 1931, which were in force before and after the War. The 23 defendants were charged with crimes against humanity without any reference to the Guidelines in force. In his opening statement, Gen. Taylor spoke of the German law passed in 1933 for preventing cruelty to animals. Gen. Taylor said:

"If the principles announced in this law had been followed for human beings as well, this indictment would never have been filed. It is perhaps the deepest shame of the defendants that it probably never even occurred to them that human beings should be treated with at least equal humanity."

It is clear that the prosecution was ignorant to the Guidelines, and the defendants and their lawyers made no attempt to remind them, if they themselves were aware of the law of the land. At the end of the trial the medical experts, Drs. Leo Alexander and Andrew Conway Ivy handed over a ten-point memorandum entitled 'Permissible Medical Experiments' to the Judges on the tribunal. With modifications, this memorandum went on to be known as the Nuremberg Code. This code calls for standards such as voluntary consent of patients, avoidance of unnecessary pain and suffering, and that experimentation should not end in death or disability of subjects.

The United States acknowledges the pre-eminence of the code and states that "The Nuremberg Code is the most complete and authoritative statement of the law of informed consent to human experimentation. It is also part of international common law and may be applied, in both civil and criminal cases by state, federal and municipal courts in the United States."

The code is however not free of faults. Firstly, it is a static document, and has not undergone any revision. Since concepts of ethics change with time, any code to remain relevant has to be revisited. There are also some controversies about the language used in the code, which leaves it open to interpretation. As of today, the code is of historic value, but little else.

The World Medical Association (WMA) developed The Declaration of Helsinki as a set of ethical principles for the medical community regarding human experimentation, and is widely regarded as the cornerstone document of human research ethics. The Declaration was originally adopted in June 1964 in Helsinki, Finland, and has since undergone six revisions (the most recent at the General Assembly in October 2008) and two clarifications, growing considerably in length from 11 to 32 paragraphs. The Declaration is an important document in the history of research ethics as the first significant effort of the medical community to regulate research by itself, and forms the basis of most subsequent documents.

The Declaration developed the ten principles first stated in the Nuremberg Code, and tied them to the Declaration of Geneva (1948), a statement of physician's ethical duties. The Declaration more specifically addressed clinical research, reflecting changes in medical practice from the term 'Human Experimentation' used in the Nuremberg Code. A notable change from the Nuremberg Code was a relaxation of the conditions of consent, which was 'absolutely essential' under Nuremberg. Now doctors were asked to obtain consent 'if at all possible' and research was allowed without consent where proxy consent, such as a legal guardian, was available.

The greatest contribution of the DOH stemmed from two of it's articles; 10 and 15. Article 10 states that "No national or international ethical, legal or regulatory requirement should reduce or eliminate any of the protections for research subjects set forth in this Declaration." As a result of this, most signatories are bound by the DOH and countries that have signed the document have to take care not to trespass over any protection given by the DOH.

Article 15 states that "The research protocol must be submitted for consideration, comment, guidance and approval to a research ethics committee before the study begins." The concept of Ethics Committees, also known as the Institutional Review Board (IRB) or Independent Ethics Committee (IEC) was been introduced, in the first revision of the Declaration. Thus if any code has had maximal impact on clinical research in recent times, it is the DOH.

The DOH is not a legally binding instrument in international law, but instead draws it's authority from the degree to which it has been codified in, or influenced, national or regional legislation and regulations. It's role was described by a Brazilian forum in 2000 in the following words:, "*Even though the Declaration of Helsinki is the responsibility of the World Medical Association, the document should be considered the property of all humanity*".

It is paradoxical, that while the US was spearheading the movement for ethical research, it's own Public Health Service (PHS) was involved in one of the most unethical trials. Initiated in 1932, the U.S. PHS sponsored a trial to investigate the prognosis of untreated syphilis. Initially, 399 men with syphilis were chosen as the experimental group and 201 on infected controls were recruited. These people were followed up for 40 years, and though the death rate in the syphilitic group was twice as that of the control group, no treatment was given to the syphilitic group.

In 1940s, penicillin became freely available, and is still the drug of choice for syphilis, yet these people were denied treatment. Since most of the patients were poor, illiterate and black, they did not even demand it. The study continued, under numerous supervisors, until 1972, when a leak to the Press resulted in it's termination. The study had repercussions on the numerous men who died of syphilis, wives who contracted the disease, and children born with congenital syphilis.

The uproar that followed the exposé, forced the U.S. Government to pass the National Research Act, and the United States Department of Health, Education, and Welfare (which was renamed as Health and Human Services) was asked to frame guidelines for research. The report, known as the Belmont report was published in 1979, and is one of the finest guideline on this subject.

This report gave importance to three principles; respect for persons, beneficence and justice. Respect for persons dictates that the individual's wishes, should be respected and every person shall be free to decide whether to take part or not in a trial, and having taken part whether to continue or not. In other words, a subject should join a research trial and continue in the trial at his/her own free will. This decision by any person must be reached after being briefed of the advantages and disadvantages of the research, and the burdens on the subject. Respect also means that confidentiality shall be maintained with respect to identifiable data.

It is accepted that every person is unable give such consent at some part of the life, such as infancy and childhood. Some persons are never able to give an informed consent due to disease or other medical condition that precludes such a decision. Such people with diminished autonomy are known as vulnerable subjects. In these situations, additional protection needs to be offered to such individuals.

People from the financially weaker sections of the society, those with lesser education and at a lower station in life have less autonomy than others. Wars, starvation, poverty and deprivation all reduce the autonomy of individuals. There is a difference in autonomy of individuals in different regions of the world. In large parts of the Arab world, women have very few rights and their status is often akin to second-class citizens. Widows, in In some parts of the world, widows and separated women are not given the same rights as other women. These differences ought to be considered before deciding upon the protection given to subjects in different regions of the world.

The principle of beneficence dictates that concern of the subject must override all other considerations and the investigators must maximize the benefits and minimize the risk to the subjects. In simple terms, if the investigator can reduce the risk of gastric intolerance to non steroidal anti inflammatory agents (NSAIDs) by advising their use after a light meal only, then the investigator must do so. Another example of maximizing benefits and minimizing risks involves cooling of the scalp during chemotherapy for cancer. Scalp cooling helps reduce hair loss following treatment with anthracyclines and taxanes, which is a distressing side-effect for young women. Failure of an investigator to inform the subject about this would amount to unethical practice.

Certain randomization schemes, such as the response adaptive schemes offer more benefit to subjects, by increasing the chances of a subject getting the better drug. Such schemes may be considered more ethical than those where a subject has equal chance of being randomized to any arm of the trial.

The third principle in the Belmont Report is that of Justice, which is the most important and the most difficult one. Justice is defined as a concept of moral rightness based on ethics, rationality, law, natural law, religion, fairness, or equity, along with the punishment of the breach of said ethics. Justice has been debated for long in history and we are yet to come to a unanimous understanding about it. The Belmont report states that benefits and risks of research should be distributed in a just fashion. As a principle of ethics one should be just, but what does justice mean? It could mean any one of the many ways of distribution, equally, according to need, as per merit or as per status.

There is no unanimity as to how to distribute the benefits and risks or research. Plato had argued that treating unequal people equally is perpetuating inequality. People are by nature unequal and it is very difficult to formulate or follow a scheme which will ensure just distribution of benefits and risks. In the past the concept of justice was applied to punishments and did not really apply to research. However, in the past, it was the poor who participated in the research, while benefits flowed to the rich.

The report suggests that equal distribution of risks and benefits is fraught with confusion. Equal distribution could mean many things, such as (a) equal distribution to all people (b) distribution proportional to need (c) distribution proportional to contribution (d) distribution proportional to merit and (e) distribution proportional to effort. The concept of justice is a complex one and has vexed humanity throughout.

Given this historical background, it is clear that the concepts of justice are relevant to research involving human subjects too. The selection of research subjects could be made just by avoiding automatic selection of underprivileged people such as welfare patients, particular racial and ethnic minorities, or persons confined to institutions. Subjects should not be chosen merely on basis of their availability and their compromised position, nor their manipulability, rather than for reasons directly related to the problem being studied.

Some authors add the principle of absence of malfeasance to the three existing ones (autonomy, beneficence and justice). Malfeasance is the opposite of beneficence, and both these concepts are mutually exclusive. Thus when one includes beneficence, malfeasance is automatically excluded. The Belmont Report excels in being brief, but comprehensive, and represents today one of the best practices to follow along with the DOH. It's efficacy in curbing unethical research is a question worth examining.

The Council for International Organizations of Medical Sciences (CIOMS); an international, non-governmental, not-for-profit organization was the next body to develop a code of ethics, which surprisingly is not considered very important. The original guidelines were developed in 1993 and updated in 2002. The original guidelines had 15 points which now have been enlarged to 210. These guidelines are comprehensive and extensive; it is therefore unfortunate that the guidelines does not carry the importance it should.

The Indian Government asked the Indian Council for Medical Research (ICMR) to formulate the guidelines for research and the ICMR published its guidelines in 2000. These guidelines were developed by a committee headed by Hon. Justice M. N. Venkatachaliah, (Former Chief Justice of India and Chairperson of the National Human Rights Commission).

These guidelines were reviewed and revised by a committee headed by Dr. M. S. Valiathan, Chairman, Central Ethics Committee on Human Research. These guidelines address issues other than those encountered in clinical testing of drugs and sub-sections have been added on the following issues:

1. Clinical Evaluation of Drugs/Devices/Diagnostics/Vaccines/Herbal Remedies.
2. Epidemiological Studies.
3. Human Genetics and Genomic Research.

4.   Research in Transplantation.

5.   Assisted Reproductive Technologies.

The role of all these codes and guidelines is to prevent violation of human rights and ensure ethical treatment of research subjects. Theoretically, an understanding of what is moral and what is immoral should be adequate for doing so, but views of morality itself differ from individual to individual. Not all those who do injustice on others are aware of how wrong their actions are. Most wrong-doers justify their actions, though others may not buy this justification.

Unethical Research

History is replete with examples of unethical research. We believe that what has happened in the past will not happen again, but this is wishful thinking. It is necessary to study and learn from history, the statement 'those who cannot learn from history are doomed to repeat it' is actually a variant of George Santayana's statement. 'Those who cannot remember the past are condemned to repeat it', and is extremely relevant in this field.

The earliest record of unethical research is the work of Cleopatra, to which reference has been made earlier. In order to investigate whether male and female fetuses develop at different rates, she got her slaves impregnated, and then sacrificed them at different stages of pregnancy to study the fetuses. If queried, she would have probably frowned at the suggestion of being unethical, since in her time, the life of a slave was of no consequence. A slave was the property of the owner, and had no freedom or choice to decide his or her fate. Viewed from today's stand-point, the studies were unethical and no modern society would permit it.

Such research work continued on slaves for a very long time. More evidence is available from experiments conducted on slaves in America. Dr. J. Marion Sims believed that African slaves had a high tolerance for pain and hence required no pain-relief during surgery. Sims experimented on 11 (eleven) slaves at one time, subjecting one slave to 30 surgeries, none of which the woman needed. Since slaves were plenty and cheap, Sims had an almost inexhaustible clinical material for his experiments.

The experiments conducted by Sims were well-known to the medical world; yet he was elected as the President of the American Medical Association, and the American Gynecological Association in 1876, suggesting that most physicians did not find fault with his work, even if they did not endorse it freely.

The greatest violation of research ethics occurred around the World War II at the hands of the Nazis. The Americans gathered adequate evidence of murders, tortures, and other atrocities committed in the name of medical science, to convict 23 doctors and officials after the war.

The Nazis conducted medical experiments without the subjects' consent, upon civilians, political and war prisoners, and on individuals considered unwanted, in the course of which experiments they committed murders. brutalities, cruelties, tortures, atrocities, and other inhuman acts. Such experiments included, but were not limited to the following:

1.   High-Altitude Experiments.

2.   Freezing Experiments.

3.   Malaria Experiments.

4.   Lost (Mustard) Gas Experiments.

5. Sulfanilamide Experiments.

6. Bone, Muscle, and Nerve Regeneration and Bone Transplantation Experiments.

7. Sea-Water Experiments.

8. Epidemic Jaundice Experiments.

9. Sterilization Experiments.

10. Spotted Fever (Fleckfieber) Experiments.

11. Experiments with Poison.

12. Incendiary Bomb Experiments.

There was a therapeutic goal for the first ten types of experiments, but the last two were conducted only to find more efficient way of killing people, hence cannot even be called medical research.

No one knows how many people were maimed or killed in these experiments, but estimates are that hundreds of thousands such people died and only a handful survived to tell the tale. After the war, 23 doctors and officials were tried and convicted for crimes against humanity, 7 were hanged and the rest sent to prison for varying lengths of time.

There are photographs, documents and films full of records of Nazi Medicine, but little is known about similar experiments conducted by the Japanese during the war. The Japanese too committed similar and probably even more horrible crimes, but they traded the data they had collected for immunity from prosecution. Nazi war trials were responsible for bringing their deeds in public domain, but the Japanese scientists faced no prosecution and their deeds remain hidden.

Rivaling in size Germany's notorious Auschwitz-Burkenau death camp was Unit 731's facility located at, Pingfan, Manchuria. The entire programme was headed by Shiro Ishii, a young captain, who rose to the rank of a general through his sheer inhuman behaviour. This isolated location was chosen for secrecy and security. Pingfan's compound was spread across 6 square kilometers. It housed administrative buildings, laboratories, workers' dormitories, barracks, an autopsy-dissecting building and a special prison to house human test-subjects. Three giant furnaces handled "disposal" of human carcasses. Subjects chosen for human testing were humorously referred to as "logs" or "lumber." A smaller camp at Mukden in Manchuria, housed American, British, Australian and New Zealand PoW's. Here too, hideous experiments were performed in in secrecy.

Constructed by forced labour, the first major BW facility was built at Beiyinhe, some 70 kms. outside Harbin. Known locally as the "Zhong Ma Prison Camp," the Chinese labour force was required to wear eye-shields, to prevent them from seeing what they were building. Conditions were harsh. At the centre of the compound a large building known as "Zhong Ma Castle" housed prisoners and a human experiment laboratory. Numbering between 500-600, the "logs" were a mixed bunch. Ranging from "bandits," "criminals" through to Orwellian "suspicious persons," their routine was severe. Shackled hand and foot they were, nonetheless, well-fed and exercised regularly. Healthy specimens were vital for scientific experimentation.

In an experiment, prisoners were subjected to Phosgene gas, injected into a brick-lined room, some were injected with 15 mg of Potassium cyanide. Others burned under 20,000 volts of electricity. Not a fatal dose, they were later disposed of by poison injections. Still others were slowly roasted to death by lower but continuous voltages. All experiments were subject to meticulous record keeping.

The Unit was also keenly interested in "frostbite" experimentation. This was a particularly important project. Frostbite degraded military efficiency during the bitter Manchurian winters. By this time BW research facility was relocated to the massive Ping Fan complex in 1939 and frostbite tests were routine. Emulating similar work by the notorious Nazi, Dr. Josep Mengele, naked prisoners - males and females - were subjected to sub-freezing temperatures. It was usual for these "logs" to have their limbs beaten with sticks until they resounded with a hard, hollow ring - signifying the completion of the freezing process was complete. Later they were "defrosted" by a range of experimental techniques.

Other experiments involved "hanging material" (i.e. humans) upside down to determine the time taken for subjects to choke to death. Another involved injecting air into prisoners to test for the onset of embolisms. Almost indescribable was the practice of injecting horse urine into the kidneys of prisoners. A common practice was feeding "logs" with food and drink heavily laced with cholera, heroin and castor oil seeds and other pathogens. All these studies thankfully ended with the surrender of the Japanese in 1946.

While all these studies were conducted on prisoners, in the US, studies were conducted on free citizens. The most notorious of these was the Tuskegee study, which brought out not only the callous attitude of investigators, but also their rabid racism. All the syphilitic patients selected for observation in this trial were poor, mostly uneducated and black. The study was also pointless, and added nothing to existing knowledge about the disease or its treatment.

Peter Buxtun, a venereal disease investigator working with the Public Health Services questioned the ethics and morality of the study in 1966, only to be rebuffed by the CDC. Buxtun finally went to the press in the early 1970s. The story broke first in the Washington Star in 1972. It became front-page news in the New York Times the following day. Senator Edward Kennedy called Congressional hearings, at which Buxtun and other officials testified. As a result of public outcry, in 1972, the CDC and PHS appointed an ad hoc advisory panel to review the study. It concluded that the study was medically unjustified and ordered it's termination. This study also led to the Belmont Report in 1979 and the establishment of the Office for Human Research Protections (OHRP). It also led to the regulation requiring Institutional Review Boards for protection of human subjects in clinical research.

The Willowbrook School, a state institution for mentally-retarded individuals conducted studies on Jaundice between 1963 and 1966. These studies were designed to gain an understanding of the natural history of infectious hepatitis and subsequently to test the effects of gamma globulin in preventing or ameliorating the disease. The subjects, all children, were deliberately infected with the hepatitis virus; early subjects were fed extracts of stools from infected individuals and later subjects received injections of more purified virus preparations.

Investigators defended the deliberate injection of these children by pointing out that the vast majority of them acquired the infection anyway while at Willowbrook, and perhaps it would be better for them to be infected under carefully controlled research conditions. During the course of these studies, Willowbrook closed its doors to new inmates, claiming overcrowded conditions. However, the hepatitis programme, because it occupied it's own space at the institution, was able to continue to admit new patients. Thus, in some cases, parents found that they were unable to admit their child to Willowbrook unless they agreed to his or her participation in the studies.

A number of studies violating the rights of the research subjects continue to surface from time to time. In India too, ICMR was involved in a study of cervical dysplasia, the ethics of which have been questioned. In an attempt to study rates of progression of uterine cervical dysplasia to malignancy, the Indian Council of Medical Research during 1976-88 allocated 1158 women with varying degrees of cervical dysplasia to long term follow-up. The development of carcinoma *in situ* was defined as the end point for treatment.

The investigators, from the Institute of Cytology and Preventive Oncology in New Delhi, said that they did not obtain written consent on the grounds that most of the women in the study were illiterate and that written consent was not mandatory when the study was launched. The study has helped India evolve screening guidelines for the National Cancer Control Programme.

The trials of an anti-cancer molecule at the Regional Cancer Center in Thiruvananthapuram and psychiatry trials in which a company known as Cogtest was involved have been implicated in fraudulent and unethical research. Fraudulent research must be included in a discussion on unethical research, since unscientific trials are unethical so should be fraudulent ones.

When human subjects are used in research, there is some amount of risk that the participants are taking. They do so for a variety of reasons, but the presence of an altruistic motive cannot be denied. Any study that poses even a minimal risk should not be undertaken unless there is reason to believe that the results will add to our knowledge of a disease or it's treatment.

When frauds are committed in research, the data obtained could be misleading and hence does not extend our knowledge about the disease or it's treatment. Such a research is therefore unethical. Additionally, experiments conducted by Nazis to find a more effective and economic way of killing people was not only unethical but also criminal, since the end point of the study was illegal.

There are many theories which try to explain why people behave unethically or carry out unethical and illegal orders. The foremost explanation is self-interest, people do so, to prevent personal loss or for personal gain. Psychiatric disturbances are another powerful reason for such behaviour. Finally it comes to individual character, but whether this is inherited or acquired during development is not clear, in fact the debate between nurture and nature is still on.

Vulnerable Populations

The Berlin Code and the Guidelines for Human experimentation of 1931 suggested utmost care while conducting research on children. The Nuremberg Code went a step ahead and elaborated that informed consent be taken from subjects and they should be able to exercise their free will. The Declaration of Helsinki went a step ahead and provided addition protection for vulnerable individuals.

It is often thought that vulnerable individuals mean those who are vulnerable to the adverse effects of drugs, but that is not true. Vulnerable really means those who are vulnerable to manipulation, and cannot exercise their free will. The question arises, as to who are these vulnerable individuals, and is there an internationally acceptable definition of vulnerability.

The place of an individual in a society depends upon the society, and not the individual. The chief of a tribe in Africa could be the most respected and revered individual in the village, but would be a misfit and an outcast in a corporate boardroom. Vulnerability status changes from society to society. For example, women are extremely vulnerable to exploitation in Afghanistan, but not in, say, France. For this reason, there cannot be a universal definition of vulnerability.

Any person who lacks autonomy (the power to decide) is vulnerable. Such persons are either legally incompetent to take decisions, or they are in a condition that they cannot take a decision. Some of these persons may not have the freedom to take a decision, since they could be forced through coercion or blackmail to do what is wanted of them. Emotional blackmail is commonly used by family members to make a person bend to the will of the family.

There are certain classes of individuals who are vulnerable universally. These groups can be defined, and they are:

1.   Children,
2.   Prisoners,
3.   Unconscious patients,
4.   People who are dependent on others,
5.   Mentally incompetent individuals.

Though universally, children are considered vulnerable, all children are not equally vulnerable and there are subsets of children who are more vulnerable than others. Orphans, mentally or physically handicapped children are far more vulnerable than healthy children living with their biological parents. In addition to orphans, India is home to 45 million street children. These are runaways, orphans or deserted, and live on the streets. They have no 'legally authorized representatives' or guardians, hence are highly vulnerable.

Similarly, though all prisoners are vulnerable, not all are equally vulnerable. A prisoner in a jail in Afghanistan is much more vulnerable than one in Sweden. In some countries, political prisoners are worse-off, in others they enjoy lavish lifestyles even in the jail. In a single country, vulnerability may change with time; in India, during the emergency (1975-1977), political prisoners were extremely vulnerable, though they are not so now.

Some guidelines consider pregnant and lactating women as vulnerable subjects. Yet in many societies these women are looked after much more than other women. In our own country, the status of women changes drastically from state to state. A married woman with sons has the highest status, higher than one who only has daughters. A widow (especially a young one) has the lowest status as does a divorced woman. The status of women changes with property and family background. Overall, this is a complex issue and needs careful consideration of the society she lives in to understand her level of vulnerability.

Patients who are unconscious or mentally incapable of understanding consent procedures are also vulnerable. Illiterate patients can be explained the process and they may be recruited, but by their very inability to read they can easily be misled into volunteering for a study which they otherwise would not have. These people are as vulnerable as children.

There is another set of patients who pose a problem to investigators, and these are psychiatric patients. A schizophrenic may listen, understand and comprehend the informed consent process on one day, while totally denying on another day that he ever went through the same. This also applies to patients with Alzheimer's disease or has dementia.

When the subjects to be recruited are vulnerable, the investigators have mechanisms available to them to ensure that the interests of the subjects are well protected. For an incompetent person to take a decision, a Legally Authorized Representative may give proxy consent on behalf of the subject. Since there are no guidelines do not define who an LAR is, they leave the definition to the local laws. Investigators are also at times unable to identify the LAR, and hence they are often reluctant to include such patients. If some guidelines could be formed for the correct identification of LAR, it will benefit both investigators and vulnerable subjects.

A subject who is perfectly able to take a decision, may often be unable to document the same due to blindness or illiteracy. In such a situation, the ICF should be read out to the individual and the consent obtained. A witness (who could be a relative of the subject or a third party) should attest that the process was conducted in his/her presence.

There is a world of difference between a witness and a proxy. A proxy takes decision on behalf of the subject, while a witness attests that the subject took the decision in his/her presence.

Since the quality of the consent is the responsibility of the investigator, each PI should assess the vulnerability of subjects using available information. No doubt, extra protection must be granted to those who are declared as vulnerable in the guidelines. The PI may take extra care to protect subjects who he/she may consider vulnerable. The guidelines define the minimum amount of protection to be granted, but do not limit the protection to other subjects.

The Institutional Review Board (IRB or the IEC) plays an important role in the protection of subjects and special care of vulnerable subjects. When a trial plans to recruit vulnerable group of subjects, certain conditions are put on the trials, such as:

1.　The trial should be expected to produce direct benefit to the subjects.
2.　Trials on vulnerable groups are preceded by other trials.
3.　If results can be obtained by using other subjects, vulnerable subjects should not be used.

The IRB should ensure that due precautions are taken to avoid undue risk to the vulnerable subjects and that adequate protection is available to prevent their abuse.

How a society treats its weakest members is a benchmark of it's development. Protection to the weakest members is essential in a society if all members are to live a free and fearless life.

Informed Consent

An unambiguous consent from the subjects is essential before recruiting them for any clinical trial. This condition has appeared in every code of research ethics, from the Berlin Code to the latest one. Yet this is the issue that is most hotly contested and most violations happen in this area. Informed consent itself has two parts, one is the document (ICF) and the other is the process, or the way the consent is obtained.

The ICF has become progressively longer and the fear of not providing all the required information is making it still longer. Many authorities have identified all the elements which need to be included in the ICF, a discussion on each might be of use. The recommendations of ICH given in the guideline E6 are given below with clarification on each point.

(a)　That the trial involves research.
(b)　The purpose of the trial.
(c)　The trial treatment(s) and the probability for random assignment to each treatment.

(d) The trial procedures to be followed, including all invasive procedures.

(e) The subject's responsibilities.

(f) The aspects of the trial that are experimental.

(g) The reasonably foreseeable risks or inconveniences to the subject and, when applicable, to an embryo, foetus, or nursing infant, if any.

(h) The reasonably expected benefits. When there is no intended clinical benefit to the subject, the subject should be made aware of this.

(i) The alternative procedure(s) or course(s) of treatment that may be available to the subject, and their important potential benefits and risks.

(j) The compensation and/or treatment available to the subject in the event of trial-related injury.

(k) The anticipated prorated payment, if any, to the subject for participating in the trial.

(l) The anticipated expenses, if any, to the subject for participating in the trial.

(m) That the subject's participation in the trial is voluntary and that the subject may refuse to participate or withdraw from the trial, at any time, without penalty or loss of benefits to which the subject is otherwise entitled.

(n) That the monitor(s), the auditor(s), the IRB/IEC, and the regulatory authority(ies) will be granted direct access to the subject's original medical records for verification of clinical trial procedures and/or data, without violating the confidentiality of the subject, to the extent permitted by the applicable laws and regulations and that, by signing a written informed consent form, the subject or the subject's legally acceptable representative is authorizing such access.

(o) That records identifying the subject will be kept confidential and, to the extent permitted by the applicable laws and/or regulations, will not be made publicly available. If the results of the trial are published, the subject's identity would remain confidential.

(p) That the subject or the subject's legally-acceptable representative will be informed in a timely manner if information becomes available that may be relevant to the subject's willingness to continue participating in the trial.

(q) The person(s) to contact for further information regarding the trial and the rights of trial subjects, and whom to contact in the event of trial-related injury.

(r) The foreseeable circumstances and/or reasons under which the subject's participation in the trial may be terminated. The patients would certainly like to know this.

(s) The expected duration of the subject's participation in the trial.

(t) The approximate number of subjects involved in the trial.

All efforts should be made to abbreviate the ICF. It is easy to add yet another element in the ICF, but it becomes difficult to remove one. Excessive information actually means depriving people of information. At no time should an information overload be allowed.

There is a worldwide concern over the increasing complexity of ICF, and lack of comprehension by the subjects. While ICFs are meant to give a thorough understanding of the subject about what is going to be done during the research trial, the length and complexity of the forms have actually reduced the understanding.

Four simple steps have been suggested to make the ICF more comprehensible to subjects:.

1. Consent forms must be shortened.

2. A clear description of research and its purposes, compared to clinical care must be displayed prominently in the consent form.

3. Except in instances of minimal risk or emergency settings where immediate action is necessary, there must be a 'contemplation' or 'cooling down' period between the presentation of the informed consent and its acceptance or rejection.

4. Comprehension of core elements of the research must be assessed before and during the course of the trial.

Another point in ICF is whether one should have such a detailed written document for the perusal by the subject. For all practical purposes, a video or a PowerPoint presentation would possible convey the information better.

The use of a checklist by the PI and the IRB ensures that the ICF meets the requirements and that all the essential elements are contained therein. The IRB members should have an access to this checklist by which they can review the ICF and ensure its completeness.

The Informed Consent Process

The ICF is the backbone of the consent process, but it is not the whole process. The method in which the informed consent is obtained from the subject is equally if not more important. Each site has a different method of administering the consent, and it is the responsibility of the PI to ensure that the process is conducted properly. There are a number of guidelines available for the administration of the process, issued by the various organizations is put together and a comprehensive guideline is presented below:

An initial meeting should be held, when members of the study team provide the subject with the informed consent document and explain it to the subject. The subject can bring a family member or friend for support, and to help the subject keep track of the information presented. This information should be given logically and at a comfortable pace, with plenty of time for the subject to consider it and ask questions. It is okay for the subject to tell the research team anything the subject doesn't understand.

The subject should be given adequate time to digest the information. It can be very difficult to absorb all of this information in one sitting, especially if it is a stressful time. The subject should be given a copy of the document so that the subject can take it home, review it as many times as needed, and discuss it with family, friends, social workers, clergy, a patient representative, or other trusted advisors as appropriate. There is no definition of what is adequate time and the PI should decide what time may be given, generally there should be no limit on this.

The individual concerned with the process should assess the level of the subject's understanding. The research team should take some steps to ensure that the subject understands the information about the study, either by having the subject fill out a questionnaire, asking the subject questions, or having the subject explain certain aspects of the study in the subject's own words. The subject should tell the study team members about anything the subject does not understand. If the subject finds that the document is written in words that are too difficult, the subject should not hesitate to let them know.

Responsibility of Informed Consent

The quality of informed consent is the responsibility of the PI. Therefore the PI must ensure that the ICF is as per the requirements, and that the process is carried out by staff that is well trained. The PI should also ensure that adequate number of consent forms (of the correct version) and translations are available at the site when recruitment begins.

The informed consent may be administered by any member of the investigator's team. The person who takes this responsibility should be able to explain the trial and answer the question, or clear the doubts of the subjects. For this person, it might be preferable to have a medically qualified person administer informed consents; however there is no hard and fast rule about this.

The names of the persons, who are given the responsibility of administering consents, must be documented in a responsibility log, so that the monitors and auditors are clear about the responsibility and accountability. A person whose name does not appear in the responsibility log is not allowed to administer informed consents.

As per the guideline, when a subject is in a dependent relationship with the PI, a physician, not involved in the trial is required to administer the consent. However, the value of this arrangement is unclear. Should the subject refuse to participate, the information would reach the PI, who holds some power over the subject, and the subject will be at a loss. Nonetheless, the use of an independent physician may allow a subject to ask some questions which could not be asked of the PI (with whom there is a dependent relationship). The involvement of the independent physician should be recorded in the trial file. The informed consent process is constantly under scrutiny, and when violation of ethics is noted, most of them are found in this process. It becomes necessary to give extra attention to this process and ensure that the discussions, the documentation is as perfect as possible. Most allegations (including the

Consent of Special Populations

1. **Non-English speaking persons** must have the information presented in a language that they comprehend. The ICF should be translated in the required language and back-translated to ensure that the translation is accurate. For potential research subjects who are unable to understand English:

   (i) The research subject should be provided with a "short form" consent document, written in the potential subject's native language that summarizes the basic elements of informed consent.

   (ii) The standard (i.e., IRB-approved, full-description) informed consent document should be presented verbally to the subject in his/her native language and all questions answered.

2. **Illiterate and/or blind subjects:** Whether a subject is illiterate or blind, the subject cannot read the ICF, in such a situation the ICF should be read out to the individual and the consent obtained. A witness (who could be a relative of the subject or a third party) should attest that the process was conducted in his/her presence.

3. **Subjects incapable of providing the consent:** Subjects may be incompetent to provide consent due to a variety of reasons such as:

   (i) the subject is unconscious.

   (ii) the subject is mentally unsound or has severe psychiatric disability that prevents taking a conscious decision.

(iii) the subject is too ill, (though not unconscious) to comprehend the consent process or sign the form.

In all the above conditions, proxy consent may be obtained from a relative of the subject. The PI and the site staff may decide who could be the legally authorized representative since the guidelines do not specifically define an LAR. The LAR chosen should the person who is likely to take a decision keeping the best interest of the subject in mind.

4.   Subjects legally not authorized to consent: Subjects below the age of consent have no legal authority to consent. Some psychiatric patients might also be considered to fall in this category. However the largest group in this category is children. A child below the age of consent cannot sign the consent form and another person must be asked to provide the consent if such a subject is to be included in the trial.

Children above the age of 10 or 12 (the cut-off age is not specified in any guideline and is at the discretion of the PI and IRB) may be asked to assent to the trial, after the consent has been given by the LAR. In case of children, the LR should be a parent (preferably a biological parent). Special caution should be exercised if the trial is likely to pose significant risks to the child.

5.   Subjects with diminished autonomy: Poverty, illiteracy, imprisonment, wars, terrorism and totalitarian governments reduce the autonomy of the people. While using subjects that fall into these vulnerable groups, extreme care should be taken to protect their rights and well-being. Investigators have a sacred duty to protect all human subjects and this duty should not be relegated to a second place in the search of scientific proof.

Prisoners have very often been the victims of unethical and cruel research. Even in democratic governments, the treatment of prisoners often falls short of humane. The PIs and IRB should ensure that prisoners are not forced to participate in research. Commutation of prison sentences may often prove to be irresistible incentives for prisoners to participate and should be avoided. Prisoners should be counseled and wardens and other authorities warned not to coerce prisoners to participate.

ICH guidelines suggest that pregnant and lactating subjects are more vulnerable than their non-pregnant or lactating counterparts. The PI should assess whether this is true for their subject population.

Waivers to Informed Consent

The earlier codes of ethics made the informed consent essential for all clinical trials. However, later it became clear that informed consent may be waived in certain conditions. The power to waive the consents vested in the IRB and this power should be used with great discretion. In general, consent may be waived if:

*   the research involves no more than minimal risk to the subjects;
*   the waiver or alteration will not adversely affect the rights and welfare of the subjects;
*   the research could not practicably be carried out without the waiver or alteration; and
*   whenever appropriate, the subjects will be provided with additional pertinent information after participation.

Minors: Sub-section D of the Common Rule allows that parental consent or "permission" for a minor child to participate in research, as well as the "assent" of the child can be waived just as waivers may be granted for research on subjects competent to give consent.

Requests to waive some or all of the Informed Consent elements must be fully documented, addressing each of the criteria above. Examples of times when a waiver may be appropriate are when anonymous questionnaires or secondary data are used.

Anonymous Questionnaires Surveys: Anonymous questionnaires and surveys, where the only link to the subject would be the signed Consent Form, allow for written consent to be waived because the subject is better protected without the existence of a signed document.

Secondary Data: If an investigator receives secondary data about human subjects or biological samples from human subjects where no possible personal identifiers are transferred to the researcher, written Consent may be waived.

Behavioural Research: A large amount of research is in progress when human responses to certain situations are measured. If the subject knew that the situation is unreal or that his/her responses are being measured, it would alter the responses. In such a situation, the informed consent could be waived.

The power to waive the consent is vested in the IRB and on every occasion the IRB must thoroughly review the application to waive the consent before granting it. When it is expected that vulnerable subjects are likely to participate or that LARs or witnesses are going to be used, the PI should inform the IRB while applying for approval of the project.

The Institutional Review Board (IRB)

The concept of having the research projects reviewed by an independent group of people was first proposed in the Declaration of Helsinki at it's first revision in 1975. Subsequent changes in the Declaration, taken together with the Belmont Report and other guidelines, have been responsible for making the IRB what it is today. This body could be set up by the institution (site where the trial is performed) or could be an independent one (known as the Independent Ethic Committee – IEC). There is great similarity between the roles and responsibilities of the IRB and IEC and in many publications the two terms are used interchangeably.

The main difference between the two is in their relation to the institution. As is clear, an IEC is an independent body, and it can accept the responsibility of trials going on at any site. An IRB is formed by an institute and it would generally take responsibility of trials conducted at the institute. In many parts of the world, institutes have branches at different locations. The IRB of such an institute may take responsibility for trials conducted at the different branches.

Reading into the spirit of the Guidelines, it is clear that the IRB should have the following characteristics:

1. **Independent**

The IRB may have members of the institute, but it should not be unduly influenced by the policies of the institute.

2. **Knowledgeable**

Members of the IRB should be able to understand the basic concepts of research.

3. **Scientific and non scientific members**

The IRB must have both scientific and non-scientific members. This is essential since non-scientific members can often focus on issues that are overlooked by scientists.

4. Gender representation

There should be an equitable representation of both genders. This requirement does not appear in the definition but is given in almost all guidelines.

Indian guidelines given in Schedule Y (to the Drugs and Cosmetics Rules, 1945) have more requirements, such as:

1. Chairperson of the IRB should preferably be from outside the institute.
2. An individual with judicial or legal background should be included in the IRB.
3. There should be a philosopher, theologist or a member of an NGO on the board.

Membership

The head of the institute is authorized to invite individuals to serve on the IRB. The invitation should mention the position the individual would hold and the term of membership. The invitation letter and the letter of acceptance by the invited person is a part of the IRB records.

On completion of the term of membership, the person may be re-appointed; there is no limit to the terms an individual may serve on an IRB. A member may be asked to leave the IRB if, in the opinion of the chairperson he/she does not contribute to the functioning of the IRB or does not attend the meetings when convened.

At any time, the IRB should have a roster of existing members for the examination of the sponsors or their representatives.

Meetings

The IRB should hold regular meetings, and the schedule would depend upon the trial applications to be reviewed.

Domain experts may be invited to present clarifications or their opinions on scientific issues relating to the trial. These experts are however, not allowed to vote while the final decision is taken.

Applications to be discussed at the meeting should be forwarded to members in advance, so that they have adequate time to study the documents before they come for the meeting. Most IRBs declare a deadline for submission of documents, usually three weeks before the scheduled meeting.

Quorum for Meetings

Different guidelines suggest different quorum for meetings. Indian regulations demand a quorum of five members for conducting a meeting. The guidelines also suggest that the quorum must have the following members:

(a) basic medical scientists (preferably one pharmacologist).
(b) clinicians
(c) legal expert
(d) social scientist / representative of non-governmental voluntary agency /philosopher / ethicist / theologian or a similar person
(e) lay person from the community.

Documents for review

The IRB generally reviews the following documents:

(a) The protocol and its amendments,
(b) The informed consent form, its amendments and translations,
(c) Investigator's Brochure,

(d)   Patient Information sheet (or Brochure) and its translations,

(e)   Insurance for subjects,

(f)   CVs of investigators,

(g)   Advertisement material if any to be used,

(h)   Any other document that the members may like to see.

Responsibilities

The IRB has the responsibility and the authority to approve/ reject or ask for modifications in the trial. While rejecting a proposal, the IRB is required to give reasons for refusing the approval.

The investigators are required to forward to the IRB all Serious Adverse Event reports, which the IRB should evaluate to check whether subjects are at undue risks. In the absence of Data Safety Monitoring Boards, the IRB can provide oversight of the safety of the drugs under trial. All Suspected Unexpected Serious Adverse Reaction reports should also be forwarded to the IRB for review.

The IRB should also review studies in progress periodically. The periodicity of such a review would depend upon the duration of the study and the likelihood of risk to the subjects. In any case, the studies should be reviewed at a frequency of not less than one year.

The protocol to be followed is the one that has been approved by the IRB. If any amendments are made to the protocol, each amendment must be reviewed by the IRB before being implemented. Only if the amendment is for the benefit of the subject or reduces risk to the subject, can the amendment be implemented prior to the IRB approval; a post facto approval can then be sought.

Prior to implementation of an amendment, the IRB's approval must be sought. However, minor or administrative changes (change in telephone numbers or changes in junior members of the investigational team may be cleared by the IRB through an expedited review. Full IRB meetings are not required to approve such changes.

Expedited Reviews

The Chairperson of the IRB may, under certain circumstances, refer a trial proposal for expedited review. This is carried out by one or two senior members of the IRB, chosen by the Chairperson. After these members give their opinion, the Chairperson may accept it and clear the proposal, in case the Chairperson disagrees, the proposal may be referred to the full IRB for a review. As per US laws, an expedited review may be conducted by the IRB chairperson or by one or more experienced reviewers designated by the chairperson from among members of the IRB.

Expedited reviews are permissible for some trials in which the risk to subjects is minimal. US FDA has drawn up a list of trials which may be cleared by an expedited process, which includes:

(A) Research activities that

(1)   present no more than minimal risk to human subjects, and (2) involve only procedures listed in one or more of the following categories.

Waivers for Informed Consent

Informed consent documentation may be waived by the IRB, on application from the PI, if it meets the following conditions:

1.   That the only record linking the subjects and the research would be the consent document and the principal risk would be potential harm resulting from a breach of confidentiality. Each subject will be asked whether the subject wants documentation linking the subject with the research, and the subject's wishes will govern;

2. That the research presents no more than minimal risk of harm to subjects and involves no procedures for which written consent is normally required outside of the research context. In cases in which the documentation requirement is waived, the IRB may require the investigator to provide subjects with a written statement regarding the research;
3. The waiver or alteration will not adversely affect the rights and welfare of the subjects;
4. The research could not practicably be carried out without the waiver or alteration.

Proxy Consents

Often the subject is not in a position to sign a consent form, which could be due to the fact that the subject is legally incompetent to do so, or physically or mentally incapable of doing so. In these situations, the IRB may permit the use of proxy consent by a Legally Authorized Representative (LAR).

When research studies are conducted on children, proxy consent by parents is the norm and assent of the child is required if the child is of an age at which it can convey its wishes to the investigators. There is no recommended age for assent, and the IRB may decide at which age the child's assent is essential.

Proxy consents could be used for patients who have medical conditions that prevent them from taking a decision for themselves. Disorders like schizophrenia, Alzheimer's disease, severe mania, coma render the subject incapable of taking a decision on their own; here LARs may be used.

No guideline defines the LAR but the Belmont Report states: 'The third parties chosen should be those who are most likely to understand the incompetent subject's situation and to act in that person's best interest." With this in mind the IRB can help the PI choose the right LAR, though not much help comes from the guidelines.

In some situations, a subject can take a decision to participate or not, but is unable to document the decision. This could be due to illiteracy, inability to see, or inability to sign the document. In such situations, a witness is used to attest that the subject did consent and consented in the presence of the witness. The witness should preferably an independent person and not related to the investigation team.

There is a world of difference between a witness and a proxy. A proxy takes decision on behalf of the subject, while a witness attests that the subject took the decision in his/her presence.

In cases where trials relate to acute conditions requiring immediate therapy, consents may have to be delayed till the subject recovers adequately to take a decision or a proxy is found to decide on behalf of the subject. Delayed consent usually occurs in emergency situations, when obtaining informed consent might make the study impossible. For example, it may be needed for research undertaken:

*   at the roadside in the event of an accident.
*   at a cardiac arrest.
*   during the early stages of a patient's emergency admission to an accident and emergency department.

IRB Meetings

As stated earlier, IRB meeting should be held regularly and at a periodicity befitting the trial work load. The Member Secretary (MS) of the IRB convenes the meeting at a suitable location and time and informs all members of the same. The MS also circulates the documents received from the PI for study by the members.

The GCP guidelines state that the responsibility of communication with IRB is that of the PI or designated members of the team. The sponsors or the CR should generally not contact the IRB, however if any communication takes place, that is not a crime. Guidelines are not as rigid as some would like to believe.

During the IRB meeting, free discussion should be allowed. Members should be free to voice their opinions with little regard to seniority or education. If a member wishes his or her point to be specifically mentioned in the minutes, the member is allowed to do so. Such a situation may arise when only one or two members dissent to a common decision, but wish their dissent to be recorded.

As stated, as IRB members are not expected to be experts in every field of medicine, they may invite experts for clarifying certain points that escape their comprehension. The PI may also be invited to elaborate or clarify doubts the members may have. However, the experts or the PI shall not vote for or against the trial proposal.

It often happens that some IRB members are PIs too, which is quite common. In such a situation, the member whose proposal is under discussion should excuse himself/herself and abstain from voting. The MS will make a note of the presence of the member, but also show that the member did not vote.

IRB Decision

The IRB may take a decision on the basis of majority opinion or any other formula the members arrive at. This decision is to be conveyed in writing to the PI, as early as possible, since the PI may be waiting only for the approval to begin recruitment. There is a standard format in which the approval has to be conveyed and the format may be developed by the members of the board.

In case the IRB has some suggestions to make regarding any aspect of the trial, they are free to record them in their letter of approval. If the IRB is rejecting the proposal then reasons for rejecting the same should be included in the letter.

IRB Documentation

The IRB must retain all correspondence with its members, beginning with letters inviting them to join the board and their acceptance letters. At any given time, the IRB files must contain an updated list of members serving on the board, which states their names, qualifications, affiliations and even their gender. While Indian sponsors may be able to differentiate between names of men and women, some foreign sponsors or regulators may not be able to do so.

The Secretariat of the IRB must retain a copy of all correspondence with the PIs, including their letter seeking approval, a set of documents submitted by them, any queries raised by IRB members and the response of the PI to the same.

The IRB must have written Standard Operating Procedures (SOPs) regarding its functioning. This would generally include method for invitation of members, fees of the IRB, meeting schedule, documents to be submitted, format etc. Often, sponsors may request for a copy of the SOPs; however SOPs are generally considered confidential documents and the IRB is not obliged to supply copies of the SOPs to anyone.

Regulatory Initiatives on Ethics

In addition to the IRB and the investigative team, there are other agencies too, who are responsible for ensuring that clinical research that takes place is ethical. An important agency which ensures that human research is ethically conducted is the Regulatory agency. In our country, the Drugs Controller General (India) (DCGI), and elsewhere the International Conference on Harmonization (ICH) have codified regulatory requirements in such a way that data from unethical research is not acceptable. Once the data becomes unacceptable, such research becomes automatically useless and hence not done.

Often, investigators and sponsors do make the mistake of conducting trials that do not satisfy ethical requirements, but the regulators generally come down heavily on them. Even if such persons are not jailed, they lose their standing among their peers, and generally have to suffer for it.

The ICH GCP Guidelines require that all clinical trials be conducted in accordance with the ethical principles of the Declaration of Helsinki. This is also echoed in the Schedule Y (Drugs and Cosmetics Rules, 1945). The ICH guideline E6 goes on to state that:

"Compliance with this standard provides public assurance that the rights, safety and well-being of trial subjects are protected, consistent with the principles that have their origin in the Declaration of Helsinki, and that the clinical trial data are credible."

The regulators require that no investigator may begin the trial unless it has been approved both by the regulator and the IRB. The Investigator has to give a commitment to that effect in Appendix VII to the Schedule Y of Drugs and Cosmetics Rules, (1945).

The IRB is required to ensure that the rights and well being of the subjects are protected before, during and after the trial. If there are ethical issues before the approval by IRB, the approval would be withheld. Should an ethical issue arise after the approval of the trial by the IRB, the IRB is well within it's right to withdraw the approval and terminate the study.

The DCGI also requires that the Investigator, while preparing the Clinical study, report to confirm that the study was conducted in accordance with the ethical principles of the Declaration of Helsinki.

The DOH has put yet one more hurdle for anyone contemplating to undertake an unethical study. Para 30, while speaking about the responsibility of authors, editors and publishers says, "Reports of research not in accordance with the principles of this Declaration should not be accepted for publication."

With these checks and balances, it is clear that a trial which is not ethical would be stopped at various stages. When the system works well, it would be blocked by the following mechanisms:

1. Regulatory approval of the trial.
2. IRB approval of the trial.
3. Midway in the trial, through IRB review.
4. Submission of the Clinical Study Reports.
5. Regulatory acceptance of data.
6. Publication of data.

Conclusion

There have been numerous violations of human rights in the name of medical research. Following every such exposé, there has been an uproar and governments have responded by issuing codes and guidelines for research. Many mechanisms have now been put in place which ensure that unethical research does not take place. It is absolutely essential to protect human subjects of research, and failure to do so will be detrimental to science and medicine.

Laws and codes are however not sufficient to protect humans subjects, every individual involved in human subject research must remain vigilant to prevent violation of rights of subjects. Ethics after all, comes from the heart and any number of books cannot teach it, if it is not in the individual's heart.

REFERENCES

1. Auel JM The Clan of the Cave Bear, Crown Publishers 1980.

2. Morris D., The Naked Ape, McGraw Hill, 1967

3. Harnett JD and Neuman R, Research Ethics for Clinical Researchers, in Methods in Molecular Biology, Clinical Epidemiology, Vol. 473. Humana Press, 2009

4. Sass H-M, Reichsrundschreiben 1931: Pre-Nuremberg German Regulations Concerning New Therapy and Human Experimentation, Journal of Medicine and Philosophy 1983 8(2):99-112

5. Grimes, Higgins v. Kennedy Krieger Institute, Maryland Court of Appeals. Aug. 16, 2001. Online at:http://www.courts.state.md.us/opinions/coa/2001/128a00.pdf p. 49.

6. Human D., and Fluss SS. The World Medical Association's Declaration of Helsinki: Historical and Contemporary Perspectives, 5th draft. World Medical Association; 2001 Jul 24.

7. Shamoo AE and Khin-Maung-Gyi FA Ethics of the use of Human Subjects in Research Garland Science, 2002

8. Steinbrueck S. Seeking Truly Informed Consent, The Monitor, 2010, 24(3):31-35.

Chapter ... 4

RESEARCH REGULATIONS

| *Good laws have their origins in bad morals.* | **Ambrosius Macrobius** |

INTRODUCTION

The ultimate goal of clinical research is to develop new medicines to address unmet therapeutic needs. This is achieved through testing the efficacy and safety of new therapies before they could be brought to market and made available for the general population. The risk of exposing human subjects to experimental therapy is thus inherent to any clinical research activity. Therefore, the scientific and ethical quality standards of all clinical research activities require close regulatory scrutiny in order to ensure the safety and well-being of trial subjects.

On one hand, the role of regulations in clinical research is to protect future patients from harmful medication, while on the other hand, it is to facilitate the availability of potentially beneficial medicines to patients. Hence regulatory oversight on clinical research must have a balance of regulatory control and pro-developmental policies so as to safeguard the well-being of human subjects and at the same time promote development of new medicines. To this extent, various national and international guidelines have been brought into force and capable regulatory agencies at national and international levels have been created. In the following sections, we will be providing a brief account of various guidelines pertaining to clinical research regulation and will also discuss structure and function of various regulatory agencies (RA).

The Investigational New Drug (IND) and New Drug Application (NDA)

At the outset, it is essential to have basic understanding of the clinical development process for a New Molecular Entity (NME). As per International Conference on Harmonization (ICH) Good Clinical Practice (GCP) guidelines, a clinical trial or clinical study is defined as any investigation in human subjects intended to discover or verify the clinical, pharmacological and / or other pharmacodynamic effects of an investigational product, and / or to identify adverse reactions to an investigational product, and / or to study absorption, distribution, metabolism, and excretion of an investigational product with the objective of ascertaining its safety and / or efficacy. Hence, all clinical trials essentially involve human subjects for study of drug effects.

Once pre-clinical animal study results suggest that an NME is fit for human study, an application for conducting clinical trial, known as the Investigational New Drug (IND) is submitted to the regulators for approval. The IND application covers all information on the NME (Table 4.1), which is pertinent for the regulatory authorities to review the IND application.

Table 4.1: Data Contained in IND Application

- Information on composition, formulation, and source of the drug.
- Chemistry, manufacturing and control (CMC) information.
- All data from animal studies (i.e., animal pharmacology and toxicology).
- Proposed clinical plans and protocols.
- Any previous human experience with the drug (if available).
- Names and credentials of physicians (investigators) who will conduct the clinical trials.
- Compilation of the key data relevant to study the drug in man.

Upon completion of phase III, the sponsor submits a New Drug Application (NDA), which is a formal request by the sponsor to regulators for marketing and registration of the drug. The NDA contains detailed information on the drug including composition, manufacturing details, stability data of finished product, intended use as indicated in proposed package insert, and results of all pre-clinical and clinical studies. All NDAs in ICH regions, i.e., the United States (US), European Union (EU) and Japan, should conform to the Common Technical Document (CTD) format, to harmonize dossier submission across the globe. The CTD modules are listed in Table 4.2.

Table 4.2: CTD Modules

- **Module 1:** Submitting country-specific administrative and prescribing information.
- **Module 2:** Overviews and summaries for modules 3, 4 and 5.
- **Module 3:** Quality (chemical and manufacturing) data.
- **Module 4:** Non clinical study reports.
- **Module 5:** Clinical study reports.

Once approved by the regulators, the drug can be marketed and post-marketing or phase IV studies initiated to collect data on the safety and efficacy of the drug in real-life conditions. A schematic diagram of the clinical development phases is provided in Fig. 4.1.

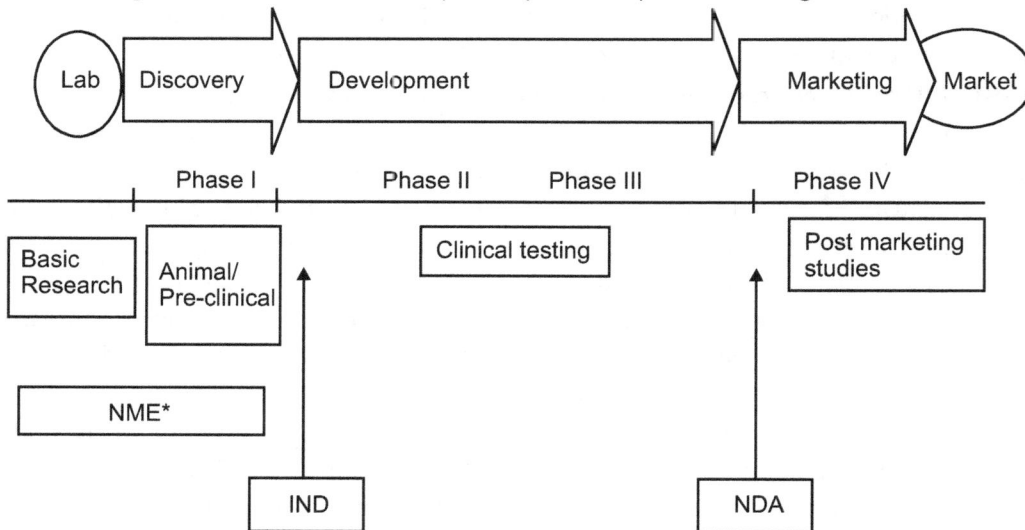

Fig. 4.1: Phases of Drug Development:

Investigational New Drug (IND) and New Drug Application (NDA)

REGULATORY AGENCIES - STRUCTURE AND FUNCTIONS

The United States

In the US, the Food and Drug Administration (FDA), an agency under the Department of Health and Human Services of the Federal Government, is charged with the responsibility of protecting public health. The FDA operates under certain laws and regulations as listed in Table 4.3.

Table 4.3: Clinical Research Laws and Regulations in the US

- **Laws:** Legislations passed by Congress and signed by President; example:
  - Food Drug and Cosmetic Act (FDCA).
  - Prescription Drugs User Fee Act (PDUFA).
  - FDA Amendments Act (FDAAA).
- **Regulations:** Rules issues by FDA consistently with laws, published in Federal Register and contained in Code of Federal Regulations (CFR); example:
  - 21 CFR 312 – IND.
  - 21 CFR 314 – NDA.
  - 21 CFR 50 – protection of human subjects.
  - 21 CFR 56 – Institutional Review Board (IRB).
  - 21 CFR 50 – Informed Consent.

Headed by the FDA Commissioner, the agency consists of six product centers, one research center, and two offices with diverse activities as listed in Table-4 [3]:

Table 4.4: Structure and Activities of Various Divisions of the USFDA

- **Center for Drugs Evaluation and Research (CDER):** Regulates over-the-counter and prescription medications.
- **Center for Biologics Evaluation and Research (CBER):** Regulates products such as vaccines, blood products, and gene /cell therapy products.
- **Center for Devices and Radiological Health (CDRH):** Regulates medical devices and electronic products that give off radiation.
- **Center for Food Safety and Applied Nutrition (CFSAN):** Regulates most foods (except meat and poultry), food additives, infant formulas, dietary supplements, and cosmetics.
- **Center for Tobacco Products (CTP):** Regulates cigarettes, cigarette tobacco, roll-your-own tobacco, and smokeless tobacco.
- **Center for Veterinary Medicine (CVM):** Regulates feed and drugs and devices used in pets, farm animals, and other animals.
- **National Center for Toxicological Research (NCTR):** Supports FDA's product centers by providing innovative scientific technology, training, and technical expertise.
- **Office of Regulatory Affairs (ORA):** Conducts inspections and enforces FDA regulations.
- **Office of the Commissioner (OC):** Provides leadership and direction to all above mentioned FDA divisions.

The primary responsibility of the FDA is to protect public health by ensuring drugs, devices, vaccines and other biological products intended for human use are safe and effective. This is achieved by close scrutiny of the sponsors' clinical development programme by the FDA review team, having diverse expertise. For IND review, the FDA focus relates to safety, wherein the agency attempts to assess: (1) that human subjects are not exposed to unnecessary risk; (2) that the pre-clinical programme was adequate in terms of providing scientific evidence that the drug is reasonably safe to administer in man; and (3) that the CMC procedures ensured that the drug is adequately reproducible and stable. The FDA has a 30-day time-line for IND review. There is no formal approval process for IND and clinical trials can begin upon expiry of the 30 day period, unless FDA issues 'clinical hold' prohibiting sponsor from initiating trials.

For NDAs, the FDA is likely to grant marketing approval only if 'adequate and well-controlled studies' have demonstrated 'substantial evidence' of efficacy and safety. The FDA has a 10-12 month timeline to review standard NDA and a 6 month timeline for review of priority NDAs, which include molecules perceived to have substantial therapeutic gain or improved safety / efficacy profile over existing drugs and molecules intended for life-threatening illnesses, such as cancer and HIV.

The FDA often encourages sponsors to have regular and frequent communications / meetings with the agency during the development phase in order to communicate new data / findings, discuss specific issues /concerns and to find solution for any anticipated difficulty. These meetings include pre-IND meeting to discuss acceptability of investigational plan; end-of-phase II meeting to confirm early efficacy and to decide on phase II plan; pre-NDA meeting to agree on NDA approach and labelling meeting to negotiate final labeling / prescribing information.

Furthermore, the FDA conducts inspections of manufacturing facilities / processes for FDA-regulated products, sites conducting clinical trials and laboratories conducting animal studies, with an aim to assess quality. Such inspections are conducted at various time points in the product-development cycle: pre-approval inspections after a company submits an NDA to the FDA to market a new product; routine inspections of a regulated facility; and, for-cause inspection to investigate a specific problem that has come to FDA's attention.

As a competent regulatory agency, the other aspect of FDA's functioning involves advancing public health by helping speed product innovations. To this extent, FDA continuously issues various guidance and advisory documents to clarify requirements, specific to therapeutic areas or technical disciplines to help the industry in better planning of its clinical development programme.

The European Union (EU)

The European Medicines Agency (EMA) is the regulatory authority for the EU region, which includes over 40 countries, and is governed by the European Commission (EU Commission). The EU Commission, headed by commissioners appointed by member state governments, ensures proper implementation of laws across EU. The EU regulatory environment is governed by regulations, directives and recommendations / guidelines as defined in Table 4.5.

Table 4.5: European Regulatory Documents

- **Regulations:** Direct legislations that apply across EU without the need for national enactment. e.g., the Medicines for Human Use (Clinical Trials) Regulations.

- **Directives:** Define objectives to be achieved by member states and directed to national authorities; national authorities have flexibility of choosing the means of implementation of the directive; required to be enacted into national legislation. e.g., the EU Clinical Trial Directive.

- **Recommendations / Guidelines**: Provides guidance only; not legally binding. e.g., various 'notes for guidance' on product development on specific therapeutic areas.

The EMA is headed by the Executive Director and comprises 5 units; each unit consisting of further sectors and sub-sectors. Additionally, the agency contains six scientific committees which evaluate applications from pharmaceutical companies to determine whether or not their products meet necessary quality, safety and efficacy requirements, to ensure a positive risk-benefit balance. These committees are listed in Table 4.6. The agency also contains a number of working parties and expert groups, which can be consulted by the scientific committees on issues relating to their particular field of expertise.

Table 4.6: Scientific Committees Contained in the EMA

- Committee for Medicinal Products for Human Use (CHMP).
- Committee for Medicinal Products for Veterinary Use (CVMP).
- Committee for Orphan Medicinal Products (COMP).
- Committee on Herbal Medicinal Products (HMPC).
- Paediatric Committee (PDCO).
- Committee for Advanced Therapies (CAT).

The CHMP plays a key role in reviewing centralized marketing authorization applications for medicines and is responsible for preparing the agency's opinions on all questions concerning medicines for human use. Although all pan-EU regulatory activities take place within the EMA, the member states' national regulatory agencies play key roles in: (1) aassessing and reviewing Clinical Trial Applications (CTA), (2) providing members to CHMP and EU panel of experts for scientific committees and (3) reviewing national, decentralized and mutual recognition marketing authorization applications.

The CTA process in the EU is regulated by EU Clinical Trials Directive, which aims to simplify and harmonize the provisions governing clinical trials, to protect trials subjects, to improve quality of research and to produce credible data. Sponsors are required to collate technical data in an Investigational Medicinal Product Dossier (IMPD), and submit to the Ethics Committee (EC) and a competent national agency of each EU member state where the clinical trial is planned to be conducted. Also, obtaining a European Union Drug Regulating Authority Clinical Trial (Eudra CT) number by registering the protocol in the EMA website is a pre-requisite for all submissions. Both EC and a national authority have a 60-day timeline for review of the CTA.

While the CTA process is solely governed by national agencies, the Marketing Authorization Application (MAA) / registration process involves both national and EMA authorities. In EU, Marketing Authorization (MA) could be either a National Authorization (through national, decentralized or mutual recognition application procedures), issued by the national agency of a member state and valid only in the issuing country, or, a Community Authorization (through centralized application procedures), issued by the EU Commission (via EMA) and valid across EU. The procedures for applying for MA in the EU could be one of the four listed in Table 4.7. Use of centralized procedure is obligatory for biotechnology-derived products, products for AIDS, cancer, neurodegenerative disorders, and diabetes and orphan drugs and optional for products which constitute significant therapeutic, scientific or technical innovation. For other products, submission may be any either national, or decentralized or by mutual recognition process.

Table 4.7: Procedures for Filing MA Application in EU

- **National procedure:** MA granted by competent national authority for products that are intended to be marketed solely in that particular member state.
- **Decentralized procedure:** Parallel / simultaneous submission of MAA to competent national authorities' of two or more member states.
- **Mutual recognition procedure:** Here, a MA already exists in one member state; the goal is to obtain recognition of this MA by competent authorities' of other member states.
- **Centralized procedure:** MA is submitted directly to the EMA for assessment by CHMP and marketing authorization, once approved, is valid across all EU member states.

Applications for MA need to be submitted in the CTD format and average approval time is 10-12 months. In-line with the US FDA, the EMA also encourages sponsors to have frequent dialogue with the agency and provides formal scientific advice on drug development path upon request.

Quality assurance for trials is provided by carrying out inspections of trials sites, manufacturing facilities, analytical laboratories and sponsors' premises by inspectors from the respective member states.

United Kingdom (UK)

The competent national regulatory agency in the UK is the Medicines and Healthcare products Regulatory Agency (MHRA), a government agency under the UK Department of Health. The MHRA is responsible for ensuring that medicines and medical devices work, and are acceptably safe. The MHRA consists of various divisions as listed in Table 4.8.

Table 4.8: Divisions of the MHRA

- **Licensing division:** Responsible for assessing and approving applications for clinical trials and national, decentralized and mutual recognition marketing authorizations.
- **Vigilance and Risk Management of Medicines (VRMM) division:** Responsible to protect public health by promoting the safe use of marketed medicines.
- **Inspection, Enforcement and Standards division:** Responsible for ensuring compliance with the standards that apply to the manufacture and supply of medicines in the UK market.
- **Devices division:** Responsible to ensure that medical devices are fit for purpose and are used safely.
- **Communication division:** Responsible for clear, accurate and timely communication with all stakeholders.
- **Operations and Finance division:** Responsible for financial infrastructure and advice .
- **Human Resource division:** Responsible for hiring efficient staff.
- **Information Management division:** Responsible for overall information management.
- **Policy division:** Responsible for taking an overview of MHRA policies.

Overall, the MHRA functions to assure safety, quality and efficacy of medicines and devices; authorizes their sale or supply in the UK for human use and regulates clinical trials for medicines and devices.

India

In India, the regulatory authority for all clinical trial related activities is the Central Drugs Standard Control Organization (CDSCO), which comes under the Director General of Health Services (DGHS), Ministry of Health and Family Welfare (MOHFW) of the Government of India. The basic regulation followed by the CDSCO is the Drugs and Cosmetics Act, which is an Act to 'regulate the import, manufacture, distribution, and sale of drugs and cosmetics in India'. This Act contains various rules, defining terminologies such as new drug (rule 122E) and clinical trial (rule 122DAA) and various schedules, most importantly, the Schedule Y, entitled 'permission to import and / or manufacture of new drugs for sale or to undertake clinical trials'.

The CDSCO, headed by the Drugs Controller General of India (DCGI), has it's headquarters in New Delhi with zonal and sub-zonal offices spread across India. Besides these, the CDSCO has also established port / airport offices and central drug testing laboratories in various places across India. The hierarchical structure of CDSCO includes Joint Drugs Controller, Deputy Drugs Controller and Assistant Drugs Controllers who work in coordination with each other to assist the DCGI. The structural composition of CDSCO is shown in Figure 4.2.

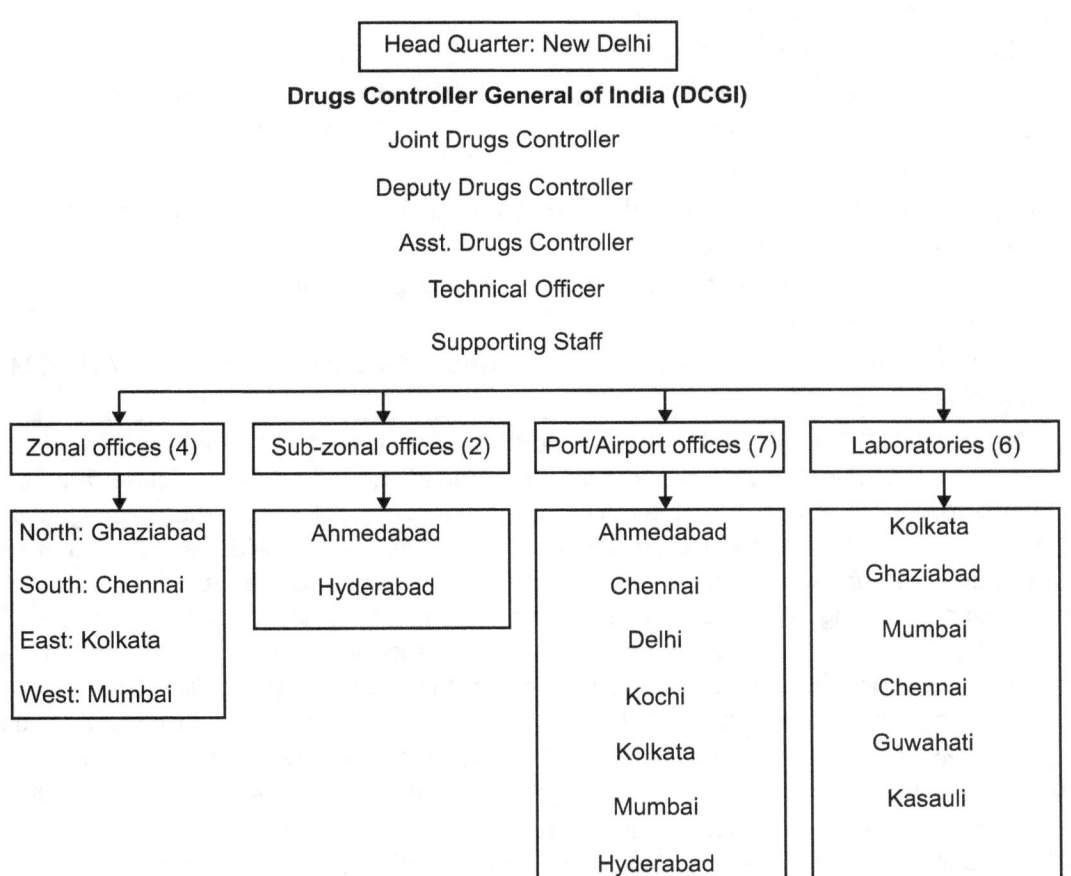

Fig. 4.2: Structure of Central Drugs Standard Control Organization (CDSCO)

Under the Drugs and Cosmetics Act, the regulation of manufacture, sale and distribution of drugs is primarily the concern of the state authorities (i.e., State Drug Control Organization) while the central authorities (i.e., the CDCSCO) are responsible for approval of new drugs, clinical trials in India, laying down the standards of drugs, and several other functions as listed in Table 4.9.

Table 4.9: Functions of CDSCO

- Laying down standards of drugs, cosmetics, diagnostics and devices.
- Laying down regulatory measures, amendments to acts and rules.
- Regulating market authorization of new drugs.
- Regulating clinical research in India.
- Approving manufacturing license for blood banks, large volume parenterals, vaccines and sera as Central Licence Approving Authority (CLAA).
- Regulating the standards of imported drugs.
- Work relating to the Drugs Technical Advisory Board (DTAB) and Drugs Consultative Committee (DCC).
- Testing of drugs by Central Drugs Laboratories.
- Publication of the Indian Pharmacopoeia.
- Monitoring Adverse Drug Reactions (ADR).
- Conducting training programmes for regulatory officials and government analysts.
- Distribution of quotas of narcotic drugs for use in medicinal formulations.
- Screening drug formulations available in Indian market.
- Evaluation and screening of applications for granting No Objection Certificates (NOC) for export of unapproved or banned drugs.
- Coordinating the activities of the State Drugs Control Organizations.
- Guidance on technical matters.
- Participation in the World Health Organization's Good Manufacturing Practices (WHO GMP) certification scheme.

In 2001, the CDSCO published the Indian Good Clinical Practice (GCP) guidelines, streamlining ethical and scientific standards of trials conducted in India. The India GCP guidelines are in sync with international ethical norms of International Conference on Harmonization GCP guidelines and also take into consideration local socioeconomic realities. Starting with definitions and study pre-requisites, the Indian GCP describes the study protocol; talks about ethical and safety considerations, including ethical principles and the EC, the informed consent process, subject confidentiality and compensation, and selection of special groups as research subject. Furthermore, it defines the roles and responsibilities of the sponsor, monitor and investigators in the conducting clinical trials; provides guidance on record-keeping and data handling, quality assurance measures, and on biostatistics. Besides drugs, the Indian GCP also provides guidance on conduct of clinical trials with vaccines, contraceptives, diagnostic agents and herbal remedies.

The requirements for conduct of clinical trials in India are defined in the 2005 Amended Schedule Y and are listed in Table 4.10. For drugs of life threatening / serious diseases / special relevance to India, these requirements might be abbreviated, or omitted as deemed appropriate by the DCGI.

Table 4.10: Schedule Y (2005) Requirements for Conduct of Clinical Trials in India

- **New drugs discovered in India:**
  - Trials to be conducted in India right from phase I.
- **New drugs discovered outside India:**
  - To conduct Phase I in India: Sponsor must submit phase I data from other countries. Concurrent Phase I with global sites is not allowed.
  - To conduct concurrent Phase II/III: sponsor to submit data from earlier phases — permission is usually granted for Phase II/III trials concurrent with global sites.
- **For marketing new drugs in India:**
  - Phase III must be carried out in India before marketing permission is granted.

For conducting global trials in Indian sites, CTA dossier is to be submitted for DCGI review and approval. This dossier should contain all data stipulated in Appendix I of Schedule Y and in the CDSCO global trial checklist, as listed in Table 4.11.

Table 4.11: Data / Documents Required for CTA Dossier

- Name (generic as well as chemical name) of the drug; dosage form, composition and formulation.
- Analytical and stability data.
- Animal pharmacology and toxicology data.
- Data from earlier phases of trial, if available.
- Rationale for selecting proposed dose and indication.
- Name of the sponsor / applicant.
- Objectives and phase of the study.
- Name of participating countries (if multi-national) and sites.
- Total number of patients to be enrolled globally and from India.
- Number of sites proposed from India.
- Regulatory / IRB approval of participating countries.
- Status of the trial in other countries.
- Safety data from other countries.
- Regulatory status of the study drug in other countries.
- Various affidavits stating that the data contained in the IB is factual (the IB affidavit), and that the study has not been withdrawn from any country (the withdrawal affidavit).
- The proposed protocol, IB, CRF, informed consent documents in vernacular and the investigator's undertaking.

The CTA application is to be made in Form 44; in trials where the study drug is to be imported from a foreign country, an application for import / test license (T-license) is to be made in form 12. In studies where biological samples are to be exported to foreign country for laboratory analysis of safety, efficacy, pharmacokinetic or other parameters, an application is to be made for granting No Objection Certificate (NOC). The expected time frame for review and first response from DCGI is about 45 days from the submission of completed CTA dossier. Besides the DCGI, trial approval from ECs of the proposed trial sites and registration of the trial in Indian clinical trial registry (www.ctri.in) is required before the first patient can be enrolled in the trial. For marketing of new drugs, following completion of phase III in India, NDA dossier is to be submitted for DCGI review, containing the information listed in Table 4.12.

Table 4.12: Data required for NDA Dossier

- Chemical/pharmaceutical information on the drug.
- Animal and clinical testing data (phase I to III).
- Flow chart on manufacturing method.
- Active substance specification.
- Drug product stability data.
- Study report (from India).
- Global regulatory approval status of the drug.
- Patent status.
- Copies of proposed package insert and labels.
- Samples of finished products to be sent to Central Drug Laboratory (CDL) for testing.

Once approved by the DCGI, the drug can be locally manufactured in India; for this the application for manufacturing license to be submitted to local state FDA. Alternatively, if the drug is manufactured in a foreign site, the site needs to be registered and registration certificate obtained from DCGI. In this scenario the commercial Import License application is to be made for import of drugs.

In case of special drugs – vaccines or biotech drugs, besides DCGI, the review is also done by other government bodies - Indian Council of Medical Research (ICMR), Department of Biotechnology (DBT), and Genetic Engineering Approval Committee. (GEAC)

Guidelines on Clinical Trials

The fact that clinical trials involve exposing human subjects to experimental therapy underscores the importance of having standard guidelines for conduct of every aspect of such studies. Incidences such as the Nuremberg trial of Nazi doctors and the Tuskegee syphilis study are classic examples of violations of trial subjects' rights, safety and well-being. Various guidelines (the Nuremberg Code, the Declaration of Helsinki, the Belmont Report) have been issued from time to time to make all trial stakeholders aware of these issues. With drug development process reaching global dimensions involving various countries, each with their own set of guidelines, a need was perceived to harmonize regulatory requirements. This idea was implemented when the US, European Union and Japan met at the International Conference on Harmonization (ICH) of Technical Requirements for Registration of Pharmaceuticals for Human Use. The ICH subsequently published a set of guidelines, namely, Efficacy (E), Safety (S), Quality (Q) and Multidisciplinary (M), encompassing all phases of drug development. ICH continues to revise and update these guidelines to meet the demands of changing scientific and ethical milieu. Of the various ICH guidelines, the Efficacy (E) guidelines relate directly to the conduct of clinical trials and pharmacovigilance. E6 describes Good Clinical Practice (GCP) guidelines. Some of the important Efficacy guidelines are listed in Table 4.13.

Table 4.13: Important ICH Efficacy (E) Guidelines

- **E2A: Clinical Safety Data Management:** Definitions and Standards for Expedited Reporting.
- **E2B: Clinical Safety Data Management:** Data Elements for Transmission of Individual Case Safety Reports.
- **E2C: Clinical Safety Data Management:** Periodic Safety Update Reports for Marketed Drugs.
- **E2D: Post-Approval Safety Data Management:** Definitions and Standards for Expedited Reporting.
- **E2E:** Pharmacovigilance Planning.
- **E3:** Structure and Content of Clinical Study Reports.
- **E6: Good Clinical Practice:** Consolidated Guideline.
- **E8:** General Considerations for Clinical Trials.
- **E9:** Statistical Principles for Clinical Trials.
- **E10:** Choice of Control Group and Related Issues in Clinical Trials.

Principles, Structure and Function of the ICH-GCP

The ICH GCP guidelines were published in 1996 and were subsequently adopted by the ICH regions in the following year. The guideline defines Good Clinical Practice (GCP) as a standard for the design, conduct, performance, monitoring, auditing, recording, analyses and reporting of clinical trials to ensure that the data generated in the trial is credible and accurate and that the rights, integrity and confidentiality of trial subjects are protected. The principles prescribed by ICH-GCP are listed in Table 4.14.

Table 4.14: Principles of ICH-GCP Guidelines

- Trials be conducted in accordance with the ethical principles defined in the Declaration of Helsinki [R] and consistent with GCP norms and applicable regulatory requirements.
- A trial should only be initiated and continued if the anticipated benefits justify the risks.
- The right, safety and well-being of the trial subjects should prevail over the interests of science and society.
- Non-clinical and other available data should be adequate to support the proposed clinical trial.
- Trials should be described in a clear, detailed protocol.
- Trial protocols must have received prior approval / favourable opinion from IRB / IECs of the proposed sites, before trial can be initiated.
- The staff involved in clinical trials are adequately qualified by education, training or experience to perform their trial related duties.
- The medical care and medical decisions made on behalf of trial subjects are the responsibility of a qualified physician or dentist, as appropriate.
- Freely given informed consent be obtained from every subject prior to clinical trial participation.
- All clinical trial information should be recorded, handled, and stored in a way that allows it's accurate reporting, interpretation and verification.
- Confidentiality of the subjects be protected.

- Investigational products are manufactured stored and handled in accordance with applicable good manufacturing practice (GMP) and that they are used only in accordance with the approved protocol.
- Systems and procedures are implemented to ensure quality of every aspect of the trial conduct.

Section one and two provide introductory overview of the terms used in the document (glossary) and the principles of ICH-GCP, respectively. The glossary section defines sixty-two terms used in the subsequent sections of the document, with the aim to give a clear understanding and interpretation of these terms to the reader. Section two explains the principles underlying the ICH-GCP (see above). Sections three, four and five define various roles and responsibilities of the three major stakeholders of clinical research, namely the Institutional review Board / Independent ethics committee (IRB/IEC), investigator and sponsor. Sections six and seven focus on the two most important documents of clinical trial: the trial protocol and the investigator's brochure (IB) and provide guidance to the structure and content of these documents. Finally, section 8 relates to essential documents for trial conduct, defined as documents that permit evaluation of the conduct of a study and the quality of the data produced. This section lists all essential documents that are required before the clinical phase of the trial commences, during the conduct of the trial and after completion or termination of the trial.

REFERENCES:

1. http://www.ich.org/LOB/media/MEDIA482.pdf.
2. Pituk TL (2006) in Clinical Research Manual, eds Luscombe D, Stonier PD (Euromed Communications, England), pp 5.1-5.31.
3. http://www.fda.gov/AboutFDA/Transparency/Basics/ucm194884.htm.
4. http://www.fda.gov/AboutFDA/Transparency/Basics/ucm194888.htm.
5. Smith JK (2007) in Clinical Research Manual, eds Luscombe D, Stonier PD (Euromed Communications, England), pp 4.1-4.30.
6. http://www.ema.europa.eu/ema/index.jsp?curl=pages/about_us/general/general_content_000217.jsp&murl=menus/about_us/about_us.jsp&mid=WC0b01ac0580028c77.
7. http://www.mhra.gov.uk/Aboutus/Ourstructure/OurDivisions/index.htm.
8. http://www.mhra.gov.uk/Aboutus/Whoweare/index.htm.
9. http://cdsco.nic.in/html/law.htm.
10. http://cdsco.nic.in/html/organisationalchart.htm.
11. http://cdsco.nic.in/html/Drugs_ContAd.html.
12. http: //www.cdsco.nic.in/html/GCP1.html.
13. http://cdsco.nic.in/html/schedule-y%20%28amended%20version-2005%29%20original.htm.

Chapter ... 5

CLINICAL TRIAL COMPLIANCE

"Compliance has the power of making things easy which seem impossible".   **Saint Teresa**

INTRODUCTION

The principal attributes of any item that decide it's quality are different, and we assess the quality of that item by measuring the relevant attribute. Assessment of the qualities of any item can be performed in many ways, so is it with drugs. In case of drugs, the two main attributes for assessing their benefit are safety and efficacy, and there are numerous methods to study these.

Clinical trials are those studies conducted on human subjects for assessing the safety and efficacy of drugs. Additionally, other parameters may also be assessed, but the focus is mostly on safety and efficacy. Generally these studies are conducted on a comparative basis where, in addition to the drug treated group; there is another group of patients who are being treated with a placebo or a standard therapy.

The methods of assessing the safety and efficacy of drugs thus are many and it becomes necessary for the investigators who perform the actual studies to be absolutely clear about the materials, method, statistics etc. to be used. To convey all the conditions of testing, there are protocols and other such documents.

Studies are often simultaneously conducted at a large number of centers, and there needs to be uniformity in the method of testing at each center, hence there are often Standard Operating Procedures that ensure that the tests are conducted in an identical manner, that there are no intra-center or inter-center differences.

Study Designs

There are two principal methods of comparing drugs, either retrospective or prospective. Retrospective studies can be used for comparing data obtained from comparisons done in the past, but in case of new drugs, this is virtually impossible. Most new drug trials are therefore prospective in nature.

Studies could either be non-comparative or comparative. In non-comparative studies, a drug is administered to a group of volunteers or patients and the effect of the drug on the subjects or patients observed. This method has been demonstrated to be undependable since one cannot separate the effect of the drug from the natural course of the disease. Patients of a number of self-limiting diseases tend to get cured, whether treated or untreated, and it becomes very difficult to say to what extent the drug was responsible for the improvement of the patient. For these reasons, most drug trials are comparative, where the drug under test is administered to one group of patients while a similar group of patients receives either the placebo or the standard drug.

In any comparative study, it is essential that both the groups of patients (the drug treated and control) are similar. A race is fair only when all the competitors begin from the same point. In order to ensure that this trial is fair, it is necessary to have all or most participants having a similar severity of the disease. To achieve this, a population of patients is identified and divided into the two groups, and each receives the test and the comparator. Since the investigators are humans, there often creeps in a bias in dividing the patients into two groups for treatment, leading to the groups being unequal. To eliminate this bias, division of the population and their allocation to treatment groups is done randomly, so that the trial is randomized and also becomes relatively less biased.

The response of the patient often depends upon his/her knowledge of what he/she is getting. Patients on placebos often fail to do well and hence cause an exaggerated estimation of the drug effects. The psychological effect of the knowledge that a placebo or an old drug is being can be minimized by blinding the patients toward the treatment. Blinding simply means not letting the patients know what treatment is being administered.

Knowledge of the therapy not only affects the patient's response but also the physician's assessment of the patient. It becomes necessary to keep the investigator also blind towards the treatments. Thus, blinding technique is applied to both the patient and the investigator. When the patient is blinded towards the identity of the therapy, the trial is said to be single blind and when the investigator is also blind toward the therapy, the trial is double blind. Some authors use the term triple blind to mean that the patient, investigator and data analysis personnel are all blind towards the therapy. Obviously in blinded trials, careful records about allocation of treatments and identity of patients in each treatment groups are maintained by a third person,.

As stated earlier, patients treated with one drug should be compared with a control group treated with another drug or placebo. If control groups are left untreated, this group feels left out and their recovery or course of their disease gets affected by their psychology. In the past, a placebo was used to prevent the negative psychological impact. However it has now been decided that the use of placebo is not the best option, since it amounts to cheating the patient, who has approached the doctor for treatment of his illness. The Declaration of Helsinki (2008 version) states that it is improper to use placebos in trials except when there are no current treatment for the disorder, or if scientific and logistic reasons require their use. Thus for most trials, standard drugs will be used for comparison and such trials are known as standard controlled trials.

Treatment of patient groups could either be parallel or cross-over. In parallel trials, both the groups receive the allotted therapies right up to the end of the trial when the results are tabulated and analyzed. In cross-over trials, somewhere in the middle of the treatment, the treatments are switched. The group receiving drug A is switched to Drug B and vice versa. Obviously, cross-over trials can be used only for stable chronic conditions, and not those which fluctuate wildly or are self-limiting. The advantage of such studies is that the total number of subjects required is lesser, and there is lower variance between the two groups. The disadvantage being that the trials take longer to complete. Depending upon the availability of patients and the type of disease, either the parallel or cross over designs could be used.

Compliance

Compliance has a number of meanings. The extent to which a patient follows the orders of a doctor is compliance. When a trial complies with all requirements, it is also known as compliance. Here, trial compliance means a trial conducted within the limits prescribed by various regulatory and legal authorities.

Most clinical trials are conducted to collect data that would support an application for permission to market the drug. It stands to reason that a trial that is not acceptable to Drug Regulatory authorities is of little use to anyone. The International Conference on Harmonization describes the Good Clinical Practice as "A standard for the design, conduct, performance, monitoring, auditing, recording, analyses, and reporting of clinical trials that provides assurance that the data and reported results are credible and accurate, and that the rights, integrity, and confidentiality of trial subjects are protected."

Every trial conducted on new drugs should therefore meet the criteria of GCP, and in fact the type of trial that has the maximum scientific and regulatory acceptance is the prospective, standard-controlled, randomized, double blind trials. These trials may be parallel or cross over.

Prior to 1996, different countries had widely varying rules for new drug development, and often, even after a drug had been approved in one country, a large number of studies were required before another country would approve it. Additionally, different countries had different languages in which they would accept the drug application; hence companies would have to spend time and money into getting the documents translated in various languages if they wanted to file applications worldwide.

In 1989 US, Europe and Japan got together and began discussing the development of a common set of rules. In April 1990, at a meeting in Brussels, the International Conference on Harmonization was established, and ICH developed guidelines for drug development which covered all the aspects. ICH Guidelines fall in four categories as Q- Quality Guidelines, S- Safety Guidelines, E- Efficacy Guidelines and M- Multidisciplinary Guidelines.

The Q Guidelines mainly refer to quality of drug substances. This series is further subdivided into 11 topics as shown under:

Guidelines	Topic	Guidelines	Topic
Q1A-Q1F	Stability	Q7	Good Manufacturing Practices
Q2	Validation	Q8	Pharmaceutical Development
Q3A-Q3D	Impurities	Q9	Quality Risk Management
Q4-Q4B	Pharmacopoeias	Q10	Pharmaceutical Quality System
Q5A-Q5B	Quality of Biotechnological Products	Q11	Development and manufacture of Drug Substances
Q6A-Q6B	Specifications		

The S Guidelines refer to safety aspects of drugs, which are further divided into ten topics as shown below:

Guidelines	Topic	Guidelines	Topic
S1A- S1C	Carcinogenicity Studies	S6	Biotechnological Products
S2	Genotoxicity Studies	S7A-S7B	Pharmacology Studies
S3A-S3B	Toxicokinetics and Pharmacokinetics	S8	Immunotoxicology Studies
S4	Toxicity Testing	S9	Non Clinical Evaluation for Anticancer Pharmaceuticals
S5	Reproductive Toxicology	S10	Photosafety Evaluation

The E Guidelines are devoted to Efficacy of drug substances and are further divided into topics as shown below:

Guidelines	Topic	Guidelines	Topic
E1	Extent of Population Exposure	E9	Statistical Principles
E2A	Clinical Safety Data Management	E10	Choice of Control Groups
E3	Clinical Study Reports	E 11	Pediatric Studies
E4	Dose Response Studies	E12	New antihypertensive drugs
E5	Ethnic Factors	E14	Qt/Qc Evaluation
E6	Good Clinical Practice	E 15	Genomics
E7	Special Populations	E16	Biomarkers for Biotechnology Products
E8	General Considerations		

There are 8 multi-disciplinary M Guidelines and they are:

Guidelines	Topic	Guidelines	Topic
M1	MedDRA Terminology	M5	Standards for Drug Dictionaries
M2	Electronic Standards	M6	Gene Therapy
M3	Non Clinical Safety Studies	M7	Genotoxic Impurities
M4	Common Technical Document	M8	Electronic Common Technical Document

The ICH guidelines were adoptec at various times around the year 1996. Although only the US, Europe and Japan were partners to ICH; the rest of the countries have realized that these countries among them hold very large part of the pharmaceutical market share and have prepared their own guidelines much on the lines of the ICH gu delines and now, ICH guidelines are followed in drug development throughout the world. It is clear that if one hopes to do business with countries of the ICH region, the ICH guidelines are better followed.

Most countries have now adopted guidelines very much on the lines of the ICG guideline, so that drugs developed by them could easily registered in countries of the ICH region. India too has introduced the CDSCO GCP which mirrors the requirements of the ICH. An additional benefit to all countries is that documentation submitted to ICH countries may be made in either English or

French. The Practice guidelines forms one of the boundaries of the playing field in which this activity has to be completed. The other boundaries are shown in the figure below:

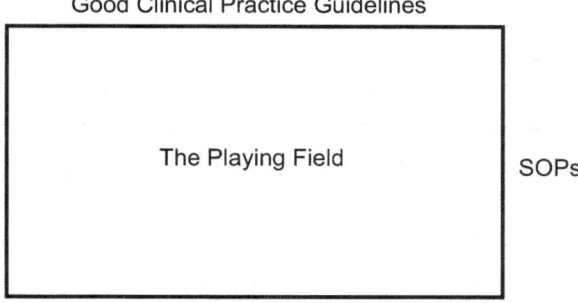

Good Clinical Practice Guidelines

The Playing Field

SOPs

Regulatory Laws

Fig. 5.1

The GCP Guidelines, SOPs, the Trial Protocol and the Regulatory Laws define the playing field for clinical research. Any attempt to step out of this boundary constitutes non-compliance. These conditions are described below:

Regulatory Laws

Every country has it's own laws regarding medical practice and clinical research. Every stakeholder in clinical research has to follow the laws of the country of residence and those of the country where the data may be submitted. A detailed description of regulations is available in this book in the chapter on Regulations.

Standard Operating Procedures

Some procedures in industry and research are simple and repetitive; which can be executed by any individual who has received relevant training. A written document describing the way the procedure is to be carried out is known as a Standard Operating Procedure (SOP). An SOP is to be made for those procedures that are simple, repetitive and can be delegated to others. Thus in the field of surgery, there should be an SOP on how to wash and sterilize surgical instruments, but an SOP on how to perform brain surgery is not required, since surgery is not delegable.

An organisation should set up a system to create SOPs, and must take the following steps:

1. Set up Management of the SOP system.
2. Create an SOP of SOPs.
3. Define Organisational responsibilities.
4. Create a system for classification and numbering of SOPs.
5. Set up a method for issue, storage, review of SOPs.
6. Set up a document control system.
7. SOP Training.

Set up the Management of the SOP System

The management of the organisation must be convinced that the organisation requires the SOP system, and must provide whole-hearted support to it. In the absence of the management's involvement, employees are likely to drop the system even before it becomes effective. An individual with experience must be made in-charge of running the system who must be provided with the required resources and time to set up the system.

SOP of SOPs

Since the whole exercise is about standardisation, it is clear that even SOPs need to be standardized. The organisation must take a call about how an SOP is to be prepared. This includes the paper on which it is to be typed, the format used, the fonts used, structure and sub-headings. The SOP may also contain details about the method of initiating the preparation of an SOP, the method of writing, reviewing and authorization.

Define Organisational Responsibilities

Smooth functioning of an organisation demands that the responsibilities of each individual are well-defined and known to all concerned. The formation of an organisational chart helps in this. It tells where there is a duplication of authority and where this is a gap. It helps people lower down the organisational hierarchy in knowing who is in authority and who is not. This ensures not only fixing responsibility but also accountability.

Classification of SOPs

Since many of the organisation's departments will have SOPs, these SOPs need to be classified and numbered functionwise or departmentwise. The numbering system should help to rapidly identify the Department and the function which the SOP subserves. It should be remembered that SOPs will be continually added to the system, hence the system must be robust enough to add more SOPs without having to change the classification and numbering system every time a new SOP is prepared.

Issue, Storage and Review of SOPs

SOPs are live documents in that they have a fixed life. They must be periodically reviewed to test their relevance and if found necessary must be replaced. At times it may be necessary to do away with a SOP without even replacing it. Often it may be necessary to leave the SOP unchanged and a few such SOPs even survive for decades.

Document Control

Whenever an SOP is revised, it gets a new version number, and then it becomes essential to ensure that all concerned staff has the new SOP and not the old one. Document control is therefore required to ensure that all people carry the same version of the SOP. The person in charge of document control should retrieve all old versions of the SOP before issuing the new one.

SOP Training

Since SOPs are meant to standardize all operations, relevant staff needs to be trained on the particular SOP. Here it should be remembered that all SOPs are not relevant to all staff. Only the staff expected to use the SOP should be trained on that SOP. Only when the training on the SOP is complete should the SOP be implemented. The date for implementation of the SOP should therefore be decided after giving adequate time for training of staff.

SOPbased systems help organisations run their operations smoothly. However, in the initial period of its implementation, the system just consumes resources without giving any apparent benefits, and organisations often give up the system. It should be remembered that these systems needs to be properly implemented and a lot of work is required before it starts yielding benefits to the organisation.

Good Clinical Practice Guidelines

GCP forms an important boundary of the playing field in clinical research. The acceptability of a research report depends upon whether the GCP has been followed or not, hence it is in the interest of the sponsors to ensure that GCP guidelines are scrupulously followed.

While conducting trials that are sponsored by overseas sponsors, it would be necessary to follow the GCP guidelines of the sponsor's country (or of ICH) in addition to the guidelines issued by the Government of India. By and large, the Government of India guidelines are in sync with those of ICH; in fact they are more stringent than those of ICH, thus when one follows the Indian Guidelines, the ICH guidelines are automatically followed. The Indian guidelines are to be found at http://cdsco.nic.in/html/GCP.htm.

The Protocol

ICH GCP guidelines define the protocol as a document that "describes the objective(s), design, methodology, statistical considerations, and organisation of a trial. The protocol usually also gives the background and rationale for the trial, but these could be provided in other protocol referenced documents. Throughout the ICH GCP Guideline the term protocol refers to protocol and protocol amendments."

Protocol writing is both an art and a science, and it is usually done by the sponsor after deliberations with a range of experts. By the time it reaches the investigator, it may have undergone a few revisions and amendments. This protocol subsequently becomes the key document that guides the clinical trial.

The protocol is built on a template which is adapted by the sponsor for it's own use, and while there are variations between those developed by different sponsors, there are a lot of similarities too. The National Institutes of Health (US) have provided a sample protocol template which can be used by anyone. This template is attached as an appendix. Each point is explained briefly for the benefit of the reader.

A. Introduction

This section gives a brief introduction to the clinical trial, the need and the scope. It includes a brief abstract of the proposed trial, including the hypothesis with which the work has been started and what the sponsors hope to achieve. This section describes the purpose of conducting the study.

B. Background

This section describes the background information, what is known so far and how the new study is likely to bridge the gaps in knowledge.

C. Study Objectives

Every study has primary and secondary objectives. The study results would meet either of the stated objectives which are in line with the purpose of the study.

D. Investigative agent

This section gives the details of the drug under investigations, the data that has been obtained from chemical, pharmaceutical, pre-clinical and any other study that has been carried out. Essentially, data on safety and efficacy is what the investigator would be interested in.

E. Study Design

This section contains the details of how the trial is going to be conducted on what sort of subjects, using what methods, contro s, precautions etc. This is probably the largest section of the protocol and it covers trial ethics, recruitment of subjects etc.

F. Study Procedures

This section discusses the method used in conducting the trial, the schedules of examination of patients, investigations etc. The methods to record outcomes and adverse events/reactions are also discussed.

G. Statistical Plan

The method of data analysis is decided even before the trial commences and this section discusses the various ways in which the data will be analyzed.

H. Data Handling and Record Keeping

Clinical data is a precious resource. It needs to be collected and protected from corruption during the trial and even later. This data is often required to be stored for 10 to 15 years' there need be foolproof methods to handle this data and keep records which can be accessible whenever required.

I. Study Monitoring, Auditing and Inspecting

As a part of due diligence, the sponsor must monitor and audit the study periodically. These activities are essential to ensure that the study is proceeding on the lines required and that it is in compliance with the required regulations and guidelines. Inspections are conducted by regulators and these activities ensure that there are no surprises when regulators inspect the study.

J. Study Administration

Most international studies conducted today are multi-national studies conducted in a large number of sites across many continents. Administration of these studies is a major challenge of logistics and management. This section describes how the studies will be managed and administered.

K. Publication Plan

It is now essential to make a publication plan as when and in whose name the publication(s) will be made. Such a plan prevents gift authorship and other undesirable practices which often take place in this area of activity.

L. References

This section lists important reference for the protocol.

Non-Compliance

Every activity done during the conduct of a trial should strictly be according to the rules and guidelines. The question is, in practices does it ever occur that the investigator of the investigative team steps out of the playing field defined? The answer to this, in all honesty, is yes. The next questions that comes in mind, is does this make the trial data invalid or unacceptable? Well, not exactly.

There are numerous situations where the investigative team's actions are beyond those prescribed by regulations and guidelines. Most often these are due to ignorance of the regulations or guidelines and these have little consequences. Such minor deviations from the normal are known as non-compliance. Whenever such an incidence is detected, the representative of the sponsor should bring it to the notice of the principal investigator and ensure that the perpetrator is identified.

The perpetrators of noncompliance need not be disciplined, but should be made aware of their error and if necessary, trained in trial or other procedures so that such incidences are not repeated. In most cases, a repetition of the noncompliance does not take place.

In rare situations, incidences of noncompliance go on repeating despite all remedial actions,including warnings. These incidences are no longer due to ignorance but are knowing, intentional violation. These are termed as misconduct. When detected, misconduct must be immediately controlled, and the perpetrator disciplined. It might become necessary to dismiss the individual from the team, because misconduct may cause irreparable damage to the entire trial, which puts the entire team in loss.

The reasons of misconduct are not very clear, and they could be many. Disgruntled employees, disruptive elements, or any other factor could case misconduct. The difference between noncompliance and misconduct is that noncompliance is a one off incident while misconduct is intentional and repetitive in nature.

In some instances, when financial profit is at the root of misconductit is known as fraud. Obviously, the incidence of fraud is very low, much lower than misconduct and noncompliance, but the impact of fraud is very high. Any intentional deviation from the norm with an aim to make profit out of it is termed as fraud. The consequences of fraud are immense and the punishment is often severe.

In July 2009, a trial site was closed down in India after a fraud was detected. Glenmark and Omnicare found that an investigator based in Jamnagar committed a fraud. While the company has not declared the details of the case, the investigator is being investigated by the police for cheating and the company has discarded all data received from the site.

In the U.S., an investigator was jailed for 57 months and fined US$ 925,000 for falsely showing almost 400 recruitments when in fact none had been done. The sponsor as well as the FDA faced flak over the issue of Ketek, all due to the fraud committed by the investigator.

The clinical trial industry is a highly regulated one, probably next only to the aeronautical industry. Clinical trials; whether conducted in Pune or Pennsylvania, Chennai or Chicago are subjected to the same level of oversight. After all, it is human life that is involved and if a bad drug comes to the market, it endangers the life of thousands of patients.

REFERENCES:

1. Weng C., McDonald D.W., Sparks D., McCoy J. and Gennar J.H. Participatory design of a collaborative clinical trial protocol writing system. Intl. J. Med. Informatics. 2007, 76 S. No. 1: 245-51.
2. DeMets D.L.; Distinctions between fraud, bias, errors, misunderstanding, and incompetence. Controlled Clinical Trials 1996, 18 (6): 637-50
3. Glenmark Brings to the Notice of the Authorities Irregularities of the Clinical Investigator at its Jamnagar Site in Gujarat.
    http://www.prnewswire.co.uk/cgi/news/release?id=262259
4. Kris Hundley, Drug's chilling path to market.
    http://www.sptimes.com/2007/05/27/Business/Drug_s_chilling__path.shtml

APPENDIX

PROTOCOL TEMPLATE
TABLE OF CONTENTS

3.e   Subject Compliance Monitoring

3.f   Prior and Concomitant Therapy

3.g   Packaging

3.h   Blinding of Study Drug

3.i   Receiving, Storage, Dispensing and Return

F   STUDY PROCEDURES

F1   SCREENING FOR ELIGIBILITY

F2   SCHEDULE OF MEASUREMENTS

F3   VISIT 1

F4   VISIT 2 ETC.

F5   SAFETY AND ADVERSE EVENTS

5.a   Safety and Compliance Monitoring

5.b   Medical Monitoring

i   Investigator only

ii   Independent expert to monitor

iii   Institutional Data and Safety Monitoring Board

iv   Independent Data and Safety Monitoring Board

5.c   Definitions of Adverse Events

5.d   Classification of Events

i   Relationship

ii   Severity

iii   Expectedness

5.e   Data Collection Procedures for Adverse Events

5.f   Reporting Procedures

5.g   Adverse Event Reporting Period

5.h   Post-study Adverse Event

F6   STUDY OUTCOME MEASUREMENTS AND ASCERTAINMENT

G   STATISTICAL PLAN

G1   SAMPLE SIZE DETERMINATION AND POWER

G2   INTERIM MONITORING AND EARLY STOPPING

G3   ANALYSIS PLAN

G4   STATISTICAL METHODS

G5   MISSING OUTCOME DATA

G6   UNBLINDING PROCEDURES

H   DATA HANDLING AND RECORD KEEPING

H1   CONFIDENTIALITY AND SECURITY

H2   TRAINING   **ERROR! BOOKMARK NOT DEFINED.**

✳✳✳

Chapter ... 6

CONDUCT OF CLINICAL TRIALS

"It doesn't matter how beautiful your theory is, it doesn't matter how smart you are. If it doesn't agree with experiment, it's wrong".
Richard Feynman

Conducting clinical trials requires good planning and organizing skills, appropriate resource allocation and coming together of a set of professionals with diverse strengths across different functions to form a well synchronized team.

Operational aspects of a clinical trial begin with synopsis and protocol finalization, pre-feasibility and feasibility studies, creation of supporting clinical operations documents such as the monitoring plan, Case Record Form (CRF) completion guidelines; identification of vendors for allied services – Clinical Research Organizations (CROs) for monitoring and operations management, Interactive Voice Response System (IVRS) or Interactive Web Response System (IWRS) service providers, central laboratory, any other specialized service providers such as centralized reading of various tests (e.g. ECG, pulmonary testing, etc.). It involves good interplay between the regulatory, investigational, product management, legal, finance, project management, data management, outsourcing/purchasing and the clinical operations teams.

A successfully conducted clinical trial will generate good quality data within a given timeline with optimal utilization of available resources and in accordance with the relevant company policies, standard operating procedures, governing rules, regulations and Good Clinical Practice (GCP) guidelines.

A bird's eye view of some of the key steps in the conduct of clinical operations of a clinical trial are discussed below and usually refer to the scenario in India, for clinical studies (not including medical device studies) conducted under an Investigational New Drug (IND) application, United States Food and Drug Administration (US FDA).

Investigator and Site Identification

This is one of the most critical factors in determining the success of the clinical trials, both in terms of achieving recruitment targets and the quality and integrity of data. Two preliminary factors that would influence the choice of the Investigator/site are the complexity of the protocol and the target recruitment rate.

As per 21CFR 312.53, a sponsor shall select only those Investigators qualified by training and experience as appropriate experts to investigate the drug. Although no minimum qualifications are specified, it is expected that the Investigator is well qualified in the area of research and is able to provide evidence of such qualifications and has adequate clinical experience and expertise. While selecting Investigators for a study, it is good to make a note of the past experience in conducting clinical research studies, the type of studies conducted as in local/global, the phases, single centre/multi-centric studies, audits and inspections if any, etc.

The FDA maintains a list of debarred Investigators on it's website and which must be checked. Some sponsors maintain a database of Investigators indicating if there were any quality issues with the Investigator in the past. Inputs from colleagues in marketing and medical affairs may also be considered. Is the Investigator a key opinion leader, does he/she have a large circle of influence amongst peers, the potential business consequences in case of an unpleasant experience during the course of a trial are some of the points that a sponsor's clinical operations team needs to be cognizant of. Expected remuneration for services rendered can be looked at as well to see how this impacts the study budget.

Other site specific points that can be looked at are:

- **Qualification of the site staff:** Staff should be qualified to perform the delegated tasks as required by the study.

- **Database of subjects:** It is worth investing resources in mining through the database to get a realistic idea of potential recruitment.

- **Infrastructure:** Check if the site meets study specific requirements for equipment, emergency situations, investigational product storage, dispensing and destruction, secure place for storage of study specific documents and materials.

- **Source documents:** It is important to ensure that original source documents would be available during the monitoring visits for source data verification and reviewing compliance to other study requirements. It is also good to note if electronic source data will be used and their compliance to applicable regulations and availability for review during the monitoring visits.

- **Ethics committee:** It is important to ensure that the EC meets the Schedule Y requirements for constitution and has Standard Operating Procedures (SOPs) in place. It is also good to enquire about their meeting frequency and approval timelines. Ethics committee approvals in some Institutes may take an inordinately long period of time which could affect study timelines.

- **Number of studies ongoing:** The Investigator should be able to adequately manage and supervise the studies that are going on at the site along with the usual clinical practice.

- **Competitive studies:** It is good to know which studies will be competing for the same subject pool at the time of recruitment as this will impact the recruitment rate.

- **Stability of the site staff/attrition:** Frequent turnovers can leave the study in a limbo. Stability of staff enables continuity in site operations, building relations with subjects and a comfort level with them ensuring retention.

- **Requirement of Site Management Organization (SMO) support:** Some sites require services of a site management organization to ensure compliance to protocol and relevant data capture and transcription in a timely manner.
- **The geographical location and accessibility:** It should be conveniently accessible for Clinical Research Associates (CRA) to comply with the monitoring plan and for delivery of investigational products. It should also be accessible to the subjects.

Investigator and other agreements/undertakings

Agreements are a means to document, share and accept (or reject) terms and conditions for a particular service, and therefore should be detailed enough to avoid unnecessary ambiguity and allow flexibility where appropriate so that a fresh agreement is not required with small changes.

There are several types of agreements in a clinical trial. Some of these are listed below:

1.   Confidentiality agreement: This is usually the first agreement to be signed between the sponsor and the Investigator or vendor/service providers prior to sharing of synopsis/protocol/Investigator's brochure (IB) or other confidential documents and as the name indicates, it is to ensure confidentiality of data and protect intellectual property. It is a legal contract and is sometimes known as non disclosure agreement or confidentiality disclosure agreement.

2.   Financial disclosure: This is required as per Code of Federal Regulations (CFR), Title 21, Part 54. Each clinical Investigator is required to attest absence of financial interest with a completed Form FDA 3454 or a disclosure of all financial interests by completing the Form FDA 3455. FDA may consider both the size and nature of a disclosed financial interest, including a potential increase in the value of the interest if the product is approved and steps that have been taken to minimize the potential for bias. It can be a ground for considering the study or data inadequate. Usually however, study designs utilize multiple Investigators (most of whom do not have a disclosable interest) blinding, objective endpoints, or measurement of endpoints by someone other than the Investigator and thus adequately protect against any bias created by a disclosable financial interest.

The sponsor has to obtain a commitment from the Investigator that the latter will promptly update this information if any relevant changes occur during the course of the investigation and for 1 year following the completion of the study.

The financial records of clinical Investigators are required to be retained for 2 years after the date of approval of the application and should be made available for inspection when required by the regulatory agency.

3.   Financial agreement: This is an agreement that outlines the payment to the Investigator and/or Institute per subject screened/enrolled/completed in the study, maximum number of subjects that can be enrolled and the breakdown of payment milestones. The agreements are usually bipartite or tripartite with the Institute/Hospital as the third party. It is in the best interest of all concerned to get the financial agreement fully executed prior to start of any study procedures.

4.   Protocol agreement: This agreement indicates the Investigator's consent to conduct the study as per the protocol. With any amendment to the protocol, the agreement has to be signed again.

5.   FDA Form 1572: The Statement of Investigator, Form FDA 1572, is an agreement signed by the Investigator to assure that he/she will comply with FDA regulations related to the conduct of a clinical investigation of an investigational drug or biologic.

The 1572 has two purposes:

- to provide the sponsor with information about the Investigator's qualifications and the clinical site that will enable the sponsor to establish and document that the Investigator is qualified and the site is an appropriate location at which to conduct the clinical investigation, and
- to inform the Investigator of his/her obligations and obtain the Investigator's commitment to follow pertinent FDA regulations.

One of these commitments is that the Investigator will ensure that the requirements relating to Institutional Review Board (IRB) review and approval in 21CFR56 are met. For studies conducted in India or outside US under the IND, the sponsor can apply for a waiver from this commitment. The IRB waiver request should contain a description of alternative mechanisms for assuring human subject protection. If the waiver is granted by the US FDA, the Investigators can attach a copy of this letter to the signed 1572 as a record.

A common concern is who should be listed as the sub-investigators in section #6 of the form. As per the FDA website and section 21CFR312.53, the Investigator is expected to provide a list of names of the sub-investigators who will assist the Investigator in the conduct of the investigation(s). Only individuals who will make a direct and significant contribution to data, are directly involved in the performance of procedures required by the protocol and collection of data should be listed on 1572. Hospital staff who provide ancillary and intermittent care but who do not make a direct and significant contribution to the clinical data, do not need to be listed individually.

Additional information on completion of the Form 1572 is found on the FDA website:

http://www.fda.gov/downloads/RegulatoryInformation /Guidances/UCM214282.pdf

The Form 1572 is available at

http://www.fda.gov/downloads/AboutFDA/ReportsManualsForms/Forms/UCM074728.pdf.

Investigators should be aware that making a willfully false statement is a criminal offense.

6.   Investigator Undertaking: As per Schedule Y of the Drugs and Cosmetics Rules 1945, the Investigator Undertaking is a commitment by the Investigator to conduct the study as per the applicable laws and regulations. Undertaking by all participating Investigators has to be submitted to the Health Authorities in India along with the application for conducting a clinical trial in India. Appendix VII of Schedule Y lists the format of the Undertaking by the Investigator.

There can be several other types of agreements in the conduct of a clinical study e.g. agreements with different vendors such as Clinical Research Organizations for outsourcing fully/partially the conduct and monitoring of a clinical trial. The transfer of any or all obligations has to be in writing and any obligation not covered by the written description would not be deemed as transferred (21CFR312.53). It is important to note that this does not exempt the sponsor from being responsible for the conduct of the study as per ICH-GCP and applicable regulations.

Other common vendor agreements could be with service providers like Site Management Organizations, Investigational product management, translation agencies, IVRS/IWRS services, specialized central services such as laboratory, ECG / radiological readings, insurance or liability coverage service.

From an audit perspective, it becomes important to document the criteria for selection of the vendor. Developing a plan for vendor management that ensures good oversight, regular meetings with documented minutes and an audit schedule is recommended.

Regulatory and Ethics Approvals

In India, Clinical trials are governed by the Drug and Cosmetics Rules, 1945 and the Schedule Y details the requirements and guidelines to undertake clinical trials in India. Applications for permission to undertake clinical trials are to be made in Form 44 of the Drugs and Cosmetics Rules, 1945 and accompanied with data which includes the chemical and pharmaceutical information, animal pharmacology and toxicology data, human clinical pharmacology data, regulatory status in other countries.

For new drug substances discovered in India, clinical trials are required to be carried out in India right from Phase I. For new drug substances discovered outside India, phase I data from studies conducted outside India has to be submitted, subsequent to which permission may be granted to repeat Phase I trials and/or conduct Phase II trials and subsequently Phase III trials concurrently with other global trials. Phase III trials are required to be conducted in India before permission to market the drug in India is granted. The sample size for the study must keep in mind the regulatory requirements for that indication, to obtain approval for marketing in future.

Other documents that should accompany the application generally include the Investigator's brochure, protocol, CRF, ICF, Investigator's undertaking and EC clearance if available. Usually, an import license to import the investigational product into the country and an export no objection certificate to transfer samples to a central laboratory are needed. The application for both these documents is made simultaneously along with the application for permission to undertake clinical trials.

The timelines for approval vary and may be influenced by approvals from other countries. Success is based on close collaboration between the operations team, regulatory team and the liaison officer. As the time for approval varies depending on the policy of the DCGI, it is good to study the recent trends in approval timelines and evaluate the time remaining to meet the recruitment target and rework recruitment strategies.

The trial has to be registered on Clinical Trials Registry of India (CTRI) prior to enrollment of the first subject. The Clinical Trials Registry - India (CTRI), hosted at the ICMR's National Institute of Medical Statistics (NIMS), is a free and online public record system for registration of clinical trials being conducted in India. Since 15 June 2009, prospective registration of trials in India has been made mandatory by the Drugs Controller General (India) (DCGI).

Protocol amendments have to be notified to the health authorities in writing. No deviation from or changes to the protocol should be implemented without prior written approval of the EC and the licensing authority except when it is necessary to eliminate immediate hazards to the trial subject or when change involve only logistic or administrative aspects of the trial. Administrative or logistic changes in the protocol should be notified to the licensing authority within 30 days. As per Schedule Y, all other changes to the study such as additional sites, additional subjects, changes in inclusion/exclusion criteria or any major protocol change to study design, dose or treatment require prior approval of the health authorities. Unexpected Serious Adverse Events (SAE's) have to be notified within 14 calendar days to DCGI and other Investigators.

The Sponsor is required to submit an annual status report to the health authorities from the receipt of study approval until the end of the study. There is no format specified however, basic information which includes study name and title, brief outline of the study, current status (number of sites, subjects enrolled, ongoing etc.) and any other relevant information needs to be submitted.

If the study is prematurely discontinued, a summary report is to be submitted within 3 months with brief description of the study, number of subjects exposed to the drug, dose and duration of exposure, details of adverse drug reactions, if any and reason for discontinuation of the study or non-pursuit of the new drug application.

A final clinical study report (CSR) must be submitted at the end of the study as per the format given in Appendix II of Schedule Y.

Ethics Committee Approvals

All clinical trials have to be approved by the Ethics Committee (EC) prior to study initiation. Schedule Y of the Drugs and Cosmetics Rules, 1945 outlines the criteria for EC members: Minimum number of people in EC = 7, Quorum for approval = 5, representations from different backgrounds required including scientist/pharmacologist, clinicians, legal expert, social scientist, NGO, philosopher, theologian, and lay person. At least one member must be independent of the institution/trial site and at least one member should be non-scientific. The Chairperson must be from outside the institution.

The approval letter must mention the study code, protocol title and version number, other documents reviewed, list of members present at the meeting, quorum of five members as per Schedule Y, date, time and venue of the meeting and have the signature and date of member secretary/Chairman. Appendix VIII of Schedule Y lists the requirements of EC in India and the recommended format of the approval letter.

EC submissions must include protocol, ICF, IB, recruitment techniques, PI CV, Insurance, Investigator agreement with the sponsor and the Investigator's undertaking. Usually, the ethics committee submissions occur parallel with HA submissions. Time for Ethics committee approval is one of the criteria for site selection. Usually 1-3 months is the average time for EC meetings and approvals. All documents that would be given to the subjects such as Informed consent documents, subject diaries and advertising material/recruitment strategies must be approved by the EC. The EC fees have increased substantially over the last few years and must be borne in mind while budgeting.

Document submission is usually done via paper, though some of the ethics committees are now open to electronic submission also. Encryption to ensure security and confidentiality of data is important with electronic submissions for EC/IRB review.

Some observations with respect to ECs include inappropriate quorum/constitution of EC, lack of documentation supporting adequate review of study documents with the requisite quorum, inadequate documentation citing approval or rejection of the study, no minutes of the meetings conducted, lack of SOPs and/or failure to follow the SOPs.

Investigator and Initiation Meetings

Investigator Meetings (IM) are organized by sponsors for a multi-centric trial. It is usually conducted prior to site initiations and it is a good platform to train various participating sites at one go. The timing and venue of the Investigator meeting is crucial to ensure maximum attendance. It should not clash with any annual international meeting. Attendance by at least 80-85% of the site members intended could be considered as a successful turnout. It should be timed close to site initiations so that it is fresh when the actual study starts.

The agenda should cover the protocol in detail, the molecule, CRF/eCRF completion guidelines, safety and adverse events reporting, safety events and reporting, adverse events of special interest, IP accountability, IVRS/IWRS, monitoring schedule, recruitment targets and strategies, study timelines, Investigator responsibilities, database lock timelines and other key milestones, Data Monitoring Committees (DMC) and their role, medical monitoring if any, etc. It could cover training of devices, demonstration of investigational product delivery and other study specific procedures. It is important to train the Investigators and sites on GCP and local regulations and document the training. The discussion and questions can be compiled in a FAQ format and shared with the sites.

A thank you letter is usually sent out to participants - it is important that these are sent out only to the attendees and not to the invited members. 'Lessons learnt' from the IM can be discussed post-meeting to understand what worked well and what can be improved for next time. Investigator meetings provide a good opportunity to participating sites to interact with each other and the sponsor representatives and are a good way to kick-start the study.

Initiation meetings are held subsequent to regulatory and EC approvals and timed close to start of subject screening and recruitment. It provides an opportunity to train the whole study site staff team, particularly the ones who could not make it to the Investigator meeting. The agenda is similar to that of an Investigator Meeting but can include detail review of the site component of the trial master files, safety reporting guidelines, GCP training and compliance, CRF completion guidelines, etc.

It is particularly important to emphasize on source documentation requirements. Common observations with source documentation include retrospective entries, entries not signed, initialed or dated, several changes to data with no explanation, overwriting and original data not readable, sometimes use of whiteouts (which may not be intentional but more because it is a hospital/institute practice-it is still not acceptable), inadequate progress notes, investigational reports missing the name or number or a subject identifier. This is particularly common with ECG tracings – there may not be an identifier and the time does not necessarily correlate with the outer ECG card to which the trace has been stapled, the X-ray films may not have an identifier and the date the investigation was carried out may be missing.

Sometimes, there is inconsistency between two entries in the same medical record. A common example of this is a mismatch in the timings recorded for a particular activity. This could be because the hospital staff may refer to their wrist watches and there is no standard reference clock/atomic clock to which all study site staff refer to for noting the time. Source documentation must fit the 'ALCOA' criteria where A = Attributable, L = Legible, C = Contemporaneous, O = Original and A = Accurate. Other common findings include delayed review of investigational reports. The review of reports may have been done in a timely manner but there is no documentation and it is signed and dated at the time of the visit of the monitor. It is important to emphasize to the site staff and Investigators that in clinical research, what is not documented, is considered not done.

Source documentation in out-patient subjects is relatively easier and it may be more difficult to standardize and ensure compliance in an in-patient set up. Organizing trainings in source documentation and GCP at the start of each shift to include ancillary site staffs that make entries in the subject's medical file may help to prevent some of the commonly observed source documentation issues.

Initiation visits are also an opportunity to set up the electronic equipment or devices such as laptops and electronic subject diaries, ensuring appropriate storage of investigational product, review of laboratory kits for different visits, and any other study specific procedures.

This is a good time to share expectations with respect to frequency and dates of monitoring visits and other key company requirements such as travel policies, payment schedules, etc.

Attendance and documentation of training is important and supports fulfillment of regulatory requirement for training of Investigators and site staff. A copy of the site initiation visit report is filed at the site detailing the activities covered during the visit and in the follow up letter. The site is now ready to recruit.

Recruitment and Retention of Subjects

Recruitment of subjects in a clinical study rarely matches the original forecast. Unfortunately, several factors are dependent on accurate forecasting of recruitment – one of the most important ones being availability of investigational product. The production and availability of an investigational product has to match the requirements as per recruitment forecasts at different sites across the world. Accurate forecasting also helps in ensuring that we have the right number of sites on the study to meet our target recruitment and resources to finance, monitor and manage the study. Recruitment rate and cost of clinical trials tend to be inversely related.

Forecast of recruitment occurs initially at the time of site selection. The inclusion and exclusion criteria determine the recruitment rate and the complexity of the protocol from the subject's point of view (too long and too frequent visits, too many investigations and cumbersome procedures, investigational product versus an approved and available oral medication, etc.) and duration of the protocol impacts subject retention. If there are significant delays in startup, it is important to re-forecast the recruitment rate. New competing studies which were not anticipated at the time of site selection may have started at the site which could impact recruitment.

If it is a study targeting a chronic disease, the existing patient database is a good indicator. If it is an acute disease, a review of footfalls at the site can give some indication. Recruitment strategies may include review of database, referrals or advertising in media, newspapers, fliers (not so prevalent in India) and regular contact by the CRA. Weekly e-mail/fax of screening logs helps in keeping the study on top of the minds of site staff. Sometimes, a quick reference card with the inclusion-exclusion criteria is shared with other medical colleagues for referral purposes.

Newsletters with performance graphs of different sites in India and performance of India vis-à-vis other countries can be a motivating factor.

National Coordinators may be appointed in some studies. Usually, a National Coordinator is an Investigator who is also a key opinion leader or has a large circle of influence. Teleconferences and sometimes an Investigator meeting may be held to discuss recruitment issues and strategies.

Services of vendors specializing in recruitment services and referrals can be availed too. Recruitment strategies need to be planned early enough as a part of the study plan itself with adequate budget allocation.

One of the concerns with the recruitment process is screening or pre-screening procedures conducted without prior written informed consent documentation. Procedures that are to be performed as part of the practice of medicine and which would be done whether or not study entry was contemplated, such as for diagnosis or treatment of a disease or medical condition, may be performed and the results subsequently used for determining study eligibility without first obtaining consent. On the other hand, informed consent must be obtained prior to initiation of any clinical screening procedures that are performed solely for the purpose of determining eligibility for research, including withdrawal from medication (wash-out). When wash-out is done in anticipation of or in preparation for the research, it is part of the research.

One of the most common and crucial GCP issues during the recruitment phase is the process of informed consent. Other observations include incorrect inclusion of subjects, and repeated error in inclusion on account of delayed identification, usually due to a late first monitoring visit or due to poor training or performance of the CRA.

Retention strategy

Retention of subjects is important in order to have complete subject data. Retention is relatively easy in studies of shorter duration and can be a challenge for studies that are ongoing for a long period of time. It is important to select the subjects who not only fit the inclusion-exclusion criteria but can also make the visits as per protocol. Subjects who stay in remote villages and have to travel a couple of hours to the site to make the visits are more likely to drop out. If the subject has the support of family, it helps in ensuring compliance to the protocol.

Clear communication regarding the number and frequency of visits, duration of each visit, the procedures to be carried out, information about the investigational product and possible side-effects, storage conditions (this can be an issue for temperature-controlled medication as many households in India do not have a refrigerator), etc. at the very start of the study prior to signing the informed consent ensures that the subject is fully aware of what it entails logistically to be a part of the study. It helps to give a schedule/timetable of all forthcoming visits so they can plan holidays around it, give a next appointment card or a fridge magnet, reminder calls or messages on cell phone, reimburse travel cost, etc.

Additional things that can be done to make the subject comfortable are providing snacks, television/magazines to read in case the visit duration is long, minimal waiting time, same coordinator for the subject each time to facilitate rapport and comfort levels, and a smooth flow of events for the subject at the site. New platforms of communication such as social networking sites could be evaluated for increasing engagement of the study participants.

'Lost to follow up' of subjects is avoidable and must be minimized at all costs. It is required to follow up with a registered/certified mail and to document all efforts to contact the subject. It helps to keep the contact information of close family members/relatives and neighbours of subjects to facilitate contact/get update on subject's status in case they do not come for appointments and are not reachable.

If the protocol is too tedious (too many blood draws) or too uncomfortable (IP involving injections) or if the adverse events (nausea, headache, vomiting, etc.), disrupt the quality of life, then it is likely that the retention will be difficult.

Medical reasons for potential discontinuation:
- Lack of efficacy of the drug.
- Intolerable adverse events.
- Serious adverse events.
- Subject's condition deteriorates.
- Subject develops an inter-current illness (an illness other than the one under study but which occurs during the course of the trial).
- Pregnancy.
- Abnormal laboratory value.
- Did not meet original entry criteria (discovered after study entry).

Subjects' reasons for discontinuation:
- Moved out of the area.
- Use of non-approved concomitant medications.
- Subject does not understand the importance of remaining in the trial even when disease condition has improved.
- The subject does not get along with some of the study staff.
- Difficulties with transportation, childcare or time off from work.
- Friends or family are unhappy about participation in the trial.
- Subject has a change in personal situation.

A Sponsor may terminate a trial because of safety concerns, business reasons, or the Investigator may no longer be able to continue with the trial as he/she may have moved and suitable replacement may not be available or if the Investigator did not comply with the regulations.

Investigator Responsibilities

The Investigator is responsible for the conduct of the clinical trial as per the protocol, GCP Guidelines and in compliance with the Undertaking as per Appendix VII of Schedule Y and the USFDA Form 1572. He/She is responsible for protecting the rights, safety and well-being of subjects under his/her care and for control of the investigational product.

The Investigator is responsible for:

- complete understanding of the protocol, the investigator's brochure, the risks and benefits of the investigational product.
- conducting the clinical trial in compliance with the protocol after obtaining necessary regulatory and ethics committee approvals.
- personally conducting and/or supervising the study.
- ensuring adequate qualification and training of study site staff and informing them about their obligations, and any study specific changes.
- reporting all adverse events to the Sponsor as per the guidelines and regulations.
- providing adequate medical care to the subject and which includes any period that he/she may not be available by ensuring delegation of responsibility for medical care to a specific qualified physician in his absence.
- reporting all unexpected serious adverse events to the sponsor within 24 hours and to the ethics committee within 7 days of occurrence.
- ensuring appropriate and adequate informed consent documentation process, maintaining accurate documentation and availability for inspections and audits.
- maintaining confidentiality of participating subjects and security and confidentiality of data.

He/She must have documented standard operating procedures for the tasks performed at the site for study related activities. Often, sites do not have documented SOPs - consultants and sometimes, SMOs offer to provide this service.

The Investigator must appropriately delegate study-related tasks by ensuring qualification, training and experience of the concerned person and document it with the dates of involvement in the study. The Investigator is also responsible for study-related activities conducted by someone who is not his/her direct employee – e.g. Study coordinator provided by an SMO service. A Sponsor who retains an SMO shares responsibility for the quality of the work performed by the SMO. If the performance of the study coordinator is not adequate, the Investigator needs to document the observed deficiencies in writing to the study coordinator's supervisor and inform the sponsor. Depending on severity of deficiencies, the clinical trial may need to be voluntarily suspended until the personnel can be replaced.

If the Investigator retains the services of a facility to perform study assessments, the Investigator should take steps to ensure that the facility is adequate (e.g., has the required certification or licenses).

There is an increased focus of the regulatory authorities on the involvement of the Investigator in the conduct of clinical studies. In order to ensure adequate supervision of the study, the USFDA guidance document suggests having routine meetings with staff to review trial progress, adverse events and updating staff of any changes to protocol/procedures and routine meetings with the sponsor's monitors.

In addition, a plan outlining the procedures for the following can be developed as applicable:

- timely correction and documentation of problems identified by study personnel, outside monitors or auditors, or other parties involved in the conduct of a study.
- documenting or reviewing the performance of delegated tasks in a satisfactory and timely manner.
- ensuring that the consent process is being conducted in accordance with 21 CFR Part 50 and that study subjects understand the nature of their participation and the risks.
- ensuring that source data are accurate, contemporaneous, and original.
- ensuring that information in the source documents is accurately captured on the case report forms (CRFs).
- dealing with data queries and discrepancies identified by the study monitor.
- ensuring study staff comply with the protocol and adverse event assessment and reporting requirements.
- addressing medical and ethical issues in a timely manner that arise during the course of the study.

Apart from the above, adequate documentation of Investigator's involvement in the study through regular progress notes, review of investigational reports and meeting minutes with the site study team is recommended.

CRC Responsibilities

The clinical research coordinator's responsibilities will depend on the delegation by the Investigator. The clinical research coordinator (CRC) should be qualified and trained to conduct the duties delegated to him/her and these should be documented.

In the start-up phase, CRCs may help in assisting the completion of feasibility questionnaires, budgeting study costs, setting up infrastructure at the site to ensure smooth flow of events as per protocol, coordination with sponsor for all requisite documents for regulatory submission (Investigator undertaking, CV, medical license), liaisoning with the ethics committee for all study - related submissions and tracking them for approval.

Once the study starts, the CRC can assist with recruitment strategies and identification of subjects as per the inclusion/exclusion criteria (to be validated by the Investigator), disseminating information about the study, ensuring all activities are completed as per protocol (laboratory tests, measurements, logistics of screening number, randomization, etc.) completing CRF/e-CRF, accurate recording and reporting of AEs and SAEs, timely resolution of data queries, ensuring appropriate storage of IP and accountability, communication with sponsor, EC, maintenance of the local site study file and all other details that go into making a successfully conducted study at site and as per the delegation by the Investigator. If the CRC is medically qualified, his/her responsibilities could include taking vitals and other medical decisions as delegated by the Investigator.

The CRC is the link between different players at the site (Investigator, sub-investigator, nurse, pharmacist, phlebotomist, laboratory, CRA, subject, ethics committee, etc.) and can ensure smooth functioning of the site. It thus becomes important for the CRC to understand the protocol and translate it to a logical flow that will ensure continuity and compliance to the protocol.

CRA Responsibilities

As per 21CFR312.53, selecting a monitor qualified by training and experience to monitor the progress of the investigation is the responsibility of the Sponsor and selecting the right monitor is as important as selecting the right Investigator.

CRA responsibilities vary depending on the organization, the phase of the study and experience of the CRA. In some organizations, the role may have scope to contribute to protocol development, creation and validation of supporting operations documents such as the operations manual, monitoring plan, CRF completion guidelines, IVRS/IWRS specifications, Central laboratory manuals, etc. It may involve supporting the vendor selection process, collaboration with the investigational product supply department in finalizing the packaging and labeling specifications, collaboration with regulatory, legal and insurance agencies, budget finalization and negotiations, management and update of clinical trials management systems and other applicable tools, vendor management and line management.

The study start-up phase would involve site selection, study and site budgets, Investigator meetings, site initiation visits, investigational product supply logistics, ethics committee submissions, customizations of documents and ensuring adequate training for site staff. The recruitment phase would focus on confirming the correct process for informed consent and verification of subjects' inclusion as per the protocol. The first monitoring visit must be made as soon as possible after inclusion of the subject in the study and prior to the next subject in order to ensure that errors if any, are caught and not repeated in another subject. It is important to motivate the site to meet the planned recruitment goals. Once recruitment is closed and the study is ongoing, CRA must continue monitoring to ensure compliance as per protocol and applicable regulations and guidelines. Close-out and archival phase would be initiated after database lock and it would involve retrieval or destruction of used/unused investigational product, study supplies, informing the ethics committee and regulatory agencies, records retention information, completion and archival of the trial master file.

Good monitoring practices help to ensure good quality of data and protection of safety and rights of the subjects in accordance with the protocol, regulatory and GCP guidelines. Each site visit should be preceded by a written agenda. The visit itself would involve a meeting with the Investigator, review of the Investigator study files, informed consent process and eligibility criteria, source data review and verification, compliance to protocol, ensuring adequate capture of adverse events, review of investigat onal products accountabi ity and storage and a closing meeting with the Investigator to communicate significant observations and actions required.

Monitoring visits are as per the monitoring plan but can be more frequent if warranted. It is important to generate accurate monitoring visit reports and upload them within the timelines. Follow up letters need to document all key activities completed by the CRA during the visit, the observations and actions required on part of the site. Subsequent follow up letters must list the previous issues and mention if they are closed out or still open.

A successful CRA meets or exceeds the recruitment targets, has minimum data queries (reflection of training given by CRA to sites) and few open issues and for a shorter duration, is well aware of the logistics (availability of investigational product at site, translated ICFs, etc.) and is ready for an audit anytime. He/she works together with the site to ensure success and compliance and does not act as a "MONITOR" who is out to point out faults.

Good communication skills with an ability to discern the important from the not-so, management or escalation of issues in time, to be able to provide 'reliability' to Sponsors about the quality of monitoring at his/her s tes, are some of the factors that are key to success in this role.

Some common observations include failure to comply to the monitoring plan, delayed completion of monitoring visit reports and follow up letters, inadequate or missed review of monitoring visit reports by superiors, missed data in monitoring visit reports (all data in follow up letters must be present in the monitoring visit report, but not vice-versa), inadequate source data review and verification, missed review of data points across visits, inadequate documentation of contacts with the site, failure to identify incorrect inclusion of subjects in the study, inadequate training records, delayed or missed escalation of significant GCP issues and issues of protocol non compliance.

Adverse Event reporting

As per ICH-GCP, an Adverse Event (AE) is any untoward medical occurrence in a patient or clinical investigation subject administered a pharmaceutical product. It does not necessarily have a causal relationship with this treatment. An AE can therefore be any unfavourable and unintended sign (including an abnormal laboratory finding), symptom or disease temporarily associated with the use of a medicinal (Investigational) product. As per 21CFR312.64, it is an Investigator's responsibility to ensure accurate, timely and complete reporting of adverse events during a clinical trial. Ensuring that th s is done by the Investigators and sites is one of the most important responsibilities of a CRA.

When an adverse event is an unintended noxious response with a reasonable possibility of a causal relationship with the investigational product, it is also termed as an adverse drug reaction.

As per 21CFR312.32, adverse events can be termed as serious adverse events if they comply with one or more of the following criteria:

- Death.
- Life-threatening adverse drug experience.

- Inpatient hospitalization or prolongation of existing hospitalization.
- A persistent or significant disability/incapacity.
- Congenital anomaly or birth defect.
- Important medical event.

All serious adverse events (SAEs) are expected to be reported immediately to the Sponsor , usually within 24 hours. A detailed report usually follows the initial reporting. Sponsors are expected to report the SAEs to the regulatory authorities within 14 calendar days as per Schedule Y and 15 calendar days as per 21CFR312.32. Under 21CFR312.32, sponsors must promptly review information about the safety of the investigational drug obtained or otherwise received by the sponsor from any source, foreign or domestic and notify FDA and all participating Investigators in an IND safety report of any adverse experience associated with the use of the drug that is both serious and unexpected. Sponsors usually notify all participating sites regarding the serious adverse events that occur in a study by Dear Investigator Letter or DILs. Tracking of DILs is important to ensure that all DILs are sent in a timely manner to all sites.

The informed consent document may have to be modified and subjects re-consented in case of new adverse events that can alter the risks to the subjects participating in the study.

Adverse event reports have to be submitted to ethics committees as per their requirements.

Delayed reporting to sponsors or regulatory agencies or the ethics committees is sometimes an observation. Steps that may be taken to ensure timely reporting during the conduct of a clinical trial include:

- Study documents - Protocol must clearly outline the possible adverse events, adverse events of special interest and serious adverse events that need to be captured and the method of reporting.
- Training of site staff during the Investigator meetings, site initiation visits and repeat emphasis during monitoring visits is important. Providing laminates with quick reference numbers, dedicated reporting cell and fax numbers or email IDs helps.
- Accurate, thorough source data review and verification to ensure that all relevant data is captured in the CRFs. Review of patient diaries for adverse events, concomitant medications give an indication of adverse events that may have occurred but not reported by the subject to the site.
- Adequate time given to subjects during their visits to listen to them, examine them and encouraging them to report adverse events also helps.
- Tracking dates of adverse events, submission to ethics committees and receipt of acknowledgements helps ensure that there is no delayed reporting.

Trial and Site Master Files

The objective of maintaining trial and site master files is to ensure documentation of the conduct of study in a self-explanatory manner. The site files indicate the course of events at the site and include signed informed consent documents, regulatory approvals, ethics committee approvals and correspondence, correspondence and communication with the sponsors including follow up letters and documentation of telephonic conversations, a copy of study documents such as the protocol/protocol amendments along with signed agreement, IB, sample case record forms, informed consent documents and any other written information given to subjects, advertisements if used, insurance information, central and local laboratory reference ranges, certifications and accreditation for laboratories, information regarding investigational product including receipt, dispensing and decoding in case of emergencies, communication regarding serious adverse events and study logs such as screening, enrolment, subject identification log, retained body fluids records, etc.

The sponsor file is a mirror image of the site file at each site and a central/general file. The differentiating documents include regulatory submission and approval documents, monitoring visit reports, agreements with different vendors, master randomization list, specifications for IVRS/IWRS, etc.

The right time to start the files is at the start of the study. At the Sponsor's end, the files can be collated with the feasibility data. The CRA can train the site staff on the importance and method of maintaining the site files at the site initiation visit and reinforce it during the first monitoring visit.

Well-maintained files on a real time basis save time during archival, reduce the chances of lost documents, keep the sponsor and site ready for audits and make handovers hassle-free during change in the site/sponsor staff. Unfortunately though, filing and review can easily become a neglected activity and it helps to link review of TMF as an activity required prior to obtaining approval for a regular operational activity, e.g. approval of a travel request to conduct a monitoring visit.

Several companies are now going for electronic TMFs. This is environment-friendly, promotes regional/home work offices and certainly the way forward.

Investigational Product Storage and Dispensing

As per 21CFR 312.57 and 312.53, a sponsor is required to maintain adequate records for the receipt, shipment, or other disposition of the investigational product. These records are required to include, as appropriate, the name of the Investigator to whom the drug is shipped, along with the date, quantity, and batch/code mark of each shipment. It is the Sponsor's responsibility to control the distribution of investigational product and ship it only to Investigators participating in the investigation. As per 21CFR312.61, an Investigator shall administer the drug only to subjects under the Investigator's personal supervision or under the supervision of a sub-Investigator responsible to the Investigator. The Investigator shall not supply the investigational drug to any person not authorized to receive it.

As per ICH-GCP, the Sponsor should determine acceptable storage temperatures, storage conditions, storage times, reconstitution fluids and procedures and devices for product infusion, if any. The Sponsor needs to inform all involved parties (e.g. monitors, Investigators, pharmacists, etc.) of these determinations.

Usually, the investigational product is manufactured in limited amounts and shipped to different study sites either directly or through an affiliate office or through vendors, as per the recruitment forecast and recruitment rate. During the initial phase, investigational product packaging and labeling to cover regulatory requirements of different countries needs to be addressed. Shipment is usually done through well-known courier agencies with a proven track record of managing temperature-controlled shipments. In India, test license or import license would be required to import the investigational product manufactured outside the country. Often, third-party clearance vendors are involved to facilitate clearance through customs. Once at a central depot within the country, the investigational product would be shipped to different sites after receiving the necessary documents and approvals to start recruitment. Subsequent shipments would be as per IVRS/IWRS generated requests and is recruitment triggered. Shipment would be via couriers, usually with a material safety data sheet (MSDS).

It is important that the templates are switched off as soon as the investigational product is received at the site and checked for temperature excursions during transit. Any deviation should be reported to the Sponsor as per company policies and written permission obtained prior to use.

At the site, the study drug must be stored in a secure area under desired conditions, accessible only to study site staff. Temperature logs must be maintained. One of the common observations is that the study name is not mentioned on the temperature log, or dates and temperatures seem to have been recorded at one time instead of each day. Thermometers must be calibrated.

Accountability of each and every investigational product needs to be ensured by the Sponsor and the Investigator and appropriate logs must be maintained. The Monitor must ensure investigational product accountability at each monitoring visit.

At the end of the study, as per 21CFR312.59, the sponsor must assure return of all unused supplies of the investigational product from each Investigator whose participation in the investigation is discontinued or terminated. The Sponsor may authorize alternative disposition of unused supplies of the investigational product provided this does not expose humans to risk from the drug. The Sponsor is required to maintain written records of any disposition of the drug in accordance with 21CFR312.57.

Common observations related to investigational product during the conduct of a clinical trial include lost or missing investigational product, inappropriate handling or preparation by an unqualified person, incorrect dosage or missing start and stop dates of altered doses, inadequate/incomplete temperature logs, thermometers not calibrated, storage area not secure, templates not stopped in time and template data not checked etc.

In case of some logistical issues or inadequate oversight, there can be instances where the subject is due for a study visit or has come for the study visit, but the investigational product is not available for dispensing. This should be avoided at all costs. Sometimes, the procedures for tracking dispensed, returned and destroyed investigational product are very detailed and if not managed on a real time basis, the backlog can quickly pile up and accountability may become an issue.

Trial Close out

Close out activities start with the successful database lock and include closing-out of different sites participating in the study, collation of the trial master files, reconciliation and destruction of investigational product, and notification to ethics and regulatory agencies. Once the data is analyzed and a clinical study report generated, it can be distributed to different sites, ethics and regulatory agencies.

Some of the key points to remember are:

- **Records retention:** As per 21CFR312.57 and 21CFR312.62, the Sponsor and the Investigator are responsible for maintaining records for a period of 2 years following the date a marketing application is approved for the drug for the indication for which it was being investigated; or if no application is to be filed or if the application is not approved for such indication, until 2 years after the investigation is discontinued and the FDA is notified. The archival location of the records should be clearly mentioned. As per 21CFR 56.115, the IRB or ethics committee is expected to retain records pertaining to the study for at least 3 years after completion of the study.

- All records must be accessible in case of an audit/inspection.

- The Investigator must be informed about the policies of the company with respect to publishing of the data.

- Financial payments to participating sites, Investigators and vendors must be completed.

- Electronic databases such as the clinical trial management system (CTMS) must be completed for sponsor and study specific details such as closure of all open issues, etc.

- Official websites hosting clinical trials information (www.clinicaltrials.gov and www.ctri.in) posted by the sponsor must be updated as per the requirements.

Section 8 of ICH-GCP guidelines is a good reference for the list of essential documents that are normally generated before the clinical phase of the trial commences, during the conduct of the clinical trial and after completion / termination of the trial.

A final closeout can be done when the monitor has reviewed both the Investigator and institution and Sponsor files and confirmed all documents are in the appropriate files. These must be available for audits by Sponsors or inspections by regulatory agencies.

Conclusion:

Conduct of clinical trials is like multiple players completing a 3-D jig-saw puzzle. All pieces have to fit-in perfectly to form a perfect picture. The consequences of inappropriate conduct are too many - for Sponsors , it could lead to delay in timelines, increase in cost, inadequate or inaccurate data, halting of clinical programme, rejection of the new drug, etc. Sponsor staff/CRAs could lose their jobs and/or reputation. For Investigators, they could be blacklisted, criminally punished, face litigation and may lose potential clientele. Study subjects may undergo irreversible and fatal health consequences. However, there are sufficient detailed regulations and guidelines available and if these are well-understood and adhered to, then the outcome is a well-conducted clinical trial which may contribute invaluable medical data and bring forth innovation in health care.

REFERENCES:

1.   US FDA website for Code of federal regulations:
     http://www.accessdata.fda.gov/scripts/cdrh/cfdocs/cfCFR/CFRSearch.cfm
2.   Guidance for industry – E6 Good Clinical Practice consolidated guideline (April 1996)
     http://www.fda.gov/downloads/Drugs/GuidanceComplianceRegulatoryInformation/Guidances/ucm073122.pdf
3.   Schedule Y:
     http://cdsco.nic.in/html/schedule-y%20(amended%20version-2005)%20original.htm
4.   Information Sheet Guidance for Sponsors, Clinical Investigators, and IRBs – Frequently asked questions: Statement of Investigators (Form FDA1572):
     http://www.fda.gov/downloads/RegulatoryInformation/Guidances/UCM214282.pdf
5.   Clinical Trials Registration of India (CTRI) website:
     http://ctri.nic.in/Clinicaltrials/cont1.php
6.   Information Sheet – Screening Tests prior to study enrollment:
     http://www.fda.gov/RegulatoryInformation/Guidances/ucm126430.htm
7.   Ginsberg David (2004) in Becoming a successful clinical research Investigator, Ed. Sara Gambrill (Centerwatch) pp 111-129.
8.   Guidance for Industry : Investigator Responsibilities — Protecting the Rights, Safety, and Welfare of Study Subjects:
     http://www.fda.gov/downloads/Drugs/GuidanceComplianceRegulatoryInformation/Guidances/UCM187772.pdf
9.   Clinical Trials website by US National Institutes of Health: http://www.clinicaltrials.gov/

RECOMMENDED READING:

1.   A Guide to Informed Consent - Information Sheet; Guidance for Institutional Review Boards and Clinical Investigators:
     http://www.fda.gov/RegulatoryInformation/Guidances/ucm126431.htm
2.   Recruiting Study Subjects - Information Sheet: Guidance for Institutional Review Boards and Clinical Investigators:
     http://www.fda.gov/RegulatoryInformation/Guidances/ucm126428.htm
3.   Information Sheet Guidance for Institutional Review Boards, Clinical Investigators, and Sponsors: Clinical Investigator Administrative Actions – Disqualification:
     http://www.fda.gov/downloads/RegulatoryInformation/Guidances/UCM214008.pdf
4.   Information Sheet Guidance For IRBs, Clinical Investigators, and Sponsors: FDA Inspections of Clinical Investigators:
     http://www.fda.gov/downloads/RegulatoryInformation/Guidances/UCM126553.pdf

5.   Financial Disclosure by Clinical Investigators :Guidance for Industry - Financial Disclosure by Clinical Investigators:

http://www.fda.gov/RegulatoryInformation/Guidances/ucm126832.htm

6.   Information Sheet Guidance For IRBs, Clinical Investigators, and Sponsors

FDA Institutional Review: Board Inspections

http://www.fda.gov/downloads/RegulatoryInformation/Guidances/UCM126555.pdf

7.   Guidance for the industry: IRB Review of Stand-Alone HIPAA Authorizations Under FDA Regulations:

http://www.fda.gov/downloads/RegulatoryInformation/Guidances/UCM126952.pdf

8.   Guidance for Clinical Investigators, Sponsors, and IRBs Adverse Event Reporting to IRBs Improving Human Subject Protection

http://www.fda.gov/downloads/RegulatoryInformation/Guidances/UCM126572.pdf

9.   Guidance for Industry and Clinical Investigators: The Use of Clinical Holds Following Clinical Investigator Misconduct

http://www.fda.gov/downloads/RegulatoryInformation/Guidances/UCM126997.pdf

✱✱✱

Chapter ... 7

CLINICAL TRIAL MONITORING

> *"Research is to see what everybody else has seen, and to think what nobody else has thought"*
> **Albert Szent-Gyorgyi**

INTRODUCTION

The ultimate objective of conducting clinical trials is to obtain data to be submitted to regulatory authorities to approve of an investigational drug. These authorities need an assurance that the clinical trial is conducted as per Good Clinical Practice (GCP) and applicable regulations, the rights and welfare of human subjects are protected and the data quality is acceptable. Hence, here is the emergence of the role of a clinical research 'Monitor', also often called as the Clinical Research Associate (CRA). This role basically involves overseeing the conduct of a trial and assuring data quality.

(a) Roles and Responsibilities of the Monitor

Until recently, the role of a Monitor revolved only around one activity i.e. monitoring the site. However, today there is a paradigm shift in the Monitor's role, and the concept of total site level management is largely accepted. The Monitor's role has thus changed to that of a Site Manager. In order to manage the site(s) well, a Monitor needs to understand the expectations from all the stakeholders - the Sponsor and/or Contract Research Organization (CRO), the site (Principal Investigator and his team) and the regulators.

Attitude is the Key

The most important skill set required for a Monitor is the right 'Attitude'. A Monitor must not only love the job but also be proud of it, enjoy interacting with people, travelling (and the long waits at the airport..............), and has lots of patience (managing sites is indeed challenging!). It is only the right attitude that will help a Monitor face all the challenges, big and small, and lead to success. A Monitor should 'own' up the responsibilities and also each site. There should not be any pre-assumptions or inhibitions about any site. There is nothing like a 'problem' site; rather such a 'problem' site where a previous Monitor has faced obstacles (or actually given up!) should be looked upon as an opportunity by a Monitor with the 'right' attitude, and display adequate site management skills to convert it into a 'most liked' site. In order to taste success, apart from the scientific/technical knowledge, a Monitor also needs to have/acquire the right blend of communication skill, professionalism, discipline, time management, confidence, humbleness, an eye for detail and to top it all - has to breathe ethics!

Monitor - The Super Hero and the Face of the Sponsor

To present an analogy here - a clinical trial is like a movie, produced and directed by a Sponsor/CRO. The success of this movie is decided by the audience i.e. the site, based on the performance of the hero of the movie, the Monitor. Hence, the movie/trial's success is the director/Sponsor's success which largely depends on the Hero, our Monitor. A Monitor is indeed the Super Hero, managing a homogeneous number of activities, tackling all odds and translating them into the desired outcome. The image of the Sponsor lies solely in the hands of the Monitor, and the Monitor should always remember that he/she is shouldering this additional baggage at all times. A Monitor is the sole member responsible to steer the trial through rough waters and sail to success.

Understanding the Responsibilities of a Monitor

A Monitor has to do various jobs and is loaded with a lot of responsibilities in trial management (ICH-GCP 5.5.1; 5.18.4). To enlist the most important ones:

- Assist in preparing the trial plan and identify Investigators.
- Conduct pre-trial visits to assess and evaluate the investigational sites.
- Verify that the Principal Investigator has adequate qualification (by education and training) and resources that would remain adequate and stable throughout the trial period, including the site facilities, infrastructure, laboratories, equipment and staff.
- Plan and conduct Investigators' meeting.
- Be the main line of communication between the Sponsor/CRO and the Investigator.
- Develop trial budgets and payment schedules.
- Review Investigator/Institution agreements.
- Collect the essential documents.
- Arrange for the investigational product (IP).
- Conduct site initiation visits.
- Verify that the Investigator has delegated site duties appropriately to qualified and trained site staff.
- Verify that the Investigator and site staff are performing the trial responsibilities as per the trial protocol/amendments and any other written agreement between the Sponsor and the Investigator/Institution.
- Ensure protection of the rights, safety and well-being of the trial subjects.
- Verify that the Investigator is enrolling eligible subjects only and written, informed consent is obtained before every subject's participation in the trial.
- Ensure that deviations from the protocol, standard operating procedures (SOPs), GCP and applicable regulations are communicated to the concerned authorities and appropriate corrective action initiated to prevent recurrence.
- Conduct monitoring visits.
- Continuously train and mentor new members of the site staff.
- Maintain and track the recruitment rate; assist in developing recruitment strategies.
- Ensure that the Investigator receives current trial documents.

- Ensure that the Investigator maintains and updates the essential documents throughout the trial duration.
- Verify that the Investigator provides all the required reports/notifications to the Ethics Committee (EC)/Institutional Review Board (IRB).
- Ensure that the scientific integrity and confidentiality of the collected data is protected and verified.
- Check the accuracy and completeness of case report form (CRF) entries, source documents and other trial-related records against each other, ensuring that:
  - data is accurately captured on the CRFs and is consistent with the source documents.
  - any dose modifications are well-documented.
  - adverse events (AEs), concomitant medications and inter-current illnesses are reported on the CRFs in accordance with the protocol.
  - visits, tests and examinations that are missed or not performed are clearly reported on the CRFs.
  - any subject withdrawal/dropout/lost to follow-up from the trial are reported.
  - appropriate data corrections are made adequately by delegated site personnel.
  - all AEs are appropriately captured and reported within the regulatory timelines.
- Track and reconcile the IP while ensuring that:
  - storage conditions and access is secured and controlled.
  - supplies are adequate throughout the trial.
  - IP is supplied only to subjects who are eligible to receive it and at the protocol specified dose.
  - subjects are adequately instructed on proper usage, handling, storage and return of the IP.
  - receipt, use, return and destruction of the IP at the site is tracked with adequate documentation.
- Track the data queries.
- Track the site payments.
- Assist during trial audits/inspections.
- Conduct close-out visits and perform post trial follow-up.
- Archive the trial files.
- Remain updated with all the applicable SOPs, guidelines/guidance documents and regulations.

Time Management

In order to accomplish all the trial responsibilities, a Monitor should be able to successfully utilize the most important resource i.e. time. As quoted by Henry David Thoreau, "It's not enough to be busy, so are the ants. The question is, what are we busy about?" As per Pareto's 80/20 rule, 80% of what we achieve takes only 20% of our time and effort. Hence, one needs to utilize the 20% time to it's optimum. A few suggestions for the Monitor to manage time effectively:

- Use 'To Do' lists
  - these lists being dynamic, prefer to have them in an electronic form; status to be updated regularly, easy retrieval - anytime, anywhere (as compared to paper 'to do lists/post-its').
  - an MS-Excel sheet is a good option - suggest to have one excel file with as many sheets per trial and per site.
- Prioritize activities - as per Stephen Covey's 'urgent and important grid'
  - urgent and important (category A).
  - urgent and non-important (category B).
  - non-urgent and important (category C).
  - non-urgent and non-important (category D).
- Identify time-wasters, both at the office and at the site (wasted time can never be recycled!).
- Delegate tasks and ensure proper execution.
- Right The First Time (RTFT) - a great time saver principle applicable in all areas of life.
- Quality of job – each accomplished task should have one's quality assurance or 'seal of quality' to ensure completeness and accuracy of task.

(b) Planning of Monitoring Visits

Different types of visits are conducted at different stages of the trial i.e. site selection, site initiation, contact visit, monitoring visit and site close-out visit. In this chapter, these visits are grouped under the common term of 'monitoring visit'. The plan of monitoring a given trial would depend on a number of factors and this is described in the trial document 'Monitoring Plan'. The objective of the Monitoring Plan is to ensure that all Monitors be consistent in their activities for a trial, across multiple sites/countries. This document also serves as a guide to the Sponsor/CRO team as it lists out all trial-related activities to be performed during monitoring and trial management.

Monitoring Plan

A typical Monitoring Plan would include at least the following:

- Trial details and the number of patients to be recruited.
- Maximum number of patients to be recruited per site/country, if applicable.
- Topics to be covered during site-initiation visit.
- Requirements and responsibilities for site monitoring and management.
- Type and frequency of site visits at different stages of the trial (site selection, initiation, monitoring, contact and close-out visits) - usually a monitoring visit frequency of four to six weeks is common, but could vary across trials. Provision for altering visit interval is to be specified in cases of high/low recruiting sites, no new subject enrolled since the last visit(s), site staff unavailable for visit, CRF not completed, etc.
- Details of SOPs or work instructions to be followed for the trial.

- Tools/Forms/Templates/Checklists to be used for trial activities e.g.
  - ○ site visit log.
  - ○ delegation of duties log/signature log
  - ○ subject screening/enrolment log
  - ○ subject identification log
  - ○ randomization worksheets
  - ○ safety reporting procedures
  - ○ IP accountability and temperature logs
  - ○ visit report templates
  - ○ clinical trial management system used, if any.
- CRF and data query transmittal process for data retrieval (for paper CRF studies) - this can be a separate document by itself i.e. CRF Completion Guidelines.
- Electronic CRF (eCRF) management.
- Plan for source data verification (SDV).
- Data Safety Management Board specifications or timelines for data collection, if any.
- Process for handling site issues and escalation.
- Process for handling and reporting deviations to the Sponsor and EC/IRB.
- Trial procedures and logistics e.g. handling and turnaround time for CRFs/data queries, handling of IP and pharmacogenetic-pharmacokinetic specimens and samples, managing Interactive Voice Response System (IVRS), adjudication procedures.
- Temperature monitoring for IP, biological samples and specimens.
- Process for collection of essential documents.
- Training requirements for the Monitor(s) and site staff.
- Communication plan.
- Review of Investigator Site File and Trial Master File (TMF).
- Report writing, review and approval.
- Post monitoring follow up.

Scheduling Monitoring Visits

A Monitor should visit the site frequently enough to assure that:

- The trial is being conducted as per the protocol, SOPs and applicable regulations.
- The facilities used by the Investigator continue to be acceptable for the purpose of the trial.
- The trial protocol/protocol amendment is being followed.
- Any changes to the protocol have been approved by the EC/IRB and reported to the Sponsor.
- Accurate, complete and timely trial progress reports are submitted to the EC/IRB.
- Appropriate trial duty delegation records are maintained and duties performed only by qualified and delegated site staff.

A Monitor at any given point of time may be expected to manage about 10-12 sites (or more at times!), depending on the complexity of the protocol/therapy area and trial management, phase (phase I-IV) and stage (site selection/recruiting/follow-up/data base lock, etc.) of the trial, geographical location of the sites and Monitor's experience. The only key to successfully manage several sites across different trials is by chalking out a quarterly comprehensive 'visit plan' for all the trial management activities. A buffer time needs to be considered for any unanticipated activities popping up at the last minute. Vacations and holidays also need to be considered during the planning stage. Once a plan is drawn, the Monitor needs to confirm appointments for the visits with the Investigator. The visit date(s) should be planned in such a way that in case of a slight delay (as is the case most of the times....) the visit frequency does not deviate from the trial Monitoring Plan. To plan and execute all the activities is nothing less than displaying the best juggling skills. The Monitor has to juggle a number of activities and adopt a monitoring strategy for each site - on one hand he/she is handling and managing all sorts of communication (emails, IVRS/safety faxes, telephone calls, IP requests), outstanding issues, handling Investigator grievances, reporting to the Project Manager, teleconferences with trial teams across the globe, tracking import/export licenses for IP/biological specimens, shipment of biological samples, interim analysis, data base lock, Investigator meets, training of new site staff, updating essential documents, review of in-house trial files, tracking CRFs/data queries, completing visit reports; and on the other hand, he/she is trying to manage some work-life balance. Hence, in order to ensure a smooth sailing, a visit plan is a pre-requisite and the only key to success.

While scheduling monitoring visits, a few other factors which can impact the visit plan need to be considered as follows:

- Sponsor's monitoring SOPs.
- Experience of the Investigator/site staff - naïve Investigator and/or site staff or less experienced site.
- Monitor's experience and effectiveness.
- High recruiting site (more visits!).
- Low recruiting site (need motivational visits to re-establish interest and priorities).
- Site performance - non-compliant site with a number of issues.
- Large turnover of site staff.
- Site planning to recruit the first patient - an immediate visit may be a must to ensure proper compliance to trial procedures and protocol.
- If the Monitor discovers serious site-related problems, the frequency of visits may be increased with appropriate follow up.

Once again, the golden rule for the Monitor - do it 'Right The First Time'. As quoted by Henry Wadsworth Longfellow, "It takes less time to do things right than to explain why you did it wrong". Though this habit can be inculcated with a lot of practice, patience and learning from one's own and other's mistakes, it saves a lot of valuable time and efforts in the long run.

While scheduling the visit plan, additional visits should be planned at non-compliant sites in order to stay on top of the activities and gain control. When such additional visits are not possible, other means of maintaining contact should be planned (e.g. telephone calls, e-mails) to manage and resolve site issues. It should also be ensured that such contacts are documented.

Duration of Monitoring Visits

The duration of each visit would again depend on the complexity of the trial design and logistics, data transmittal process, SDV plan and phase of the trial. At a minimum, the duration could range from about four to six hours, to one to two days, or more. Considering all the above factors, a Monitor should try to club visits to several sites within the same geographical zone in a single trip. The actual monitoring visit dates should not deviate too much from the Monitor's visit plan; and the monitoring agenda and strategy for each site should be developed before executing the visit.

Preparation for Monitoring Visits

After having the initial communication with the Investigator for confirming the visit date(s), an agendum needs to be forwarded around three to four weeks in advance, which at least includes the following:

- Time required for planned meetings with the site staff (specifying names of staff).
- Request time with the Principal Investigator to discuss.
    o recruitment at the site.
    o adherence to protocol.
    o overall trial conduct.
    o any other matter.
- SDV - requesting medical records for required subject numbers.
- Completed CRFs required for review.
- Status of outstanding issues from last visit, if any.
- Other trial activities planned to be performed e.g. IP accountability, Investigator Site File review, collection of updated essential documents, laboratory facilities/certifications, collection/storage/ handling/shipping of laboratory and/or biological specimens.
- Review of EC/IRB submissions/notifications/approvals.
- List of any trial documents to be collected from the site.
- Change in site staff - any new staff on-board.

Other Visit Logistics

- **Travel Itinerary:** Apart from managing the sites, a Monitor also needs to plan the personal travel itinerary well in advance. Adequate instructions to be forwarded to the travel desk for ticketing and accommodation arrangements.
- **Trial Kit:** As the Monitor is on a continuous move, it is worth preparing and carrying a time saving trial-specific kit to the site, thus ensuring availability of all required trial resources with the Monitor. The basic contents of the kit could include:

  o   Mini-handbooks of trial documents e.g. protocol, Investigator's Brochure, CRF completion guidelines.
  o   copies of trial forms/templates (also the electronic versions of all documents and presentations should be on the laptop for easy retrieval/reference/printing).
  o   latest listings of AEs, recruitment status, data queries, CRFs to be reviewed/retrieved, IP inventory.
  o   an MS-Excel tracker with the contents of TMF.
  o   trial payment status for the site.
  o   an electronic copy/online access to a medical dictionary and generic/brand names of drugs along with their indications.
  o   adequate stationery (post-its, flags, multi-coloured pens, highlighters, stapler, pins, note pads.......).

Trial Monitoring Process

The monitoring process starts when the Monitor reaches the site. The Monitor should be formally dressed, well-organized and not spread personal belongings beyond the table space provided at the site. Most important of all, one needs to be punctual and respect other's time as well (needless to say, the mobile phone should always be on a silent mode and personal calls to be avoided!).

A Monitor should have a scheduled activity plan for each day at the site. After meeting the Study Coordinator, the sequence of activities for the day depending on the availability of the site staff needs to be decided. Proper time management is required to allocate adequate time for each activity in order to accomplish all items on the agenda. The monitoring process would include activities like SDV and review of consent forms, safety reports, CRFs, protocol specific procedures, IP accountability/reconciliation, laboratory facilities, and Investigator site files.

(c) Source Data Verification (SDV)

The primary objective of SDV is to ensure that the rights and well-being of human subjects are protected; the data collected and reported is accurate, complete and verifiable from source documents; and that the trial is conducted in compliance with the protocol/protocol amendments, GCP and applicable regulations. SDV is the process of verifying the original source document and confirming the corresponding data entered on the CRF. The plan for SDV would be described in the trial Monitoring Plan, and it could be 100% SDV for all subjects or there could be a random SDV plan with about 20-25% of the subjects being 100% verified.

The Investigator is required to prepare and maintain adequate, accurate case histories that record all observations and other data pertinent to the subject's investigation and protocol specific procedures. If the source data is to be recorded directly on the CRF (i.e. no prior written or electronic record of data), separate supporting documentation is not required; but identification of such data should be well-described in the trial design itself.

For SDV, the site should specify the source document for various data fields on the CRF and its location (Source Data Location List) e.g. vitals, demography, AEs, progress notes, concomitant medication, IP administration, nurses chart, measurement of bone lesions, etc. The list should specify if original or certified copies of originals would be available as source for specific information (e.g. past medical history of patient). If copies of electronic medical records are printed to serve as a source document, these also should be certified by appropriate site staff and the electronic record should be available for verification as well. While performing SDV, the Monitor should also confirm the subjects' existence and eligibility for trial participation. All protocol-specific procedures, safety and efficacy information should be documented and performed only by site staff delegated by the Principal Investigator.

Source documents would comprise of the following examples:

- Hospital records.
- Medical notes.
- Clinical and nurses' charts.
- Laboratory notes, test reports, diet charts.
- Pharmacy dispensing and accountability records.
- Recorded data from automated instruments.
- Scans/microfilm/X-rays/negatives/other diagnostic media.
- Subject diaries/evaluation checklists.
- Copies or certified transcriptions.

Source Data Requirements

The principle of 'ALCOA' should be applicable to all source documents as follows:

- **Attributable:** This is the 'who, when, why' part of the source document i.e. who created a record and when; who amended a record - when and why.
- **Legible:** All source notes as well as any corrections should be legible. You could meet some Investigators who refuse to improve their writing, but then it should be explained to them that 'if data is not readable, what good is it?"
- **Contemporaneous:** In simple words, data should be recorded in real time as it is observed. This is very important to reconstruct the occurrences around the data. Needless to say, all recorded dates should be the current date at the time of entry and late entries should be clearly designated and explained as such.
- **Original:** All records are expected to be original. In case of previous medical history of the subject in some therapy areas (e.g. diabetes, oncology), these could be attested by the Investigator to be treated as 'original'. It should be noted that any additional source documents like chits of paper/paper tissues/post-its should also be preserved in the trial file.
- **Accurate:** Data should be accurate and complete. The records should speak for themselves and narrate the entire sequence of events e.g. blood pressure readings cannot always be rounded off as 120/80, 140/90, etc. One should be accurate in reporting them as recorded i.e. 124/82, 144/98......

The principle of ALCOA can be applied similarly to electronic source data as well:

- Accurate - validated system.
- Legible - electronic capture.

- Contemporaneous - date and time-stamped.
- Original - compare transformed date to original.
- Attributable – unique-user identification system and passwords.

CRF Entries and Corrections

All entries and corrections in the CRF should correspond to adequate contemporaneous information/notes on the source documents and be attributable. Corrections should be justified and properly signed and dated by responsible staff listed and delegated on the duties log. eCRF entries should also have adequate audit trail for every entry and correction.

Review of Informed Consent Forms

Inadequate informed consent process is one of the top five GCP findings from regulatory inspections and it should be understood that consent administration is not a one-time activity, but an ongoing, interactive process throughout the trial duration. The informed consent administration can be divided in two parts - the process and the documentation. The consent process is the exchange of information and includes recruitment material, verbal instructions, question/answer sessions and measures of patient understanding. The consent process should ensure that adequate explanation is provided by the delegated site staff to the patient on the trial's purpose, procedures, risks, potential benefits, and the rights as a participant to assist the decision about trial participation. Once the consent process is complete and the patient decides to participate, the consent form should be personally signed and dated by the patient or the patient's legally acceptable representative (LAR) or in the presence of an impartial witness; or in case of a child, the parent(s) or legal guardian or an assent (as applicable). The consent should be administered prior to any trial specific procedures being performed and administration of any IP.

The first activity that a Monitor needs to perform at the site is to review the screening and enrolment logs, and then request for the signed informed consent forms for screen failure as well as enrolled subjects. It should be verified that the consent forms are the appropriate versions approved by the EC/IRB, adequate time was given to the patient and the consent process is documented in the source documentation. It should be verified that a copy of the signed informed consent form and information sheet has been handed over to the subject.

The number of subjects recruited into the trial should be commensurate with the Investigator's agreement/contract with the Sponsor/CRO.

Tips for Reviewing Consent Forms

- All the consent forms should be placed in such a way that the signatures of the subject and Investigator for each consent form can be viewed at one glance. The Monitor should look out for any particular pattern across all the signatures e.g. trends in signatures like shaky writing, whether all subjects' signatures look alike or resemble the hand writing of any site staff.
- The Investigator's signature on the consent form should be compared and verified against the signature on the Delegation of Duties Log.

- It is a good practice by the Investigator to include a contemporaneous note in the medical notes describing the consent process and also a statement that the subject received a copy of the signed consent form.

Compliance with Inclusion-Exclusion Criteria

Supporting source documentation should be available for every inclusion/exclusion criteria. Inclusion of the patient as a subject into a trial should be adequately reflected in the source notes. The patient's qualifying diagnosis for the trial should be supported by medical reports and assessment by the Investigator.

Review of Protocol-Specific Records

The Monitor should ensure that the protocol/protocol amendment used has been approved by the EC/IRB. Adherence to protocol/protocol amendments should be verified. All protocol-specific procedures should be appropriately supported by source notes/hospital chart. Administration of the IP as required by the protocol should be appropriately captured on IP logs or adequate source document. Other concomitant medications administered or taken by the subject should be reviewed thoroughly to ensure that the subject is not receiving exclusionary medications. All other concomitant medications permitted as per the protocol should be adequately documented with their start and stop date, route of administration and dose. It is preferable to capture generic names of concomitant medications in the source and CRFs to maintain consistency in multi-centric global trials. Also ensure that medications administered during AEs are adequately documented and captured on the CRFs. Laboratory abnormalities, if clinically significant, should be marked on the laboratory report as 'Clinically Significant or CS' and should not go unreported as AEs. If these events qualify for any seriousness criteria, these should be reported as a serious adverse event (SAE) within the expedited regulatory timelines. Laboratory abnormalities which are not clinically significant should be assessed as 'Non-clinically significant or NCS' on the laboratory report. Efficacy endpoints and other treatment emergent adverse events (TEAEs) which have been identified in the protocol may be specified as not to be captured as AEs/SAEs. Diagnostic reports should be available for diagnostic tests performed as per protocol or in the event of any SAEs or otherwise during the trial period. All subject reports e.g. ECGs, diagnostic reports should have a subject identifier and 'reviewed by' signature and date by the Investigator. Signatures across all documentation should be personally dated by the signatory only.

(d) Investigational Product Accountability and Reconciliation

IP is an integral and important part of any clinical trial since the quality of data submitted to the regulatory authority decides the fate of the investigational drug. Hence, it is the responsibility of the Monitor to ensure that the IP is handled and managed appropriately by the site. There should be accurate records for each step of handling and managing the IP i.e. the receipt, storage, dispensing, return and destruction of the IP.

Receipt and Storage of IP

The IP should be received, quantity confirmed with the shipment form and stored as per storage conditions specified in the protocol, in a secure area with controlled access. The first IP shipment should not be sent to a site unless all appropriate approvals and essential documents are in place. Sites are to be trained to fax receipt notifications for every shipment on a real time basis to the Sponsor/CRO. The IP of one trial should not be stored with the IP of another trial, nor with any other marketed products used by the Investigator. Expired IP should be stored separately, but still under secured and controlled conditions. The shipment receipts and records of transit temperature from temperature monitoring devices, temperature monitoring records of the IP cabinet/refrigerator should be filed in the Investigator Site File. IP receipt and storage conditions e.g. cold chain maintenance needs to be verified. Some common IP storage issues to look out for are e.g. IP stored at a site is accessible to a site/hospital staff not listed on the trial delegation log, an untrained individual receives and stores the IP or IP shipment reaches the site and lies unattended for several hours.

Dispensing

Records to be verified to ensure that the IP is dispensed to trial subjects only. The total amount of IP dispensed should coincide with the number of subjects and the doses administered. In randomized blinded trials, emphasis to be laid on dispensing correct kit numbers and maintenance of the blind. Subject's compliance and adherence to storage and dosage regimen needs to be verified. IP accountability logs and CRFs to be verified for accuracy, completeness and also against actual physical count at the site (records for both used and unused IP must tally to the last unit level).

Return and Destruction

Adequate accountability logs to be maintained when returning IP to the Sponsor/CRO or dispatching IP for destruction. Authorization from the Sponsor/CRO would be needed before proceeding for destruction. The destruction could take place at the site or the Sponsor may reconcile all the IP and destroy it centrally (depends on the type of IP e.g. cytotoxic drugs are usually destroyed at the site). A destruction certificate should be obtained and filed in the appropriate trial file.

(e) Safety Report Monitoring

Players in monitoring drug safety include the subject, Sponsor/CRO, EC/IRB, regulators, and the Investigator. The Investigator has the prime responsibility of assessing, interpreting and reporting the AEs. A Monitor needs to verify that all AEs have been assessed by the Investigator, captured in the source notes along with its description, management, outcome and applicable supporting documents (laboratory reports, hospitalization records, scans, etc.). Abnormal laboratory findings, if not categorized as clinically significant/insignificant, should be discussed with the Investigator; and if significant, should be reported. AEs are to be followed up until complete resolution or until the condition is stabilized or returned to baseline. Any AE qualifying for the seriousness criteria should be reported within the expedited timelines to the Sponsor/CRO and the EC/IRB (ICH-GCP 5.17). Adequate SAE follow-up reports should be available. The data captured on the SAE report/CRF should be compared with the source documentation. The Monitor should have quick reference tools to check for concomitant medications/indications in safety reporting. While reviewing the source notes, the Monitor should also look for any potentially unreported SAE and if there is any, should ensure that it is immediately reported. The

Investigator and the trial team should be re-trained on the significance of timely reporting of AEs and training should be documented in the visit report.

The Monitor also should check for timely receipt and reporting of the Suspected Unexpected Serious Adverse Reactions (SUSARs) to EC/IRB. As applicable, it should be verified if the new safety information which could affect a subject's decision to participate in the trial is passed on to the subjects by the Investigator.

(f) Laboratory Facilities, Normal Ranges and Certifications

A Monitor needs to verify whether there is any change in the laboratory facility/specifications, validity of the laboratory certification and normal ranges. If yes, the changes to be verified and appropriate documents are to be collected for the Sponsor's file, and a copy to be filed in the Investigator Site File. To check if all the protocol-related tests have been conducted in the laboratory facility specified for the trial only. To discuss and ensure adequacy of procedures for sample/specimen collection, labelling, tracking, storage, processing, analysis, reporting and adequate data capture on CRFs. The Monitor should emphasize on temperature monitoring of all facilities (ensuring adequate auxiliary power back-up) and to verify the temperature logs. Ensure that the specified laboratory follows all the SOPs for testing, maintenance and calibration of equipments.

(g) Delegation of Duties and Training of Site Staff

Though the Principal Investigator is solely responsible for personally conducting or supervising the clinical trial, he is permitted to delegate some trial specific tasks to his Investigators and site staff. Nevertheless, the Principal Investigator should ensure adequate supervision of his staff and their performance. There is no chance for a blame game if his staff fails to perform adequately in the trial, resulting in regulatory violations. The Monitor should ensure that all trial duties have been appropriately and adequately delegated to qualified, trained and experienced personnel; and documented on the Delegation of Duties Log by the Principal Investigator. All trial-related duties should have a mention on the delegation log. Only a qualified physician should be responsible for all trial-related medical decisions and care. Adequate staff to be delegated for 'out of hours' cover too e.g. after office hours, leave/vacation/holidays. Inexperienced personnel should be appropriately trained before initiating any trial activities. The date of a staff's appointment on the trial and training should precede the date of any actual duty performed on the trial. Refresher trainings should be conducted as and when required throughout the trial period. Additional training to be provided and documented for protocol amendments released throughout the trial period. If the Monitor is unable to visit the site for imparting training, other modes of training should be adopted e.g. audio/video/WebEx conferences. All records of training imparted by the Principal Investigator and/or the Monitor should be filed at the site and also recorded in the monitoring visit report.

(h) Investigator Oversight

Regulatory agencies are greatly concerned about the Principal Investigator's involvement in the trial and need adequate records during inspections to support their level of involvement. Even though the Principal Investigator would have delegated most of the trial related duties to qualified site staff, the overall responsibility/accountability of the trial cannot be delegated.

Adequate documentation should be available and verified at the site indicating the Principal Investigator's involvement e.g.

- Routine meetings with site staff to review trial progress, protocol compliance, AEs/SAEs, and update staff on any changes to the protocol or other procedures.
- Assessment of inclusion-exclusion criteria, laboratory reports for clinically significant findings, primary/secondary efficacy end points.
- Routine meetings with the Monitor.
- A procedure for timely correction and documentation of problems identified by site staff, Monitor/auditor/other parties involved in the trial conduct.
- A procedure for documenting/reviewing the performance of delegated tasks in a satisfactory and timely manner (e.g. observation of the performance of selected assessments or independent verification by repeating selected assessments).
- A procedure for ensuring that the consent process is being conducted in accordance with 21 CFR § 50 and that subjects understand the nature of their participation and the risks.
- A procedure for ensuring that source data follows the ALCOA principle.
- A procedure for ensuring that information in the source documents is accurately captured on the CRFs and dealing with data queries/discrepancies identified by the Monitor.
- A procedure for addressing medical and ethical issues in a timely manner that arise during the course of the trial.

(i) Clinical Trial Files

A trial file has two parts - a Sponsor/CRO File and an Investigator Site File. The table of contents of any file would slightly vary from Sponsor to Sponsor, but basically includes all the documents listed under the ICH-GCP Section 8. More and more Sponsors/CROs are slowly moving towards electronic filing system. The basic principle in maintenance of trial files would remain the same, be it paper or electronic filing. A few tips on the maintenance of files:

- A trial file (Sponsor/Investigator file) should ideally be prepared as soon as a trial/site is allocated. This would enable all documents from day one to be compiled and filed at one place, thus preventing chances of misplacing/missing them.
- The site should be trained into a habit of filing the documents in the file itself, rather than scattering them all over at the site. Training for filing should be provided at the initiation visit itself.
- The filing of documents is an ongoing process. Documents received on a day-to-day basis should be reviewed for completeness prior to filing. In case of any discrepancy, the Monitor should request the site to forward the corrected document. The Monitor can have site-wise floating files to temporarily place the reviewed documents and have a regular plan to visit the documentation room for transferring the documents from the floating file to the trial file.
- An incorrect document should never be filed; chances are that it would never get corrected for a long time. It would be preferable to let it remain in the floating file until rectification.

- Each file should have a tracker or detail index of the contents. A Monitor should carry this tracker to site during monitoring visit and check if both files have the required documents.

A Monitor should also ensure that the storage area of trial files/records is appropriate with secured and controlled access; and the Investigator has a designated area with adequate environmental control for the archival of trial records (both paper as well as electronic) for the specified number of years as per regulations.

Use of Notes to File

This is a very dear topic of every Monitor and the site, since for every deviation/inappropriate action/unusual incident one tends to prepare a note to file e.g. unusual decision made, instructions from the Sponsor, problem experienced in executing a particular part of the protocol. Great attention needs to be paid to draft the contents of a note to file. In the absence of a note to file, such incidents could be interpreted in the worst possible way by different personnel (e.g. new site staff/new Monitor or auditors/inspectors). But it should also be remembered that a note to file does not serve as a record to endorse or approve any deviations/errors.

Some do's and don'ts for preparing notes to file:

- A note to file should narrate the following:
  o problem incident in brief (what, where, who, when, how, why) and it's significance.
  o root cause/investigation.
  o action taken to correct and prevent the problem from re-occurrence, in brief (e.g. any kind of retraining given to the team).
- It should provide clarity, save time in understanding/interpreting/reconstructing the incident and establish accountability.
- A note to file should not document any incident that is already documented elsewhere in the trial documents. Such a note would be redundant as it would not provide any additional information (e.g. an error in a date entry on the consent form corrected by the subject at a later date - such corrections are obvious and need no additional explanatory note).
- If any additional or revised information needs to be added to a note to file, a new note should be created giving reference to the first note.

(j) Debriefing Meeting with the Site Staff

The Monitor's pre-visit letter should have identified the need to schedule a meeting to discuss pertinent monitoring findings with the site staff. The Principal Investigator, Investigators and other site staff should preferably be present for the debriefing. Each site may determine appropriate additional participants for the debriefing. If the Principal Investigator is unavailable, a telephone call should be scheduled at the earliest after the visit for debriefing, and documented as a contact report and/or an email. The Monitor should briefly highlight the main issues and issues which need follow-up. Mutually agreed timelines should be discussed for issues that need follow-up. Critical issues, if any, should be discussed at length, along with the need for any re-training to be provided to the site staff concerned. The date(s) of next monitoring visit should be confirmed.

(k) Monitoring Reports and Follow up

A Monitor should make notes (electronic or paper) during the visit itself as this would help in writing the monitoring visit report. An ideal way of functioning would be to draft the report at the end of the visit day itself when events are fresh in the memory. Every site visit would need a report, including the basic details i.e. date, site, name of the Monitor, name of the Principal Investigator and other members contacted at the site (ICH-GCP 5.18.6). Some quick tips for report writing:

- Write logical, accurate, detailed reports that would convey the necessary information.
- Do not criticize or add undue emotion in the writing.
- Do not include subject data or identifiers in the reports.
- Include a summary of what has been reviewed.
- Write only the facts and not what you think them to be or what could have happened in the situation.
- Be brief in writing the observations, deviations or deficiencies; conclusions, actions taken, to be taken or recommended.
- Describe critical issues which need to be followed up for resolution and document issues which have been closed during the visit.
- Pay attention to formatting, margins and space.
- Write full sentences, not abbreviations or phrases. The report should serve as an independent document. It should be understood by someone years later and should represent the facts or help reconstruction of the events during the trial.
- Be sure to spell-check and proof read before forwarding it for review.

A brief and precise follow-up letter needs to be sent to the Principal Investigator, listing all the activities reviewed during the visit and the observations (open, closed and to be followed up for resolution). Issues awaiting resolution should be followed-up appropriately until the next visit.

(l) Confidentiality

Since the early days of medicine, maintaining privacy and confidentiality have been the cornerstone of the patient-physician relationship. It is also crucial in the area of clinical research i.e. the subject-Sponsor relationship. A breach of confidentiality violates the subject's privacy and poses a risk of dignitary harm, ranging from social embarrassment, shame, stigmatization and even damage to social and economic status.

In 1993, the Council for International Organizations of Medical Sciences (CIOMS) and the World Health Organization (WHO) published the Ethical Guidelines for Biomedical Research Involving Human Subjects, which provide explicit provisions for respecting the privacy of research participants and maintaining the confidentiality of their personal information. Privacy refers to the right of individuals to limit access by others to their personal details that can include identifying information and also information contained in bodily tissues and fluids. Privacy relates to the subject's direct disclosure to the researcher; confidentiality relates to the extent to which the researcher protects the subject's private information. Confidentiality is the process of protecting an individual's privacy.

Patients will not volunteer for research unless the researchers can ensure that, as much as possible, the information they disclose will not be released to others without their knowledge and consent. A researcher's obligation to protect confidentiality is higher than a clinician's since research often does not provide benefit to the participant and provides no compelling reason to become involved in the research. Disclosure of personal information may be required for public health interests in disease registration, communicable disease investigations or vaccination studies. Balancing societal interests in research must be carefully considered by the Investigator and approved by the EC/IRB. Hence, confidential data needs to be de-identified before being utilized for various research purposes.

For example:

- Names, social security numbers, or other unique identity proofs.
- Telephone numbers, fax numbers and other contact details.
- Electronic mail addresses.
- Medical record numbers and health plan beneficiary numbers.
- Biometric identifiers, including finger and voice prints.
- Full-face photographic images and any comparable images.

The United States' Health Insurance Portability and Accountability Act (HIPAA), 1996 became effective in 2003; thus, for healthcare providers covered by the HIPAA law, informed consent involves not only the confidentiality of subject records but also the privacy of subjects' identifiable/protected health information, which is broader than records only. It is any health information by which a person can be identified. In general, the informed consent regulations require that every informed consent document have a statement describing the extent to which records that identify the subject will be kept confidential, noting that the Sponsor/EC/IRB/ regulatory authorities may view the records.

All trials require protecting privacy and maintaining confidentiality of data even if they are not covered under the HIPAA Privacy Rule. It is important to have a specific Data Protection Plan to identify the accessibility, maintenance of data and a contingency plan for dealing with any breach of confidentiality.

(m) Scientific Misconduct

Scientific misconduct means falsification of data in proposing, designing, performing, recording, supervising or reviewing research, or in reporting research results. The FDA uses the terms "fraud" and "misconduct" interchangeably. It is the violation of the standard codes of ethical behaviour in scientific research and can be committed by the Investigators, nurses, Study Coordinators, Monitors/Sponsors, laboratory personnel, data management team, EC/IRB staff and trial subjects as well.

Falsification could include both the acts of omission and commission:

- **Omission:** Consciously not revealing all data e.g. reportable AEs, concomitant medications.
- **Commission:** Consciously altering or fabricating data e.g. laboratory values, blood pressure readings, biological specimens.

A broad categorization can be done as follows:

- **Non-compliance:** It is the failure to comply, and most of the time it could be unintentional in the initial stages.
- **Misconduct:** Deliberate or repeated non-compliance with trial requirements, GCP and/or regulations.
- **Fraud:** It can be termed as fabrication or making up of data/results and recording or reporting them. This would also include falsification/manipulating research material, equipment, or processes, or changing or omitting data or results such that the research is not accurately represented in the research record.

As per the FDA, deliberate or repeated non-compliance with the protocol and GCP can be considered as fraud, but is secondary to falsification of data.

Possible Reasons of Misconduct

- Lack of resources at the site (not enough time or staff).
- Competition to recruit.
- Complex protocol, difficult to recruit.
- Lack of GCP training or awareness.
- Laziness, loss of interest.
- Money, greed.
- Peer pressure to recruit, perform, and publish.
- Lack of awareness on regulatory obligations (e.g. Form FDA 1572) and consequences.

Consequences of Misconduct/Fraud

Any kind of scientific misconduct can lead to serious consequences which can impact everyone concerned with the trial. Also, the consequences of scientific misconduct can be severe at a personal level for both the perpetrators and any individual who exposes it. In addition, there will always be public health implications attached to the promotion of medical or other interventions based on dubious research findings.

- Investigator - disqualification, fines, incarceration, legal expenses.
- Institution - lawsuits.
- Sponsor - data validity compromised, submission jeopardized, additional costs.
- Subject - safety at risk, loss of trust in clinical trial process.
- Fraudulent Investigators can have a broad impact on many submissions made by multiple Sponsors on multiple trials.

Scientific misconduct can occur at any time during the phase of a trial - before, during and after. It can include, but is not limited:

- Lack of or inadequate informed consent process/SOPs.
- Inadequate consenting/re-consenting process.
- Incomplete and/or incorrect signatures/dating pattern.
- Different handwriting and ink for Investigator's signature and date on the consent forms.

- Subject's handwriting and/or signatures are inconsistent across trial documents (consent form and subject diaries).
- The dates on the signed consent forms matching the site staff's handwriting.
- Incomplete, incorrect or missing consent forms.
- Inadequate delegation of informed consent and other trial responsibilities.
- Enrolling ineligible participants who do not meet protocol-specific inclusion/exclusion criteria.
- Falsification of records/data e.g. making identical prints of x-rays with different subject names, using old ECG tracings to qualify the patient, changing dates in hospital records to match the wash-out period required per protocol, preprinted subject identifiers altered/obliterated on ECGs/laboratory reports, continuous ECG strip run on a single patient torn into two and represented for two patients).
- Use of pencil in source documents.
- Data not attributable or contemporaneous e.g. in between entries made in source notes in a different handwriting and ink without initials and date.
- Data on source documents not present at previous monitoring visit but appears at a future visit.
- Documents signed and dated by Investigator/site staff with date before the first day of joining the trial or after leaving the trial.
- Corrections not initialed and dated.
- Investigator/site staff on vacation/holiday but entries present in trial documentation on the days of vacation e.g. subject visits conducted on Sundays, holidays, staff vacations.
- Underreporting of data e.g. AEs.
- Abnormal laboratory values not reviewed by Investigator.
- Consistently same physical examination data for the subject.
- Alarmingly high lost to follow-up cases.
- Failure to follow the trial protocol e.g. not performing protocol specific procedures/tests which affect primary/secondary endpoints or performing them out of window period.
- Failure to adhere to protocol specific concomitant medication requirements.
- Consistently out-of-window subject visits.
- Failure to report significant protocol violations to the EC/IRB.
- Unethical conduct by a member of the site staff.
- Same subject recruited multiple times on the same or different trials.
- Subject visits cannot be traced from the hospital entry register/medical chart/appointment schedule/billing records.
- Discrepancies in drug dispensing log.
- Discrepancies between the subject diary and IP dosing records.
- Subject diary card information written-over/altered by site staff.
- Handwriting same for subject diaries of several subjects.

A Monitor should always look for suspicious records or behavior of team members at the site. The site staff should be given a primary knowledge of scientific misconduct, and it should be ensured that members are not pressurized for 'not to report the misconduct'. The Monitor should be trained on how to report any suspicion of scientific misconduct, which could be based on the company's policies. Sponsors, site staff and Monitors must be alert for any possible actions which could lead to scientific misconduct. If anyone suspects scientific misconduct, it must be reported to an appropriate group such as an EC/IRB, a regulatory agency, and the Sponsor as appropriate.

Methods of Detecting Scientific Misconduct

- Look out for signals e.g. too clean data or subject diaries, missing or replenished pages in subject diaries, too many errors, too fast recruitment, Investigator unaware of trial status, site staff trying to cover up errors, being defensive when queried, subject records missing/replaced, different version of explanations by different staff for a situation, use of ink whiteners/obliteration of data, site staff signing for records on all holidays, CRF entries and subject's signatures on consent forms have a similar handwriting, similar pattern of signatures on all consent forms, same/rounded off temperature readings for IP temperature logs, tracking of clinical specimens in order to detect substitution, laboratory instrumentation, high staff turnover, no screen failures.

- Data indicators or outliers - look for any particular pattern/trend at site:
  - No AEs/SAEs reported.
  - Too many SAEs reported as compared to other sites.
  - 100% IP compliance.
  - Perfect efficacy responses for all subjects.
  - Identical laboratory/ECG results.
  - Not a single deviation in visit schedules.
  - All rounded figures for IP temperature logs, blood pressure readings, constant body weight for all subjects through a trial of long duration.
  - Compliance with subject diaries - real time completion or 'hoarding' (completing all entries at one time).

- Ask for all information (data) pertinent to the trial (CRFs, trial specific source worksheets, clinical charts, sign-in sheets, laboratory requisitions, shipping records, etc.).

- Accept no copies - review original whenever possible.

- Be technical - read laboratory reports, X-rays, ECGs - don't just be happy with a physical presence of the record.

- Ask a lot of questions until you are satisfied - question all missing/altered/inconsistent data e.g. dates, times - request or offer to retrieve records.

- Don't be intimidated by the Investigator - request for copies of suspected data, seek explanation on the suspicious data.

- Be suspicious of blame shifting.

- Cultivate whistle blowers at the site - pay attention to staff complaints, listen to grievances, establish rapport and be approachable.

Monitor - The Whistle blower

Very often a Monitor faces a 'shoot the messenger' situation. As the Monitor is the only member aware of all intricate details about a site, he would be the first one to blow the whistle. But a Monitor is the one who faces the music when it comes to escalating the matter to his superiors. The organization should trust the Monitor and analyze the story, and in fact put the burden of proof on the Investigator. The overarching rules that follow apply throughout the whistle-blowing process, but especially in coming to a decision on whether to blow the whistle:

- Consider alternative explanations (especially that you may be wrong) – remain open to information provided by the site.

- Ask questions, do not make charges - the situation could be a perceived misconduct and sufficient evidence is needed to confirm it. Before charging/accusing anyone, pose your concerns as questions, permitting the fact that you might have misunderstood or misinterpreted the situation.

- Figure out what documentation supports your concerns and get copies of them - instead of getting into "he said", 'I said', look at actual facts and records. Try re-constructing the situation.

- Don't be overwhelmed by anger, frustration, anxiety, or resentment.

- Seek advice and listen to it – Maintain your calm and discuss with superiors so as to open up various possibilities or ways to analyze the situation.

- Report your concerns - blow the whistle.

Prevention of Fraud

A Monitor can actually set the platform for the smooth conduct of a trial. A few precautions from the beginning of the trial as follows will set the right tone:

- Emphasize the company's policy and the FDA's stance on fraud at the Investigators' meet and/or initiation visit itself.

- Conduct GCP training at the initiation visit and also throughout the trial, as necessary, to highlight the deficiencies or opportunities for improvement at the site.

- Include case studies and warning letters in GCP training to bring about more awareness on the consequences of misconduct and Investigator disqualification (21 CFR § 312.70).

- Make the Investigator aware of the regulatory authority's inspection process i.e. FDA's procedures on inspections, handling Establishment Inspection Reports (EIR; NAI, VAI, OAI - No Action Indicated, Voluntary Action Indicated, Official Action Indicated, respectively), issuance of 483's/warning letters, consequences of fraud (restrictions, assurances, debarment, prosecutions, convictions, imprisonment, fine, etc.). Notice of Initiation of Disqualification Proceedings and Opportunity to Explain (NIDPOE).

- Be an expert on protocol and get trained by your Medical team, specifically on the eligibility criteria and primary efficacy parameters where things can be manipulated.

- Do not let the site take you for granted.

- Identify the errors and request the site to have a corrective and preventive action plan from the beginning itself, rather than at the end of a trial.
- Train and re-train the site at regular intervals on protocol amendments or trial procedures so as to avoid possible protocol deviations.
- Minimize the use of enrolment incentives.
- Make sure that the site has necessary resources and support to conduct the trial.
- Accept no photocopies (could vary across situations!).
- Challenge suspicious data and seek explanations.
- Look out for mistakes/changes/inconsistencies in data and its frequency or pattern.

REFERENCES:

1. http://www.ich.org/fileadmin/Public_Web_Site/ICH_Products/Guidelines/Efficacy/E6_R1/Step4/E6_R1__Guideline.pdf International Conference on Harmonisation Harmonised Tripartite Guideline for Good Clinical Practice, E6(R1), May 1996

2. http://www.fda.gov/ScienceResearch/SpecialTopics/RunningClinicalTrials/GuidancesInformationSheetsandNotices/ucm113709.htm U.S. Department of Health & Human Services, Food and Drug Administration-Information Sheet Guidance for Institutional Review Boards (IRBs), Clinical Investigators, and Sponsors

3. http://www.fda.gov/downloads/Drugs/GuidanceComplianceRegulatoryInformation/Guidances/UCM187772.pdf U.S. Department of Health & Human Services, Food and Drug Administration-Guidance for Industry-Investigator Responsibilities-Protecting the Rights, Safety, and Welfare of Study Subjects, Oct 2009

4. Smith-Tyler, 2007, Informed Consent, Confidentiality, and Subject Rights in Clinical Trials. *The Proceedings of the American Thoracic Society* 4:189-193

5. Stone et al., 2002, Patient Non-compliance with Diaries. *British Medical Journal* 324:1193-1194

6. Miracle V.A., 2008, Scientific Misconduct. *Dimensions of Critical Care Nursing* 27(2):90-91

7. Gunsalus, C.K., 1998, How to Blow the Whistle and Still Have a Career Afterwards. *Science and Engineering Ethics* 4:51-64

8. http://ori.hhs.gov/misconduct/inquiry_issues.shtml, U.S. Department of Health & Human Services, Office of Research Integrity-Handling Misconduct-Inquiry Issues

9. http://www.fda.gov/downloads/RegulatoryInformation/Guidances/UCM214008.pdf

   U.S. Department of Health & Human Services, Food and Drug Administration-Information Sheet Guidance for Institutional Review Boards, Clinical Investigators, and Sponsors, Clinical Investigator, Administrative Actions- Disqualification, May 2010

Disclaimer

The views and thoughts expressed in this chapter are solely of the author and do not necessarily represent the employer organization; Vanthys Pharmaceutical Development (P) Ltd.

Chapter ... 8

CLINICAL TRIAL DOCUMENTATION

INTRODUCTION

The principal objective of therapeutic research is to obtain regulatory approval for a drug or a device. The regulators cannot observe each trial, but would depend on the trial documents and results to decide whether the new drug or device has an acceptable risk benefit ratio or not. The trial documents are both a resource and an outcome; they are the outcome of the study and a resource for the regulators.

The regulators therefore demand that the trial documents be prepared thoroughly, accurately, completely, and honestly. It is also in the interest of the Sponsor to prepare the documents as required by the regulators. The documents should be such that they provide a trail of the trial, so that the regulators can follow the way the trial was conducted merely by studying the documents. Clinical research professionals also subscribe to the dictum '**what is not documented is not done**'. There is a particular way of collating documents which has been well-explained in the ICH Guideline E6, and the same system is followed herein. Documents are generated or collected at various stages of the trial, before, during and at the end of the trial. The names of the documents and their required location is given in Appendix I at the end of this chapter.

A word of caution concerning amendments;, most documents undergo revision before and during the trial. This means that the sites would have copies of different versions of the documents. Version control becomes necessary and the person responsible for documentation should ensure that all superseded versions are withdrawn and then issue the latest version. This precaution holds good for all documents whether they are protocol, informed consent forms or investigator's brochure.

Trial Master File (TMF)

Guideline E6 states that Trial Master files should be established at the beginning of the trial, both at the investigator/institution's site and at the sponsor's office. A final close-out of a trial can only be done when the monitor has reviewed both the investigator/institution and sponsor files and confirmed that all necessary documents are in the appropriate files. The file maintained at the site is often called the Site Master File. This file is generally the responsibility of a designated member of the investigating team at the site and of the monitor at the sponsor's office. In case a CRO is involved, the TMF is the responsibility of one of the members of the CRO's staff.

The site master file is almost a copy of the trial master file. The differences being, some documents are at the Sponsor's office but not in the site office, likewise there are some documents which are in the site office but not in sponsor's office. These files are the first that will be examined by the monitors, auditors and inspectors, and hence should be kept updated all the time. Appendix I gives the list of documents and where they are to be stored.

Protocols and their Amendments

The master document of the trial is the protocol. The Guideline ICH E6 (1.44) defines the protocol as 'a document that describes the objective(s), design, methodology, statistical considerations, and organization of a trial'. The protocol usually also gives the background and rationale for the trial, but these could be provided in other protocol-referenced documents also. Throughout the ICH GCP Guideline, the term protocol refers to protocol and protocol amendments.

The protocol sometimes undergoes changes before the trial initiation and sometimes even after the trial initiation. It is essential for the investigators to ensure that they are following the current protocol and not a superseded version. It is also necessary to ensure that the current protocol is the one that has been approved by the IRB. In any case, if there is an amendment to the protocol, the same should be put up before the IRB for approval before it is implemented. The essential elements of the protocol have been discussed in Chapter 14 and shall not be repeated here. A signed copy of the current protocol must be present in the site master file and the trial master file.

Appendix II (6) of Schedule Y to Drugs and Cosmetics Rules (2005) implies that all clinical trials have to be carried out as per the conditions laid down in the Declaration of Helsinki (DOH). Despite this being informed and explained to the investigator, the investigator may subsequently claim that he/she was unaware of the DOH, or its contents. For this reason, it may be appropriate to cut and paste the DOH on the last page of the Protocol. The investigator is required to sign the protocol below the DOH with a declaration that he has read and agrees to all conditions stated above.

Informed Consent Form

The informed consent form (ICF) is an important document that provides evidence to the voluntary nature of recruitment. This form lists out the possible adverse effects which the subject could suffer and details the burdens on the subject. At the end of the form, the subject is provided with telephone or other contact details in case he has some queries regarding the trial or his/her own rights.

The ICF needs to be translated into languages with which the subjects are comfortable and in a multilingual country like ours, it is not unusual to have the ICF in ten or twelve languages. To verify the accuracy of translation, a back translation is done from a different translator. The translation needs to convey the same meaning as the original subject; it need not be a word-to-word-translation. Additionally, though some words, are more easily understood by the population in English than their vernacular meanings, they should be left as such.

Each subject recruited in the trial will sign a consent form. All these forms need not be kept in the site master file; one copy of the IVF is adequate, while individual ICF are filed with source documents of the subject. The sponsor will not receive a copy of the ICF signed by subjects, but will have a single unsigned copy. The signed copies of the ICF will remain with the site and not be transferred to the sponsor, since such a transfer will violate the confidentiality and reveal the identity of the subjects.

The ICF may not highlight the benefits of the drug under study , but it must highlight the burdens on the patient, and the expected adverse events, following therapy. The ICF must detail every procedure that is likely to be viewed as a burden by the subject. However, care should be taken to ensure that the ICF does not scare the patient, else there would be no subjects available for the trial.

Majority of the findings at audits and inspections relate to the ICF, hence great care should be taken to ensure that the consent is properly administered and recorded. The dates and signatures of subjects should match with each other, as these are the documents which an Inspector or an auditor is going to carefully scrutinize.

Investigators' and Patients' Brochures

The Sponsors need to make two different brochures- one for the Investigators and one for subjects or patients, giving them information of how the trial is to be conducted. No investigator can be expected to take up for study a drug about which he has little knowledge. Investigators would necessarily have to be briefed about the data accumulated on the drug to date, before one can expect them to even accept to do the trial.

Thus, in a number of situations the Investigators' Brochure (IB) may have to be handed over to the investigator even before the investigator agrees to conduct the trial. In such a situation, handing over the IB to a physician who has not yet accepted to be an investigator could be dangerous for the confidentiality of the project. It is therefore customary to get a Confidentiality Disclosure agreement signed before handing over the IB.

The IB must contain all information required by the investigator for the following:

1. Decide whether to accept the responsibility of the trial.
2. Understand the risks involved in the use of the new drug/device in his/her patients.
3. Understand the possible benefits of the use of the new drug/device.
4. Carry out the trial as per the protocol.
5. Capture the expected and unexpected adverse events to the extent possible.
6. To complete the objectives of the trial,

Thus the IB must contain the following information:

1. All pre-clinical data obtained with the drug/device.
2. All human data, whether obtained by the sponsor or someone else on the drug/device.
3. Information on chemistry of the drug, and its relation to other drugs in use, so that class effects, if any, are detected and managed.
4. A total analysis of risk benefits of the drug/device, so that the investigator may manage his/her subjects better.

As the drug goes through different phases of the trial, the information given in the IB goes on increasing. The IB for Phase I will contain only the pre-clinical information, while that for Phase II will contain data obtained from Phase I trial along with the preclinical information. The IB for the Phase III will contain data obtained from Phase I and II. For the Phase IV trial the IB need not be very elaborate, since by this time, the Summary of Product Characteristics, package insert and a variety of published information is available for the use by the investigators.

Even during a particular phase of the trial, new information keeps coming in, and the IB needs to be revised, in any case the IB has to be revised at least annually. It is assumed that all investigators are familiar with English language, hence in India it is not a practice to translate the IB into regional languages.

The Patient Brochure (sometimes known as the patient information sheet) is quite a different document, since it is meant for use by patients. This needs to be prepared in a simple language, which an average patient can understand. This could be replete with graphs and pictures, for better understanding, and should be translated in to languages that the patients understand. It should be remembered that patients are not experts in medicine and hence the language used has to be kept simple.

The PIS should make it very clear that recruitment is purely voluntary and the subject can withdraw from the study at any time, without having to give any reasons for doing so. Typically, the PIS should answer the following questions.

1. What the research is about?
2. What is the condition or treatment under study?
3. What will happen to the participant during and after the trial?
4. What usual treatment may be withheld?
5. What are the participant's responsibilities?
6. What are the potential risks?
7. What are the inconveniences or restrictions balanced against the potential benefits and the alternatives?

The PIS should also give details of payments, whether they are reimbursements, or compensation for adverse effects or insurances. The patient may like to know whether the study has received approval from authorities and which authorities have reviewed the study.

The patients should never be hurried, rather should be given ample time to decide whether to enter the study, allowed to ask questions and seek advice of friends and relatives, so that the consent of the patients is truly voluntary.

US guidelines suggest different types of PIS for adults and children; they also suggest giving PIS for children between 6 and 12 and those above 12. The main problem in using PIS for children below 12 is that they have a fear of hospitals and doctors and a low attention span. PIS for female patients should make the issue of pregnancy clear during trial. Also, men should be told that pregnancy in their partner during the trial period is not desirable.

Source Documents

ICH Guideline E 6 (1.52) defines source documents as original documents, data, and records (e.g., hospital records, clinical and office charts, laboratory notes, memoranda, subjects' diaries or evaluation checklists, pharmacy dispensing records, recorded data from automated instruments, copies or transcriptions certified after verification as being accurate copies, microfiches, photographic negatives, microfilm or magnetic media, X-rays, subject files, and records kept at the pharmacy, at the laboratories and at medico-technical departments involved in the clinical trial).

The patient's file, with all its contents, nurses' notes, doctors' prescription, laboratory reports etc. all form the source documents. These are the papers from which data will be transcribed into the CRF, and this transfer has to be accurate. The Monitors will, from time to time compare the data in the source documents with that in the CRF. This is known as source data verification.

Source documents are generally confidential, and should not be made available to all and sundry. However, before the trial begins, the sponsor should make it clear that the investigators must make the source documents available to the monitors for verification. After the end of the trial, the source documents must be archived for a very long time. Though the guidelines specify the period for which archiving is necessary, documents need to be stored virtually forever . It would also be a good idea if source documents are copied and a copy stored in a different location than the original one.

ICH Guideline E6 states that essential documents should be retained until at least 2 years after the last approval of a marketing application in an ICH region and until there are no pending or contemplated marketing applications in an ICH region or at least 2 years have elapsed since the formal discontinuation of clinical development of the investigational product.

The Investigator is quite clear if the decision has been taken to formally discontinue the drug development, but would never know if another application (for a new indication) is going to be filed in the future, hence destroying the documents at any time could be hazardous. In any case, the Investigator should ask for a written consent of the sponsor to destroy the documents, and this written permission should be stored forever .

Agreements

This is an era of legal wrangling. There is a need for everyone to protect themselves from being sued on one count or another. Though this is more common in the United States, the bug of suing companies over every adverse drug reaction is spreading worldwide. What is strange is that some lawyers make money by not going to court, but merely threatening to do so.

In a trial there are a variety of agreements that need to be signed, by various parties. The sponsor or CRO may also sign an agreement with a courier company to carry their documents, but that sort of agreement will not be covered in this chapter. Those agreements which are strictly essential will be covered, though there will be a debate as what is essential and what is not.

Confidentiality Disclosure Agreement (CDA)

Such an agreement is generally signed when two parties exchange information which they do not want falling in other's hands. In this type of agreement, the matter to be kept confidential is clearly defined, and non-disclosure to parties other than those required by law is agreed upon. This is a relatively simple agreement, but care should be taken to include clauses that keep information already in public domain out of this agreement. The agreement also defines the people to whom the information may be disclosed and under what circumstances.

When a sponsor or a CRO approaches an Investigator for conducting a trial (which could be when they are studying the feasibility of the trial), the investigator would demand some information about the drug. It is at this time that a CDA is signed. This is so since, the Investigator has not yet agreed to do the trial, yet will be privy to certain information of the drug. At a later stage when the investigator takes on the trial, a much larger amount of information will be disclosed to the investigating team. A fresh CDA is then signed between the Sponsor/CRO and the Investigator and a separate one between the Investigator and other members of the investigating team.

Trial Agreement

This agreement is signed between the Sponsor/CRO and the investigator. If these are the only two parties to the agreement it is a bipartite agreement, and can be signed if the Investigator is a private practitioner and does not involve a larger hospital or clinic. If a hospital is involved, the hospital has certain responsibilities. The hospital may have to take over the trial if the investigator leaves the hospital or dies. Additionally, the hospital may have to archive the documents if the investigator leaves the institution.

In Government and Municipal hospitals, transfers of doctors are common, and if the trial does not go with the doctor, then another doctor from the same institute may take over the trial. In order to meet such an eventuality, the institute becomes a party to the trial agreement, which becomes tripartite.

Such an agreement must specify:

1. Roles and responsibilities of the investigator and those of the Sponsor/CRO.
2. Time frames for the trial, recruitment and treatment of subjects.
3. Making source documents available for checks during monitoring visits.
4. Financial arrangements between the involved parties.
5. Material that will be made available to the investigators for the trial and the unused material which needs be returned to the Sponsor/CRO.
6. Monitoring and audits to be conducted during the trial.
7. Payments to subjects and other vendors.
8. Insurances of subjects and investigators alike.
9. Post-trial record retention.

Some of these issues may be covered in the protocol and may not appear in the trial agreement. Some sponsors may like to separate all financial matters and have a separate agreement for that. There is no hard and fast rule for what the agreement should contain and what it should not.

When finances are included in this agreement, it is prudent for both parties to remember that the trial may go on for a few years, and exchange rates can change during this time. A mechanism to dampen the effect of these changes should be included. Over a period, inflation may make a trial unviable for the investigator, and hence there should be an in-built mechanism to buffer this.

Vendor Agreements

A number of vendors will be used to provide services to the investigator; this could be laboratories where samples are tested, couriers to transport the samples, legal advisors on both side, and many others. The investigator should ensure that each of the agreements with these parties is signed and the agreement retained during the trial.

Sample Investigations

Investigation on samples may either be performed in a central laboratory or in the laboratory affiliated to the site. A separate agreement may be signed with laboratory after collecting the required documents such as:

1. Certification of the laboratory
2. CV of the Chief analysts
3. Normal reference ranges
4. List of equipments or schedule of tests

Bulk rates can be negotiated since most laboratories offer heavy discounts for bulk samples.

Logs and Checklists

Logs and checklists are essential to ensure that all activities required to be performed are done so, in time, and responsibility is delegated to individuals who are held accountable for the same.

In a clinical trial, various activities need to be completed in time for the timely completion of the trial. The PI therefore delegates a large number of responsibilities to members of the investigational team. In the responsibility log, each individual's responsibility is spelt out and that individual is asked to sign the responsibility log. Thus, the individual is forced to accept the fact that he/she has indeed accepted the responsibility and is therefore accountable for the same. It is best to assign the responsibility of a particular task to one or two individuals at a time, joint responsibility also means joint irresponsibility.

In clinical trials, there are many tasks and functions which are to be performed, some of them simultaneously and some in tandem. Unless a proper checklist is drawn, one of more tasks may remain incomplete which could delay the completion of the trial. Any of the project management principles could be employed for timely completion of the trial, including pre-defined milestones, PERT charts etc.

Financial disclosure

Every trial has a financier, and depending on who that is, there could be conflicts of interest. A financial disclosure is meant to ensure that none of the investigating team or the IRB members have any financial involvement in the trial. This document also makes clear that the money for funding the study comes from legal sources.

Annual and final reports

The IRB and the regulators may require interim reports, usually at a minimum frequency of one per year. These reports are to be prepared as per the requirements of the IRB and the regulators.

After completion of the trial, the data collected from the study is checked for completeness and consistency by the sponsor's data management group. The statistician of the sponsor's research team then undertakes the analyses as described in the study protocol. Following which, the medical writers in the sponsor's research team then prepare a clinical study report, describing the methods and results as well as the interpretation of the data.

This report generally contains the following sections:

1. Title page
2. Abstract/Summary
3. Introduction
4. Objectives
5. Clinical trial design
6. Methods
7. Results
8. Discussion
9. Conclusions
10. References
11. Tables and Figures
12. Appendices.

The clinical study report is the one which the regulators (DCGI in India) study and review before deciding whether to grant or reject the New Drug Application. In India, along with this report, the sponsor has to present the labelling and packaging details of the product and the indications to be claimed. By law, each of these need the approval of the DCGI and no changes can be after the approval.

Archiving

Essential documents of the trial have to be retained and archived for a long period. The rules make it impossible to predict how long they would have to be archived, and it appears that they may be needed forever.

There are no set standards for archiving but in general, the following conditions should be met with while creating facilities for document archival:

1. Fire-proof building in an area not prone to earthquakes, floods or other such natural disasters.

2. Fire and pest-proof rooms equipped with fire extinguishers using powder fire retardants.

3. Access control-Adequate security to prevent access to all but authorized persons.

4. No permission to withdraw documents without an authorization.

It is recommended that all essential documents be copied and one copy stored at a location different from the original. Thus, in case of accidental damage to one archive, the copy is available for study.

REFERENCES:

1. Schedule Y to the Drugs and Cosmetics Rules 1945, IInd amendment 2005.

2. Declaration of Helsinki, at: http://www.wma.net/en/30publications/10policies/b3/index.html

3. ICH Guideline E6 4.9.5

4. Grisham J. The King of Torts, Doubleday 2003.

APPENDIX I

Pre Trial Documents

Sr. No.	Name of the document	Location of Document	
		Site	**Sponsor/CRO**
8.2.1	Investigators' Brochure	X	X
8.2.2	Signed protocol and amendments if any and sample case record form	X	X
8.2.3	Information given to trial subjects:		
	Informed Consent Forms	X	X
	Any other written information	X	X
	Advertisement for subject recruitment	X	X
8.2.4	Financial aspects of the trial	X	X
8.2.5	Insurance statement (where required)	X	X
8.2.6	Signed agreements between parties		
	Investigator/institution and sponsor	X	X
	Investigator/institution and CRO	X	X
	Sponsor and CRO	X	X

Sr. No.	Name of the document	Location of Document	
		Site	Sponsor/CRO
8.2.7	Dated, documented approval/favourable opinion of IRB/IEC of the following:		
	Protocol and any amendments	X	X
	CRF (if applicable)	X	X
	Informed Consent Forms	X	X
	Any other written information supplied to the subjects	X	X
	Advertisement for subject recruitment (if used)	X	X
	Subject compensation (if any)	X	X
	Any other documents given approval/favourable opinion.	X	X
8.2.8	IRB/IEC composition	X	X
8.2.9	Regulatory approval	X	X
8.2.10	CV and other documents evidencing qualification of investigators and sub-investigators	X	X
8.2.11	Normal values/ranges of test procedures included in the protocol	X	X
8.2.12	Medical/Laboratory certification	X	X
8.2.13	Sample for label attached to Investigational Product	X	
8.2.14	Instructions for handling of IP	X	X
8.2.15	Shipping records for IP and trial related material	X	X
8.2.16	Certificates of analysis of IP shipped		X
8.2.17	Decoding procedures for blinded trials	X	X
8.2.18	Master Randomization List		X
8.2.19	Pre trial monitoring report		X
8.2.20	Trial initiation monitoring report	X	X

During the Trial Documents

Sr. No.	Name of the document	Location of Document	
		Site	Sponsor/CRO
8.3.1	Investigators' Brochure updates	X	X
8.3.2	Any revision to: Protocol/amendments and CRF Informed consent form Any written information given to subjects Advertisements for subject recruitment	X	X

Sr. No.	Name of the document	Location of Document	
		Site	Sponsor/CRO
8.3.3	Dated, documented approval/favourable opinion of IRB/IEC of the following: Protocol and any amendments CRF (if applicable) Informed Consent Forms Any other written information supplied to the subjects Advertisement for subject recruitment (if used) Subject compensation (if any) Any other documents given approval/favourable opinion.	X	X
8.3.4	Regulatory approval for: Protocol amendments	X	X
8.3.5	CV of new investigators and sub investigators	X	X
8.3.6	Updates to normal values for tests in the protocol	X	X
8.3.7	Updates on Medical laboratory certifications	X	X
8.3.8	Documentation of IP and trial related material shipment	X	X
8.3.9	COA of new batches of IP		X
8.3.10	Monitoring visit reports		X
8.3.11	Relevant communication other than site visits Letters Meeting notes Notes on Telephone calls	X	X
8.3.12	Signed consent forms	X	
8.3.13	Source documents	X	
8.3.14	Signed, dated and completed CRFs	X	X
8.3.15	Documentation of CRF corrections	X	X
8.3.16	Notification of SAE to sponsor	X	X
8.3.17	Notification of unexpected SADRs to IRB/IEC	X	X
8.3.18	Notification of safety information by sponsor to	X	X

Sr. No.	Name of the document	Location of Document	
		Site	Sponsor/CRO
	investigators		
8.3.19	Interim or annual reports to IRB	X	X
8.3.20	Subject screening log	X	X
8.3.21	Subject identification code list	X	
8.3.22	Subject enrollment log	X	X
8.3.23	IP accountability at site	X	X
8.3.24	Signature sheet	X	X
8.3.25	Record of retained biological samples	X	X

After Completion of Trial

Sr. No.	Name of the document	Location of Document	
		Site	Sponsor/CRO
8.4.1	IP accountability at site	X	X
8.4.2	Documentation of IP destruction	X	X
8.4.3	Completed subject identification code list	X	
8.4.4	Audit certificate		X
8.4.5	Trial close out monitoring report		X
8.4.6	Treatment allocation and decoding documentation		X
8.4.7	Final report by investigator to IRB and Regulatory authority	X	
8.4.8	Clinical study report	X	X

Chapter ... 9

FINANCIAL ASPECTS OF CLINICAL TRIALS

INTRODUCTION

Conducting clinical research is enormously expensive. To understand that a molecule is safe and effective to be used as a therapeutic agent takes a lot of money. It is very important to have a deeper understanding of the financial and economic factors in conducting clinical trials. It is expensive, slow and in need of constant refinements and oversight but the process is trustworthy.

In clinical research, the most important and valuable tool in planning for a clinical trial budget is the study protocol. Protocols have become more complex, calling for more procedures on average. Poorly designed protocols are always the major source of recruitment delays and cost overruns. This means that sites must be careful about whether or not they can actually afford to do a study, without losing money, and that they will need to be very selective about the projects they decide to take on. By reviewing this document carefully, the project team can get an excellent idea of all necessary procedures to be taken into account in determining the study budget. Project managers should do a proper analysis prior to deciding the sites to be selected. This will help them prepare effectively which in turn will save money.

The most difficult and critical task for any company is to understand how to calculate the research budget. In any business, a hidden cost will be always overlooked e.g., sites taking on clinical projects from Sponsor which require an estimated $7000 to $8000 in hidden costs per study may not be reimbursed. While preparing a budget, it is very necessary to include additional cost, so that it becomes easy for the investigative sites not to go in a loss. By doing so, it is unlikely that costs that might otherwise be left out of the budget will be overlooked. A budget worksheet (in many cases the sponsor will provide a worksheet) should be prepared to overcome these kind of issues.

Since each study patient will be going through the same protocol, an easy way to calculate the budget is to figure the cost of one study patient (studies are usually funded on a per patient basis) and then multiply this figure by the number of expected enrollees. Sponsors will pay for actual work, i.e., subject enrolled and subject visits. Most grants are formulated on a per-subject amount prorated for the number of visits a subject actually completes. Start the process by developing a budget worksheet, proceed through the protocol and write in each expense. It is important to remember that the figures placed on the budget worksheet are not the cost of the procedure to the institution but are instead the institution's usual and customary charge (speak with the accounting department or clinic administrator to get an idea of these costs). The amount per visit will often vary, as some visits are more labor and time-intensive than others.

It is important to remember that only those expenses which are covered by the protocol will be reimbursed by the Sponsor. Any additional procedures (not covered within the protocol) should be billed as usual to the patient or their insurance. For example, in an in-patient study, the patient would still be billed for the stay in the hospital but all procedures included in the study budget (x-rays, lab tests, drug therapy etc.) would not be billed to the patient. A procedure needs to be worked out by the study coordinator and the medical billing department within the hospital to identify the patients on study (and their expenses handled appropriately) so these items are not double-billed to the patient or their insurance. It is also important that all department heads (lab, radiology, pharmacy etc.) are informed of the protocol requirements for each patient and how their individual departments will handle the actual billing process for the study patients.

In many cases, the Sponsor will offer the institution a per-patient budget amount rather than having the coordinator decide what would be required. Figuring out the institution's costs ahead of time will allow the study coordinator to assess the fairness of the Sponsor's offer. In many cases, the Sponsor will be willing to barter if the study coordinator can show additional costs which will need to be reimbursed. Some of the costs which should be considered are listed below.

The optimal conduct of clinical research in any setting requires dedicated research staff. Having such staff increases the likelihood of success adhering to protocols and providing the best patient care. When budgeting for staff time, consider the time required for all tasks integral to coordinating the trial: screening patients, obtaining informed consent, conducting patient visits, completing accurate source documents and case report forms, maintaining regulatory documents, and communicating with the sponsor and contract research organization. Reimbursement for those costs should be included in a budget.

Budgeting for payment of the investigator and coordinator salaries during attendance at investigator meetings remains controversial. Since the site must pay it's staff during these meetings, it is believed that the Sponsor should be charged for the salaries and benefit costs associated with attendance. Often, the practice is told that attendance at an investigator meeting is "the cost of doing business." However, investigators and coordinators attend these meetings specifically for training related to the Sponsor's clinical trial. Therefore, these meetings are more appropriately considered to be the Sponsor's cost of doing business. Perhaps, if site managers unite on this issue, a change can be effected.

CLINICAL TRIAL BUDGET WORKSHEET

STUDY NAME: _____

STUDY ID: _____

SPONSOR NAME: _____

INVESTIGATOR: _____

NAME: _____

STUDY ACTIVITIES	PERSONNEL (PI/RN)	EST. HRS	FREQUENCY	TOTAL HRS. / PATIENT	FEE (USD)
Medical History					
Consent					
Screening					
Nursing Assessment/Vitals					
Phlebotomy					
Specimen prep/Collection					
Review of meds/protocol					
CRF Completion					
Queries/Monitor Visits					
EC Correspondence					
SAE Forms					
Other Study Specifics					
ECG					
X Ray					
Others					
Pharmacy Fee/Patient					
Subtotal					
Institutional Overhead (25%)					

The following items are intended to serve as a guide to Principal Investigators and administrative staff in clinical trial budgeting, and particularly in determining whether per patient enrollment fee will be adequate to cover the entire cost of the trial. Often, investigators develop a planned agreement with a pharmaceutical organization even before the clinical trial agreement is developed, in which the following types of costs can be budgeted. This phase is often overlooked and, therefore, uncompensated, although it is often one of the phases of the study when the investigator makes the most significant intellectual contributions. It is essential to be aware of all the costs associated with conducting clinical research and have the ability to document those costs to validate budget requests. Expect sponsors to negotiate on funding support, but consistently resist making budget reductions that are unreasonable. Ensure that budget and billing procedures are in place before a trial begins and that all staff, not only research staff, remain diligent in accurately budgeting and billing for research procedures. Other site costs that should be considered during budget development, and which are included in the template, are site initiation meetings, completing and faxing screening logs, third-party radiology review, central lab specimen collection and shipment, the complexity of the case report form, the frequency of monitoring visits, collection and shipment of pharmacokinetic specimens, conducting the close-out visit, and long-term storage of study documents.

CLINICAL TRIAL BUDGET WORKSHEET

STUDY NAME: _____   STUDY ID: _____

SPONSOR NAME: _____   INVESTIGATOR: _____

NAME: _____

FIXED OR ONE TIME COSTS

INVESTIGATOR START UP (Time/Effort For Protocol Assessment)	
	Fee (USD)
Protocol Review	
Site selection time with sponsor	
Investigator Time	
In-Service Staff	
Document Archival charges	
IP storage and maintenance fee	
Miscellaneous (Telephone, fax, internet charges)	
Sub Total	

FIXED OR ONE TIME COSTS

INVESTIGATOR START UP (Time/Effort For Protocol Assessment)	
Non-Refundable onetime fee	
	Fee (USD)
Ethics Committee fee:	
Pharmacy Fee	
Regulatory Fee	

BUDGETING BY ACTIVITY WORKSHEET					
Procedures	**Pre-Rx**	**During Rx**	**IV to PO**	**End of Rx**	**Total**
Clinical and Medical evaluations					
Obtaining Informed Consent					
History and Physical Examination					
Follow Up Visits and Exams					
Administrative					
Principal Investigator					
Ethics Committee, Site, sponsor activities, AE reports, Meeting time, etc					
Study Coordinator/ Research Nurse					
Initial Meeting Time					
In servicing					
Coordinator per Patient Administrative Activities					
Screening fee (estimated for 1 enrolled for 3 screened)					
Clinical Score or Efficacy calculations, if any					
AE recording					

Concomitant Medication recording					
Patient Diary review					
Dispensing and accounting for study medications					
Patient Instructions					
Scheduling of next visits					
CRF data entry					
Query resolution					
Monitoring Visits					
SAE forms					
EC correspondence					
Sponsor/site correspondence					
Sponsor Audit					
Lab Test Procedures					
Hematology					
Biochemistry					
Serology					
Urinalysis					
Pregnancy Test					
Specimen collection and handling					
Specimen shipping					
Microbiology					
Blood cultures, if any					
Sputum					
Stool sample, Others					
ECG					
X-Ray					
Patient stipend for time and travel					
Total (25% Overhead)					

FUNDING FOR CLINICAL RESEARCH

The pharmaceutical industry plays a vital role in financing research required to develop new drugs. While grants from the National Institutes of Health (NIH) fund most basic research in academic laboratories, it is largely the industry that bears the cost of identifying new molecular entities and testing them on animal models and human subjects. Clinical trials make up the largest portion of the $266 million to $802 million estimated total cost to industry for bringing each new drug to the market. Furthermore, of all funding for clinical trials in the United States, nearly 75% currently comes from corporate sponsors. In addition, scientists employed by pharmaceutical companies play an important role in evaluating the efficacy, safety, and cost-effectiveness of new drugs.

Unlike publicly-funded studies, however, clinical trials supported by the pharmaceutical industry may be adversely affected by business interests. Numerous industry-sponsored trials, for example, are prematurely terminated for financial rather than for scientific or ethical reasons. Discontinuation of a clinical trial for financial reasons thus violates the Declaration of Helsinki, a covenant that safeguards the interests of human research subjects.

Corporate financing of clinical research, which often includes incentives for academic investigators, may also create conflicts of interest that can bias study results. Some companies pay physicians for each patient they recruit into clinical trials. In other cases, clinician-researchers serve as paid scientific consultants who speak on behalf of industry or are offered shares, options, or paid positions on scientific advisory boards at the companies who fund their work.

Research supported by pharmaceutical companies may also be subject to methodological bias. Industry-funded clinical trials and cost-effectiveness analyses, for instance, yield positive results far more often than studies funded or conducted by other entities. This may reflect bias caused by enrollment of relatively healthy patients, insufficient selection or dosage of comparator drug, inadequate sample size, or inappropriate length of patient follow-up. Other problems may include reliance on invalidated surrogate end-points, inappropriate use of statistical analyses, or misleading presentation of data.

Djulbegovic et al suggest that the overwhelmingly positive results of industry-funded studies are due to violations of the "uncertainty principle," an ethical guideline stating that a randomized controlled trial should be conducted only "if there is substantial uncertainty about which trial treatments would benefit a patient most." Industry-financed studies also more frequently compare novel treatments against a placebo than against drugs that are known to be effective.

Most peer-reviewed journals mandate that reports of clinical studies conform to Consolidated Standards of Reporting Trials (CONSORT), a set of guidelines issued by physician-investigators to standardize descriptions of trial methods and to ensure inclusion of important details about the therapeutic regimen, adjunctive therapies, patient enrollment and withdrawal. With evidence that biased reporting may result from academic-industry relationships that compromise the intellectual freedom of clinical investigators, members of the International Committee of Medical

Journal Editors (ICMJE) specifically condemn all contractual agreements that deny researchers the right to independently analyze clinical trial data and prepare a manuscript for submission. In addition, the ICMJE now mandates that authors disclose all details about their role and the role of the corporate sponsor in the clinical study. Members of the ICMJE may also request lead authors to sign a statement accepting complete responsibility for the conduct, analysis, and reporting of the trial.

Although industry sponsorship of clinical trials can lead to important therapeutic advances, the potential for bias in these studies may exist at multiple levels. Academic internal review boards, US Food and Drug Administration drug advisory committees, peer reviewers, and journal editors, all play vital roles in recognizing bias in clinical research and ensuring that only drugs supported by unbiased, scientific evidence reach the market and clinic. To ensure objectivity in clinical research, some investigators have suggested that industry-academia collaborations continue only if academic medical centers assume sole responsibility for the design, conduct, analysis, and reporting of clinical trials. Others have supported the creation of conflict-of-interest committees at academic institutions to monitor the financial interests of both clinician-investigators and institutional decision makers. By establishing checks and balances for academic-industry partnerships, such proposals may help to mitigate the potential for bias in industry-sponsored research.

BUDGET DEVELOPMENT

The Sponsor will be usually providing the budget but it is not necessary that the budget would identify all the costs of the trial. Site should revise the budget from the Sponsor as needed. To survive in today's competitive clinical research market, it is very important to have a vigilant retrospective budget review and an attentive prospective budget preparation. Resources should be analyzed discussed before planning the budget.

Below mentioned are cost divisions:
- Start up Cost
- Fixed Cost
- Personnel Cost
- Procedure/Tests
- Administrative Cost

1. Start up Cost

This involves the principal investigator and coordinator. Start up cost involves protocol review, feasibility review, budget development and negotiation, site selection visits, staff training, site initiation visits.

This also includes the administrative paper work, the documents involved to be submitted to the Regulatory Bodies. Confidentiality disclosure agreement should be prepared along with financial disclosure agreement.

2. Fixed Cost

There are many types of fixed fees involved in running a clinical trial including IRB (Ethics Committee) fees, processing of amendment fees, transportation fees, courier fees, supply fees etc. There may also be a good deal of overnight mailing (establish with the Sponsor prior to accepting a study on who would be paying these shipping fees). Try to make a realistic prediction of the fixed fees involved in the study and include those fees in your budget analysis. Cost for retention of documents, pharmacy review and set-up fee, external audit fee, lab set up fee, closeout activities.

3. Personnel Cost

A database review has to be conducted for identifying the subjects. This is time-consuming and personnel will be involved in doing so.

To find subjects for the study, sometimes the investigators may have reach out to their fellow physicians to give them the protocol compliant subject. Investigators will be also sending letter to their patients who may make protocol compliant subject for the study.

Principal Investigator (PI), Co-Investigator (Co-I), Study physician and Staff Stipends:

Study will be requiring hiring study staff for conduct of the trial. While a budget should be prepared for the PI, Co-I, a fixed stipend should be paid to the study physicians involved in clinical trials for their time and effort. This must be calculated into the budget as should be stipends for staff personnel (Study nurse, phlebotomist) or the physicians who refer study patients. Budget release for the study staff can be done by time estimates or milestones (per visit of the subjects, etc.)

Study Coordinator Costs:

The study coordinator spends a good deal of time recruiting patients, working with the site monitor and training and consulting with other members of the study team. These time costs must be part of the study budget. The coordinator may also be active in patient care; assessing vitals, conducting interviews and preparing specimens for shipment and also completion of the case report forms, so this time and effort must also be factored into the budget.

Cost for every monitoring visit by the study monitor should also be a part of the study budget. All the adverse event and serious adverse event reporting to the Ethics Committee and regulatory bodies should be a part of the study budget.

4. Procedure/Tests Cost:

Visit Costs:

In clinical research, the budget for visits is always prepared on the basis of each subject visit to the site. e.g., if the subject is visiting the site on an out-patient basis, then each visit needs to be charged. A cost has to be worked out for each visit.

The initial visit of the subject for the study would require elaborate work which means this will require more time from the investigator, so the cost should be planned accordingly. The time and effort put in by the physician, study nurse, co-ordinator and other study staff should also be considered. Factor in the cost of the physical exam, medical history, and all other procedures as detailed in the protocol as well as any specialist fees (i.e.: cardiologist, neurologist) if referrals are required. Many follow-up visits may require just a short amount of the physician's time or maybe just a visit to see the study coordinator. All these costs associated with each visit need to be charged.

Procedure Costs:

These are the costs for the procedures laid down in the protocol. This may involve lab work (if a local lab rather than a central one is being used), x-rays, CAT scans, EKG's etc. It is important to factor in the costs of materials (X-ray film, syringes etc.). Specimen processing (centrifuge, refrigerator etc.) and shipping (dry ice, shipping boxes etc.) cost should be also included.

Patient Participation Cost:

In many cases, some reimbursement will be necessary for the time and effort of the study patients. This is a budgetary consideration.

Paper Work Costs:

During and following each study patient visit, the study coordinator and other members of the study team would perform a good deal of paper work. This time-consuming work needs to be included into the study budget. Paperwork is usually factored in as coordinator fee and/or institutional overhead.

5. Administrative Cost:

Additional Overhead Costs:

These are costs which exist simply because the study is taking place at the institution. Examples of these costs could include electricity, copier use, fax use, telephone, storage, square footage use etc. The most significant of these costs is usually the phone as numerous phone calls are made during the course of a clinical trial. These costs are usually calculated as a percentage of the entire budget. Depending on the institution, overhead cost ranges from 10-100%. (120% is a good rule of thumb).

Pharmacy Costs:

Although the test article will be provided for free, there would still be work performed by the pharmacy. Dispensing of the test article (especially in the case of an in-patient trial, many of which involve IV's) involves costs that must be factored into the study budget.

Advertising Costs/Study Promotions:

Depending on the type of advertising utilized to locate study patients, this may or may not be a budgetary consideration. After adding up all these costs for a single study patient, multiply that figure by the number of enrollees to arrive at the total study budget.

CRCs often help investigators when it comes to figuring a budget and determining an appropriate grant amount for a study. A good way to come up with a grant figure is to look at each study activity, attach a cost to it, add an additional overhead amount and other required activities, and total it up. The change for each item should also include the cost of time of the person performing it.

Some companies utilize their monitor (the CRA) in determining when grant monies should be paid, while others handle all grant payments in-house without the CRA's involvement. These companies usually pay in-house. Whatever the scheme, the site will want to know it is ahead of time, so it is prepared accordingly.

The Financial Agreement:

After all the budgetary details are finalized, the Sponsor and the research site must arrive at a mutual agreement on the time and method of paying the institutions for their hard work. All this will be contained in a document called the Investigator Agreement. This agreement will define what is expected by the investigator and the Sponsor.

Details usually specified in this document include:

(i) The amount of upfront money the research site would receive. In most cases, the Sponsor will forward the research site, the equivalent payment of one or two completed protocols. This money is usually paid to the site upon completion of all critical documentation and after the study initiation visit has taken place.

(ii) The time frame of payment for patients completing the entire protocol as the study progresses. In most cases, the institution will be paid quarterly for all patients who have completed the study (This is why it is vital to have all paper work completed during site visits by the study monitor). In studies which require patients to be followed for prolonged periods, sites are often paid quarterly for completion of stipulated portions of the study protocol.

(iii) Monetary re-imbursement for patients who drop out of the study or do not complete the entire protocol (these are usually paid on a pro-rated basis).

Negotiating physician fees:

Some Sponsors determine a range or a single per subject grant figure. Investigators either accept it or will not be able to do the study. Other Sponsors allow more flexibility, depending on their experience with an investigator or the geographic location. Costs do differ in different parts of the country, so it makes sense to allow some flexibility. It is also vital to be fair with physicians when negotiating their portion of the budget. Without the help of physician- investigators, the research department will be unable to operate therefore the physicians must be treated fairly.

By doing so, contract clinical research becomes a win-win scenario for everyone. It is important to explain to the study physicians that they will be paid after the patients have completed the protocol and the research department is paid by the sponsor, so there may be a lag from the time of patient recruitment until actual payment is received.

Cash flow and checking accounts:

Although contract clinical research is an exciting and dynamic arena, it is important to realize there will be an initial lag in cash flow. Upfront money from the Sponsors will not be received until the site is study-ready and the initiation visits are completed for the site's initial studies. Further, funds will not be available until the patients have completed the protocol. Therefore, it is important to be realistic about cash flow for at least the first six months after opening a research department. It is also important to keep a handle on the cash flow once the studies begin. The research department will need a checking account to pay bills and store funds collected from sponsors.

To minimize cash flow management problems, the hospital may want to assign an administrator to co-sign all checks the coordinator will be issuing. These checks will be for a variety of expenses (physician fees, patient reimbursement, study advertising/promotions etc.) and the coordinator will need ready access to funds to make timely bill payments. Careful record-keeping of all study expenses is vital. The study coordinator will need to make use of an accounting programme (preferably one that the hospital is already utilizing) to keep close records of all study debits and credits. By doing so, the study coordinator will be prepared to demonstrate the financial success of the research department to the interested administrators at annual budget meetings.

Miscellaneous costs:

1. Biostatistical or other analytical costs.
2. Computer time.
3. Equipment maintenance.
4. EC fees when changes in protocols require additional fees.
5. Dry ice/shipping costs/fax and phone costs.
6. Laboratory and specialized equipment supplies.
7. Computers.

SUBJECT COMPENSATION

Subjects who take part in clinical research should be compensated for their time and effort dedicated for the clinical trials. These might range from medical benefits, unscheduled hospital visits, transportation fee, parking fees or any out-of pocket expenses related to study participation. IRB should take care that compensation provided to the subject is fair and this does not unduly pressurize them for participating in the clinical trial.

IRB/IEC should approve any kind of payment which is provided for the subject in the trial for his/her participation in the same. Liability of sponsor and the investigator should be made very clear before the start of the study.

The Sponsor is liable to provide equitable compensation to participants in the clinical trial in case of the latter suffering any physical injury; irrespective of whether it is a temporary or a permanent disability. The subject should get full compensation if he/she withdraws from the study due to medical reasons associated with the study.

Compensation should be paid to a child injured *in-utero* utero through the participation of the parent in clinical research. Material compensation should be provided to the dependents of the trial subject if they expire during the course of the trial. The Indian Society of Clinical Research has made certain recommendations for compensation for study related injury/death. These recommendations have been published by the ICMR on their website calling for comments on the same. In case there are no serious objections, we may see these recommendations take the form of a law in the near future.

INSURANCE AND INDEMNITY

Insurance and Indemnity are liabilities related to sponsor which means claims made by or on behalf of participants taking part in the clinical trial for the personal injury which is a result of taking part in the trial. These injuries may be due to negligence incurred due to the design of the protocol or unintended harmful effect of the investigational product.

Insurance coverage is provided for the study subjects wherein they can claim the insurance amount in any case of personal injury due to participation in trial.

Indemnity coverage is applicable for the Investigator and the site staff. Indemnity excludes application of the indemnity to the extent that injury to or death of a participant is caused by negligence on the part of individuals conducting the trial.

Insurance and indemnity are an essential part of conducting a clinical trial. It is very much necessary to understand and have in place competent insurance and indemnity documents. This helps the clinical research organizations to be insured in case of a claim by the subject. If valid insurance and indemnity documents are provided to the ethics committee, it helps in getting the approvals without delays.

In India, this concept was not strict but, nowadays the Indian Drug Regulatory Body and Ethics Committees suggest insurance and indemnity coverage from the sponsor. The CROs should discuss this coverage with the Sponsor and should be reflected while making the Budget.

The Sponsor is a key stakeholder of the project and there may be more than one Sponsor for a project. The Sponsor is the person or group that provides financial resources, in cash or in kind, for the project. The project Sponsor works with the project management team, especially helping with project matters such as funding, scope clarification, progress monitoring, and influencing others in order to benefit the project.

BUDGET TRACKING

Budget tracking usually refers to monitoring expenditure. It can be looked at vertically (i.e. how money flows through a system from higher to low level), or horizontally (how are disbursements made at one point in the system, are they regular and spent as planned?). For either type of budget tracking, the focus is on whether the money is spent as detailed in the plan. If not, why not? Where does it go? Budget tracking can also link to an evaluation of the impact of a particular budget, looking at whether expenditure had the intended impact, or focusing on the impact of different departments.

Tracking through the system: With increased decentralisation of clinical research budgets, there are more and more countries where financial transfers are made from top management to the middle and junior-level executives. For the tracking process to work well, it generally needs to involve actors at three levels. At the top level, this involves engaging directly with organisation and policy makers, ensuring accurate up-to-date information about the levels of funding that should be flowing through the system, as well as information about when disbursements are made, and where the money is sent.

This can be followed up at the middle level by engaging with the executives and enquiring whether the money arrived, how much arrived, how much is allocated to each respective clinical research activities, and exploring whether this is consistent with the pre planned expenditures. This work will depend on whether there is an open information policy, and if you can access the relevant data. In general, the budget and tracking of budget is confidential and shall be made by the Manager/Director of the organisation. Budget-tracking should not be limited to actual expenditure. It is also important to consider the impact of the budget. For example, is quality research work achieved through this budget? What extra expenditure might be needed? How does the budget impact different divisions of the organisation? For this work you may collect statistical information or use personal testimonies of department heads, and other important group members. This tracking would help top the management to foresee any unexpected activities for which budget was not allocated, if any, and adjust funds accordingly.

TAXATION

A tax is a financial charge or other levy imposed on an individual or a legal entity by a state or a functional equivalent of a state.

In most countries, lots of medicines for clinical trials are not taxed because of non-commercial use by clinical trials subjects and being free for them. In Russia, VAT rate for commercial lots of imported medicines is 10%, and for non-commercial lots for clinical trials – 18%.

According to the amendments introduced by this law to article 164 of the Tax Code, VAT rate of 10% shall be applied to all imported medicines including medicines for clinical trials.

But taxation practice did not change instantly. At first, customs refused to apply VAT 10% rate for medicines for clinical trials referring to the absence of the prescription of the Federal Customs Service. Representatives of the Federal Customs Service refused to admit the right of taxpayers to apply VAT 10% rate referring to the fourth paragraph of article 164 of the Tax Code. According to it, the code list of goods named in the article 164 is to be approved by the Government of the Russian Federation. ACTO appealed to the Ministry of Finance and the Government of Russian Federation. As a result, customs began to apply VAT rate of 10% for imported medicines for clinical trials but continued refusing to apply VAT rate of 10% if there was placebo in the lot.

PROFITABILITY

Over the past 20 years, medical research has become a largely privatized, and thoroughly Taylorized, business. The largest of the new private industries are contract research organizations (CROs), which range from small niche agencies to multinational corporations that manage all aspects of clinical trials, from ethics approval and subject recruitment to the submission of clinical data to the FDA. Company A, the company that managed the study in which Dan Markingson was enrolled, is the largest, with 14 percent of the $11.4 billion global market. CROs save money for pharmaceutical companies by deploying the principles of industrial management: breaking trials down into narrow, discrete steps, which can be carried out with maximum efficiency by specialized workers who can be paid relatively low wages. According to Vanderbilt University social scientist Jill Fisher, author of *Medical Research for Hire*, very little experience is required to be a CRO "monitor" — a middle manager, often a nurse, who coordinates the various sites involved in a study. Monitors usually make less than their counterparts at universities or pharmaceutical companies, and job turnover is very rapid. Fisher says, "The goal of many monitors is to be hired by the pharmaceutical industry."

In contrast, private physicians paid to supervise clinical trials are often very well-compensated. A part-time contract researcher conducting four or five clinical trials a year can expect to earn an average of $300,000 in extra income. Yet they generally have little, if any research training. They do not generate original scientific ideas, design studies, or analyze the results. Their main role is to help recruit subjects and oversee their trial participation.

Today, if cash-strapped academic centers want to compete for the revenue generated by industry-sponsored trials, they must play by the new rules. Academic institutional review boards must approve trials quickly to compete with for-profit IRBS, and academic study-coordinators must recruit subjects quickly to compete with private trial sites. The competition is even stiffer for academic physicians, many of whom must generate part of their own university salaries by obtaining grants and contracts from external funding sources. If academic physicians want to do clinical trials for the pharmaceutical industry, they must compete with contract researchers, who offer little to the body of science but carry out industry-tailored trials efficiently. Such arrangements often reduce academic physicians to little more than industry-helpers, collecting data according to a company protocol. All these factors, it seems, were at play in the study that Dan Markingson was enrolled in when he died.

INFLATION

The cost of conducting a clinical trial for a drug is rising like mercury on a summer afternoon, a trend that researchers say is hampering the development of new medicines and is bad news for academia, pharmaceutical companies and consumers.

From the 1980s to the 1990s, the, According to the Tuft Center for the Study of Drug Development, clinical trial costs of drug development increased 5 times faster than pre-clinical costs from the 1980s to the 1990s. In 2003, some health economists in the United States estimated the average cost of bringing a drug to market at US$802 million. Estimates of typical research and development costs today are in the US$1.3 billion-to-US$1.7 billion range, though some health researchers dispute these numbers. Though there is much debate about the numbers, there is little debate that they are getting bigger, which has some researchers worried.

In a recent article, Dr. Johnston, director of the University of California, San Francisco Neurovascular Disease and Stroke Center wrote that the average cost of developing a drug had, over the previous 20 years, risen at a rate 7.4% higher than inflation and that clinical trials were responsible for most of the increase. To combat rising costs, some drug companies have off-loaded their research and development responsibilities to contract research organizations, which are believed to conduct trials more efficiently. Companies are also searching for inefficiencies in the clinical trial process, in the hope of streamlining it by focusing on key elements.

EXCHANGE RATE

When comparing Clinical Research cost studies across nationally and internationally, the common practice has been to use official currency exchange rates. In the long run, official exchange rates reflect the relative rate of overall inflation between two economies. In the short run however, official exchange rates can deviate substantially from this value and can fluctuate widely in response to financial and political factors. In addition, the relative prices may differ between the overall economy and the health care sector, as in the United States. Finally, the way in which the resources are organized to produce the health care services and the relative prices of these resources may differ between countries. An index that is considered to be more accurately reflect underlying rates of resource allocation and relative prices than the official exchange rate.

REFERENCES:

1. *Understanding Clinical Trials; April 2000; Scientific American Magazine; by Justin A Zivin.*

2. *Industry Funding of Clinical Trials: Benefit or Bias? Sameer S. Chopra, A.M. Vanderbilt, University School of Medicine, Nashville, Tenn, July 2, 2003—Vol 290, No. 1.*

3. *Draft Guidelines on Compensation for Research Related Injury in India.*
   ICMR, New Delhi. 2011.

Chapter ... 10

BASIC BIOSTATISTICS

INTRODUCTION

Biostatistics forms one of the most important and conclusive aspects of clinical research and basic knowledge of biostatistics is a "must know" for all students of clinical research. One of the most wrong perception about biostatistics is that it comes only after the study has been completed. In fact, application of biostatistics is required right at the stage of planning of a study. This chapter deals with the basic concepts of biostatistics and is aimed to provide working knowledge of biostatistics for clinical researchers.

Variation in biological phenomena

The word 'statistic' means a numerical fact, a measurement. Any statistic is classified as being either descriptive or analytical. Descriptive statistics measure by describing something and analytical statistics measure by comparing things. Why do we need statistics at all?

We need statistics to deal with the variation shown by all biological phenomena.

For example, what is the normal level for serum creatinine levels in humans?

There is no single value that be considered as a normal serum creatinine level as the levels vary to some extent even amongst healthy individuals. The levels may change due to age differences or sex differences. Further, the values are not the same in a given individual at different points of time. Thus, normal serum creatinine values vary in a normal biological range. There are intra-individual and inter-individual biological variations.

However, in a patient with renal failure the serum creatinine levels are above normal. Similarly, what is the normal weight for a given height? Weights of individuals of a given height vary according sex, ethnicity etc. Thus, normal weight for given height varies in a normal biological range.

Biostatistics

Biostatistics is a branch of statistics developed for the study of life sciences. Biostatistics can be used for several applications while dealing with a biological data.

- It can be used to describe a given set of data. This is known as descriptive statistics.
- It can be used for analyzing whether a given set of data differs from the rest of the population or some other sample significantly, or the difference is just a part of normal biological variation.

- It can be used for calculating an appropriate sample size for a study.

- It can also be used for validating a given test for a tool as a diagnostic measure.

- Finally, biostatistics can be used for assessing association and correlation between two or more variables.

Observational and Experimental Studies

A study can be done by mere collection of observations or by analyzing the observations statistically to draw conclusions. Various surveys and epidemiological studies of the natural history of the disease fall into this category. As against this, in experimental studies, an intervention is performed in order to change the outcome.

Experimental studies may include *in vitro* studies or animal studies or clinical trials.

Observational studies are often conducted to find out the association between a risk factor and a disease or impact of a preventive strategy on the occurrence of the disease. Case-control study and cohort study are the two important types of observational studies.

In a case-control study, a group of cases and a group of controls are traced back in time to find out how many of them were associated with a particular risk factor.

E.g. In a case-control study, 100 cases of lung cancer were investigated for history of smoking. 70 out of 100 patients were reported to be chronic smokers. In the control group of 100 subjects, only 30 were reported to be smokers.

In a cohort study, a large group of individuals exposed to a particular risk factor are followed in the course of time and incidence of the disease in question is recorded. This is matched with a control cohort in terms of demography which is also followed up for occurrence of the disease.

E.g. A cohort of 1000 smokers (smoked at least 5 cigarettes per day for at least 10 years) and demographically matched control cohort of 1000 non-smokers are followed up for next 10 years for incidence of lung cancer.

Case-control studies are retrospective in nature, usually contain lesser number of subjects and include number of bias or confounding factors as the case and control groups are not matched. Hence, it is not always possible to draw very solid inferences from case-control studies. However, case-control studies are easy to conduct, not time-consuming and at times can provide some important conclusions.

On the other hand, cohort studies are more systematic and large-scale studies which are useful to calculate several important statistical parameters such as relative risk or number needed to treat. However, they are tedious and more time-consuming than case-control studies.

Types of data

Quantitative (numerical) and qualitative (categorical) can be considered as two main sub-types of data. Quantitative data is the one for which one asks "how much?" and qualitative data is the one for which one asks "what type?". The classification of subtypes of data is presented in Table 10.1.

Table 10.1: Types of Data

Quantitative (Numerical)	
Continuous	**Discrete**
• Data can take any value in the given range • Often measured and not counted • E.g. Age, weight	• Data can take only whole integer number • Often counted and not measured • E.g. Number of adults in the family
Qualitative (Categorical)	
Nominal	**Ordinal**
• Unordered categories • It may be binary e.g. male or female • Blood groups – A, B, AB and O	• Ordered categories • E.g. Grades such as mild, moderate and severe

Types of data may be inter-convertible

Numerical data can be converted into categorical data.

e.g. 120, 130, 134, 110, 140, 150, 144

This set of numerical data consists of values of systolic blood pressure. However, considering the cut-off value of 140 mm Hg, this data can be converted into categorical data such as: Hypertensive and non-hypertensive.

It is important to realize the differences between numerical and categorical data as the statistical analyses are different for them.

Descriptive statistics or summary statistics

For numerical data

This helps to summarise important information in the data into few numbers which can be communicated easily. This can be done by using, together, two kinds of measures, measures of central tendency and measures of dispersion.

Measuring central tendency

One measure of central tendency that everyone knows is the average. For example, average monthly family income, average annual rain fall.

The average, also known as the mean, is a statistic which describes the central tendency of a group of values. The mean equals the sum of the values in a group divided by the number of values in that group.

Following is the formula for mean:

$$\bar{x} = \frac{x_1 + x_2 + x_3 + x_4 \ldots + x_n}{n}$$

Other descriptive measures of central tendency are the median, which is the middle value in a group, and the mode, which is the most frequent value in a group. Although, mean or average is the most common summary statistic used to describe central tendency, a major disadvantage associated with mean is its sensitivity to outliers.

E.g. For the given data set,

1, 2, 3, 4, 5, 6, 7, 8, 10

Mean is 5.11 and median is 5. Replacing the value 10 with 100 will change the mean to 15.11, but the median will remain unchanged.

Measures of dispersion

The simplest form of measure of dispersion is range which is difference between the lowest and the highest value. Although, it is easy to calculate range, it does not give much information about the average spread of data around the mean.

Here comes the role of variance and standard deviation. Let us first understand the term variance. Variance is sum of the squares of differences between the individual values and the mean divided by the number of observations minus one.

$$\text{Variance} = \sqrt{\frac{\Sigma(x - \bar{x})^2}{n - 1}}$$

E.g. For the given data set,

1, 2, 3, 4, 5, 6, 7, 8, 9

$$\text{The mean is } \frac{1 + 2 + 3 + 4 + 5 + 6 + 7 + 8 + 9}{9} = 5$$

$$\text{Variance} = \frac{(1 - 5)^2 + (2 - 5)^2 + (3 - 5)^2 + (4 - 5)^2 + (5 - 5)^2 + (6 - 5)^2 + (7 - 5)^2 + (8 - 5)^2 + (9 - 5)^2}{9 - 1}$$

$$= \frac{(-4)^2 + (-3)^2 + (-2)^2 + (-1)^2 + (0)^2 + (1)^2 + (2)^2 + (3)^2 + (4)^2}{9 - 1}$$

$$= \frac{16 + 9 + 4 + 1 + 0 + 1 + 4 + 9 + 16}{9 - 1}$$

$$= \frac{60}{8}$$

$$= 7.5$$

Standard deviation is nothing but the positive square root of variance.

$$\text{Standard deviation (SD)} = \sqrt{\frac{(\Sigma x - \bar{x})^2}{n - 1}}$$

Hence, for the given dataset,

$$\text{Standard deviation (SD)} = \sqrt{7.5}$$

$$= 2.738$$

By taking the squares of differences and then taking their positive square root, standard deviation always comes out to be a positive number. Instead, had we added just the differences, the positive and negative values may balance out to zero.

Degree of freedom

Why do we have to divide the numerator by n-1 and not the total number of observations? For understanding this, one must use the concept of the degree of freedom.

Degree of freedom tells us about the number of choices we have while randomly selecting a value from the given dataset. We have a choice, until we reach the last value of dataset in which case we are left with no choice. Hence, the degree of freedom is always one less than the total number of observations.

E.g. In a box containing 10 marbles, one has to choose one marble every time and put it aside. After selecting 9 marbles, there remains a single marble left in the box for which one has no alternative choice.

Hence the degree of freedom is 10-1 = 9.

Inter-quartile range is another measure of dispersion which takes into account the range between the first and the third quartiles. If we place the data in ascending order then the point below which 25% of the values lie is known as the first quartile and the point below which 75% of the values lies is defined as the third quartile. At the centre of inter-quartile range lies the median. Median along with the inter-quartile range has also been used to describe the data.

For categorical data

Binary data can be best represented in the form of a 2 X 2 contingency table which helps to calculate risk reduction, odd's ratio, number needed to treat and also apply required statistical analysis to the data.

E.g. There was an observational study regarding the preventive efficacy of a novel vaccine against influenza given to a community of 1000 individuals. Of the 1000, 550 had received the vaccine. Amongst the total number of cases (400), 230 had not received the vaccine and 170 had received the vaccine.

The 2 × 2 contingency table for this set of data can be made as follows:

	Cases	Controls
Vaccinated	170	380
Not vaccinated	230	220

Such tables can be made for categorical data which is not binary (2 × 3, 3 × 3, 4 × 4 contingency tables). For the ease of understanding, we would deal with binary data.

Odds of an event has the ratio of probability of occurrence of an event to the probability of non-occurrence of the event.

If p is the probability of occurrence of an event then,

Odds of the event $= \dfrac{p}{1 - p}$

So, for the given example, the probability of occurrence of influenza in spite of vaccination is 170/550.

Hence, odds of occurrence of influenza in spite of vaccination is

$\dfrac{170/550}{1 - 170/550} = 170/380$

The probability of occurrence of infection in the absence of vaccination is 230/450.

Hence, the odds of occurrence of influenza in the absence of vaccination is

$\dfrac{230/450}{1 - 230/450} = 230/220$

The ration of the odds of occurrence of infection in spite of vaccination to the odds of occurrence of infection in absence of vaccination can tell us about the protection offered by preventive vaccination. This is nothing but Odd's Ratio (OR).

Odd's Ratio (OR) for occurrence of influenza in spite of vaccination

$$= \dfrac{P_1/(1 - P_1)}{P_2/(1 - P_2)}$$

$$= \dfrac{170/380}{230/220} = \dfrac{170 \times 220}{380 \times 230}$$

$$= 0.42$$

Odd's ratio is often used in the analysis of case-control studies with a rough measure of relative risk.

Relative risk or risk ratio (RR)

Relative risk is defined as the ratio of the risk of occurrence of an event in the experimental group to the risk in the control group.

In the given example, the risk of acquiring influenza infection with vaccination is 170/550 (P_1) and the risk of acquiring influenza infection without vaccination is 230/450 (P_2).

Hence the relative risk is $P_1/P_2 = \dfrac{170/550}{230/450} = 0.6$

The relative risk of less than one indicates that the risk in control group is more than in the experimental group. Relative risk is often used in the cohort studies. Odd's ratio can approximate the relative risk closely in case the absolute risk is low.

Absolute risk reduction (ARR)

This is the difference between the risks in control group and experimental group.

ARR $= P_2 - P_1 = 230/450 - 170/550 = 0.51 - 0.31 = 0.20$ or 20%.

Thus, the absolute risk of acquiring infection is reduced by 20% by prior vaccination.

Number needed to treat (NNT)

Number needed to treat is the number of patients required to be treated in order to prevent occurrence of disease in one patient.

NTT $= 1 / P_1 - P_2$ or $1 / ARR$

For the vaccine example,

NTT = 1/ 0.20 = 5.

Hence, 5 individuals should be prior treated with the vaccine in order to prevent one case of influenza in the future.

Graphical representation of data

Some of the commonly used data display methods are as follows:

- **Dot-plot:** This is useful for displaying a small amount of data.
- **Box-whisker plot**: This is a graphical representation of the median with inter-quartile range. It is useful for comparing the distributions of two datasets and observing any outlier values.

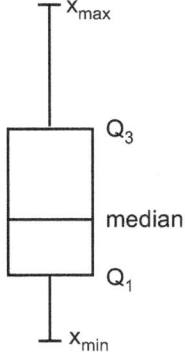

Fig. 10.1: Box-Whisker plot

- **Histograms:** Histograms are useful for representation of continuous data. They can be plotted from a frequency distribution table. If the midpoints of histograms are joined they give a frequency polygon.

- **Bar diagrams:** Bar diagrams are useful for display of discrete variables.

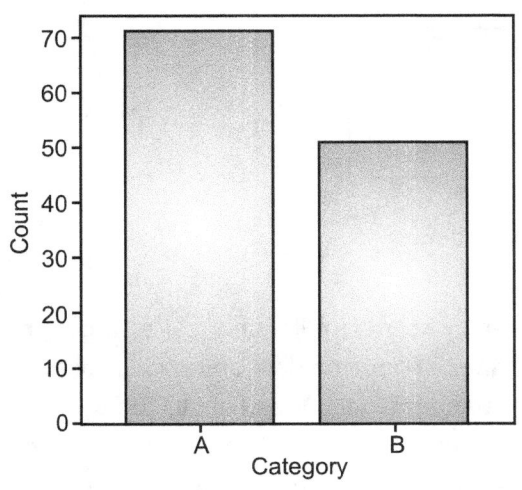

Fig. 10.2(a): Example of Bar Chart   **Fig. 10.2(b): Bar Diagram and Histogram**

- **Pie charts:** Pie charts are used for display of categorical data, especially data in percentages.

Normal distribution

Normal distribution is represented by a family of curves defined uniquely by two parameters namely mean and standard deviation. The curves are bell-shaped and are also known as binomial or Gaussian distribution curves.

Many biological variables have been shown to follow normal distribution. E.g. Heights of girls and boys of a given age. The normal distribution curve tells us about the extent of normal biological variation that exists regarding the given biological variable.

Mean forms the centre of this curve and standard deviations provide the extent of scatter around the mean.

Typically, if observations follow normal distribution curve, then mean ± 1 SD cover about 68% of the observations, mean ± 2 SD cover about 95% of the observations and mean ± 3 SD cover about 99.7% of the total observations. Thus, if data is known to follow normal distribution then with the help of mean and standard deviation, we can estimate the range of values that are expected to include 68%, 95% and 99.7% of the observations (Exact 95% values are distributed within 1.96 times of standard deviations).

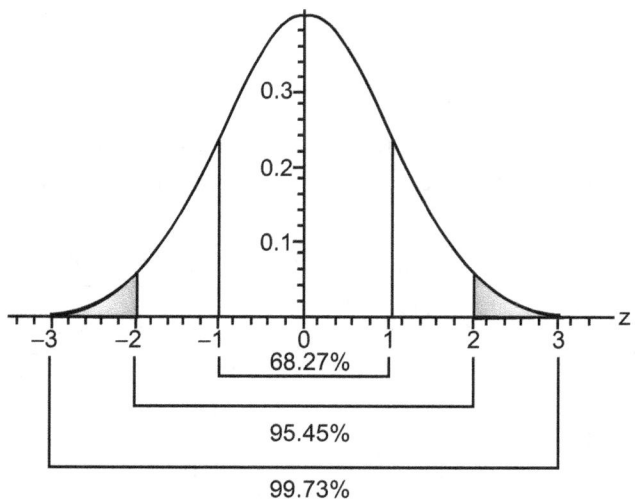

Fig. 10.3: Normal Distribution

A numerical data containing large numbers is generally seen to follow normal distribution. The numerical data that follows normal distribution is called parametric data and numerical data that does not follow normal distribution is called non-parametric data. A categorical data by it's virtue is non-parametric in nature. The importance of knowing whether the data is parametric or non-parametric is that the tests of significance applicable for parametric as well as non-parametric data are different.

For a normally distributed data, the mean, median and mode coincide.

Population and sample

The meaning of population in statistics is different from its meaning in routine English. Population in statistics is the large group of individuals for which a study estimates results. Population is thus an aggregate of cases, creatures, observations and so on.

It may not be possible to count the exact number of individuals in a population.

E.g. the number of adult hypertensives in India.

As a population contains too many individuals, it is not feasible to include all in a study. Instead, a convenient sample is chosen from the given population which is best representative of the population. A well-chosen sample from the population can have parameters similar to the whole population and results derived for the sample can be extrapolated for the whole population. Thus, it becomes important to select the correct sample before conducting any study.

Before drawing any sample, an investigator has to first define parameters for a population e.g. Patients with known diabetes mellitus since at least past 2 years. Randomness is an important attribute while choosing a sample so that every individual in the population has an equal chance of getting selected in the sample. Thus, randomization achieves unbiasedness while choosing a sample.

There are different ways in which a sample may be chosen:

E.g. Every fifth patient may be included in the sample (systematic random sampling).

Males or females, patients of different age groups may be selected in different proportions to as to match their relative proportions in the given population.

Series of samples chosen from a population may differ from the population as well as from one another to some extent. A small sample drawn from a population is less representative of the population. As the sample size grows, it becomes more and more representative of the population. Also, variations between two samples chosen from a population reduce with increase in sample size.

Standard error of mean

Now, we know that series of samples chosen from the same population may vary within a closed limit. If means of these samples are taken, then they are seen to follow normal distribution even if the individual samples are not normally distributed. This is known as "central limit theorem."

If we treat these series of means as a sample and derive standard deviation for the same, this will represent variation between the means of various samples. This value is given the name "standard error of mean" (SE). This tells us how closely the samples are distributed.

If standard deviation for a given sample is SD and the number of observations are n, then SE can be calculated as follows:

$$SE = SD / \sqrt{n}$$

Although this is a hypothetical calculation, it tells us about the range in which a sample mean can vary if repeated random samples are taken from the same population. Again, with large n, the SE reduces.

Just like SE for mean, SE can also be calculated for proportions.

If p represents one percentage and 100-p another then

SE for proportion or percentage $= \sqrt{p(100-p)/n}$

SE can be used to study significance of difference between two mean or two proportions.

Difference between Standard Deviation and Standard Error of Mean

A standard error is often used instead of standard deviation while describing a dataset, only because it looks more precise. However, standard error is not the correct measure to describe the variation of values in the given dataset. In fact, it estimates the variation of the sample mean from the actual population mean. Hence, it is incorrect to use it in place of standard deviation. Standard deviation is used to describe data where as standard error (or confidence interval) is used to describe the outcome of a study.

P value, reference range and confidence interval

We now know that in normal distribution, the range between mean ± 2 SD contains about 95% of the observations and 5% of the observations lie outside this range. This provides basis for the concept of statement of probability or p value.

So, if we randomly choose an observation from the given sample distributed normally, there is a 95% probability or chance that the observation would lie within the 95% range and there is 5% probability that the observation would lie outside this range.

E.g. In a sample of 100 patients, the mean fasting blood glucose is 115 mg/dl with the standard deviation of 15 mg/dl.

The calculation of mean ± 2 SD generates lower and upper limits for 95% range as in the following example:

Lower limit = 115 − (2 × 15) = 85 mg/dl

Upper limit = 115 + (2 × 15) = 145 mg/dl

Thus, for 95% of the individuals in the given sample, fasting blood glucose value would lie within the range of 85-145 mg/dl. There is a 5% chance (p = 0.05) that an individual would have a fasting blood glucose outside this range.

For biological variables that are distributed normally, 95% reference range is taken as the normal range and something that lies outside this range is taken as abnormal. The reference range can be widened to 99% by taking into consideration values up to 3 standard deviations.

Confidence Interval

Just in the way standard deviations can give us reference ranges, standard errors are used to calculate confidence intervals. Mean ± 2 standard errors give us confidence intervals. Thus, if series of samples are taken from a given population then 95% of the means would lie within this interval and the common mean would be close to the population mean. Thus, confidence interval helps us estimate the difference between sample mean and population mean.

Confidence intervals can also be counted for percentages. Although it is possible to calculate confidence intervals for all values, it's use should be restricted only while describing the best outcome of a study. Confidence intervals can be used for assessing difference between means or difference between proportions.

What is null hypothesis?

Before starting any research study, one has to assume a null hypothesis, which states that there is no difference between the study groups under consideration.

E.g. If we compare the diastolic blood pressures of obese men and men with body mass index in normal limits, then the null hypothesis states that there is no significant difference between the diastolic blood pressures of the two groups. At the end of the experiment, we either accept or reject the null hypothesis. If there is a significant difference between the two groups, then the null hypothesis is rejected and when the study does not detect any significant difference, then the null hypothesis is accepted.

Now, what is meant by "significance"? Even if we choose two samples from the identical population, there is bound to be a difference between the means of the two samples as a result of chance or random variation.

In the given example, whether the difference between the mean diastolic blood pressures of obese and lean men is as a result of random variation or there is a true difference? To determine this, we need to define the confidence limits or interval.

Within 95% confidence interval, the random variation would be possible between mean -2 SE and mean + 2 SE of the reference sample; in this case the group of men with normal body weight. If the mean of the second group lies outside this range, then we can say that there is a 'significant' difference between the groups.

However, it needs to be noted that acceptance of null hypothesis does not mean that the two groups are 'equivalent'. It just means that the study failed to detect any significant difference between the two groups. Statistical principles for setting of null hypothesis testing for equivalence and non-inferiority trials are different from that of superiority trials.

P value and significance level

P value defines nothing but the probability of occurrence of an event. It is designated by the letter p. P value is an important concept in biostatistics which tells us about whether the difference observed between two samples is a real difference or just by chance.

Suppose there are two samples with different means. We have to find out whether they arise from two different populations or the difference observed is just a result of random sampling from the same or identical population (by chance). If the p value is 0.01 it means there is 1% chance of getting this difference despite the two samples originating from same or identical population. On the other hand, there is 99% chance that the two samples have originated from two different populations.

At 95% confidence intervals, the p value of 0.05 is taken as the significance level.

The concept of confidence intervals can be used to find out whether the difference between means of two samples is statistically significant. For this, we need to know how many times of the SE does the difference between means represent. This ratio is denoted by the alphabet "z". Different values of z represent different probabilities of occurrence of event by chance.

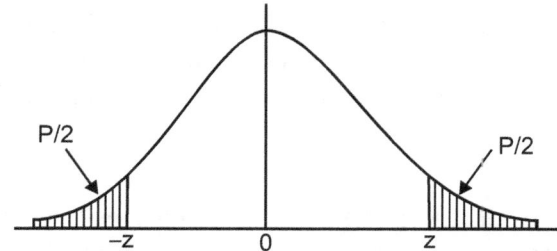

Fig. 10.4: Z Values and Two Sided Probability Values

E.g. 1.96 value of z represents a two-sided p value of 0.05 as the 3.29 value of z represents p value of 0.001.

If in the example of obese and normal men, the difference between means is 10 mm Hg and the SE of the sample of individuals with normal body weight is 2 mm Hg, and $z = 10/2 = 5$, then the difference between the means is five times SE. This will represent the p value of even less than 0.001 which means that this event is very rare to occur by chance and the difference is statistically significant.

Types of Errors and Power of the Study

Type I error

As we have set our limits at 95% confidence intervals, there is still 1 in 20 possibility (5%) that we may be wrong or the difference detected is just as result of chance. That means, we have detected a significant difference between the two groups when there is actually no difference. This is known as type I error where we wrongly reject the null hypothesis when it is actually true. Type I error depends upon the confidence limits chosen and the levels at which it is declared significant is known as type I error rate or α. At 95% confidence limits, α is 5%. At 99% confidence limits, α is 1%. Lower is α, lesser is the possibility of false positive results.

Type II error and power

On the other hand, type II error is said to have occurred when there is a true difference between the two groups and our statistical test fails to detect it. In other words, the null hypothesis is false but it is wrongly accepted. Type II error represents probability of false negative results. It is represented by the alphabet β. Now, $(1-\beta)$ represents the probability that the null hypothesis is rejected when there is a true difference. This is known as power of the study and it represents the ability of the study to detect a true difference. The most commonly used values of power are 0.8, 0.85 or 0.9. The most common reason for type II error is small size of the study.

Table 10.2: Type I, type II errors and power

Test Results	Null Hypothesis	
	False	True
Significant	Power	Type I
Non-significant	Type II	----

Calculation of sample size

Calculation of sample size is one of the most important aspects of biostatistics. A sample size for the study has to be calculated right at the planning stage. Adequate sample size powers the study to detect a desired difference or effect size and also avoids recruitment of large patient population that would lead to wastage of resources. Calculation of the sample size depends upon following factors: α, β, variability of the given data and effect size.

Amongst these variables, α and β are usually assumed as 5% and 20% for majority of the studies. A larger effect size will require smaller sample size and vice-versa. Determination of effect size is very critical which is based on the previous literature about the efficacy of the comparator group, the clinical relevance of the difference and availability of research funds. E.g. For a clinical trial on hypertension, an effect size of 4 mm Hg would not be of clinical relevance. In short, calculation of effect size not just involves statistics but also takes into consideration the scientific goal, ethical concerns and practicability of the project.

Variance of the data can be calculated from past studies or running a pilot study. Variance of the data is directly proportional to the sample size.

A simple formula for calculation of sample size at 5% α and 80% power is as follows:

Sample size = $16 \, \sigma^2/d^2$

Where σ is variability of the data and d is the effect size.

Sample sizes can be calculated from various statistical software that require filling of the above-mentioned variables. This also requires information about the study design or the types of data being analysed.

E.g. Epistat, GraphPad Statemate, WinPep Compare 2.

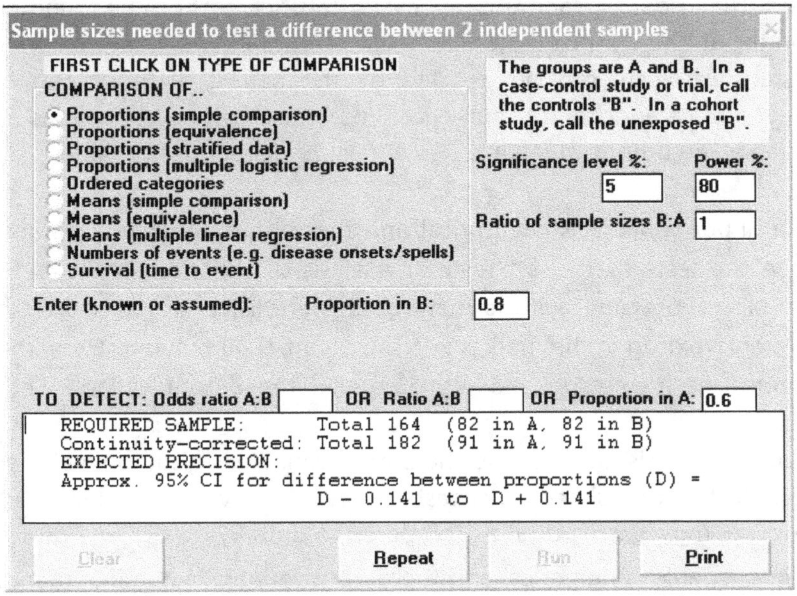

Fig. 10.5: An example of sample size calculation in WinPep Compare 2 for proportions

Calculation of sample size should involve the primary efficacy variable and should be large enough to detect a clinically significant difference in the primary efficacy variable.

At times, the sample size is already fixed due to budget restraint. In such case, do we need sample size calculations? The answer is yes. This is to show whether sample size used is adequate enough to detect a clinical relevant effect size at 80% power and 5% alpha error. This can be called a retrograde or post-hoc power-calculation.

So far, we discussed the sample size calculations for superiority trials. The process of sample size calculation for non-inferiority or equivalence trials is beyond the scope of this book.

Hypothesis testing

Before analysis of any study data, one must know the primary study hypothesis based on which the study is designed. Hypothesis reflects into the study design as well as the statistical analysis of the study data. A study can ideally test only one hypothesis.

Steps in testing of the hypothesis are as follows:

- Select a research design and sample size appropriate to the hypothesis to be tested.
- Decide the test of statistical significance that is to be applied.
- Determine the p value from the results one has observed.
- Compare it with the critical value of p, say 0.05 or 0.01.
- If the p value is less than the critical value, reject the null hypothesis.

Choice of statistical test

The choice of statistical test depends upon a number of factors. Statistical tests can be applied to those studies which involve hypothesis testing i.e. comparison, association, correlation. No statistical tests can be applied for epidemiological studies designed only find out the incidence or prevalence of a condition.

This discussion is aimed to help the readers to assess which test should be applied for the given type of data. The in-depth elaboration of every statistical test can be found elsewhere.

Choice based on input and output variables

Choice of statistical tests can be decided by the nature of input and output variable i.e. whether they are categorical or numerical in nature. Input variable is also known as independent variable and output variable is also known as dependent variable.

Some examples:

1. When the input variable is categorical and the output variable is parametric numerical data, then the tests used are t tests or analysis of variance (ANOVA). E.g. Decrease in diastolic blood pressure with a new antihypertensive as compared to an existing antihypertensive drug in the market in a sample of 1000 patients. Here, the input variable is categorical i.e. new drug and old drug and the output variable i.e. diastolic BP is numerical.

2. If the input variable is nominal and the output variable is also nominal then the test used is Chi-square test or Fisher's exact test. E.g. How many patients achieved fasting blood glucose < 126 mg% with drug A as compared to drug B?

3. If the input variable is numerical and the output variable is nominal then the test used is logistic regression.

4. If both the input and output variables are numerical, the test used is linear regression (if parametric) and Spearman's or Pearson's coefficient (if non-parametric).

Comparison of two or more groups

For most of the comparative efficacy studies, the input variable is categorical. In such cases, following are some important factors deciding the choice of statistical test:

- Objective of the study – comparison, association, validation or assessment of survival trends (cancer studies).
- Number of study groups.
- Whether the output variable is paired or unpaired?
- Whether the output variable is categorical or numerical?
- If numerical whether parametric or non-parametric?

Based on these questions, commonly used statistical tests for comparison are shown in Table 10.3.

Table 10.3: Choice of statistical tests for paired and unpaired data

Type of output variable	Comparison of unpaired data	
	2 groups	*> 2 groups*
Numerical-parametric	Unpaired t test	ANOVA
Numerical-nonparametric	Mann-Whitney	Kriskal Wallis
Categorical	Chi-square (2x2)/Fisher's exact	Chi-square for trend
	Comparison of paired data	
	2 groups	*> 2 groups*
Numerical-parametric	Paired t test	Repeated measures ANOVA
Numerical-nonparametric	Wilcoxon sign rank	Friedman
Categorical	McNemar	Cochran' Q

In case of multiple comparisons e.g. ANOVA , the initial test is followed by a post-hoc test like Tukey's test or Bonferroni's test or Dunn's test. The initial test results tell us whether there is any significant difference between any of the groups and post-hoc test gives the individual p values between each pair of groups.

Chi-square and Fisher's exact test are the most commonly used tests for categorical data. But, Fisher's test is applicable when n < 40.

Testing relations between two or more variables

The degree of association is measured by a correlation coefficient. E.g. Pearson's correlation coefficient. The choice of statistical tests for association are as follows:

When both variables are parametric – Pearson's correlation coefficient.

One of the variable is nonparametric - Spearman's or Kendall's coefficient.

For 2×2 categorical data – Odd's ratio or relative risk.

For categorical data larger than 2×2 – Logistic regression, Chi-square for trend.

Assessment of survival trends

Assessment of difference between survival trends is required to be assessed in mainly oncology studies.

The statistical tests used are Mantel- Haenszel test in case of 2 groups and Log rank test or Mantel-Cox test in case more than 2 groups are compared.

How to assess normality of the given data

A categorical data is always non-parametric, whereas numerical data needs to assessed for normality. Usually samples more than 100 in size approximate normal distribution and can always be analysed with parametric tests.

Some methods to analyse normality are:

✓ Mean, median and mode are very close to each.

✓ Distribution of the sample data simulates normal distribution curve.

✓ Goodness of fit (Shapiro-Wilk test, Kolmogorov-Smirnov test).

✓ Samples have the same variance i.e. drawn from the same population (homogeneity of variances assessed through Levene's test).

Statistical packages

Microsoft Excel

Excel is a common and easy to use function of Microsoft Office that can be used for capturing data in spreadsheets for graphical representation and also for simple statistical tests. Excel is most useful for data presentation and statistical analysis.

E.g. calculation of mean, standard deviation, standard error of mean, percentage.

GraphPad

Graphpad is an extremely user-friendly software for beginners in statistics. Graphpad Instat is used for simple, commonly used statistical analysis including comparison of means, correlation and regression as well for analysing contingency tables. The datasheets are compatible with Excel. It provides the choices of statistical tests for the given type of data. Graphpad StatMate is a useful and easy to use software for calculation of sample sizes.

SPSS

SPSS is another useful software that has been used since decades now. It has datasheets that are compatible with Excel and the results as well as the graphs can be easily exported into PowerPoint presentations or word documents. However, users need basic training for operating SPSS. SPSS can be used for advanced statistical analysis.

SAS

SAS is a standard software that has been used commonly just like SPSS. It's advantage is that it can handle large datasets and can do comprehensive statistical analysis.

REFERENCES

1. Swinscow T.D.V., Campbell M.J. Statistics at square one. Tenth edition, 2003, Viva publications.

2. Chan Y.H., Biostatistics 101: Data presentation. Singapore Med J 2003 Vol 44(6) : 280-285.

3. Length R.V. Some practical guidelines for effective sample size determination. Downloaded from http://www.stat.uiowa.edu/techrep/tr303.pdf accessed 11-11-11.

✷✷✷

Chapter ... 11

CLINICAL DATA MANAGEMENT

"Everything that can be counted does not necessarily count; everything that counts cannot necessarily be counted".
Albert Einstein

INTRODUCTION

A huge amount of data with respect to the drug or device is generated in the clinical trial phase of a drug development process. All the data generated by the trial and trial-related data is known as Clinical data. Pharmaceutical companies invest a lot of money for these trials. So for any company, this is an asset on the basis of which the company would get approval to conduct further trials or market the drug. Review and approval of new drugs by regulatory agencies is dependent upon a trust that the clinical trial data presented is of sufficient integrity and supports the stated conclusions.

Drug development is becoming more and more global. There are parallel multi-centric and multinational trials going on worldwide, leading to simultaneous regulatory submissions. With increase in globalization and consequent need for increased data management expertise needed for global submissions, data management organisations are being set up all over the world.

Clinical Data Management refers to compiling all of the data and evidence collected during the trial. Once the data is collected, it has to be reviewed, processed and verified, so that it is accurate, reproducible and truely representative of the drug/device.

If the data is well-recorded and well-processed, the probability of a drug or a device to be approved for marketing increases. Therefore, data management has become a critical element in the steps to prepare a regulatory submission and obtain approval to market a treatment.

Data management entails:

- Planning the data needs of the study.
- CRF Designing.
- Data collection.
- Data entry.
- Data validation and checking.

- Data manipulation.

- File backup.

- Data file documentation.

- Data Security.

- Quality Assurance.

- Data Retention and Record Keeping/Archiving.

The locked database undergoes statistical analysis after which it is ready to be submitted to the regulatory authority for approval.

Processes used to support clinical data must be clearly defined and documented. Before a CDM unit gets functional, a clinical data management plan must be prepared so that every process is in place and there aren't any ambiguities.

Traditionally, paper case records were used. But over past five years, much attention has been given to the use of computers for medical records management. Many software companies have started developing software to capture clinical trial data. These companies also customize the CRF as per the client's requirements, providing CRF as required by the client to capture protocol-specific data.

Paper CRF's:

Paper Case Records Forms (CRFs) are used to collect data generated during the course of the trial. Data from the source documents is transcribed on Paper CRF's. The CRF's are then sent to the data management team for cleaning and verification. Any discrepancies and inconsistencies found in the data are pointed out by the data processors. They fill the Data Clarification Form (DCF) and send it back to the site. The site responds to the query and the data processors would close the query if the answer has been satisfactory with respect to the protocol and sponsor-specific SOP. If the answer does not fulfil the criteria, the query would be re-issued to the site for some more clarification. Most of the paper case record forms have been replaced by electronic case record forms, but a few companies still use paper CRF's because of it's its ease of use (for investigators who might not be very savvy with the electronic software) and also because of low cost as it does not involve much investment as compared to e-CRF's.

e-CRF's:

Electronic case record forms are widely used to capture electronic records. Software companies customize the software for the Sponsor as per the trial data required to be captured.

Data Management Software

Clinical Trials conducted in the past were small and simple, and the data generated was small in volume. It was possible to analyze the data using calculators and even log-books. After computers became freely available, trial sponsors began using packages like Lotus and later MS Excel for data analysis. Use of computers made it easier to arrange and analyze data. Subsequently, trials became more complicated and newer software were used to manage data.

The present-day trials have 5000 plus subjects and the complexity of trials has gone up. Every subject is subjected to 150 tests at the least. Additionally, these tests have to be conducted generally before midway in the trial, and at the end of the trial. This means that there would be around 2.25 million data points. This volume of data cannot be handled manually and nor by software programmes like Lotus and Excel. The special software needed was provided by packages like Oracle, Symetric, Progeny etc., while statistical assistance was provided by packages like SPSS and SAS. Some software went beyond just managing data, they managed the trials too.

Almost all clinical software systems are also highly adaptable and extremely user-friendly. Since medical data changes frequently, which allow users to customize them to update and replace data efficiently. Any clinical data management software system that works in conjunction with other systems is often invaluable, since two or more systems can communicate without any effort on the part of a software user.

In some cases, a clinical data management software system may also be used to store vital patient information. When it comes to managing patient medications, these systems can be life-saving. Very often, patient medications become mixed resulting in a dangerous dosage, or unforeseen side-effects. These common errors rarely occur when specialized patient software has been utilized.

As stated, another advantage of data management software (they are often called trial management software or clinical data management systems) is that they help in the management of the trial too. The software helps in scheduling visits, planning projects and even keeps track of payment schedules. These versatile software are expensive but they make the life of trial managers easy by providing them skilled assistance.

Choosing the right clinical data management software system for any medical facility can be challenging, as so many different options exist. While some software may be universal, specialized software often proves to be a far better choice. This way, a hospital or clinic can customize software to suit trial specific needs. In addition, some types of generalized software may include complex programme additions that are not necessary for all medical facilities. Some examples of software tools available for data management are InForm®, Oracle Clinical®, RAVE®, Clintrial®, and Pheedit®. Also there are software specialized to capture safety data. Softwares like ARGUS®, AERS (Adverse Event Reporting Systems) are used for safety of data. AE and SAE reconciliation is then done between the Clinical data management system and safety software. These tools can be customized as per the protocol requirements.

Desirable Features of Clinical Data Management Software:

- It should be user friendly.
- It should have audit trial functionality for each and every update made from the first data entry till the last data entry, irrespective of the number of entries in the middle.
- It should also capture deletions and erased (the data erased after submitting, not the items erased before submitting the data in the system) data in the audit trial.

- It should have functions like report generation, view outstanding queries and view closed queries.

- It should have functionalities like view list of patients along with their visit status, list of patients per site.

- The CRF pages should be arranged in a logical sequence and it should be easy to search a particular page of CRF on the screen.

- It should get updated as soon as data is entered in the system.

- It should have all the data elements required to be captured as per the protocol.

- It should be able to retain all the data if there is a change in the version of the software or a change control.

- The software provider should have 24x7 IT support for helping users with technical difficulties, like account-lock, unable to enter data, or system crash.

- It should have features like auto-save so that if there is power cut, the data that was entered remains, without requiring the person to re-type it.

- It should have a portal which would contain essential documents like protocol, IB along with their amendments. Also it should have a user manual for the use of software with FAQ's on how to enter data, edit data, delete data, submit data and update data.

- It should have spelling check functionality.

- It should have an eraser icon, otherwise the backspace button has to be used, which deletes one character at a time or the words need to be selected and then deleted, both of which are time-consuming. Instead, an erase icon would save time, which on a click would delete all the matter written in that data field. This is especially useful for AE or SAE narrative or comments.

- It should have features like allowing a comment to be written in addition to the text boxes on the CRF. This could be utilized by the investigator in case if he feels some more data is essential to be captured other than the data already captured in the software.

- Radio buttons and drop-down boxes should be used, which make the data easy to capture rather than having empty test boxes everywhere for the investigator to fill by typing. This would make data entry easier and faster.

For example: Discrete value groups like Gender could be represented in two forms:

1. Use of radio buttons

Male   ○
Female   ○

2.   Use of drop down menu

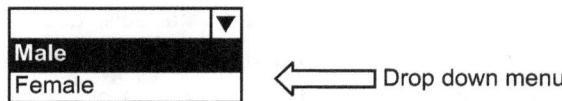

*   Preferably, open queries, closed queries, incomplete data should be indicated with different colours. For example, In InForm® tool (version 4.5) an open query is indicated with a red traffic light, closed query is indicated with a green traffic light and yellow indicates incomplete or missing data. A white light or a null traffic light indicates blank CRF pages which have been initiated but not filled. This helps in having a quick view of all the patients and visually gives the status of pending or completed work to the data processing team. So the screening page consisting of all the patients and their modules have a traffic light. The colours would indicate which forms are completed, which need resolutions and which need to be queried for missing data.

*   It should comply with 21CFR Part 11 which is now a regulatory requirement.

*   It should be web-based and since sites and data processors would be working on the software for many hours per day, the software should have an appealing look to the eye, so that interest can be sustained for longer time.

*   It should have features like data transfer into different formats.

*   It should have security and data-encryption/decryption features for safe data transfer. (Would be dealt with in detail in Data Security section)

It is very difficult to find single software with all the desired features. Most importantly, the software is tailor-made for a particular protocol, so that no data is left un-captured. The Software should contain all the required elements, since it is a costly affair to get the eCRF revised, if any data elements are found missing. So, CRF designing, and programming edit checks should be done simultaneously and dummy data should be entered to see if it is functioning in the fashion it was expected to. It's up to the companies to decide which tool would be the best for their protocol-specific needs.

Validation of Software: The task is not over once the software has been selected as the software has to be validated, without which the costliest software would be redundant. Regulatory authorities demand clinical data management systems to be validated prior to clinical trial use. Software validation plans are prepared and followed extensively. FDA defines validation as "Establishing documented evidence which provides a high degree of assurance that a specific process will consistently produce a product meeting its predetermined specifications and quality attributes." By validating software, evidence is established that the software is fulfilling protocol-specific needs; it is working the way it is supposed to and will continue to do during the entire trial process. Software testing is therefore a necessary activity.

The validation process starts at the very beginning of system development or implementation when information is collected on the design and intent of the system. Before it is released, the system is thoroughly tested to document it's working and problems. When it is in production use, information on how the application should be used (manuals, guidelines, standard operating procedures [SOPs]) further helps assure continued quality of the product of the application. Usually, dummy data or mock data is entered to check whether it is functioning as intended before the software goes live. SOP's are prepared for data validation and validation checks are run throughout the process. The date of validation and validation reports are well documented.

DATA ENTRY METHODS

Introduction:

Once clinical trial data has been collected, it has to be transferred to a computer system or software for easy accessibility, review and final storage. The data transcribed from the paper CRF to computer system is known as Data Entry. Data entry can be done in several ways. All methods have their pros and cons. It is up to the pharmaceutical company to decide what their objective is and which data entry method would help them achieve their objective. Data entry could be done manually or it could be automated by using an Optical Character Recognition system (OCR).

Regardless of the method used to enter data, following things should be kept in mind while choosing a data entry method.

1. Selecting a method to transcribe data.

2. Determine how much the data should match the CRF.

3. Create processes to detect and deal with problematic data.

4. Editing data and making changes without losing credibility and accuracy.

5. Quality control of the data entry process.

Entering data:

Transcribing the data could be done by the following methods:

A. First Pass Entry

1. Single data entry with heads up.

2. Single data entry with heads down.

B. Second Pass Entry

1. Double data entry with second person resolving discrepancies.

2. Double data entry with third part reconciliation of discrepancies.

3. OCR as first entry with one or more subsequent entry or review passes.

Irrespective of the method used to transcribe the data and transcription errors reduced to a minimum, there remains some variation in what an accurate transcription means. Data entry guidelines and the company specific SOP's should mention whether the data should be an accurate duplicate of source or some variations are permitted.

A. First Pass Data Entry:

It refers to data being entered to database for first time. Data entry operator enters all data of each document and releases work item. It can be done in two ways heads up and heads down.

1. Single data entry with heads up:

In this method of data entry, the data entry personnel reviews the data while entering it and raises a flag in case of any discrepancies or inconsistencies found. They have the liberty to enter comments called as "Operator Comments", for a particular data point. Operator comments are entered when data entry operators are not sure about any illegible or unclear text. Also, operator comments can also be recorded if data is recorded in an erroneous way,. It is more time-consuming than heads down. If data is entered by this method, it doesn't go to the second pass for entry as this is the first and the final data entered.

2. Single data entry with heads down:

In this method of data entry, the data entry personnel enters the data without reviewing. The data is entered as seen on the CRF. Data entry is faster as they follow natural flow of CRF.

This method emphasizes on number of keystrokes made and specific training is provided on database to be utilized. Only a few checks are provided while entry is made, for e.g., only numeric values entered in a text field where number is expected and no text entered. The aim is to enter the data with great speed and accuracy (with less typographical error). Any discrepancies or inconsistencies would be checked by the second data entry operator.

B. Second Pass Data Entry:

Second pass entry is done by another data entry operator, following the first entry. When he is entering data, the system gives an alert notification if he enters anything different from first pass.

Discrepancies can be resolved by second data entry personnel or by a third person. The second or the third person would confirm the correct value and enter it.

1. Second data entry with second person resolving the discrepancies:

The second entry operator resolves mismatches. After first pass entry, the second entry operator selects a set of data and begins to re-enter it. If the entry application detects a mismatch, it stops the second operator who decides what the correct value should be or whether to register a discrepancy to be resolved. This method is known as second pass with heads up.

2. Second data entry with third person resolving the discrepancies:

In this double-entry method, the two entries are made and both are stored. After both passes have been completed, a comparison programme checks the entries and identifies any differences. Typically, a third person reviews the report of differences and makes a decision as to whether there is a clear correct answer (for example, because one entry had a typo error) or whether a discrepancy must be registered because the data value is illegible or is in some other way unclear. This method of double entry is sometimes known as "blind" double entry since the operators have no knowledge of each other's work.

Usually, first pass with heads down and second pass with heads up or blind double entry are the preferred methods for data entry. The advantages of these methods are that they are fast, more reliable and give nearly accurate data. This becomes first quality check in CDM process. Both DEO and system contribute to this first quality check in CDM process.

3. OCR as first entry with one or more subsequent entry or review passes:

Optical Character Recognition (OCR) is a technique whereby software converts scanned image to machine-readable and editable text. It is equivalent to keying-in text by hand. OCR is used as a first pass entry. Any data like number scales or text boxes which could not be detected by the computer is filled in manually. A second DEO visually checks the values entered by the OCR. The advantage of this method is that it saves a lot of time, as it is an automated first pass entry.

Dealing with Problem Data:

Data-entry problems are bound to happen irrespective of however well a CRF may be designed. Problems may be due to illegible data, or confusion in the mind of the person entering the data. Methods to deal with these problem data are usually given in the company specific data entry guidelines.

Illegible Fields:

Illegible writing on CRF is always a problem for data entry staff, CRA's, data processors and data managers. While trying to deal with such data, data entry people should have a pre-defined method to deal with such data. Data entry guidelines should clearly state, whether DEO's are allowed to make educated guesses for illegible fields, or can the CRA's take a decision on the available medical information.

If data is illegible, data clarification form is filled and sent to the investigator via monitor for review and resolution.

Modifying data:

After data entry, a lot of errors would be noticed which would require modification of the data. This could be due to flags raised by data entry operators, CRA's or data processors. These would be resolved and then updated by the investigators. For paper CRF's, where queries are resolved on the data clarification forms, a responsible person should transcribe the data from DCF to CRF. Ideally, a person designated should be allowed to do the data changes. In many organisations, data-modification privileges are given to specific people only. Whenever a data point is modified, the old value as well as the new value should be visible alongwith the username of the person who brought about the change. Usually companies prefer having an audit trail, which is a record of activities performed on a data point. It records what data is entered, when it was entered, when it was deleted, altered or updated.

Electronic Data Capture

Data capture can be defined as a collection of clinically-significant data by investigators for clinical trials, on behalf of the sponsor in a sequential manner, to process the same and generate reports at a later stage for submission to regulatory authorities for various purposes is known as data capture.

Data capture can be of two types:

*   Paper based data capture.

*   Electronic base capture

Paper-based data capture:

It is the most widely used form of data capture. In this, traditional paper Case Report Forms (CRF's) are used. Data is entered manually by site personnel on three-part NCR paper CRF's. One copy is retained with the investigation site and two copies are sent to Sponsor or CRO's Data Management department.

Advantages:

1. Easy to enter data.

2. Requires simple training.

3. Logistically patient's bedside may not be the right place for a computer to enter data.

Disadvantages:

1. Since data need to be archived as required by regulations, storing huge amount of paper is a problem.

2. It is time-consuming as data is entered on paper CRF's and if there are any errors or illegible data, a DCF has to be filled, sent to the site and wait for their response. So the query turn around time is long.

3. Cost of printing and distribution/ imaging if applicable.

4. Lack of real time reporting as the data entered has to reach the sponsor for review and then action has to be taken.

5. It becomes slightly difficult to maintain confidentiality of the drug etc. as chances of accidental disclosure of information to an unauthorized person are high.

Electronic based capture:

Electronic Data Capture (EDC) systems deliver clinical trial data from the investigation sites to the sponsor through electronic means rather than paper CRF's. The site enters the data in an electronic case record form. The site may first record the information on paper and then enter it in electronic form. The paper in this case may be normal site source documents or special worksheets provided by the sponsor; the paper is not a CRF and is not sent to the sponsor.

Before EDC evolved, there was a pre-EDC era where Remote Data Entry (RDE) came into being and took over the paper technology. RDE, which can be done both online and offline became more popular due to the advantages it offered. The early RDE systems used "thick-client" software which is software installed locally on a laptop to collect the patient data. The system could then use a modem connection over an analog phone line to periodically transmit the data back to the sponsor and to collect questions from the sponsor that the medical staff would need to answer.

Though effective, RDE brought with it several shortcomings as well.

➢ Hardware (e.g. a laptop or computer) needed to be deployed, installed, and supported at every investigation site.

➢ It was expensive for sponsors and complicated for medical staff.

➢ This model resulted in a proliferation of laptop computers at many investigation sites that participated in more than one research study simultaneously.

Rise of the Internet in the mid-1990s gave obvious solutions to some of these issues. One of which was the adoption of web-based software that could be accessed using existing computers at the investigation sites. EDC represents this new class of software.

EDC is defined as any electronic capture of trial data including electronic patient notes, IVR systems, eCRF's, patient diaries, centralized lab reporting, etc. In most current EDC systems, the site is online with a central computer and the data is stored only on a central computer. As data is entered, eCRF gets updated. Certain software have the feature of changing the refresh time of the web pages. The refresh interval is shortened during timeliness and before database lock.

EDC systems are optimized for site activities during a clinical trial and typically feature:

- eCRF's for the entry of data.
- Single-field and cross-field checks on the data.
- Tools to allow sites to review and resolve discrepancies.
- Features permitting the Sponsor, data management team to raise manual discrepancies while reviewing data.
- True electronic signatures, so that the investigator can sign for the data.
- Reports about patients for the sites and reports for the sponsor about sites.
- A variety of ways to extract data for review and analysis.
- Tools to track queries to check status of their resolution for the sponsor and the data management team; and to check the number of outstanding queries for the site to answer.
- An audit trail tracking all the events in a chronological order.
- Tools to pull out reports like number of patients enrolled, number of withdrawals, number of visits completed by each patients, deaths, AE reports, SAE reports, missing data reports and query metrics.

Pre-requisites of EDC system:

1. **Study set up:** In traditional paper based studies, patient enrollment can begin and trial related procedures can be started once the CRF has been designed and approved. But if EDC is being used, then the systems have to be set at the sites, the sponsors end and for the data management team. In EDC systems, no patients can be enrolled until the entire application has been built, tested, and approved. The application also includes all of the key patient-based edit checks.

2. **Training:** After the database system has been set up, sites have to be trained for data entry. Data management team is also trained for issuing queries and submitting them in the system, for generating reports etc.

3. **Data Repositories:** Usually these EDC systems support multiple trials, so its essential to have a data repository, so that the data can be stored and archived. Usually, data go into a server computer which may be the sponsor's or one outsourced to a vendor. Usually, sponsors prefer a vendor managing it, as EDC applications require a sophisticated technical infrastructure to support high-bandwidth access to the server with 24/7 availability and very high quality security and emergency planning. Many companies do not have the expertise to provide this kind of environment.

4. **Coding:** The medical terminologies used to describe the AE's, SAE's need to be coded in a standard known and accepted terminology. EDC systems may support robust automatic coding and maintenance of synonyms and provide tools for making manual assignments of codes.

5. **Multiple data streams:** Data comes in not only from the sites but from many other sources like laboratories (both local and central), data from IVRS, e-diaries or patient diaries. Data obtained from all these sources should reconcile with the patient data present on the eCRF.

6. **Access administration:** Only authorized persons have the data entry and data edit rights.

7. **Data Security:** Protection against data manipulation, back-ups and contingency plans and readability of current and previous data after data edit.

8. **User support:** Adequate training for users. Support "hot line" of the provider for any software related issues or login failures etc.

9. **UAT Testing:** Sponsor companies should emphasize on user acceptance testing. Any group (vendor, host, or Sponsor) that builds the EDC application for a study is responsible for validating it. Their process usually requires a user acceptance test (UAT) whereby the company using the system tests the application for that particular study. It is critical that the Sponsor performs such a test and goes over the study application thoroughly before it is released to the site. If a CRO is conducting the study using an EDC system, the CRO has to perform the UAT for the sponsor.

While working on an EDC system, data is easily accessible immediately after the data is entered. The data coming in from the sites is very active in the sense that it can be entered, changed, reviewed, and monitored nearly all at once. This impacts not only data managers but also clinical research associates (CRA's) and biostatisticians.

The following decisions need to be taken before data processing starts:

- Should data management or biostatistics team decide on the dataset specification.
- Should data processing start after source data verification is over or simultaneously.
- Should data transfer/extraction be done by data management or the biostatistics team and frequency and interval for the same.
- Should coding would be done by DM or some other team delegated by the Sponsor and who would coordinate with the coding queries.
- Who would decide whether the data is clean, the DM team or biostatistics team.

Advantages of EDC:

The main advantage of using EDC is not data entry, because data would be entered in the same way as in paper, except that the data is entered at the site and it is entered only once. The main advantage of EDC is discrepancy management. It hastens the process of query resolution by scrappingthe DCF's. Instead, as the data is entered on the eCRF, it is visible to the data managers and they can raise queries on the eCRF. Site would review outstanding queries and reply to them. The data management team would then action the queries, either close them if the answer is satisfactory or reissue them if there are still some inconsistencies. In this way EDC reduces the query turn around time. It makes it possible for CRA to raise queries directly on the CRF if there is any inconsistency between source data and CRF, that too as soon as the data is captured on the CRF. The Sponsor can review the status of the study online, pull reports and set prospective milestones.

Another advantage of using EDC is that there are edit checks in place, so data is checked automatically against predetermined standards during data entry itself. This alerts the site of possible errors in data entry. So it leads to faster correction of issues and immediate site education. The site would be more vigilant while entering similar data for another patient. Many EDC systems also include screen level checks that look at data across the fields on an eCRF screen and some can also do more complex checks across screens. Manual queries are also raised by features like aggregate checks run over larger datasets, listing reviews, coding, analysis of lab data. Due to edit checks, SAS checks and manual queries the data generated is of high quality and is available faster for review and processing, thereby faster submission also. EDC shortens the time between 'last patient last visit' and 'database lock'.

Common problems with EDC:

Companies that use EDC feel that it hastens the process of achieving clean data and so is cost effective and preferred over paper-based studies. So companies that have not ventured into EDC have realized the advantages of EDC and are trying to shift to EDC trials. However, companies do admit that there are some problems encountered with them too. Most of them are with the site, technical problems or a combination of both.

Site management with EDC goes beyond the already challenging procedures for paper studies. First of all there is a slight resistance by sites to upgrade and learn to use an EDC tool. Sites need adequate training on the how to enter data, review queries, answer queries. They need to undergo a certification after which they have access to the study specific EDC tool. Investigators find it cumbersome. In addition to all regulatory compliance and protocol requirements, sites need to have electronic signatures and ongoing training in the EDC application. They must also be trained in appropriate procedures (21 CFR 11) for using the system and maintaining their accounts. The site may have several questions, despite the training about the design of EDC or the method of entering particular data. All EDC studies must be supported by a well-staffed help desk that can provide technical support and direct callers to someone to answer their questions. Not only must the site staff be trained and supported, site computers must also be qualified; that is, the EDC host must verify that the site can actually use the EDC system and make a reliable connection.

While all software applications have limitations, Sponsors using EDC report that the most significant problems have to do with study maintenance and application software upgrades. Most traditional CDM databases will need at least some minor changes during the conduct of the study. If the protocol changes significantly, database changes may also be significant. CDM databases are generally set up to handle these changes and companies have processes in place to test and then release them. When changes are needed in an EDC application, it is a more serious undertaking. Any change must be made carefully and it should be immediately available to all sites when it is moved into production. If training or notification is needed for the changes, all the sites must be prepared before the change is made available.

Software upgrades are a big deal for traditional data management systems because they require validation, they sometimes require data migration, and they always require careful planning for down-time when the production data itself is upgraded. If sites forget their passwords and type in a wrong password a couple of times, then the account gets locked. The password has to be reset and they may need to contact the help desk or IT support. This again brings in some delayed.

Despite all these difficulties, EDC trials are a huge success and since it makes data available faster, it is being widely used. Software companies are learning from every trial and are coming with even more user-friendly, customized software for the sites for efficient data capture.

Data Cleaning and Query Management

The biggest task for any data management team for a paper or electronic based study is not data entry, but resolving the inconsistencies or discrepancies. Discrepancies are any inconsistencies in the clinical data that require research or investigation. Discrepancies are generated after the application of edit checks/validation procedures, to the entered data in the database or even by manual review of data. Most commonly, they are identified by the data management systems automatically at entry or after entry via rules defining acceptable data. Discrepancies may also be identified through reporting or analysis in systems external to the data management application e.g. by the biostatics team or by running external SAS checks. Discrepancy may not mean wrong data; rather it is the data not satisfying the desired protocol or acceptable ranges. These inconsistencies found in the clinical trial data need to be corrected as per the study protocol.

Data in clinical trial should be congruent with the study protocol. Each discrepancy is registered or stored in some way until it can be resolved. The process or system to store discrepancies can be called a discrepancy management system. This feature is available in the EDC systems used. CDM systems store discrepancy, tracks it's status, and records it's resolution or type of resolution.

Discrepancy can be resolved in-house by the data management team or by CRA. If it is sent to the site, it is known as a query. A query can be sent on a data clarification form for paper-based study or via fax or email. In EDC trials, queries can be issued, answered by the site and tracked on the eCRF. When forms are used, the site resolves the query by writing directly on the query form and returning that form to the data management group. Data management then updates the data.

In electronic case record forms, the queries are answered by the site on the eCRF itself and the value is updated by the investigator itself. Sometimes, the investigator may mention the value as a comment and not update the value in the data field. In such a case, if a standard clarification agreement with the sponsor is in place, the data management can edit that data field. This SCA holds good only for obvious errors. A few senior data managers could be given edit rights as per SCA. This is done to hasten the process of data cleaning and also to reduce the number of queries sent to the site. For example, if the site has entered the value in comment, then raising a query one more time may confuse the investigator and make him enter a wrong value. Fig. 11.1 enlists the steps involved in data cleaning and validation.

It is very essential to identify discrepancies and look for their resolution. For better query management, one has to know the source or origin of discrepancies.

Discrepancies can come from several sources:

- Manual review of data and CRF by data managers.
- Source data verification by monitors. Monitors are also given access to the CDMS, where they too can raise queries if they find any inconsistencies between source data and CRF.
- Computerized checks of data by the data management system or entry application.
- Computerized checks or analysis by data management or biostatistics using external systems.

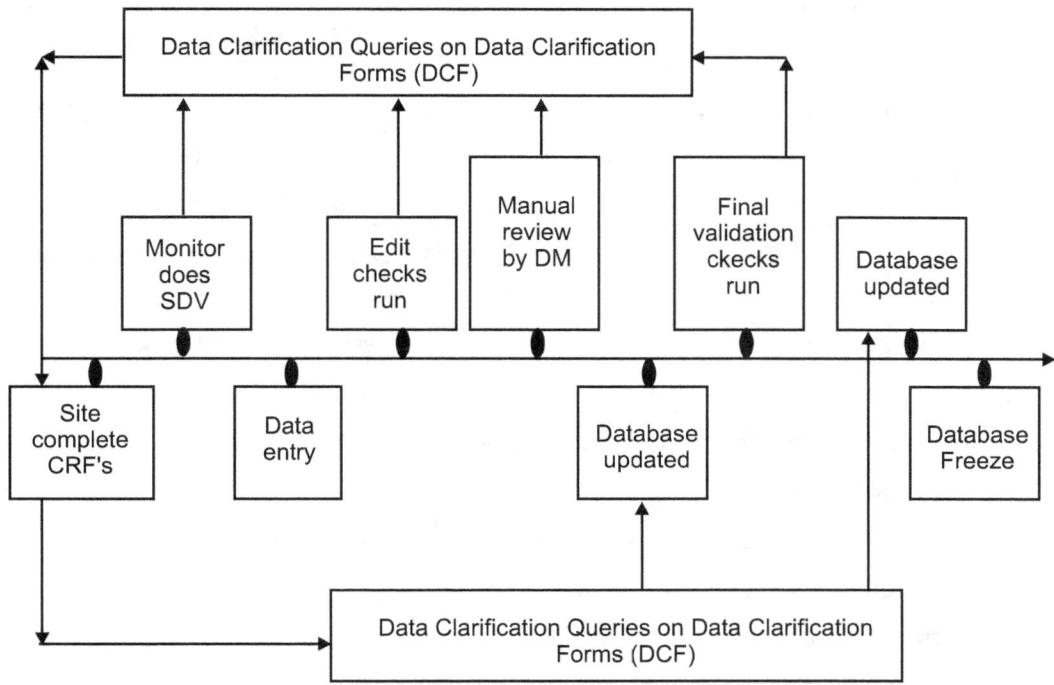

Fig. 11.1: Steps involved in Data Cleaning and Validation

Automated checks used to identify discrepancies are called "edit checks". In order to perform the same checks on all the data consistently throughout the course of the study, data management groups create a list of checks at the start of the study, often called an "edit check specification." or "data validation procedures". These specifications typically take the form of tables or Excel spreadsheets with one row per check. Each check is identified by the CRF page and/or the module or table in which the value being checked appears. The logic of the check is mentioned with less technical words and more user-friendly or understandable language. With the help of these edit checks, queries are auto-generated when they find a value which is not in the protocol specified ranges. Table 11.1 below enlists a few examples of such edit checks.

Table 11.1: Examples of edit checks.

Page Number	Module	Check Name	Edit Check	Edit Check Description	Type
1	DEMOG FORM	DOB_MISSING	DOB is not entered or incomplete	Date of birth is missing or incomplete. Please update.	AUTO
1	DEMOG FORM	AGE_RANGE	Age is not in the range of 18-65 years	As per the DOB, the age does not fall in the acceptable limit. Please verify and update.	AUTO

Contd. ...

Page Number	Module	Check Name	Edit Check	Edit Check Description	Type
2	VITAL SIGNS	WEIGHT_ RANGE	Weight is not in the range of 50-100kgs.	Weight is outside the acceptable range (50-100kg). Please verify and update.	AUTO
3, 4, 5, 6, 7, 8, 9,10	VISIT DATE	VISIT_DATE	Date of Visit is before the previous visit.	Date of Visit 1 is before screening visit. Please verify and update.	AUTO

The types of edit checks found in an edit check specifications are as follows:

1. **Missing values:** Checks for empty fields, for example, BP value missing for a visit.

2. **Simple range checks:**

   (i)   Dose given in an appropriate range like 100 mg to 500 mg.

   (ii) Discrete value checks: e.g., gender

   (iii) One value greater then or equal to another. e.g., PK value greater at 0 hr than 1 hour.

3. **Logical inconsistencies:** e.g., is the event serious is marked NO, but one of the options certifying the event to be serious (life threatening) has been marked.

4. **Checks across modules:** e.g., AE form mentions action taken due to AE as "dose of investigational product (IP) reduced". But IP dosing form does not show a dose reduction for those dates. It is not always possible to have automated checks linking more than two modules. For linking more than two modules SAS checks are designed, listings are run and compared or manual queries are raised.

5. **Protocol violations:** e.g., Visits not in compliance with protocol, or subject taken in study with co-morbidity which excludes the patient from participating in the study.

6. **Quality control checks:** e.g., to check if dates are in a logical sequence.

7. **Compliance and safety tests:** Checking lab values against normal ranges. (Auto queries would fire only if the values are below the lower acceptable range or higher than the upper acceptable value).

Manual Review:

Manual review of CRF's may be done by the data managers, but if a CRF is lengthy and there are many subjects in the trial, it becomes a tedious and non-reliable task. So, for this purpose data managers can run listings. Data managers use these listings to identify unusual texts that have passed entry but do not appear to make sense. They also review the list of medications listed in medical history which should have been mentioned in the concomitant medications list and vice versa. They cross-check medications against the listed AE's.

Data managers and statisticians may manually review certain key numeric values and dates looking for odd patterns or inconsistencies that have not been programmed into the edit checks. Statisticians may also run some simple analyses looking for outliers. It does not make sense to get all the data reviewed manually as we have edit checks, SAS checks and listings checking most of the data. So rather, only those data points which are not taken care of by any of the automations mentioned above should be reviewed manually and other complexly related data points which cannot be linked by edit checks.

To take another example, Tumor Response is mentioned as a "Progressive disease". So the relevant fields which should be checked are: actions taken with drug, has the treatment been terminated and the reason for termination, list of CONMEDS taken for any listed AE's, medical history, tumor size when screened, tumor responses in all visits (values over time), patient compliance with IP. These data points are all related. These may be linked by two or three edit checks or SAS checks. If not, it should be studied as a whole case and careful manual review should be done for the same. Since these are directly linked to the safety and efficacy endpoints, a lot of checks would be programmed so that such important information does not go unnoticed. Not only a data manager but everyone should keep in mind to relate data fields and understand the case.

Whatever be the source of the manual discrepancy, it must be registered in the system so that it can be tracked. In order to enforce careful checking and consistency, companies typically have data managers create the actual discrepancies regardless of who identifies them. The data management group must be very careful to review all existing discrepancies associated with the same data before creating a manual discrepancy and sending it to the site as a query. Sites find it very annoying when they get two queries for the same data point.

External checks:

Systems external to the data management application are frequently used to review and analyze clinical data, for which, package such as SAS® are used. These applications may be run by data management specifically to check data, or may be used by other groups to review data and analyze it. Problem data may become apparent from any of these reports, analyses, or graphs and must also be registered as a discrepancy. Just as with the discrepancies that arise during listing reviews, data managers usually register these discrepancies manually.

Common features included in discrepancy management systems:

- Source of the discrepancy
- Date and time it was identified
- Linked or duplicate discrepancies
- Status of discrepancy in the system
- Data and time when query was sent to investigator

- Query form identifier
- Final resolution
- Date and time of resolution
- Source of the resolution
- Audit trail

Discrepancy Management:

All discrepancies that are identified automatically by the system are looked upon by the data managers and the ones which require verifications or amendments are sent to the site via queries. The queries which could not be resolved internally i.e. by senior data managers, subject matter experts, CRA's need to be sent to the site in the form of a query.

Registering a query:

Clinical Data Management staff send out "Data Clarification Forms" (DCF's) in the process of query management. Other names given to this form are:

- Query forms
- Correction forms
- Discrepancy forms

The site responds with the correct values on these forms and the data managers update the CRF. But in EDC trials queries are registered on the eCRF.

Creating queries:

Data managers should keep the following things in mind before raising a query:

- They should have a good understanding of guidelines.
- Knowledge about Protocol.
- State the problem in a simple and concise manner.
- Be precise or to the point while wording the query text.
- Use proper punctuation and grammatically correct sentences.
- Avoid repetition of words in query text.
- Raise a query at the relevant data point and not at any data point which makes site surf the CRF's and lose track of what he was looking for.
- Query should not be raised if a query is outstanding at a relevant data point. For e.g., Action taken for AE is CONMED administered and the CONMED form is not updated. So if there is an outstanding query on AE form saying "Please enlist the drugs taken to manage the AE", then we need not query on CONMED form asking for updating of CONMED form.

- The query should not be a leading one. E.g. the unit for weight has not been entered but you are aware looking at the value that it is not in pounds, it has to be in kg. So if it is queried as "Is the unit of weight kg? " This becomes a leading query and it is quite possible that the weight was in pounds and the numeric value entered was wrong. So the query should be framed as "The unit of weight is missing, kindly update the same. This way, the site must go to the source document and check the value rather than just automatically say "yes."

Resolving queries:

Site replies to DCF's and data managers update it in the CRF. DCF with the response is an important document as it becomes a source for that discrepancy, so it is filed with other documents in the patient files at the site. As for CDMS, the site views the list of outstanding queries and answers them. Data managers can then filter the queries and have a look at the list of queries answered by the site. If the answers are satisfactory and data has been updated, data mangers can close the query indicating, issue has been resolved. Sometimes the site may respond in the comment box, but may not update the value in the data field. In such a case if the company has a standard clarification agreement in place; such self-evident corrections can be corrected by the data managers without bothering the site by re- querying. But they should be self-evident and this access is limited to a few senior data managers only.

For example, list of drugs used to treat AE "diarrhoea" have been mentioned. But the question "Were drugs given to treat AE?" is not answered or has been left blank. In this situation, only a tick box has to be checked with answer "YES". This is an example of self evident corrections. If the answers given by the site are not in compliance with the protocol and there is still some discrepancy noted, the site can be re-queried with the same issue describing and stating the discrepancy with more precision.

Getting Signatures:

Every DCF that is replied to by the site is signed and dated by the investigator. In CDMS, with 21CFR Part 11, investigators should electronically sign each and every CRF page. (Discussed in detail in electronic signatures).

Examples of Discrepancy types, query types, resolution types:

Query states:

- Open state: Awaiting site response.
- Answered state: Replied by the site, and to be reviewed by data managers.
- Closed: Discrepancy resolved and issue closed.
- Re issued: Query has been reissued (may be in open, answered or closed state).

Resolution types:

- Resolved (with data from site).

- As is (i.e., not a problem).

- Cannot be resolved (but incorrect).

Resolution sources:

- CRA.

- Data management.

- Site, by query form or in CDMS.

Several studies have shown that identifying discrepancies early and continuously throughout the process of data management leads to better-quality data and faster closure of studies. When discrepancies are identified early in the study, it is often possible to uncover problems with a field on the CRF or misunderstandings at a particular site. Clarifications or further training that addresses those problems can prevent the same discrepancies from occurring throughout the entire study. This is a very effective way of reducing errors and paving the way towards accurate data. Discrepancy management and query resolution is a large and resource-intensive part of data management. It is due to the discrepancy managers that companies get clean and validated data to be compiled and sent for regulatory submissions.

Data Storage and Security

Regulatory authorities are always concerned and emphasize on quality and integrity of clinical trial data. They also look into the measures taken by the companies for the same. One way of achieving this is controlling access and security of data. Be it paper or electronic trials, access to the study is only given to those people who are involved in the study.

By limiting access to the study, it's ensured that only authorized individuals get access to the trial details and only authorized individuals enter, delete and update data. This is done by generating user names and passwords for people involved in the study.

User name: Usually this is a unique name given to the individual involved in the study. It is a name by which others can easily recognize the person. The user name must uniquely identify a person and the combination of user name and password constitutes a signature.

Password: The first password is system generated, which has to be changed immediately. The password has to meet certain criteria like it should have a particular length, at least one numeric value, one special character and one capital alphabet. It should be changed frequently. For compliance the system may prompt for change of password and regular intervals. The system may not allow use of previously used passwords. Passwords should never be shared however reliable the person with whom it is being shared looks. Also, for data managers sitting together at a workplace, irrespective of whether they have access to the same study or different study, they should lock their computer when they are away from their workplace. Some companies prefer having the computer to be auto-locked, if the system is idle for a long time.

Account Management: Accounts that are used to access CDM systems provide the user with varying degrees of power, or control over data stored in the system. Only certain people are given the access to enter data, edit data and delete data. All this is again audit trailed, to ensure who is responsible and for which activities. That's the reason a username and password make an electronic signature. And that makes the person attributable to any particular activity against which he has signed. Therefore, it's very crucial to keep passwords private. Even auditors have a look at the list of people involved in the study and what kind of access they had to the system data, as it is all sensitive and expensive data and little bit of tampering be it intentional or unintentional can cause a havoc, thereby rendering the data redundant with lost integrity and authenticity.

Account managers or system administrators grant access depending on the role of the person. For example, data entry people are given the access to enter data for their particular projects. Discrepancy managers are given the authority to raise queries. They cannot enter or modify data. In this way, data is secured by limiting access only to authorized individuals. Also access needs to be revoked, when the database is locked for release.

Data Storage: Data needs to be archived for future reference, especially if there is an active product line or if there is any litigation or at least till the drug is approved and on the pharmacy shelf. Data is stored in the same platform in which it was when it was locked. E.g.: If it was stored on Oracle platform, it is also archived on a compatible version of Oracle, so that the data is easily available when required. The archived data is kept separate from production data and under high security so that anyone who needs to can read it but no one can make changes.

Few important things that need to be archived are:

- Audit trials, as they are a proof of who did what,
- database design,
- coding dictionaries,
- coding algorithms,
- derived/calculated values,
- cleaning rules.

Documents should not only be stored for retention but also for retrieval.

Quality Assurance in CDM

Clinical trial data is an evidence of a safe and effective drug. So, since this data is going to decide the fate of a drug and finally the fate of patients consuming it, it is very critical to capture good quality data, which is reproducible, credible and accurate. That is why quality assurance and control are very important processes in CDM. At every step of CDM activity, some kind of quality check is in place, because, if any error during data entry is left unobserved or unresolved, it is going to lead to a systematic error in data analyses and drawing conclusions. In order to prevent this, rigorous QC checks are used.

Double data entry is the first QC check to ensure that the data has been entered accurately and CRF transcription is as correct as possible.

For data managers, CRF pages are considered as source or raw data. The quality and correctness of the database is determined by checking the database data against the CRF and associated data clarification forms. For eCRF data, monitors do a source data verification where they verify the accuracy of the transcribed data from the raw data or source data on the eCRF. QC for data entry is usually a check of the accuracy of the entry performed by auditing the data stored in the central database against the CRF. This is referred to as "database audit". Ideally, the auditors are not people who participated in data entry for that study. They select the CRFs to be used, pick the appropriate copies and associated query forms, and compare those values against the ones stored in the central database. Results of the audit are usually given as a number of errors against the number of fields on the CRF or in the database.

To conduct an audit, there must be a plan, for that includes:

- Sampling details.
- Definition of an acceptable error rate.
- A plan for what is to be done if the error rate is unacceptable.

Also, there are edit checks that highlight data which fall out of range or are inappropriate as per protocol. Discrepancy managers look for erroneous data manually as well as by running listings. Also, there are QC processes for manual discrepancies raised by the data managers. This is a kind of check for the data management process. Before the database is locked, a checklist is made to ensure that everything has been completed in all aspects.

So, right from method of entry to the database audit, everything should be streamlined and mentioned in the data management plan. With this, the data management team ensures that data obtained from the trial sites are nearly accurate with less errors and are a true representative of the investigational molecule.

21CFR Part 11

With increasing number of trials and the increasing burden to archive trial data and evolution of electronic data capture, it has become essential to have process in place for validating electronic records and having systems to maintain its authenticity and reliability.

21 Part 11 of the Code of Federal regulations deals with the FDA guidelines on electronic records and electronic signatures in the United States. It defines the criteria under which electronic records or electronic systems are considered to be trustworthy, reliable and equivalent to paper records.

21 CFR Part 11 says that records that are "created, modified, maintained, archived, retrieved, or transmitted, must be protected by procedures and controls to "ensure the authenticity, integrity and the confidentiality of electronic records, and to ensure that the signer cannot readily repudiate the document as not genuine." Its goal is to ensure electronic records and signatures are at least as authentic and traceable as those on paper.

It has now become a regulatory requirement to comply with 21CFR Part 11. Companies should employ procedures and controls that include validation of systems to ensure accuracy, reliability, consistent intended performance, and the ability to discern invalid or altered records. So electronic tools need to be more secure and access controlled.

System Requirements Specifications:

Regardless of whether the computer system is developed in-house, developed by a contractor, or purchased off-the-shelf, establishing documented end-user requirements is extremely important for computer systems validation. End user needs and intended uses need to be considered and fulfilled for the system to be validated. Once the user needs are fulfilled, evidence should be obtained that the system implements those needs correctly and that they are traceable to system design requirements and specifications. Requirements would vary with a closed system and an open system.

1. Closed System:

It means an environment in which system access is controlled by persons who are responsible for the content of electronic records that are on the system. Controls for closed systems are:

1. The ability to generate accurate and complete copies of records in both human readable and electronic form suitable for inspection, review, and copying by the agency.

2. Protection of records to enable their accurate and ready retrieval throughout the records retention period.

3. Limiting system access only to authorized individuals.

4. Use of secure, computer-generated, time-stamped audit trails to independently record the date and time of operator entries and actions that create, modify, or delete electronic records.

5. Use of authority checks to ensure that only authorized individuals may use the system, electronically sign a record, access the operation or computer system input or output device, alter a record, or perform the operation at hand.

6. Determine that persons who develop, maintain, or use electronic record/electronic signature systems have the education, training, and experience to perform their assigned tasks.

7. The establishment and adherence to written policies that hold individuals accountable and responsible for actions initiated under their electronic signatures, in order to deter record and signature falsification.

8. Use of appropriate controls over systems documentation including:

   (1) Adequate controls over the distribution, access, and use of documentation for system operation and maintenance.

   (2) Revision and change control procedures to maintain an audit trail that documents time-sequenced development and modification systems.

2. Open System:

It means an environment in which system access is not controlled by persons who are responsible for the content of electronic records that are on the system. Controls for open systems are:

Such procedures and controls shall include those identified in previous section, as appropriate and additional measures such as document encryption and use of appropriate digital signature standards to ensure, as necessary under the circumstances, record authenticity, integrity, and confidentiality.

Electronic Signatures and its Significance:

Digital signature can be defined as a form of electronic signature that works with a public and private key encryption system and a certificate authority. To sign an electronic document with a digital signature, you use digital signature software to select the document and enter an authorization code is unique to your digital signature. The signature consists of a string of characters and the signer's name, title, company, certificate serial number, and the name of the certifying authority.

General requirements for electronic signatures:

Each electronic signature shall be unique to one individual and shall not be re-used or reassigned to anyone else. Before an organisation assigns an individual an electronic signature, the organisation shall verify the identity of the individual. Persons using electronic signatures shall certify to the agency that the electronic signatures in their system, used on or after August 20, 1997, are intended to be the legally binding equivalent of traditional handwritten signatures.

Signature manifestations:

Signed electronic records shall contain information associated with the signing that clearly indicates all of the following:

(1) The printed name of the signer;

(2) The date and time when the signature was executed;

(3) The meaning (such as review, approval, responsibility, or authorship) associated with the signature.

Electronic signatures and handwritten signatures executed to electronic records are linked to their respective electronic records to ensure that the signatures cannot be excised, copied, or otherwise transferred to falsify an electronic record by ordinary means.

Significance of electronic records:

(1) With use of electronic records, access is limited to authorized users only.

(2) Records can only be updated by users with security access.

(3) Time-stamps are recorded for each and every change.

(4) Changes are authenticated using electronic signatures.

(5) Accurate change histories are maintained for all files.

(6) Meet audit trail requirements.

(7) Traceability throughout the entire life cycle.

Since 21CFR Part 11 has become a regulatory requirement and it's compliance generates good quality data, efforts should be taken to make the computer system compliant. Investigators and others involved in research should be trained and assigned electronic signatures.

Database Lock

After the last patient's last visit, Sponsor companies desire the database to be locked as soon as possible so that they can analyze the data and draw conclusions for submission. But there are a lot of critical activities to be performed before the database lock. Once all these critical and time-consuming activities are done, the database is all set to be locked. Although undesirable, it is not uncommon for a database to be unlocked and then relocked after a few changes. Locking and unlocking is not as easy as it may sound and it is not a good practice to frequently unlock database for every minute change. Before the database is locked, lot of activities have to be done, and the time between the last patient's last visit and database lock is an important metrics for the data management team. Sponsors do keep an account of this time and prefer outsourcing the work to those organisations which have a short lag between last patient's last visit and database lock.

Few things which are to be considered before database lock are as follows:

1. **Final data collection and reconciliation:** All data generated by the trial should be collected and updated on the CRF. Final data from all the sites and external vendors should be updated in the database. Any final data obtained may have some discrepancies which need to be resolved before the final database lock. CRF tracking is done by data management team, to ensure that all the CRF pages have been received by them and AE and SAE forms should be checked for completion in all aspects... i.e. Date of event, resolution status with dates etc. It should be ensured that coding of all medical terminologies and adverse events has been done as per protocol-specified dictionaries. If there are any terms which have not been coded, a query has to be sent to the site for a standard terminology for the same. Reconciliation with external data like adverse event data, lab data, and randomization numbers should be completed. Any outstanding queries should be resolved and closed as early as possible. Frequently missing data listings should be run and the site should be queried for the same.

2. **Issuing queries:** Resolution for outstanding queries is required for completion before database lock. So the monitors increase the frequency of their visits to the site for quick query resolution. If the trial involves an EDC system, the refresh time of the website is also increased so that the amended data entered by the site is visible in almost real time to the data management team, and the data management team can act on the queries faster, so that if they need to re-issue queries, it is done as soon as possible and the query turn around time is shortened to a great extent. It is not possible to get absolutely clean data with satisfactory answers for all the questions. Also, data may not be available for certain data points. In such cases usually, the data field would be updated stating data not available. Companies classify data points as critical and non-critical, which would be enlisted in the data management plan. At this stage of data handling, companies may choose not to pursue non- critical data elements and concentrate on critical data points to be entered accurately prior to database lock. All outstanding queries from monitors, data management team, coding team need to be resolved and closed.

3. **Final Quality Control:** As quality of data affects the analyses and conclusion of data, a quality control check should be run. Since unlocking is not preferred, a final QC should be done to prevent conditions which would warrant unlocking. Database audit, running listings for discrepant data, unusual values, outliers and reconciliations are good DM practices to be performed before data base lock.

Locking:

After the above-mentioned time-consuming important tasks are over, the database is all set to be locked. Database lock means declaring that the data is clean and ready for analyses. Its a very important DM milestone and there is a lot of pressure for database to be locked on time. In database lock, data-edit rights are taken over and no deletion, amendment or data updating can be done to the data on the database. Different companies use different terminologies for database lock. Some would call it database freeze and some may call it database release. So, sub-terminologies like soft lock and hard lock may be used sometimes. Some companies refer to soft lock when all CRF pages have been received from the site. This is not a good practice, because in this case, significant event would be only hard lock or final lock. Some organisations declare soft lock at the point when last response for all queries is received from the site. This serves as intimation for the database auditor to start database audit and the final quality check. Hard lock is performed after database audit and QC findings just to ensure if anything needs to be corrected before the final data base lock.

In soft lock, the edit rights are taken away from the clinical data management team and only a person like the project manager or the database administrator of that project may have the right to add, modify or delete, which would be captured in the audit trail. And in case if a data manager's userid would be required for editing (whose edit rights have been taken away), IT support has to been contacted, which would make it possible for the data manager to gain access and edit that data; ofcourse with proper documentation for the same. Edit rights would be taken away once the correction is done.

In hard lock, edit rights are taken away from the entire CDM team including those of the respective project managers or database administrators. And the clinical data management software would not allow anyone to do any alterations to the data. If any data changes would be required, the entire database needs to be unlocked which again would be captured in audit trail. Some softwares tag the data which is locked (in case subsets of data need to be locked). Sometimes individual CRF pages may be frozen or locked. The advantage of this is that, if there are any changes to be made; only that particular page would be unlocked for editing. But it is time-consuming to lock each and every page manually. The database is released to the statistics team which accepts the data, starts analyzing it and drawing conclusions.

Unlocking:

As mentioned earlier, it is not a good practice to unlock database frequently. Sometimes if there is anything critical, the database would be required to be unlocked. Generally, database has to be unlocked only when any significant error is observed after database locking. When such a thing is observed, the data management team is intimated and impact assessment of the erroneous data on data analyses and conclusion is calculated. The database would be unlocked only if the assessor feels the need. But once the subject data is unblinded and significant error is observed, the database should not be unlocked under any circumstances. In this case, the error should be recorded and the table and listings affected by this should be documented. This document should be signed by the study statistician, project manager and study Sponsor.

Re-locking: Once the necessary amendments are made, it is relocked following the same SOP of locking.

An SOP for locking should be prepared and each and every step of the SOP should be followed with high accuracy. Once the study is locked and released to the statistical team, the study files should be updated and the data should be suitably archived and backed up. A dissemination session should be held in which experience with the software used, project milestones or troubleshooting methodology should be shared for better, more efficient and faster data processing.

With the increasing complexity of trials and stringent regulatory requirements, data management has evolved by leaps and bounds. CDM has evolved and will continue to develop in response to the special cross-functional needs due to e-clinical research, advances due to much enhanced clinical harmonization and global standardization. EDC technology has radically increased efficiency by reducing the amount of paper documentation associated with clinical trials, and streamlined the CDM process considerably. The market acceptance of EDC technology has fuelled new demands for improvement in software and intelligent features. The availability of near-real-time data through the use of EDC has opened the doors to the development of an integrated e-clinical environment. All these developments in the current biopharmaceutical arena demand that clinical data management (CDM) is at the forefront, leading change, influencing direction, and providing objective evidence. Many CDM units are coming up in all parts of the world and pharmaceutical companies, CRO's and software companies have ventured into this business leading to loads of job opportunities.

Chapter ... 12

PROJECT MANAGEMENT

> *"Because a thing seems difficult for you, do not think it impossible for anyone to accomplish."*
>
> **Marcus Aurelius**

INTRODUCTION

A project in business and science is typically defined as a collaborative enterprise, frequently involving research or design that is carefully planned to achieve a particular aim. Since most activities undertaken in clinical research fit into the definition of a project, the management approach to clinical research is similar to that of project management.

Every project is driven by quality, cost and time lines for delivery. Speed is of paramount importance in successful completion of any project. At the same time, under no circumstances should quality be compromised. This is particularly more important when managing a clinical research project, because it involves human beings and their lives.

Moreover, in clinical research, data is collected from hundreds of sites. Proper estimation of the timeline and assuring the quality of the data is of utmost importance. The molecules (drugs) that are being studied are patented at an initial stage which means that the drug has to be launched in the market as early as possible to ensure maximum profitability for the sponsor company. This can be achieved by implementing the basic principles of Project Management.

One of the important attributes of a project is it's uniqueness, which means each project is unique in nature. This is particularly true when we consider clinical trial projects. Professionals who have spent their entire lives in clinical research will testify that no clinical trial is like another. Each differs in the specifications, timeline, challenges and problems.

What is a Project?

A project is "a unique endeavour to produce a set of defined deliverables within clearly specified time, cost and quality constraints".

Projects are different from standard business operational activities as they:

- Are **unique** in nature. They do not involve repetitive processes. Every project is different from the last, whereas operational activities often involve undertaking repetitive (identical) processes.

- Have a defined **timescale**. Projects have a clearly specified start and end date within which the deliverables must be produced to meet a specified customer requirement.

- Have an approved **budget**. Projects are allocated a level of financial expenditure within which the deliverables must be produced to meet a spec fied customer requirement.

- Have limited **resources**. At the start of a project an agreed amount of labour, equipment and materials is allocated.

- Involve an element of **risk**. Projects entail a level of uncertainty and therefore carry business risk.

- Achieve beneficial **change**. The purpose of a project typically, is to improve an organization through the implementation of business change.

What is Project Management?

"Project Management is the sum total of skills, tools and management processes required to undertake a project successfully". Project Management can also be defined as "Gathering and ensuring optimum utilization of the project resources". These resources include people, their efforts, funds, tools and techniques, raw material, machinery, knowledge (skill sets), processes and even experience.

Basically, Project Management comprises:

- A set of **skills:** Projects in a particular area of specialization require a specific set of skills which may or may not be common across different areas. The skills required are both project-specific and generic. The generic skills required are: Specialist knowledge, skills and experience required to reduce the level of risk within a project and thereby enhance it's likelihood of success.

- A suite of **tools:** Various tools are used by project managers to improve their chances of success. Examples include: document templates, registers, planning software, modeling software, audit checklists and review forms.

- A series of **processes:** Various management techniques and processes are required to monitor and control time, cost, quality and scope on projects. Examples include: time management, cost management, quality management, change management, risk management and issue management.

Major activities in Project Management:

1. Project Initiation
2. Project Planning
3. Project Execution (with monitoring and control)
4. Project Closure

1. Project Initiation:

This phase starts after getting a clear-cut "go ahead" from the client. This involves signing off a non-disclosure agreement as well as signing a mutual agreement that clearly specifies milestones against the deliverables.

The Initiation Phase is the first phase in the project. In this phase, a business problem (or opportunity) is identified and a business case is defined which provides various solutions. A feasibility study is then conducted to investigate the likelihood of each solution to address the business problem after which a final recommended solution is put forward. Once the recommended solution is approved, a project is initiated to deliver the approved solution. A 'Project Charter' is completed which outlines the objectives, scope and structure of the new project, and a Project Manager is appointed. The Project Manager begins recruiting a project team and establishes a Project Office environment. Approval is then sought to move into the detailed planning phase.

2. Project Planning:

Once the scope of the project has been defined in the Project Charter, the project enters the detailed planning phase. This involves the creation of a:

- Project Plan (outlining the activities, tasks, dependencies and timeframes).
- Resource Plan (listing the labour, equipment and materials required).
- Financial Plan (identifying the labour, equipment and materials costs).
- Quality Plan (providing quality targets, assurance and control measures).
- Risk Plan (highlighting potential risks and actions taken to mitigate them).
- Acceptance Plan (listing the criteria to be met to gain customer acceptance).
- Communication Plan (listing the information needed to inform stakeholders).
- Procurement Plan (identifying products to be sourced from external suppliers).

At this point the project has been planned in detail and is ready to be executed.

3. Project Execution (with monitoring and control):

This phase involves executing every activity and task listed in the Project Plan. While the activities and tasks are being executed, a series of management processes are undertaken to monitor and control the deliverables of the project. This includes the identifying changes, risks and issues, reviewing the quality of deliverables measuring each deliverable against the acceptance criteria. Once all of the deliverables have been produced and the customer has accepted the final solution, the project is ready for closure.

4. Project Closure:

Project Closure involves releasing the final deliverables to the customer, handing over project documentation, terminating supplier contracts, releasing project resources and communicating the closure of the project to all stakeholders. The last remaining step is to undertake a Post-

Implementation Review to quantify the overall success of the project and list any lessons learnt for future projects.

The following sections provide a more detailed description of each phase and list document templates which provide the Project Manager with guidance on how to complete each phase successfully.

The initiation phase essentially involves the project 'start-up'. It is the phase within which the business problem or opportunity is identified, the solution is agreed, a project formed to produce the solution and a project team appointed. The following depicts the activities undertaken:

1. Project Initiation

1.1 Develop Business Case

Once a business problem or opportunity has been identified, a Business Case is prepared. This includes:

- A detailed definition of the problem or opportunity.
- An analysis of the potential solution options available. For each option, the potential benefits, costs, risks and issues are documented. A formal feasibility study may be commissioned if the feasibility of any particular solution option is not clear.
- The recommended solution and a generic implementation plan.

The Business Case is approved by the Project Sponsor and the required funding is allocated to proceed with the project.

1.2 Perform Feasibility Study

A formal Feasibility Study may be commissioned at any stage during or after the development of a Business Case. The purpose is to assess the likelihood of a particular solution option achieving the benefits outlined in the Business Case. The Feasibility Study will also investigate whether the forecast costs are reasonable, the solution is achievable, the risks are acceptable and/or any likely issues are avoidable.

1.3 Establish Project Charter

A project is formed after the solution has been agreed and funding allocated. The Project Charter defines the vision, objectives, scope and deliverables for the project. It also provides the organization structure (roles and responsibilities) and a summarized plan of the activities, resources and funding required to undertake the project. Finally, any risks, issues, planning assumptions and constraints are listed.

1.4 Appoint Project Team

At this point, the scope of the project has been defined in detail and the project team is ready to be appointed. Although a Project Manager can be appointed at any stage of the project, s/he will need to be appointed prior to the establishment of the project team. The Project Manager documents a detailed Job Description for each project role and appoints a human resource to each role based on his/her relevant skills and experience. Once the team is 'fully resourced', the Project Office is ready to be set-up.

1.5 Set up Project Office

The Project Office is the physical environment within which the team will be based. Although it is usual to have one central project office, it is possible to have a 'virtual project office' also, with project team members in various locations around the world. Regardless of the location, a successful project office environment will comprise the following components:

- Location (either physical or virtual).
- Communications (telephones, computer network, email, internet access, file storage, database storage and backup facilities).
- Documentation (methodology, processes, forms and registers).
- Tools (for accounting, project planning and risk modelling).

1.6 Perform Phase Review

At the end of the Initiation Phase, a Phase review is performed. This is basically a checkpoint to ensure that the project has achieved its stated objectives as planned.

2. Project Planning

By this stage, the benefits and costs of the project have been clearly documented, the objectives and scope have been defined, the project team has been appointed and a formal project office environment established. It is now time to undertake detailed planning to ensure that the activities performed in the execution phase of the project are properly sequenced, resourced, executed and controlled.

2.1 Develop Project Plan

The first step is to document the Project Plan. A 'Work Breakdown Structure' (WBS) is identified, which includes a hierarchical set of phases, activities and tasks to be undertaken on the project. After the WBS has been agreed, an assessment of the effort required to undertake the activities and tasks is made. The activities and tasks are sequenced, resources are allocated and a detailed project schedule is formed. This project schedule becomes the primary tool for the Project Manager to assess the progress of the project.

2.2 Develop Resource Plan

Immediately after the Project Plan is formed, it is necessary to allocate the resources required to undertake each of the activities and tasks within the Project Plan. Although general groups of resources may have already been allocated to the Project Plan, a detailed resource assessment is required to identify the:

- Types of resources (labour, equipment and materials).
- Total quantities of each resource type.
- Roles, responsibilities and skill-sets of all human resources.
- Items, purposes and specifications of all equipment resources.
- Items and quantities of material resources.

A schedule is assembled for each type of resource to enable the Project Managerassess the resource allocation at each stage in the project.

2.3 Develop Financial Plan

Just like the Resource Plan, a Financial Plan is prepared to identify the quantity of money required for each stage in the project. The total cost of labour, equipment and materials is quantified and an expense schedule is defined which provides the Project Manager with an understanding of the forecast spending vs. the actual spending throughout the project. Preparing a detailed Financial Plan is extremely important as the project's success will depend on whether the project is delivered within the 'time, cost and quality' estimates.

2.4 Develop Quality Plan

Meeting the quality expectations of the customer is critical to the success of the project. To ensure that the quality expectations are clearly defined and can reasonably be achieved, a Quality Plan is documented. The Quality Plan:

- Defines what quality means in terms of this project.
- Lists clear and unambiguous quality targets for each deliverable. Each quality target provides a set of criteria and standards which must be achieved to meet the expectations of the customer.
- Outlines a plan of activities which will assure the customer that the quality targets will be met (i.e. a Quality Assurance Plan).
- Identifies the techniques used to control the actual level of quality of each deliverable as it is built (i.e. a Quality Control Plan).

Finally, it is important to review the quality not only of the deliverables produced by the project but also of the management processes which produce them. A summary of each of the management processes undertaken during the execution phase is identified, including Time, Cost, Quality, Change, Risk, Issue, Procurement, Acceptance and Communications Management.

2.5 Develop Risk Plan

The foreseeable project risks are then documented within a Risk Plan and a set of actions to be taken formulated to prevent each risk from occurring and reduce the impact of the risk, should it occur. Developing a clear Risk Plan is an important activity within the planning phase as it is necessary to mitigate all critical project risks before entering the Execution phase of the project.

2.6 Develop Acceptance Plan

The key to a successful project is to gain acceptance from the customer that each deliverable produced meets (or exceeds) his/her requirements. To clarify the criteria used to judge each deliverable for customer acceptance, an Acceptance Plan is produced. The Acceptance Plan provides the criteria for obtaining customer acceptance, a schedule of acceptance reviews within which customer acceptance will be sought and a summary of the process used to gain acceptance of each deliverable from the customer.

Prior to the Execution phase, it is also necessary to identify how each of the stakeholders would be kept informed of the progress of the project. The Communications Plan identifies the types of information to be distributed, the methods of distributing information to stakeholders, the frequency of distribution and responsibilities of each person in the project team for distributing information regularly to stakeholders.

2.7 Develop Communications Plan

Prior to the Execution phase, it is also necessary to identify how each of the stakeholders would be kept informed of the progress of the project. The Communications Plan identifies the types of information to be distributed, the methods of distributing information to stakeholders, the frequency of distribution and responsibilities of each person in the project team for distributing information regularly to stakeholders.

2.8 Develop Procurement Plan

The last planning activity within the Planning phase is to identify the elements of the Project which will be acquired from external suppliers to the project. The Procurement Plan provides a detailed description of the Products (i.e. goods and services) to be procured from suppliers, the justification for procuring each product externally, as opposed to from within the business, and the schedule for procurement. It also references the process of selection of a preferred supplier ("Tender Process") and the process for the actual order and delivery of the procured products ("Procurement Process").

2.9 Contract Suppliers

Although external suppliers may be appointed at any stage of the project, it is common to appoint suppliers after the Project Plans have been documented but prior to the Execution phase of the project. Only at this point will the Project Manager have a clear idea of the role of the supplier and the expectations for his/her delivery. A formal Tender Process is invoked to identify a short-list of interested suppliers and select a preferred supplier to meet the procurement needs of the project. The Tender Process involves creating a Statement of Work, a Request for Information and Request for Proposal to obtain sufficient information from each potential supplier to select a preferred supplier. Once a preferred supplier has been chosen, a Supplier Contract is agreed for the delivery of the requisite product.

2.10 Perform Phase Review

At the end of the Planning phase, a Phase review is performed. This is basically a checkpoint to ensure that the project has achieved its stated objectives as planned.

3. Project Execution (with monitoring and control)

The Execution phase is typically the longest phase of the project (in terms of duration). It is the phase within which the deliverables are physically constructed and presented to the customer for acceptance. To ensure that the customer's requirements are met, the Project Manager monitors and controls the activities, resources and expenditure required to build each deliverable throughout the execution phase. A number of management processes are also undertaken to ensure that the project proceeds as planned.

3.1 Build Deliverables

This phase requires the physical construction of each deliverable for acceptance by the customer. The actual activities undertaken to construct each deliverable vary, depending on the type of project (e.g. engineering, building development, computer infrastructure or business process re-engineering projects). Deliverables may be constructed in a 'waterfall' fashion (where each activity is undertaken in sequence until the deliverable is finished) or an 'iterative' fashion (where iterations of each deliverable are constructed until the deliverable meets the requirements of the customer). Regardless of the method used to construct each deliverable, careful monitoring and control processes should be employed to ensure that the quality of the final deliverable meets the acceptance criteria set by the customer. Whilst the Project Team is physically producing each deliverable, the Project Manager implements a series of management processes to monitor and control the activities being undertaken. An overview of each management process follows.

3.2 Time Management

Time Management is the process within which the time spent by staff undertaking the project tasks is recorded against the project. As time is a scarce resource of projects, it is important to record the time spent by each member of the team on a Timesheet to enable the Project Manager to control the level of resource allocated to a particular activity. A Timesheet Register provides a summary of the time currently spent on the project and enables the Project Plan to be kept fully up to date.

3.3 Cost Management

Cost Management is the process by which costs (or expenses) incurred on the project are formally identified, approved and paid. Expense Forms are completed for each set of related project expenses such as labour, equipment and materials costs. Expense Forms are approved by the Project Manager and recorded within an Expense Register for audit purposes.

3.4 Quality Management

Quality is defined as "the level of conformance of the final deliverable to the customer's requirements". Quality Management is the process by which the quality of the deliverables is assured and controlled for the project using Quality Assurance and Quality Control techniques. Quality reviews are frequently undertaken and the results recorded within a Quality Register.

3.5 Change Management

Change Management is the process by which changes to the project's scope, deliverables, timescales or resources are formally defined, evaluated and approved prior to implementation. A core aspect of the Project Manager's role is to successfully manage change within the project. This is achieved by understanding the business and system drivers requiring the change, documenting the benefits and costs of adopting the change and formulating a structured plan for implementing the change. It is often necessary to complete a Change Form to formally request a change. The change request details may then be recorded within a Change Register.

3.6 Risk Management

Risk Management is the process by which risks to the project (e.g. to the scope, deliverables, timescales or resources) are formally identified, quantified and managed. A project risk may be identified at any stage by completing a Risk Form and recording the relevant risk details within the Risk Register.

3.7 Issue Management

Issue Management is the method by which issues currently affecting the ability of the project to produce the required deliverable are formally managed. After completion of an Issue Form (and logging the details within the Issue Register), each issue is evaluated by the Project Manager and a set of actions undertaken to resolve the issue at hand.

3.8 Procurement Management

Procurement Management is the process by which product is sourced from an external supplier. To request the delivery of product from a supplier, a Purchase Order must be approved by the Project Manager and sent to the supplier for confirmation. The status of the purchase is then tracked using a Procurement Register until the product has been delivered and accepted by the project team.

3.9 Acceptance Management

Acceptance Management is the process by which deliverables produced by the project are reviewed and accepted by the customer as meeting his/her specific requirements. To request the acceptance of a deliverable by the customer, an Acceptance Form is completed. The Acceptance Form describes the criteria from which the deliverable has been produced and the level of satisfaction of each criterion listed.

3.10 Communications Management

Communications Management is the process by which formal communications messages are identified, created, reviewed and communicated within a project. The most common method of communicating the status of the project is through a Project Status Report. Each communication item released to the project stakeholders is captured within a Communications Register.

3.11 Perform Phase Review

At the end of the Execution Phase, a Phase review is performed. This is basically a checkpoint to ensure that the project has achieved its stated objectives as planned.

4. Project Closure

Following the completion of all project deliverables and acceptance by the customer, a successful project will have met its objectives and be ready for formal closure. Project Closure is the last phase in the project and must be conducted formally so that the business benefits delivered by the project are fully realized by the customer.

4.1 Perform Project Closure

Project Closure involves undertaking a series of activities to wind up the project, including:

- Assessing whether the project completion criteria have been met.
- Identifying any outstanding items (activities, risks or issues).
- Producing a hand-over plan to transfer the deliverables to the customer environment.
- Listing the activities required to hand over documentation, cancel supplier contracts and release project resources to the business.
- Communicating closure to all stakeholders and interested parties.

A Project Closure Report is submitted to the Customer and/or Project Sponsor for approval. The Project Manager is then responsible for undertaking each of the activities identified within the Project Closure Report on time and according to budget. The project is closed only when all activities identified in the Project Closure Report have been completed.

4.2 Review Project Completion

The final activity undertaken on any project is a review of it's overall success by an independent resource. Success is determined by how well it **performed** against the defined objectives and **conformed** to the management processes outlined in the planning phase. To determine performance, a number of questions are posed. For example:

- Did it result in the benefits defined in the Business Case?
- Did it achieve the objectives outlined in the Project Charter?
- Did it operate within the scope of the Project Charter?
- Did the deliverables meet the criteria defined in the Quality Plan?
- Was it delivered within the schedule outlined in the Project Plan?
- Was it delivered within the budget outlined in the Financial Plan?

To determine conformance, a review is undertaken of the level of conformity of the project activities to the management processes outlined in the Quality Plan. The above results, key achievements and lessons learnt are documented within a Post Implementation Review report and presented to the Project Sponsor for approval.

Chapter ... 13

CONTRACT RESEARCH

| *"Do what you do best and outsource the rest".* | **Tom Peters** |

INTRODUCTION

A **contract research organisation**, (CRO) is a service organisation that provides support to any industry. The term is more common in pharmaceutical and biotechnology industries in the form of outsourced clinical research services (for both drugs and medical devices) and hence such organisations are often known as Clinical Research Organisations. CROs range from large, international, full-service organisations to small, niche specialty groups and can offer their clients the experience of moving a new drug or device from it's conception to marketing approval without the drug sponsor having to maintain a staff for these services.

The U.S. Food and Drug Administration regulations state that a CRO is "a person [i.e., a legal person, which may be a corporation] that assumes, as an independent contractor with the sponsor, one or more of the obligations of a sponsor, e.g., design of a protocol, selection or monitoring of investigations, evaluation of reports, and preparation of materials to be submitted to the Food and Drug Administration." [21 CFR 312.3(b)].

The sponsor (usually a pharmaceutical company or a research institute or university) may outsource any part of the New Drug Development (NDD) activity to another organisation or individual. Such outsourcing is done for a number of purposes, but those relevant to the discussion here are:

1. Need for more expertise.
2. Manpower shortage.
3. Economy.

Agencies involved in new drug development may or may not have the expertise to develop the drug and see it through all activities required prior to marketing. In such a situation, outsourcing a part, which the sponsor finds difficult to manage is the basis of this outsourcing.

The popularity of Business Process Outsourcing (BPO) industry, makes many think that outsourcing has been invented by the BPO industry. Nothing could be farther from the truth. Man has been outsourcing so many of his requirements, that outsourcing can be called one of basic tenets of civilizations. Thus, we outsource our children's education, the making of clothes, footwear, furniture and food, keeping only a small part of the required activities to ourselves.

The same principle is applied for CROs also. Sponsors outsource all or parts of NDD to various organisations. These organisations or CROs either specialise in a particular area or offer a full service to the client. For some vague reason, Site Management Organisations (SMOs), are considered a different type of organisation, though they are in fact, CROs whose function is limited to management of a site.

There is however, one difference between the setting up of an SMO and a CRO. A company or a chain of hospitals would be better off setting up an SMO rather than a CRO. Most CROs expect business from sponsors which are other pharmaceutical companies, who would be reluctant to give business to a CRO, which belongs or is owned by another pharmaceutical company. In case of a chain of hospitals, the same rule applies; the CRO set up by one hospital would find it difficult to manage trials at other hospitals since they are competitors.

There are a variety of CROs operating in India, both overseas and Indian, who are helping the Indian Clinical Research industry grow at the rate of around 30 to 35 % annually. The leading among these are Quintiles, Siro, GVKBio, PPD, Clininvent, Chiltern, Clintec, Clinsys, Clingene. Quintiles is probably the only full service CRO offering every service to the sponsor, though quite a number of other CROs too claim to do so.

Organisation

There is great variety in the organisational set up of CROs, but there are a few common factors. The factor on which these setups depend are the areas of expertise offered. These are briefly discussed below:

1. Clinical Operations

This is the key area of expertise most CROs offer. It is only the niche CROs who may not be in this area of activity. This area covers the actual conduct and management of clinical trials at various sites. Unless otherwise stated by the CRO, it can be safely assumed that this service is offered by the organisation. The trendy abbreviation of this is Clin. Ops.

2. Clinical Data Management

Receiving, entering, checking and creating a data base for clinical data is the main function of this area. Companies involved in mainly IT activities are also involved in CDM. Tata Consultancy Services (TCS), Accenture, Cognizant are among the leaders in CDM. Some CROs, including Quintiles also have their own CDM units.

3. Laboratory Services

This expertise is rarely offered by a CRO; of course Quintiles is an exception and they have set up their laboratories a few years ago. Other organisations offering laboratory services are Metropolis, Ranbaxy etc. Most other CROs use the services of these laboratories to get their clinical samples tested.

4. Quality Assurance

While most CROs do their own quality planning and audits, there are one or two niche CROs who specialize in this field. Even if the CRO has it's own QA set-up, care should be taken to ensure that the QA does not fall under the Clin. Ops or CDM, else it loses it's independence and objectivity.

5. Medical Writing

This is yet another area where many CROs operate, and again there are niche CROs who offer this service.

6. Biostatistics

In many set-ups, the CDM unit has a biostatistics cell, while in others, Biostatistics is a separate entity. It all depends upon the size and workload of each organisation.

7. Archives

Clinical research generates a lot of paper, and essential documents of each trial may have to be archived for long periods of time. While outsourcing of archives is possible, many CROs have their own archives. There are no set standards for archiving in India, but British or U.S. standards may be used to protect documents during long periods of archival.

These are a few of the technical areas which merit separate mention. The other routine areas like Human Resource Management, Administration, Finance etc. are required in all organisations.

Infrastructure

The infrastructural requirements for a CRO are minimal. A CRO is basically an office, and nothing more. Unless the CRO plans to have it's own laboratories or CDM unit, there are little requirements other than furniture for the staff and computers for working. Communication is nowadays managed through the Internet hence laptops of PCs are the main equipment required.

Since there is a concern about the confidentiality of communications and other documents, the computers should be connected to a common server and the LAN secured against unintended outflow of information. An intranet on which SOPs are loaded often helps in reducing paper work, and SOPs (Standard Operating Procedures) are available to each employee, but cannot be downloaded or mailed out of the organisation.

Since most documents are going to be stored in an electronic format, there should be adequate measures to ensure safety of the facilities against natural hazards and fire. Fire extinguishers suitable for the circumstances should be installed to prevent loss of data due to such accidents.

Every CRO should have access control using either biometric or any other equally sensitive and accurate system. Sponsors and inspectors are likely to take a dim view of those that permit free access of individuals to all places.

Thus, office space, furniture, IT software and hardware, electrical supply, storage space for documents and clinical trial material form the essential infrastructure for all CROs, while other infrastructure is more or less optional.

Those CROs that also offer CDM or Laboratory services will obviously need infrastructure to support these activities. Infrastructure requirements are thus service-specific and with greater number of services on offer, greater would be the infrastructure requirements.

Human Resource

CROs are highly human resource-intensive. People are the most essential and important part of the organisation. Since the clinical research industry thrives on talent, people with of the right type are essential for the success of the organisation;, people who are qualified by education training and experience.

Well-qualified and trained people are difficult to come by, and the industry faces a high attrition rate. This is partly due to large number of openings in every company and also due to the demand of the industry for experienced staff. Obviously, experienced staff does not come from educational institutes but from other companies. As a result, what is talent acquisition for one company is attrition for another.

Earlier, in the absence of training institutes, CROs used to hire the brightest and best graduates or post-graduates of pharmacy, medicine and life sciences. However, with the launch of clinical research training by the Institute of Clinical Research India (ICRI) and the many clones that followed, it is now possible to choose from among the 1000 plus graduates these institutes produce annually. The products of these institutes may lack practical knowledge of conducting or aiding clinical research, but have at least a basic understanding of the subject which earlier entrants in clinical research lacked.

Talent acquisition is an expensive and time consuming activity. Not many head hunters specialize in this field, and even today it is common to use contacts in the industry and research academies to get the people one wants.

Regulations concerning clinical research change dramatically, hence continuous training of staff is essential in this industry. Experience tells us that training is a continuous requirement, and however well-qualified an individual may be, he or she must undergo periodic training to stay abreast of the ever-changing face of this industry.

As in every other industry, success depends upon pinning down the responsibilities of individuals and holding them down to be accountable for their responsibilities, hence CRO employees must have clearly defined responsibilities for which they can be held responsible. Most CROs therefore have responsibility logs for each and every employee they hire.

Systems

The clinical research industry is a highly regulated one, and the regulators watch over the shoulders every action of the staff, thus there is a need for systems. Systems comprising Standard Operating Procedures, and other components of quality. Quality measures have therefore been adopted by most CROs.

Systems are tedious processes which seem to give the organisation no advantage in the short term. Initially, the systems are an irritant and only devour resources, but after a time they yield results too. Investment in systems is therefore for long-term success rather than immediate return on investments.

Setting up systems for an organisation is easier said than done. One of the favoured models is that of the ISO. The ISO based approach is one of the ways to standardize the working of a manufacturing or a service-oriented organisation. In the words of ISO, standards

- make the development, manufacturing and supply of products and **services more efficient, safer and cleaner**.
- **share** technological advances and good management practices.
- disseminate **innovation**.
- **safeguard consumers** and users in general, of products and services.
- make life simpler by providing **solutions** to common problems.

The use of Quality Systems, Plans, Standard Operating Procedures, and Formats make everybody's life easier, though initially there is a lot of resistance to this among the employees. Getting the staff involved in developing the system helps to an extent counter this resistance. One of the most important contributions of this system is that it institutionalizes individual experiences.

A highly experienced employee may do a job very efficiently, but if that employee is absent or leaves the organisation, the quality of work, suddenly suffers. If the employee were to write down each simple step involved in the completion of the job, another person would be able to complete the job with the same thoroughness; which is what the ISO system ensures. Consistency of a product or service is often better continuous improvement, which means change in deliverables.

Standard Operating Procedures (SOPs) are very essential for the smooth functioning of organisations. One of the most efficient services in India are the Armed Forces, which have SOPs for every function, which are very strictly adhered to. Many companies adopt an SOP-driven system, but often end up overdoing it. SOPs should be prepared for those processes which affect the quality of the product. Procedures which are peripheral to the ultimate product quality need not be SOP-driven.

SOPs should be developed for procedures which are routine, can be delegated and which are repetitive. In a hospital, one should have an SOP for cleaning the operation theater and for sterilizing instruments, but there need not be any SOP for brain surgery, because it cannot be delegated from one surgeon to another. For example, every priest who performs marriages must have an SOP for the entire process, simply because the priest has to perform marriage ceremonies again and again whereas no SOP is needed by the marrying couple since most individuals marry only once and very few may marry twice or thrice.

Good clinical research requires definite allocation of responsibilities, and accountability among the employees. For this, a well-defined organisation structure needs to be drawn up and respected by all. Most companies have people with extra-constitutional powers; who tend to give orders and instruction to other staff, but are never accountable for the results of their orders. Such individuals do considerable damage to the organisation, and we unfortunately come across such people in many companies, thriving at the expense of others.

There is no definite organisational structure that can be recommended, and each organisation has to establish it's own, yet there are a few common principles on which a structure should be based which are:

1. Total centralization of power as also total democracy should be avoided.
2. People at all levels in the hierarchy must follow the hierarchical system.
3. Roles and responsibilities should not overlap.
4. Quality assurance should never be reporting to an individual whose work they are to audit.
5. Work load and responsibilities should be fairly distributed, without fear or favour.

The Organisation chart shown below is just representative. . No company has probably such an ideal set up, yet this is a type of set up that a CRO should have. In any case a CRO can choose to follow any option for an organisation chart, provided they have one.

Most sponsors would like to see the organisation chart of the CRO before they outsource the trial. ISO too demands a documented chart, with responsibilities clearly defined. A poorly-defined organisation may do well at times, but the chances of a well-defined set up in succeeding are many times more.

Finance

Finance is the key resource in setting up a business, CRO or otherwise. It is at this level that most businesses fail. CRO is an industry that does not give return on investment very soon. Any individual or company wishing to set up a CRO should remember that business does not come just because a company has been set up.

There are many sources of finance, but most carry some disadvantages along with the advantages. One has to carefully weigh both these factors before choosing the finance source before setting up a CRO.

In many cases, it is a pharmaceutical company that wants to set up a CRO. While the advantages of this are many, so are the disadvantages. Other pharmaceutical companies are not very keen to outsource their trials to a CRO owned by another pharmaceutical company. The problem arises that companies who do not operate in drug discovery are not keen to enter the CRO space.

The most successful CROs are those that have no stake in drug discovery themselves, the most obvious example being Quintiles. This being a full-service CRO, offers services of almost all types, but they themselves do not have a stake in drug discovery, and thus there is rarely a conflict of interest for them.

In India, finance is not scarce, but a lot of it is unaccounted for. It is dangerous to accept capital from such sources, since the responsibility of accounting then falls on the CRO. It is best to avoid such financial support.

Banks and Non Banking Financial Companies do offer finance, but it is rare for them to finance a start-up company, since they would usually want to examine the profit and loss statements of at least two to three years whereas a start-up has no P and L statements to offer for examination.

Angel venture capitalist is yet another source, but this animal is scarce to find. The fact that the break even-point for CROs is more than 2 to 3 years makes many of them baulk at investing in a CRO. Even if they initially invest, they start asking for returns immediately after the CRO has been set up. The relation with such financiers is very tenous at best.

Before starting such an organisation, the promoters would do well by making a business plan. Such a plan should list out the expected expenses (both fixed and variable) as well as the income. Estimating the income is an exercise in prediction, based on current trends of the industry and the expected market share. Most such calculations are based on forecasts and can never be expected to be accurate.

Anyone wishing to set up a CRO should remember that sponsors prefer an organisation that has a full complement of trained staff in addition to the required infrastructure. The staff needs to be in place and trained before the first project comes their way. No sponsor would hand over a project to a company that says 'We have the staff identified and we will take them on board as soon as a project is in hand.'

It is the old chicken-nd-egg-story, which comes first or should come first. From the CRO perspective, the project should come first, but from the sponsor's point of view, a good trained staff in place comes first. Those companies who have been able to crack this old puzzle survive, while the rest perish.

Finance is often the last thing an entrepreneur thinks of. Slogans like 'there is no shortage of money in this country', are fine as slogans go, but they are useless while setting up a company. The feeling that banks and other institutions are ready to lend money at competitive interest rates is actually a fantasy. It is bizarre that in this country, car loans are cheaper than education loans. Most banks are willing to lend money to a business that is making good profits, but rarely to a start-up. In fact, banks are always keen to lend to a customer who does not need finance.

As a result, very few entrepreneurs enter this field. Only large companies can enter clinical research in a big way, but the trouble with large companies is that they carry a lot of baggage and are not nimble enough to change as required. It is a rare Louis Gerstner who can make an elephant like IBM dance. For these reasons, many entrepreneurs end up setting small CROs with limited staff and services. These small companies become stepping stones for budding CR professionals whose ultimate goal is Quintiles or PPD.

Today we have a large number of CROs in operating in India, which range from something like what was known as 'Mom and Pop' shop to professional large companies. It is expected that over time, the larger companies will survive, while 'Mom and Pop' shops give way to commercial malls.

The expression 'deep pockets' has been often quoted as an essential feature for the company that sets up a CRO. Just how deep those pockets are is a mystery to one and all. The deeper the better, but then it is not the financial stability, but a mind set of the investor that counts.

Training

Clinical research professionals often say that the three keys of success are training, training and training. This is true. It is often noted that senior people in clinical research have forgotten the basics of Good Clinical Practices (GCP)with the rise in hierarchy. Professionals in this business need to be trained periodically and continually.

The staff of a CRO or an SMO needs to be trained on not only GCP but a variety of subjects including, ethics, auditing, and a large number of activities that they have to be involved in. Since knowledge is vaporous, training reinforces the knowledge one tends to forget that one is not routinely involved with.

The dictum in clinical research is 'what is not documented is not done' hence training too needs to be documented. Maintaining records of training is as important as training itself. These records provide sponsors with evidence that the CRO staff is actually trained and are therefore up to date in its knowledge about clinical research.

Clinical research is a new discipline, and as in any new discipline that is evolving, changes are rapid. Any person trained in say 2000 would be quite out of date with the present guidelines and regulations, hence repeated training is a part of life in a CRO.

Every member of the staff of a CRO (except perhaps, administrators) should be trained in GCP, and in as many different aspects of ICH Guidelines as possible. There are a number of online certifications available and the staff should try to obtain as many certificates as possible to hone their skills in research.

The staff could also be sent to clinical research training institutes who deliver customized training modules as per the clients' requirements.

Vendors

CROs have to deal with multiple vendors including courier companies, insurance companies, translation agencies, computer hardware and software suppliers etc. While it is desirable to draw agreements with each of the chosen parties in advance, it may not be always possible to do so.

Outsourcing is the 'mantra' for business in these days. A CRO should not attempt to enter all areas of operations. Even laboratory services and CDM can be outsourced to start with, and as a CRO builds it's business, it may enter these areas. With a handful of projects in hand, both laboratory services and CDM are not economically viable if done in-house. For laboratory services, quick access is essential and most cities have branches of large central laboratories.

In case of CDM, geographical proximity is not at all essential and movement of data is very easy through e-mail and couriers. Add to this the cost of data management software and the talent required to operate them, CDM is best left to large companies like TCS, Cognizant and Accenture to handle.

Identifying and short-listing vendors is an important task that has to be undertaken before stating research activities. Selection of vendors should be based on their track record, reputation in the market and their competitiveness. Good vendors should be retained and unsatisfactory one deleted if one wants to maintain competitive edge.

Couriers are important vendors since their efficiency decides whether documents and samples reach their destination in time. In certain cases, where heat-sensitive material may have to be transported, one should check beforehand whether the chosen courier has facilities to do so.

Insurance is another very important part of the clinical research process. There are a number of companies that offer clinical trial insurance but very few who understand the mechanism of insurance. Getting a knowledgeable insurance agent is most crucial for finding and obtaining the optimal insurance coverage. Insurance is required not only to safeguard the subjects and investigators; it is also a statutory requirement.

Setting up a CRO

A decision to set up a CRO maybe taken after considering the aforementioned points. Entrepreneurs are well-advised that CRO is not a 'get rich quickly' business. It is a venture that requires patience and hard work before the pay-off begins. Break-even points may be reached at different times, and it may be three to four years before the venture starts yielding profits.

Before setting up a CRO, one should first make a business plan which should include the present scenario, and the advantages that one expects to offer in order to grab a slice of the market. A dispassionate study of the CR market and the strategies adopted by successful CROs will help in formulating this plan.

Financials form the next part of the business plan. Expenses should be divided into fixed and variable. Fixed expenses represent those expenses which have to be incurred, whether or not any business comes your way. Variable expenses are those incurred while executing the projects which are underway.

Expenses on staff are galling to a number of managements, since the staff has to be paid even when there is no work. In this period, attrition is also very high as the staff gets frustrated without any real work. It is quite common to have one turn-over of the whole staff before even the first project comes in.

Next come the projections of income, and this is an exercise in prediction. There is no historical data to go by, there is no trend that can be safely assumed, hence figures in this projection are more of guesstimates rather than estimates. Very ambitious planning can land one in as much trouble as conservative planning.

While formulating a business plan, one likes to develop a plan which is attractive to the investor. Hence projections of income and growth tend to be optimistic. This may satisfy the investor, but it puts severe pressure on the business development and operations staff. One can't be too pessimistic about income and growth, since the investor may lose interest in the project. . What one needs is a judicious mix of hope and caution, but nobody really knows how much of each of these ingredients is adequate.

Once finalized, the business plan also covers raising and repayment of loans, and calculates the profits before tax and those after tax. The plan should have provisions for staff recruitment and growth of the organisation. This plan should also help in raising money from banks or other financiers. Very often, the investor requires the plan to provide for opportunity cost.

The logic of opportunity cost is economically sound yet unfair. Let us assume that ₹ 5.00 Crores (₹ 50.0 million) are invested in a CRO. The investor estimates that this ₹ 5.00 Cr. eats into his capital which he could have invested elsewhere, and earned a Return-on-Investment (ROI) of 20 %. The investor therefore deducts 20% from any profit accruing from the CRO business. While in theory this may be right, in practice this expects a new venture to perform better than a running business.

These aspects make it difficult for new ventures to be set- up and flourish. Another issue is that the organisation that sets up a CRO should have no conflict of interest. This means that it should not be linked to any drug development programmes. If it is, then other sponsors will be wary of outsourcing their trials to them. These conditions hence require investment from an organisation that is not related to drug development activities. Most organisations are usually not interested in investing in areas in which they have no expertise or stake. This is the Catch 22 of clinical research.

Following the business plan, acquiring premises for the CRO office should begin. Sponsors today are used to a particular level of elegance and one has to keep up with their expectations while doing up the office. There should be adequate security and equipment for controlled access to the premises as well as certain restricted areas in the office.

The next activity is talent acquisition or hiring the staff. This industry has been facing one of the highest attrition rates. One of the reasons for this is that every company wants to hire experienced staff, and such staff can only come from another company. What is talent search for one company is attrition for another.

Nonetheless, some of the staff needs to be experienced as having a full complement of freshers can be disastrous. Managers and Vice-Presidents would also be people with considerable experience and have to be sourced from other organisations. Clinical Research is a very small field and most people in this field know each other. While hiring any person, it would be wise to check up his or her suitability and/or integrity with another.

As placement consultants are not of much value and their charges very high, it is better to spread word in the industry which would attract a number of people interested in making a change. In the past, most of the senior people in CROs came from the pharmaceutical industry, but with availability of Graduates from CR institutes, the situation may change after a few years.

Quality is as important in Clinical Research as in any pharmaceutical industry. Principles of quality are the same everywhere and only it's application differs. Persons for Quality Assurance could be sourced from the pharmaceutical or biotech industries. It is true that a person working in QA function in any manufacturing industry would be suitable, but persons from pharmaceutical or biotech industries have a steeper learning curve and they may be preferred.

After the staff is in place and training begins for them, business development work can begin. Marketing a CRO is not like marketing any other service. The Business Development Manager (BDM) would have to deal with R and D and Medical Chiefs of pharmaceutical companies in India and abroad. The BDM should therefore be sound in his CR knowledge. The prospective candidate for the position of BDM would be a person well-trained in both marketing and Clinical Research. A slick marketing expert with no knowledge of clinical research is as unsuitable as a technocrat with no marketing knowledge. The blend of skills are required are difficult to find.

Departments like Finance and Human Resources (HR) pose little problem. They could be sourced from any industry. Yet, a few words about HR. Few human resources departments live up to the standards they claim. Despite all psychological profiling they deploy in hiring, one finds that the wrong sort of people are hired. Despite the employee-friendly policies that are claimed to be in place, there is widespread dissatisfaction among employees. Lastly, despite the most comprehensive appraisal systems in the organisation, one finds that sour cream rises to the top. This follows the principle widely known as Peter's Principle which states that "in a hierarchy, every employee tends to rise to his level of incompetence"

Business Development

Ideally, the first person to be taken on board should be the Business Development (BD) head, because BD is going to require at least 6 months before the first contract could be landed. The entrepreneur has at least six months' time to set up the rest of the organisation. It is a policy decision as to where to look for business. One could concentrate on the Indian industry, which is developing new molecules, or on the Multi National Companies who are getting their trials done in India, or small to medium scale companies who are searching for more economical trials.

There is a lot of talk that sponsors do not come to India due to the lower prices. This might be nice to hear, but it is certainly not the truth. Take the price advantage away from India and sponsors would rush out of the country. Finally, it all boils down to money, and the pharmaceutical industry is not different from others . True, there might be some sponsors who are ready to move to India for other reasons, such as non-availability of patients in other countries, but they are few and far in-between.

When developing business, a CRO must have an understanding of what the sponsors are looking for, which is often openly declared by the sponsors, while on the other hand, many would not be so forthcoming. The trick is to guess or find out what the sponsor needs and then address the needs of the sponsor.

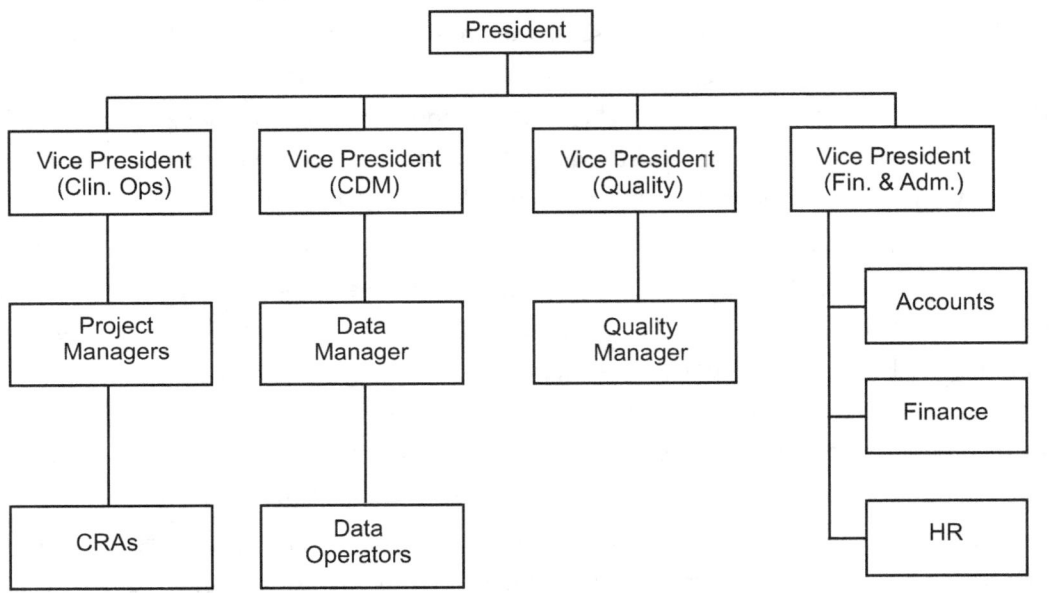

Reference: Peter, Laurence J; Hull, Raymond (1969). *The Peter Principle: Why Things Always Go Wrong.* New York: William Morrow and Company.

✳✳✳

Chapter ... 14

PHARMACOVIGILANCE

"There is no medicine like hope, no incentive so great, and no tonic so powerful as expectation of something better tomorrow".
Orison Swett Marden

INTRODUCTION

Pharmacovigilance is the science and activities relating to the detection, assessment, understanding and prevention of adverse effects or any other possible drug-related problems. The scope of the Pharmacovigilance has been to:

- improve patient care and safety in relation to the use of medicines and all medical and paramedical interventions.
- improve public health and safety in relation to the use of medicines.
- contribute to the assessment of benefit, harm, effectiveness and risk of medicines, encouraging their safe, rational and more effective (including cost-effective) use.
- promote understanding, education and clinical training in Pharmacovigilance and it's effective communication to the public. Recently, it's concerns have been widened to include herbals, traditional and complementary medicines, blood products, biologicals, medical devices and vaccines.

Pharmacovigilance also concerns sub-standard medicines, medication errors, lack of efficacy reports, use of medicines for indications that are not approved and for which there is inadequate scientific basis, case reports of acute and chronic poisoning, assessment of drug-related mortality, abuse and misuse of medicines and adverse interactions of medicines with chemicals, other medicines, and food.

Sound drug regulatory arrangements provide the foundation for a national ethos of drug safety, and for public confidence in medicines. Besides approving new medicines, the issues which drug regulatory authorities have to contend with include:

(a) Clinical trials,

(b) Safety of complementary and traditional medicines, vaccines and biological medicines,

(c) Developing lines of communication between all parties with an interest in drug safety and ensuring that they are open and able to function efficiently, particularly in times of crisis.

Pharmacovigilance programmes need strong links with regulators to ensure that the authorities are well-briefed on safety issues in everyday practice that may be relevant to future regulatory action. Regulators understand that pharmacovigilance plays a specialized and pivotal role in ensuring the ongoing safety of medicinal products. Pharmacovigilance programmes need to be adequately supported to achieve their objectives. Pharmacovigilance begins at the clinical development process of a drug product and continues throughout the life cycle of the product. Broadly; it could be divided into two phases:

(1) Pre-Marketing Pharmacovigilance Process

(2) Post-Marketing Pharmacovigilance Process

Pre Marketing Pharmacovigilance Process:

The assessment of clinical data and safety and efficacy data during the drug product development is known as the Pre- Marketing Pharmacovigilance process. It involves measuring adverse drug reactions in all the phases of clinical trials. During the clinical data, the adverse drug reaction occurances are known asexpected adverse drug reaction and those which occour during the post-marketing Pharmacovigilance process are known as the unexpected adverse drug reaction.

All the regions in the world have their own Pharamacovigilance systems based on the World Health Organisation's (WHO) guidelines. In this part, we will briefly highlight regulatory practices from a pharmacovigilance perspective from UK the Medicines and Healthcare products Regulatory Agency (MHRA), the US Food and Drug Administration (FDA), and from India, DCGI (Drug Controller General of India).

In general, regulatory pharmacovigilance follows the flow chart below, definitely deviating and adding according the need and betterment of the overall process.

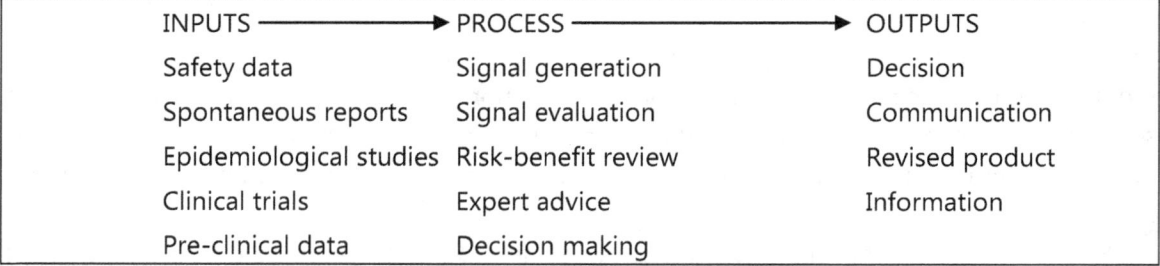

INPUTS	PROCESS	OUTPUTS
Safety data	Signal generation	Decision
Spontaneous reports	Signal evaluation	Communication
Epidemiological studies	Risk-benefit review	Revised product
Clinical trials	Expert advice	Information
Pre-clinical data	Decision making	

Fig. 14.1: Regulatory Pharmacovigilance

Spontaneous Reporting- UK

In the United Kingdom, the Licensing Authority responsible for medicines for human use consists of ministers, including the Secretary of State for Health. The Authority's executive function in the control of medicines is performed on a day-to-day basis by the UK Medicines and Healthcare products Regulatory Agency (MHRA). The MHRA was formed on 1 April 2003 by the merger of the Medicines Control Agency (MCA), previously responsible for monitoring the safety, quality and efficacy of medicines, and the Medical Devices Agency (MDA). The Agency's primary objective is to safeguard public health by ensuring that medicines, healthcare products and medical equipment in the UK market meet appropriate standards of safety, quality, performance and effectiveness, and are used safely. The cornerstone of UK's spontaneous reporting is the Yellow card scheme since 1960, following the thalidomide tragedy. In the United Kingdom, the Committee on Safety of Drugs; subsequently the Committee on Safety of Medicines (CSM) and now the Commission on Human Medicines (CHM) was set up. One of the responsibilities of this new committee was to collect and disseminate information relating to suspected adverse effects of drugs. To address this objective, the United Kingdom's spontaneous reporting Scheme was introduced in 1964.

This established four key principles of the Scheme, namely:

1. Suspected adverse reactions should be reported; reporters do not need to be certain or to prove that the drug caused the reaction.
2. It is the responsibility of all doctors and dentists to report.
3. Reporters should report without delay.
4. Reports could be made and would be treated in confidence.

With the very common limitation of these reporting systems; "under reporting", the yellow card scheme has identified many "early warnings" which has helped to take necessary action on the drugs. There are many recent initiatives to strengthen the Yellow card reporting system, mainly to curb under-reporting, which includes: Pharmacist reporting, Nurse reportingand highlighting special therapeutic areas by creating greater awareness healthcare professionals.

Spontaneous Reporting: USA

The US Food and Drug Administration (FDA) is responsible for not only approving drugs for marketing but also for monitoring their safety, post-marketing. After marketing, new information relating to drug safety usually becomes available as the product use becomes more widespread, and on occasion this may alter the benefit-risk profile of a drug. The FDA continues to assess the benefit–risk profile of approved drugs throughout the life of the drug, primarily on the basis of Adverse Drug Reaction (ADR) case reports voluntarily sent to the FDA or to the drug's manufacturer by healthcare professionals and consumers. Drug manufacturers are legally required to submit all ADR reports they receive to the FDA. Under current US regulations,(21 CFR; Code of Federal Regulations 314.80), reports of 'serious' ADRs not presently listed in the drug product's labelling must be submitted to the FDA within 15 calendar days of the company receiving them. For regulatory purposes, a 'serious' report is defined as one describing an ADR that is life-threatening or that leads to death, hospitalization (initial or prolonged), disability, congenital anomaly or required intervention to prevent permanent impairment/damage. Reports meeting the regulatory definition of 'serious' but describing events already listed in product labelling as well as all reports with non-serious outcomes are submitted to the FDA on a periodic basis that varies depending on the market age of the product. The FDA has maintained a computerized repository of these voluntarily reported ADRs since 1969. This repository and the system to manage it have grown and changed since then. In 2004, the FDA received approximately 425,000 reports, and the total number of reports in the database now exceeds 3 million, covering all marketed prescription drug and therapeutic biological products in the United States. For most over-the-counter (non-prescription) products, manufacturers are not required to submit ADR case reports to the FDA. The ADR database has evolved over the years as computer and information technologies improved. The most recent modification occurred in 1997 when the FDA redesigned the database, now referred to as the Adverse Event Reporting System (AERS), and shifted from using Coding Symbols for Thesaurus of Adverse Reaction Terms (COSTART) to Medical Dictionary for Regulatory Activities (MedDRA) coding terminology. These changes were implemented for several reasons. Agreements reached through the International Conference on Harmonization (ICH) necessitated restructuring the database to meet international standards for electronic submission of ADR reports. Identification and evaluation of safety signals from spontaneous reports may result in a range of regulatory actions. These may include one or more of the following:

- Change in the manufacturer's professional and/or patient labelling.
- Implementation of a Risk Management Action Plan (RiskMAP).
- Market withdrawal of the product.
- Further study of the safety concern.

Pharmacovigilance is the cornerstone of post-marketing drug safety activities in the United States and will likely remain so for the foreseeable future. Nearly all post-marketing labelling changes related to drug toxicity are based on spontaneous case reports. The same holds true for drug withdrawals also. Since 1980, there have been 22 major prescription drug withdrawals in the United States. Of these, spontaneous case reports and their analysis were a critical informational component contributing to the withdrawal decision in 20. Finally, advances in technology in the 1990s and the advent of the ICH process have created an environment where global pharmacovigilance is now conceivable. A remaining challenge is to make this a reality.

Pharmacovigilance in India

In India, The National Pharmacovigilance Advisory Committee (NPAC) monitors the performance of various zonal, regional, and peripheral centers and performs the functions of "Review Committee" for this programme. The NPAC also recommends possible regulatory measures based on pharmacovigilance data received from various centers. The Zonal Pharmacovigilance Centre (ZPC) and Regional Pharmacovigilance Centre (RPC) have also been established. The Central Drugs Standard Control Organization (CDSCO) is initiating a countrywide pharmacovigilance programme under the aegis of DGHS, MoH and Family Welfare, and the Government of India. The National Pharmacovigilance Centre at CDSCO shall coordinate the programme. The National Centre will operate under the supervision of the NPAC to recommend procedures and guidelines for regulatory interventions.

The National Pharmacovigilance Programme will have the following milestones:

1. **Short-term objectives:** To foster a culture of notification.
2. **Medium-term objectives:** To engage several healthcare professionals and Non Government Organizations (NGOs) in the drug monitoring and information dissemination processes.
3. **Long-term objectives:** To achieve such operational efficiencies that would make Indian National Pharmacovigilance Program a benchmark for global drug monitoring endeavours.
4. **Periodic safety update reports:** These shall be expected to be submitted every 6 months for the first 2 years of marketing in India, and annually for the subsequent 2 years. In addition, training programmes and interaction meetings shall be held every 6 months after the initial training.

ROLE OF INVESTIGATOR IN SAFETY REPORTING

Introduction

One of the key milestones in Pharmacovigilance is devising an appropriate plan for handling safety information in the investigational phase of drug development. After understanding "what" should be reported as safety information in a clinical trial and "by when", the next question is "who" will be responsible for reporting this information, and "to whom". Here is where the role of the investigator of a clinical trial comes in, as one of the primary reporters of solicited safety information in clinical research.

The ICH E6 guideline defines an investigator as "a person responsible for the conduct of the clinical trial at a trial site". The Office for Human Research Protections (OHRP) considers the term 'investigator' to include anyone involved in conducting the research with the exception of people who are involved solely in the act of providing coded private information or specimens. An investigator is the central unit in the machinery of a clinical trial; he has the deepest knowledge of the trial protocol, the drug, the indication, and the subject. By virtue of this, an investigator's duties and obligations are manifold, and it is imperative that he understand what an adverse experience in a clinical trial means, and how it is to be documented, reported, mitigated, followed-up, and evaluated.

The ICH E6 guideline describes the fundamental role of an investigator in a clinical trial from which extrapolate his/her functions as a safety reporter. It is recommended that one reads this guideline to comprehend the responsibility an investigator has towards the safety of the subjects of a clinical trial in it's entirety. However, in this chapter we will only speak about how these duties amalgamate into what an investigator is obligated to do when he receives any information relevant to the safety of his trial subjects during and following a subject's participation in a trial.

One would think that the safety of trial subject gains relevance after the subject has been administered the study drug(s), but, a subject is monitored to ensure his safety right from the time he is enrolled in the trial. The investigator is trained appropriately in the nuances of the sponsor's trial protocol, the investigational brochure's (IB) contents, and his mandatory functions in his dealings with an IRB/IEC. Before the site enrols it's first patient, the investigator provides a signature on a tripartite agreement, and assures that he will comply with the study protocol, Sponsor's written instructions and all laws and regulations applicable to the performance of the study. Here begin his safety reporting obligations.

Receipt of safety information by the investigator

At this point, we should understand that an investigator may not always be the individual who observes an adverse event (AE) as it occurs. In fact, in practice, it may be quite rare. The sub-investigator, nurses etc. are usually the ones who first receive information about AEs that a trail subject experiences. Therefore, it is made a mandatory for the investigator to employ medically-qualified staff, and to ensure that they are adequately trained in the trial protocol, IB, the sponsor's instructions and regulatory reporting requirements. However, the investigator remains responsible for all medical decisions that required to mitigate an AE.

Sources of safety information

During the course of clinical drug development and early post-approval phase, solicited safety information always reaches the sponsor from pre-defined sources. The investigator is one of the most important pit-stops in the processing of safety information. Safety information may be found in clinical examination findings, patient statements (diary), laboratory and diagnostic value changes, may also be directly sought by using questionnaires especially designed for the clinical trial. More information on this may be found in Chapter 4 of this text book, but what is relevant to this chapter is that the investigator needs to look for safety information in several places, and most importantly, document it.

Components of an adverse event report

An AE report is one which provides a picture of what AE occurred to whom, and the name of at least one suspect drug that maybe temporarily related to the ADR. The minimum elements of an adverse event report are: An identifiable source (patient), and identifiable reporter (investigator), a distinct adverse event term (is usually verbatim; coded using MedDRA after it reaches the Sponsor), and an identifiable suspect drug. The investigator's primary responsibility lies in the collating this information and reporting it to the sponsor within the timelines (and when required to the IRB) using an appropriate format).The investigator must apply appropriate medical and scientific judgment for each situation. Apart from adverse events, information that might materially influence the benefit-risk assessment of a medicinal product or that would be sufficient to consider changes in medicinal product administration or in the overall conduct of a clinical investigation also represents situations that underscore the importance of safety of information reporting. Examples include:

(a) An increase in the rate of occurrence of an expected serious AE which is considered clinically important.

(b) A significant hazard to the patient population, such as lack of efficacy with a medicinal product used in treating life-threatening disease.

(c) A major safety finding from a newly completed animal study (such as carcinogenicity).

All these events are considered reportable as AEs, and their reporting time-frames differ according to the nature of these AEs.

Causality assessment is required for clinical investigation cases, and it is the responsibility of an investigator to provide an opinion on the causality of an AE based on the temporary relationship of the AE with the drugs consumed, the confounding medical and concomitant medicinal status of the subject and the de-challenge/re-challenge testing of the AE. All cases judged by either the reporting investigator or the sponsor as having a reasonable suspected causal relationship to the medicinal product qualify as possibly/probably related to the suspect drug.

Safety event reporting timelines

Depending on the nature of safety events, the investigator is bound to report all of them that occur in clinical trial subjects with the information, and follow it up as long as the subject is enrolled in the trial, the event has resolved, all information has been received (e.g. in event of the subject's death) or the protocol requires, whichever is longer.

Expedited reporting of AEs: In general, all AEs that are both serious and unexpected are subject to expedited reporting. Expedited reporting of AEs which are serious but expected will ordinarily be inappropriate, unlessconsidered medically significant (e.g. abrupt increase in frequency or intensity of the expected AE). Similarly, non-serious AEs, whether expected or not, will usually not be subjected to expedited reporting. As per ICH guidelines, all drug regulations mandate that the investigator adhere to AEs reporting timelines as follows:

1. Death and life threatening-serious AEs: Any event leading to the subject's death or is life-threatening and not intervened wmust be reported by the investigator to the sponsor (who in turn reports it to the regulatory authority in no later than 7 days) and the IRB/IECs immediately, with as much information as available at the time.

2. All other serious, unexpected AEs that are neither fatal nor life-threatening should also be reported as soon as possible, as the sponsor has no more than 15 calendar days after first knowledge that the case meets the minimum criteria for expedited reporting.

3. All other AEs should be documented by the investigator, and the documentation should be made available to the monitors/auditors, IRB/IECs, independent data safety monitoring committees and the sponsor as and when required.

For all events, follow-up information (including event outcomes, laboratory test results and autopsy reports) should be actively sought by the investigator and submitted to the sponsor as it becomes available.

Conclusion

Thus, to summarize, an investigator's safety reporting responsibility starts from the time of a subject's enrolment, requires him to document and report all safety information to the sponsor and the IRB/IEC, and gather and report follow-up information as per regulatory and sponsor requirements.

Periodic Safety Update Report

The Periodic Safety Update Report (PSUR) for marketed drugs was designed to be a stand-alone document that allows a periodic but comprehensive assessment of the worldwide safety data of a marketed drug or biological product. The PSUR can be an important source for identifying new safety signals, a means of determining changes in the benefit-risk profile, an effective means of risk communication to regulatory authorities and an indicator of the need for risk management initiatives as well as a tracking mechanism monitoring the effectiveness of such initiatives. For these reasons, the PSUR can be an important pharmacovigilance tool. Numerous steps are involved in the PSUR process including: intake of adverse drug reaction information, case processing, data retrieval, data analysis, and medical review and risk assessment. These processes are heavily reliant on the availability of adequate resources. An overarching principle throughout the PSUR process is the need for a proactive approach to identify the critical steps in the process and have a clear understanding of the consequences of any critical 'mis-step'. With this information comes appropriate planning, building quality into each step of the PSUR process.

Periodic monitoring of it's performance will maximise the likelihood of generating a quality report. Any failure of a key PSUR process will have the opposite effect - a poor-quality report that will give little insight into emerging safety signals or provide misleading information that may adversely affect public health. A pragmatic approach that will avoid or minimise these pitfalls includes the following: adequate resource planning, training, development of 'scripts' designed to maximise the capture of key information for medically-important reactions, standardised and harmonised Medical Dictionary for Regulatory Activities (MedDRA) coding procedures, pre-specified search criteria for data retrieval, ongoing medical review, and metrics to evaluate the effectiveness and efficiencies of these processes. With these quality measures in place, the utility of the PSUR as an effective pharmacovigilance tool is greatly enhanced.

Principles of PSURs in general:

- All dosage forms and formulations as well as indications for a given pharmacologically active substance for medicinal products authorised to one marketing authorisation holder (MAH) should be covered in one PSUR. Within the single PSUR, separate presentations of data for different dosage forms, indications or populations (e.g. children versus adults) may be appropriate.

- Each MAH is responsible for submitting PSURs, even if different companies market the same product in the same country. When companies are involved in contractual relationships (e.g. licenser–licensee), arrangements for sharing safety information should be clearly set out. To ensure that all relevant data is reported to the regulatory authorities, responsibilities for safety reporting should also be clearly specified.

- For combinations of substances which are also authorised individually, safety information for the fixed combination may be reported either in a separate PSUR or included as separate presentations in the report for one of the separate components, depending on the circumstances. Cross-referencing all relevant PSURs is essential.

- All relevant clinical and non-clinical safety data should cover only the period of the report (interval data), except the regulatory status information on authorisation applications and renewals and data on serious, unlisted ADRs, which should be provided for both the period in question and as cumulative summary tabulations starting from the International Birth Date (IBD). A listed ADR is one whose nature, severity, specificity and outcome are consistent with the company core safety information (CCSI) (ICH, 1996). The safety information contained within the PSUR comes from a variety of different sources. These include spontaneous reports of adverse events from different countries, the literature, clinical trials, registries, regulatory ADR databases and important animal findings. The main focus of the report should however be ADRs.

Regulatory Requirements

ICH E2C, in conjunction with its addendum, has been adopted by the Japanese Ministry of Health, Labour and Welfare and included in Volume 9 of the Rules Governing Medicinal Products in the European Union, on pharmacovigilance (EC, 2004a). The US Food and Drug Administration

(FDA) has also introduced periodic reporting requirements based on ICH E2C, and it published guidance for industry in February 2004 (FDA, 2004). ICH E2C has therefore made it's mark in all three ICH regions. However, the reporting requirements in those regions differ as stated below:

- In the EU, the reports need to be submitted every 6 months for the first 2 years after authorisation, annually for the three following years and then five-yearly after the first renewal.

- In the United States, the FDA requires quarterly reports during the first 3 years, then annual Reports subsequently.

- In Japan, the authorities require a survey on a cohort of a few thousand patients established by a certain number of identified institutions during the 6 years following the authorisation.

By taking into account a precise denominator, a systematic information on this cohort must be reported annually. For the other marketing experience, adverse reactions which are non-serious, but mild in severity and unlabelled, must be reported every 6 months for 3 years and annually thereafter.

In India, PSURs submitted by pharmaceutical companies shall be expected to be submitted every 6 months for the first two years of marketing in India, and annually for subsequent 2 years.

The following points are the proposed content of a PSUR, while a more detailed guideline is available on the document named "Guidance for Industry Addendum to E2C Clinical Safety Data Management: Periodic Safety Update Reports for Marketed Drugs" to harmonise the data shared and the format across the globe.

EXECUTIVE SUMMARY

1.1 Introduction

1.2 Worldwide market authorisation

1.3 Update on regulatory authority or marketing authorisation holder actions taken for safety reasons

1.4 Changes in reference safety information

1.5 Patient exposure

1.6 Presentation of individual case histories

1.7 Studies

1.8 Other information

1.9 Overall safety evaluation

1.10 Conclusion

Appendix 1 Company core data sheet

Appendix 2 Marketing authorisation status

Appendix 3 Line listings of case reports

Appendix 4 Summary tabulations of events

SUMMARY BRIDGING REPORTS

The different frequency and periodicity requirements of different regulatory authorities in different countries create potential problems for the production of PSURs. Under ICH E2C provisions, regulators who do not wish to receive 6-month report are expected to accept two 6-month-reports as a substitute for an annual report or the appropriate series of reports as a 5-year report.

CIOMS V therefore proposed the use of the summary bridging report to facilitate the review of a series of reports. This is a concise document combining the information presented in two or more PSURs submitted to a regulatory authority to cover a specified period over which a single report is required. It should not contain new data or repeat the information already included in the PSURs but should only cross-reference those other reports. The format/outline should be identical to the format of the usual PSUR but the content should consist of summary highlights.

THE PSUR PROCESS

The PSUR process comprises the following steps:

- Intake of ADR information;
- Case processing
- Data retrieval
- Data analysis and
- Medical review and risk assessment.

Once an ADR has been reported (usually spontaneously to a company representative), the case is entered into a safety database, a narrative prepared and a MedDRA term assigned to ADRs described in the case. Severity and labelledness are assigned which determine if the event needs to be processed as an expedited report. Retrieving data from the Data Lock Point (DLP), generating line listings and summary tabulations are typically the most time-consuming parts of the PSUR process but are important for a thorough medical review and risk assessment. The sections of the PSUR which lend it's value as a pharmacovigilance tool, the presentation of individual case histories and the overall safety evaluation, depend critically on the data retrieval step. Data analysis is based on the traditional method of medical review carried out by trained healthcare professionals and increasingly supplemented by data mining methods which are emerging as useful tools in signal detection. Finally, the medical review and risk assessment steps force the MAH to take a critical look at it's data to determine whether the risk for the marketed product has changed and whether the product label needs to be modified or other risk management initiatives need to be implemented.

PSUR AND RISK MANAGEMENT

The 'Guideline on risk management systems for medicinal products for human use' from the EMEA, adopted in November 2005, clearly states that risk management plan (RMP) and it's updates should be submitted with the PSURs unless other requirements have been laid down as a condition of the marketing authorisation. This RMP is now requested from health authorities for all new applications.

In general, safety issues should be identified at early stages in the development of a compound, and incorporated in a RMP. This RMP can then propose different actions to counteract or better understand these issues: education (physicians, patients, sales representatives etc.), step-wise market approach, use of utilisation and/or safety databases, specific studies targeting defined issues and so on. The RMP would serve as a guiding document, and assessment of the plan will be reported in the PSUR. The PSUR is thus now the document in which all the available information on safety of a given product is gathered from all sources, such as clinical trials, observational studies, spontaneous reports and also pre-clinical experiments, and put into perspective. The consistency of a potential signal/issue across all the sources is of very high value. The PSUR will help in that analysis because it is a unique document assembling all these information from multiple sources.

CONCLUSION

The PSUR can be an important source to identify new safety signals, a means of determining changes in the benefit–risk profile, an effective means of risk communication to regulating authorities, an indicator for the need for risk management initiatives as well as a tracking mechanism for monitoring the effectiveness of such initiatives (Klepper, 2004). It is not a document for submission to regulatory authorities. One of the major strengths of the PSUR is the unique opportunity it provides to review aggregate data. If a drug is marketed in numerous countries for example, a finding of an ADR of interest across many countries has greater clinical weight than the same finding made in isolated countries. More generally, it is a chance to view all available information on the safety of a given product – that is information from clinical trials, observational studies and spontaneous reporting, as well as pre-clinical studies. The consistency (or lack of it) of a potential signal across all these information sources can be extremely valuable to a MAH. The PSUR is also a chance to detect potential problems as patient exposure increases in response to promotional efforts. For example, it may reveal ADRs in elderly people on multiple drug regimes. Such patients may be excluded from clinical trials but their number may increase very quickly after the product has been launched, and the PSUR provides a means of reviewing the relevant safety data in a regular and intelligent manner. Similarly, it is a tool for monitoring un-promoted use of a drug in sub-populations such as children, the very old and those with multiple diseases, and it can alert manufacturers or sponsors to long latency ADRs or explosive ADRs (when a handful of reports is quickly followed by dozens). The company is then in a position to respond proactively if and when such an event is reportedby shifting the promotional programme and product literature away from encouraging exposure in what seem to be vulnerable groups. To sum up, instead of considering the PSUR a tedious piece of compliance with regulatory authorities, companies should regard it as a valuable exercise in which the manufacturer or sponsor thoughtfully assesses benefit and risk and seeks to protect it's patients and products.

Information Technology and Pharmacovigilance : A beneficial bond

Risk assessment during clinical product development needs to be conducted in a thorough and rigorous manner. However, it is impossible to identify all safety concerns during controlled clinical trials. Once a product is marketed, there is generally tremendous increase in the number of patients exposed, including those with co-morbid conditions and those being treated with concomitant medications. Therefore, post-marketing safety data collection and clinical risk assessment based on observational data are critical for evaluating and characterizing a product's risk profile and making informed decisions on risk minimization. Information science promises to deliver effective e-clinical or e-health solutions to realize several core benefits: time savings, high quality, cost reductions, and increased efficiencies with safer and more efficacious medicines. The development and use of a standards-based pharmacovigilance system with integration connection to electronic medical records, electronic health records, and clinical data management system holds promise as a tool for enabling early drug safety detections, data mining, results interpretation, assisting in safety decision making, and clinical collaborations among clinical partners or different functional groups. The availability of a publicly-accessible global safety database updated on a frequent basis would further enhance detection and communication about safety issues. Due to recent high-profile drug safety problems, the pharmaceutical industry is faced with greater regulatory enforcement and increased accountability demands for the protection and welfare of patients. This changing scenario requires bio-pharmaceutical companies to take a more proactive approach in dealing with drug safety and pharmacovigilance.

Information Technology into Pharmacovigilance: A global reach

It is recognized that Information Technology (IT) has entered and transformed the world of health care and clinical medicine in which the work of doctors and the care of patients proceed with higher quality, efficiency and lower cost. It is also no secret that IT has merged with clinical safety practice and sparked the creation of worldwide pharmacovigilance systems for safety signal detection. The IT transformative force and health IT adoption have fundamentally changed the conduct of clinical research, practice of medicine, and medicinal safety monitoring. After the incidents of recent drug withdrawals,health care providers and regulators demand that biopharmaceutical or medical device firms show a demonstrated commitment to safety that goes beyond mere compliance in order to regain the trust of patients. In today's world, pharmacovigilance pushes new boundaries and it is no longer sufficient to simply report adverse events along with efficacy and quality requirements. Regulators are demanding proactive surveillance programmes which include comprehensive risk management plans and signal detection and analysis throughout a clinical product's lifecycle. Organizations that lead in developing a more proactive and long-term approach to manage the safety of their products recognize that success requires a continuous, consistent process from pre-clinical research onwards. This is achieved through developing a good clinical safety practice that shows the company's awareness and corrective action at every stage of the product/device development.

Even though partial drug safety evaluation in the post-marketing phase is widely accepted now, it's need and methodology involved is still upto the discretion of the regulators. The stronger the national systems of pharmacovigilance and adverse drug reaction (ADR) reporting, the more likely would reasonable regulatory decisions will be made for the early release of new drugs with the promise of therapeutic advances. Most have now made it essential by law to have detailed pharmacovigilance in the initial days of a new drug's release. Careful safety monitoring is not restrictedonly to new drugs or significant therapeutic advances. It plays a critical role in introducing generic medicines, andreview of the safety profile of older medicines already available where new safety issues may have arisen. While spontaneous reporting remains a cornerstone of pharmacovigilance in the regulatory environment, and is indispensable for signal detection, the need for more active surveillance has also become increasingly clear. Without information on utilization and on the extent of consumption, spontaneous reports are unable to determine the frequency of an ADR attributable to a product, or its safety in relation to a comparator. More systematic and robust epidemiological methods are required to address these key safety questions that consider the limitations of spontaneous reporting or post-marketing studies. They need to be incorporated into post-marketing surveillance programmes.

In principle, pharmacovigilance involves identifying and evaluating safety signals. Safety signal refers to a concern about an excess of adverse events compared to what would be expected to be associated with a product's use. Signals can arise from post-marketing data and other sources, such as preclinical data and events associated with other products in the same pharmacologic class. It is possible that even a single well documented case report can be viewed as a signal, particularly if the report describes a positive re-challenge or if the event is extremely rare in the absence of drug use. Signals generally indicate the need for further investigation, which may or may not lead to the conclusion that the product caused the event. After a signal is identified, it should be further assessed to determine whether it represents a potential safety risk and whether other action should be taken. Pharmacovigilance is particularly concerned with adverse drug reaction, many other issues are also relevant to pharmacovigilance science.

- Sub-standard medicines.
- Medication errors.
- Lack of efficacy reports.
- Use of medicines for indications that are not approved and for which there is inadequate scientific basis.
- Case reports of acute and chronic poisoning.
- Assessment of drug-related mortality.
- Abuse and misuse of medicines.
- Adverse interactions of medicines with chemicals, other medicines, and food.

   The specific aims of pharmacovigilance are to:

   1. Improve patient care and safety in relation to the use of medicines and all medical and paramedical interventions.

   2. Improve public health and safety in relation to the use of medicines.

   3. Contribute to the assessment of benefit, harm, effectiveness and risk of medicines, encouraging their safe, rational and more effective (including cost-effective) use.

   4. Promote understanding, education and clinical training in pharmacovigilance and its effective communication to the public.

Pharmacovigilance has developed and will continue to develop in response to the special needs and according to the particular strengths of members of the WHO programme and beyond. Such active influence needs to be encouraged and fostered; it is a source of vigor and originality that has contributed much to international practice and standards. Pharmacovigilance is gaining traction among doctors and scientists as the number of stories of drug recalls increases in the global mass media. Because clinical trials involve several thousand patients at most, less common side-effects and ADRs are often unknown at the time a drug enters the market. Even very severe ADRs, such as liver damage, are often undetected because study populations are small. Post-marketing pharmacovigilance uses tools such as data mining and electronic case report forms to identify the relationships between drugs and ADRs. In brief, an electronic data capture (EDC) system is a computerized system designed for automated support of clinical data collection, reporting, query resolution, randomization, and validation, among other features, in conducting clinical trials. Though EDC technologies offer superior advantages over traditional paper-based systems, collecting, monitoring, coding, reconciling, and analyzing safety data can be challenging. To realize the full potential of the information revolution in e-clinical research as compared with traditional paper-based studies, both the sponsor and site users will probably have to change the way their offices and days are organized, how they enter and retrieve patient information, how data is entered, the process by which they issue, answer, or close queries, and the ways in which they relate to colleagues and clinical research organizations (CROs) and interact with their patients. Safety scientists will have to find ways to understand and analyze huge volume of safety information across different studies or systems and coordinate with third party independent committees to enter adjudication results. In other words, effective use of e-technologies depends as much on managing change as it does on information management, and change has never been easy for sponsor e-clinical system implementation and integration.

The EDC technology products now being sold are intended to meet the present needs of both sponsor and site users with certain vendor-based differential functions – as would any product be that is aimed at attracting consumers in a well-functioning market. In reality understanding limitations and opportunities offered by EDC vendor, configuring EDC system to meet data capturing needs based on sponsor IT or data management profile, and collaborating with vendor to offer flexible configurations, are key to EDC implementation success. Technology innovators and EDC vendors, however, imagine a world in which electronic system meets needs that most sponsor and site users do not think they have. How to meet future needs, how to persuade EDC vendors to invest in such innovative systems, is something involving collaborative efforts from many players.

Benefits and Risks: Pharmacovigilance Technologies

The idea that randomized clinical trials can establish product safety and effectiveness is the core principle of the pharmaceutical industry. Neither the clinical trials process nor the approval procedures of the US Food and Drug Administration (FDA) provide a perfect guarantee of safety for all potential consumers under all circumstances. Despite this, there are viable pharmacovigilance technology solutions that biopharmaceutical companies can implement to systematically detect, assess, understand, and prevent adverse drug reactions. When built into clinical research and development practices, pharmacovigilance technologies assist biopharmaceutical firms in enhancing patient safety while reducing or even preventing costly safety-related withdrawals. It is recognized that clinical data mining and signal detection associated with pharmacovigilance contribute to potential benefits in providing Systematic, automated and practical means of screening large datasets. (10) Better utilization of the large safety databases maintained by the FDA, the World Health Organization (WHO) and other organizations improved efficiency by focusing pharmacovigilance efforts on key reporting associations positive contributions to public health by identifying potential safety issues more quickly and/or more accurately than traditional pharmacovigilance methods better decision support for the pharmaceutical industry and regulators potential to clarify the many complex interdependent factors (e.g. concomitant drugs and/or diseases) that can play a role in the development of adverse events in a clinical setting value by detecting disproportionalities involving multiple drugs or multiple events that would be too difficult to detect by traditional methods. Adopting good pharmacovigilance practice in clinical safety monitoring and analysis and having an aptitude to utilize the advantages pharmacovigilance technology solutions provide are key to unlock the power of pharmacovigilance and maximize clinical safety returns in an evolving drug safety environment. One needs to realize that pharmacovigilance is a tool and should be applied into clinical context to achieve it's intended functions. One critical component of good pharmacovigilance practice is centered on acquiring complete quality data from reported source on adverse events. Spontaneous case reports of adverse events submitted to the sponsor and FDA, and reports from other sources, such as the medical literature or clinical studies, may generate signals of adverse effects of drugs. The quality of the reports is critical for appropriate evaluation of the relationship between the product and adverse events.

Challenges:

There are well-known inherent issues in systematically analyzing and interpreting voluntarily-submitted data involving multiple drugs, medical conditions, and events per report, without the benefit of a research protocol, randomization, and a control group of persons taking the placebo. Other difficulties include chronic under-reporting, occasional publicity-driven and litigation-driven episodes of over-reporting and mis-reporting, incomplete information, and inconsistencies and changes over time in reporting and naming/coding practices. In addition, there is considerable uncertainty regarding the quality and completeness of the information contained in each data field, including dosage, formulation type, timing of exposure, and length of exposure and follow-up and in estimating the corresponding product exposure and background rate of adverse events. The extraction of useful information from this database presents multiple challenges, including managing, storing, querying, and analyzing such a large amount of data, resolving event and drug dictionary problems and data miscoding. There is a need for analytical methods that are capable of systematically screening this database to identify potential serious adverse events of concern in such a noisy background that properly balance the concerns for excessive signaling and accounting for background noise. Challenge area also lies in clinical process re-engineering to ensure modern pharmacovigilance technology systems are configured, tailored, and implemented in the context of addressing safety process improvements and organizational needs to support daily clinical safety operations. In the past four decades from the thalidomide tragedy to the recent drug recalls, companies have used pharmacovigilance methods to identify rare, easily-identified safety problems. During the same four decades, we have seen the growth of a fragmented clinical or healthcare system that lacks a unifying infrastructure. As a result, this system operates primarily in reaction to, rather than in anticipation of major pharmaceutical safety events. As drug consumption has increased and the public has grown to expect greater drug safety, the traditional reactive approach has proven largely incapable of addressing both the shifts in public expectations and regulatory and media scrutiny. This reality has revealed improvement areas involved in patient safety operations: organizational alignment, operations management, data management, and risk management. Last but not least, standard-based systems integration will present challenges. In sponsor corporate environment, pharmacovigilance technology system needs to establish interoperable channels with other numerous systems: Clinical data management system (CDMS), clinical trial management system, product performance system, clinical coding application, and potential Clinical Research Organisation (CRO) systems. It seems that standardization on signal definitions, common medical domains, clinical data elements, case report forms, adverse events, and medication coding are critical to ensure quality signal analysis. Standardization is also key to ensure success of pooled data analysis among all subjects in the pharmacovigilance databases used.

A peep into the future:

The challenges to manage drug safety efficiently and to adhere to regulatory requirements create the strong impression that widespread adoption of pharmacovigilance is inevitable. As an instrument of reform, pharmacovigilance has attributes that ensure its attractiveness to many groups in a politically and economically divided health care system that is struggling with seemingly insurmountable problems of cost and quality and post-marketing clinical studies as well. Perhaps the biggest uncertainty concerning pharmacovigilance is whether it will accomplish dramatic, transformational improvement in accurately and reliably detecting clinical safety signals among the millions of haystack of voluntarily reported data. It would rather be premature to assume that modern pharmacovigilance technology will offer such critical decision-making capability. Even if it does, a thorough manual confirmation would be required at the detailed clinical data levels. Sponsor management is already grappling with the fact that implementing pharmacovigilance across the corporation will require changing, quite dramatically, the work of many different functional groups including but not limited to: IT, clinical data management, safety, product performance, operations, CROs if applicable, clinical sites in order to create an operational safety framework and foster the gear switch to support the implementation of new technology. In the face of this challenge, the will to improve and prosper will be primary, the technology and innovation secondary, and patience and collaboration critical. Creating standards-based and interoperable clinical pharmacovigilance systems in which corporate management and safety staff can find the quality improvement in signal detection and cost reduction essential to accomplishing corporate financial and professional goals will be necessary to widespread adoption of modern pharmacovigilance and to assessing its transformative potential.

Conclusion

The assessment of spontaneous reports is most effective when it is conducted within the defined and rigorous good pharmacovigilance process (GPVP) framework, a functional structure for both public health, health care delivery and corporate risk management strategy. These practices are designed to efficiently and effectively detect and alert the drug safety professional to new and potentially important information on drug adverse reactions. Data mining of adverse event databases is a tool to help with the challenging task of systematically detecting signals among the over 300,000 MedWatch or other similar reports submitted annually to the FDA or similar agencies and is most effectively utilized with full awareness of the limitations and circumstances of voluntary reporting, coding, database characteristics, or quality. Data-mining signals by themselves are not indicators of problems, but indicators of possible problems. Data mining is not intended to replace traditional pharmacovigilance techniques, but to engender improvement and add efficiency. Signals are generated for a relatively small proportion of all distinct drug–event pairs in the database. These signals capture a high proportion of the total number of drug–event pairs reported, greatly facilitating more focused follow-up and prioritized risk assessment. Such practices and the overall GPVP are supported by modern internet-based systems with powerful analytical engines, workflow, security, and audit trails to allow validated systems support for proactive drug safety signalling efforts. Future pharmacovigilance technology will have more standardization and interoperability. It reasons to state that pharmacovigilance has the potential to meet the challenges of the increasing range and potency of medicines (including vaccines); however, still there are issues, concerns, challenges and risks involved in implementing and adopting modern pharmacovigilance solutions, which should be taken into consideration with the coming time and development.

Pharmacovigilance : Structural and Functional Units

This chapter elaborates different structural and functional aspects of pharmacovigilance, which go hand in hand. Starting with the definition of pharmacovigilance always help us to understand further about it in detail particularly when we are talking about its' structural and functional practices. Simply put, pharmacovigilance is a system to monitor the safety and effectiveness of medicines and other pharmaceutical products.

A pharmacovigilance system should include all entities and resources that protect the public from medicine related harm, whether in personal health care or public health services.

Product Quality

Monitoring the quality of products available in the marketplace should identify products that are defective, deteriorated, or adulterated because of poor manufacturing practices, inadequate distribution and storage, or tampering. Medicines that have lost their potency after being stored at high temperatures would fall under this category, for example, as would counterfeit products. Many studies have documented the circulation of counterfeit and sub-standard medicines, especially antimalarials, in developing countries. An example of the impact of medicine quality occurred in the mid-1990s, when almost 100 children in Haiti died from ingesting locally manufactured pain relief syrup adulterated with diethylene glycol.

Medication Errors

The National Coordinating Council for Medication Error Reporting and Prevention (NCC MERP) defines medication error as "any preventable event that may cause or lead to inappropriate medication use or patient harm while the medication is in the control of the health care professional, patient, or consumer" (NCC MERP 2009). Errors can be harmless or detrimental to the patient. Medication errors result from faulty systems, processes, and conditions that lead people to make mistakes or fail to prevent mistakes. Problems can result from illegible handwriting, use of dangerous abbreviations, overlooked interactions with other medicines, oral miscommunication, and sound-alike or look-alike products. For example; a recent number of highly-publicized injuries and deaths have involved infants receiving overdoses of heparin because of confusing labels, mixture miscalculations, or faulty verification by a health care provider (ISMP 2008); in Uganda, over 45 children were crippled from nerve damage caused by improperly injected quinine (Agiro 2009). By definition, medication errors should be preventable through education and effective systems controls involving pharmacists, prescribers, nurses, administrators, regulators, and patients. An adverse drug reaction is a harmful response caused by the medicine after it was given to the patient in the recommended manner (dose, frequency, route, administration technique). Examples include allergic reactions, effects from withdrawal, or responses caused by interactions with other medications. WHO defines a serious ADR as any reaction that is fatal, life-threatening, permanently or significantly disabling, requires or prolongs hospitalization, or relates to misuse or dependence. An ADE is caused by either the medicine itself or the medicine's inappropriate use. Therefore, an ADR is always an ADE , but the ADE category also includes results from, say, an overdose because of a dispensing error or some other error occurring when the patient is taking the medicine.

A Comprehensive system perspective

Health professionals may still think of pharmacovigilance strictly in terms of identifying and reporting previously unknown and serious ADRs related to new products. Although many national pharmacovigilance programmes are largely based on this activity, a comprehensive system should also encompass monitoring of medication errors and therapeutic ineffectiveness (related to poor treatment adherence, antimicrobial resistance, product quality problems, inappropriate use, or interactions); product quality problems; and communication of such information to health care professionals and consumers for risk-benefit decision making. For example, as a pharmacovigilance system matures, it may expand from a programme based strictly on passive ADR surveillance that relies on voluntary reports from health care providers or consumers to incorporate active surveillance methods to address priority safety concerns, such as the use of registries, sentinel sites, and follow-up of defined patient cohorts. Other system expansion efforts can include establishing a link between pharmaceutical quality assurance and ADR monitoring and developing mechanisms to communicate medicine safety information to health care professionals and the public.

A country's pharmacovigilance system should incorporate activities and resources at the facility, national, and international levels and foster collaboration among a wide range of partners and organizations that contribute to ensuring medicine safety. Figure 2 illustrates the components of a comprehensive, ongoing pharmacovigilance system with **functions** for monitoring, detecting, reporting, evaluating, and documenting medicine safety data as well as intervening and gathering information from and providing educational feedback to the reporters— prescribers, health care workers, other health care professionals, and consumers.

Once the information has been collected, **evaluators**, such as epidemiologists or pharmacologists, should analyze it to determine the adverse event's severity, probable causality, and preventability also significant data must be communicated effectively to a **structure** or entity that has the authority to take appropriate action, whether at the facility, national, or even international level. The entity may be a hospital's drug and therapeutics committee (DTC), the national pharmacovigilance center, if one exists, or the WHO Programme for International Drug Monitoring. The final function in the framework is **appropriate action**.

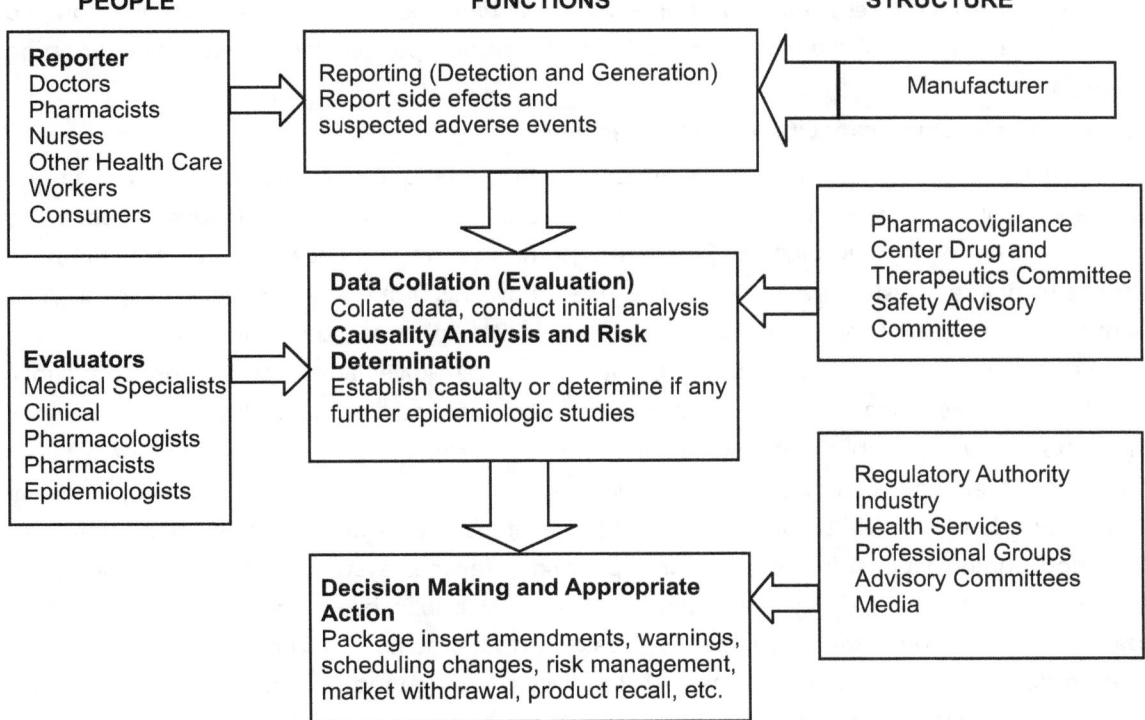

Fig. 14.2: The Pharmacovigilance Framework: relating people, functions, structures, and expected outcome and impact

If data are collected, analyzed, reported, but no one takes any action based on the data, the system is irrelevant. The risk reduction action may be regulatory (withdrawing marketing authorization, recalling a medication); managerial (revising a hospital formulary, instituting distribution controls); or educational (teaching prescribers about medicine-medicine interactions or proper product handling). To encourage continued participation in the process, interventions should be shared with the data reporters as part of a feedback loop. Follow-up data collection and analysis will then measure the effectiveness of the interventions. The outcome of a pharmacovigilance system should be decreased medicine-related problems with the ultimate impact being a reduction in morbidity and mortality. As countries move to expand the scope of their pharmacovigilance activities to include monitoring for product quality problems and adverse events related to inappropriate medicine use, they will need to establish new mechanisms for cooperation among stakeholders and build system capacity. For example, incorporating product quality surveillance into the system used for ADR reporting may require linkages between the entity responsible for collecting, compiling, and evaluating ADR reports and the national pharmaceutical inspectorate and quality control laboratory. Data collection and reporting on the three potential sources of ADE s—product quality problems, medication errors, and ADRs—must be incorporated into the overall health system, from the facility to the national level. To plan for this information system, basic questions must be answered about whether the data flow will be combined for each of these potential sources, who will be responsible for the data collection and reporting at each level of the health system, and how vertical public health programme reporting will be integrated.

Developing structural capacity and staff capacity

The medicine regulatory authority's most important role is to lead the collaboration among the various pharmacovigilance partners and to assure that information feedback loops are working. An important coordination function is to monitor performance and create a culture of responsibility in the system, whereby every partner knows his or her role and what is expected. As mentioned above, pharmacovigilance partners may include pharmaceutical procurement officials, professional organizations, media outlets, patient and care-giver advocacy groups, and public health programme managers, in addition to health care managers at the facility, district, regional, and national levels. Establishing linkages and widely disseminating medicine safety information builds. Another key component of developing a strong system is the integration of pharmacovigilance activities of public health programs, such as HIV/AIDS treatment and childhood immunizations, into the national pharmacovigilance system. Multiple ADR reporting structures tend to evolve when a country has vertical public health programmes operating; however, such fragmentation ultimately weakens the system. Conversely, a public health programme that has a well-established ADR collection and reporting structure can serve as a model and a starting point for a national system, if one does not already exist. Along with building the structural capacity having well trained staff can strengthen the pillar of pharmacovigilance any time. A common understanding of the process in general would serve the need for the practice of pharmacovigilance, and that could only be initiated by proper trained staff in different areas, like All health care providers, including physicians, pharmacists, nurses, dentists, and others, should realize that reporting ADRs and medication errors should be a part of their professional responsibility. Voluntary reporting of ADRs and medication errors requires health care providers to be active participants in a culture of safety. Even though programmes relying solely on voluntary, spontaneous reporting methods reveal only the tip of the iceberg, voluntary reporting should always be encouraged, because it helps to establish a team approach to improving patient care and reducing risks. Nonetheless, under-reporting is a common challenge in all pharmacovigilance systems at the facility, be it regional or national level.

In summary, the use of pharmaceuticals involves a trade-off between their benefits and the potential for harm. Pharmacovigilance can help minimize the risk of harm by ensuring that medicines of good quality are used appropriately and that health care providers and consumers have the information they need to make knowledgeable decisions about treatment. Countries can create a comprehensive medicine safety system through careful strategic planning that encompasses all aspects of pharmacovigilance, but uses phased implementation, and effectively coordinated technical and financial support to achieve long-term goals.

Uppsala Monitoring Center

The Uppsala Monitoring Centre (the UMC), located in Uppsala, Sweden, is the field name for the World Health Organization Collaborating Centre for International Drug Monitoring. The UMC works by collecting, assessing and communicating information from member countries' national pharmacovigilance programmes in regards to the benefits, harm, effectiveness and risks of drugs.

The work of the UMC is:

- To co-ordinate the WHO Programme for International Drug Monitoring and its more than 100 member countries
- To collect, assess and communicate information from member countries about the benefits, harms and risks of drugs and other substances used in medicine to improve patient therapy and public health worldwide
- To collaborate with member countries in the development and practice of the science of pharmacovigilance.

The main focus and source of data in pharmacovigilance are reports of ICSRs (individual case safety reports) from healthcare providers and patients in member countries of the WHO Programme. A WHO global individual case safety report database (Vigibase) is maintained and developed on behalf of the WHO by the UMC. The UMC develops and provides several tools and classifications for use by organisations involved in drug safety, including the WHO Drug Dictionary, WHO-ART (adverse reaction terminology) - with a bridge to the MedDRA terminology, tools for searching in the database, and a programme for case report management, VigiFlow. The Uppsala centre has also published books in the field of drugs safety including a regular newsletter.

Data Mining: A Computational method to extract the useful information from a large data pool.

The WHO has defined a signal as: 'Reported information on a possible causal relationship between an adverse event and a drug, the relationship being unknown or incompletely documented previously'. A signal is therefore very tentative in nature; the first expression that something might be wrong with a medicinal product, or a hint given by new information which might support or explain a medicinal product–adverse reaction relationship already known. Both quantitative and qualitative factors come into the decision of whether something is a signal or not (Edwards et al., 1990). Many algorithms have been proposed for determining causality between a drug substance and an adverse reaction, but there is no perfect way of doing this, which fits all possible situations.

Apparent causality in a single case, or even a series, is not the only issue in comprehensive early signal detection. One might exclude many of the case reports with limited information, yet, just because a case record does not allow for remote assessment of the case, does not mean that the original observer was incorrect; only that one cannot confirm the observation. Thus the quantity as well as the quality of reports of associations is valuable. The use of 'poor quality' reports as a trigger for a signal should be considered more carefully if the clinical event is serious. Early warning is more important, and a signal based on doubtful evidence should promote the search for better.

Data mining is a form of exploratory data analysis and a key component of the knowledge discovery process. Data mining can clearly be used on any dataset, but the approach seems particularly valuable when the amount of data is large and the possible relationships within the data set numerous and complex. In principle the WHO Collaborating Centre for International Drug Monitoring (the Uppsala Monitoring Centre, UMC) has been doing data mining since the mid-1970s, using an early relational database. As with many automated systems, the relational database to a very large extent replicated a manual approach. The UMC is, as the WHO Collaborating Centre for International Drug Monitoring, responsible for the technical and scientific maintenance and development of the WHO International Drug Monitoring Programme. The Programme now has more than 100 member countries, annually contributing around 2,50,000 suspected adverse drug reaction (ADR) reports to the WHO database in Uppsala. One of the main aims of the international pharmacovigilance programme is to identify early signals of safety problems related to medicines. To aid this, a new ADR signalling system has been provided for national monitoring centres and authorities based on automated exploratory data analysis. It complements the previous signal detection procedure which involved the examination of unwieldy, large amounts of sorted and tabulated material by an expert panel. Critics of data mining can reasonably suggest that, with all the possible relationships in a huge database, many medicine-adverse reaction associations will occur by chance, even though they seem to be significantly associated.

The limitations:

Data mining is intended to alert the observer to unusual relationships within a data set. It is essential to understand that in pharmacovigilance, what is reported and contained within the data set does not represent the true epidemiology of adverse reactions to medicines. There is the very well-known problem of underreporting, but more than that, many countries ask health professionals to be selective in their reporting to cut down the 'noise'. Data mining should allow for much easier and useful handling of large amounts of information. Since the 'triaging' of information is done automatically, there is no longer any need to specify that only serious and unexpected reactions need be reported. Indeed, data mining in pharmacovigilance will function better for us if there is a large amount of 'ordinary' adverse reaction information to serve as the background. If we just record the serious and unexpected, only the more serious and unexpected will stand out, progressively. Data mining has it's main future in the detection of complex patterns in the data. It is possible that, if doctors reported all the medicinal product safety issues that concern them, we would be able to identify some issues of use and poor use of medicines which could be addressed. One problem with data mining is the temptation to turn it into data dredging. There is a difference: data mining uses objectively predetermined (if flexible) logic to examine relationships in data transparently with the aim of generating hypotheses for further evaluation. Data dredging is based upon a series of prejudiced queries which might imbue chance relationships with plausibility, and in which a strict logic or strategy is not followed.

Data mining is proving to be a useful tool. It's full potential has not yet been reached, and it may be that some of the current drug regulations and attitudes may need to be reconsidered as its use becomes more widespread. In spite of it's potential as the primary search tool in pharmacovigilance, it is clear that it's use must be accompanied by the wise interpretation of the information. Since no database is representative of what truly happens, other observations, monitoring and epidemiology must continue to be used in a complementary way. Only by the interactive interpretation of findings using different observational methodology are we likely to even approach the truth.

Practical Pharmacovigilance

Ensuring the safety and efficacy of pharmaceuticals and biotechnology products is one of the topmost challenges in healthcare today. With drug recalls continuing to make headlines, consumers and other stakeholders across the healthcare ecosystem are demanding more oversight and regulators around the globe are responding to these pressures by increasing their scrutiny and compliance requirements from the industry. Despite the heightened focus on drug safety and the direct link between reactive safety and numerous risks to business — financial, regulatory, brand loss, etc. — many biopharmaceutical companies today still have inefficient drug safety operations and detect safety signals with suboptimal latency. Inefficiencies and redundancies in pharmacovigilance operations result in higher costs and undermine efforts to significantly increase overall performance. As the pharmaceutical, biotechnology and medical device industries renew their focus on becoming lean and more effective in bringing safer, newer products and therapeutic value to patients in a timely manner, they must also transform their drug safety operations. Proactive pharmacovigilance — enabled by globally integrated process, people and technologies — can help the industry achieve its objectives. This can be accomplished by:

- Rigorous analysis, interpretation and "realtime" decision making on safety signals and proactive remediation.
- Leveraging pre- and post-marketing safety patterns and insights for clinical trial design and safety analysis to balance the risk-to benefit ratio of new products, therapeutic directions and early "go, no-go" decisions advancing drug candidates.
- Allowing for convergence of the evolving regulatory environment and the integrated.

Pharmacovigilance safety operations and analytics into a source of innovation and competitive advantage.

Practical Practices to collect safety data around the globe

Systematic examination of the reported adverse events by using statistical or mathematical tools, or so-called data mining, can provide additional information about the existence of an excess of adverse events reported for a product at various stages of risk identification and assessment. There are various methods by which safety data are collected mainly depending the objective and kind of data that need to be stored for differential purposes. Below are the key methods to collect data mainly used for pharmacovigical purpose.

1. Passive Surveillance

Spontaneous Reports

A spontaneous report is an unsolicited communication by healthcare professionals or consumers (patients, pharmacists etc.) to a sponsor company, regulatory authority or other organization (e.g., WHO, Regional Centers) that describes one or more adverse events in a patient who was given one or more medicinal products. Spontaneous reports are almost always submitted voluntarily and do not derive from a study or any organized data collection scheme.

One of this system's major weaknesses is under-reporting, though the figures vary greatly between countries and in relation to minor and serious AEs. Another problem is that over-worked medical personnel do not always see reporting as a priority. Spontaneous reports play a major role in the identification of safety signals once a drug is marketed. Spontaneous reports can provide important information on at-risk groups, risk factors, and clinical features of known serious adverse drug reactions.

Stimulated Reporting

As opposed to spontaneous reporting, several methods like on-line reporting of adverse events and systematic stimulation of reporting of AEs based on a pre-designed method are used to generate safety signals. In the early post-marketing phase, companies notify healthcare professionals of the newly-marketed drug and provide known safety information, and at the same time encourage the submission of spontaneous reports when an AE is identified Data obtained from stimulated reporting cannot be used to generate accurate incidence rates, but reporting rates can be estimated. These methods have been shown to improve reporting, they are not devoid of the limitations of passive surveillance, especially selective reporting and incomplete information.

2. Active Surveillance

Active surveillance is deployed to determine the number of AEs by way of a continuous pre-organized process which is determined while drafting the risk management programme. Active surveillance involves reaching out by public authority by regular telephone calls or visits to laboratories, hospitals, and providers to stimulate reporting of specific diseases. AsI Implementing active surveillance should be limited to brief or sequential periods of time and for specific purposes only as it places intensive demands on resources. Active surveillance takes a step ahead to verify case reports and/or review medical records and other alternative sources to identify diagnoses that may not have been reported.

Sentinel Sites

Sentinel surveillance involves the collection of AE data from only part of the total population (from a sample of providers) to learn something about the larger population, such as trends in disease. The advantages of sentinel surveillance data are that they can be less expensive to obtain than those gained through active surveillance of the total population, and the data can be qualitatively better than those collected through passive systems. This is because it is logistically easier to obtain higher quality information from a smaller population. A vulnerability of sentinel systems is not being able to ensure the representativeness of the sample. Also, some major weaknesses of sentinel sites are problems with selection bias, and increased costs.

Drug Event Monitoring

In drug event monitoring, patients are identified from electronic prescription data or automated health insurance claims. Patients who fill a prescription for the concerned drug may have been asked to complete a brief survey form and give permission for later contact. A follow-up questionnaire is then sent to each prescribing physician or patient at pre-specified intervals to obtain outcome information. Although detailed information on adverse events from a large number of physicians and/or patients might be collected, drug event monitoring can include poor physician and patient response rates and the unfocused nature of data collection, which can obscure important signals. Also, in this system, maintenance of patient confidentiality might be a concern.

Registries

A registry is a list of patients with the same characteristic(s). This characteristic can be a disease (disease registry) or a specific exposure (drug registry). Both types of registries, which only differ by the type of patient data of interest, can collect a battery of information using standardized questionnaires in a prospective fashion. Disease registries can help collect data on drug exposure and other factors associated with a clinical condition. Exposure (drug) registries address populations exposed to drugs of interest (e.g., registry of rheumatoid arthritis patients exposed to biological therapies) to determine if a drug has a special impact on this group of patients. Patients can be followed over time and included in a cohort study to collect data on AEs using standardized questionnaires. Single cohort studies can measure incidence, and can be useful for signal amplification, particularly for rare outcomes. This type of registry can be especially valuable when examining the safety of an orphan drug indicated for a specific condition.

3. Comparative Observational Studies

This method of PV surveillance borrows from traditional epidemiologic methods. A number of observational study designs can prove useful in validating signals from spontaneous reports or case series. These designs are cross-sectional studies, case-control studies, and cohort studies (both retrospective and prospective).

Cross-Sectional Study

The data collected from a population of patients in a cross-sectional study can be attributed to at a single point in time (or interval of time) regardless of exposure or disease status. A drawback of cross-sectional studies is that it does not define the temporal relationship between exposure and AE (outcome). These studies are best used to examine the *prevalence* of an AE at a time point or to examine trends over time.

Case Control Study

In a case-control study, cases of AEs are identified. Patients can be identified from an existing database or using data collected specifically for the purpose of the study of interest. Controls, or patients without the AE of interest, are then selected from the source population which had reported the AEs. The controls are selected in such a way that the prevalence of drug exposure among the controls represents the prevalence of drug exposure in the source population. The exposure status of the two groups is then compared, and the relative risks of the 2 groups are computed.

Cohort Studies

In a cohort study, a population-at-risk for the AE is followed over time for the occurrence of the AE. Information on drug exposure status is known throughout the follow-up period for each patient and incidence rates can be calculated. In many cohort studies involving drug exposure, comparison cohorts of interest are selected on the basis of drug use and followed over time. Cohort studies are useful when there is a need to know the incidence rates of AEs in addition to the relative risks of AEs.

4. Targeted Clinical Investigations

When significant risks are identified from pre-approval clinical trials, further clinical studies might be devised to evaluate the mechanism of action for the AE. Some studies may be conducted to determine whether a particular dosing instruction can put patients at an increased risk of AE. Pharmacogenetic studies may be conducted to provide clues about which group of patients might be at an increased risk of AE. Furthermore, specific studies may be devised to investigate potential drug-drug interactions and food-drug interactions in patients and normal volunteers.

The role of the Life Sciences companies

In today's world a huge volume of work related to pharmacovigilance is offshored to many service providers across the globe. Many pharmaceutical companies manage their own work load of pharmacovigilance whereas others outsource it to a specialised division established specifically established in many multinationals worldwide. The amount of strategic partnership amongst the multinationals and the parent pharmaceutical companies that have grown in last few years now has a definite impact to maintain the "quality" of the data generated overall that guide the decisions at the regulatory bodies as well as the parent company for a particular drug. As with any other industry, there are huge challenges to this nascent collaboration which has a critical role to play in this particular domain. Below, we have briefly discussed the key challenges and solutional approaches which would give a better understanding of pharmacovigilance from industrial point of view.

- Establish the "safety first" vision and re-emphasize the need for proactive safety and compliance, RiskMAPs and benefits that can be realized with the entire team-both internal and partners — through structured governance/communications from executive and senior management.
- Ensure safety risk assessment as part of business risk management that is tracked and monitored for proactive remediation.
- Make informed and early decisions on "go, no-go" on products in the pipeline based on signals/safety analytics from launched products and products in advanced clinical studies.
- Implement specific actions and programmes that are focused on "getting it right the first time" to avoid intensive/overtime fire-fighting work and costs.
- Develop/refine capabilities to manage regulatory changes in "real-time" Regulators across the globe have varying and continually changing reporting requirements. To operate globally, life sciences companies must meet these requirements as well as local timelines, reporting formats and translation requirements.
- A critical activity is keeping abreast of regional regulatory changes for registration and reporting. Life sciences companies need a dedicated group of analysts and regulatory experts who follow evolving trends and provide guidance on class-wide Risk Evaluation and Mitigation Strategies (REMS), alignment between global regulatory agencies (ICH, EU, FDA, Japan, etc.), post-marketing data collection, integration and analysis, guidance on training, policies and reporting to all stakeholders.

Implementation of globally aligned processes and technology:

From the Processes perspective, in order to gather comprehensive data, life sciences companies must manage global drug safety operations and coordination of case-processing through a "single harmonized process" with options for local customization to fit regulatory requirements. These include:

- A seamless operating model that integrates case processing volumes, types and submissions timelines "demand" with a globally flexible and scalable resourcing "capacity" model, across the sponsor and the global partners/service providers.

- Identifying drug risk profiles using preclinical and relevant post-marketing data before future clinical trials are designed.

- Following up with subjects after completion of trials and analysis of adverse-event related patient withdrawals.

- Ensuring that comprehensive post-marketing process including regular case handling, reporting, labelling changes and active querying.

- Signal generation, evaluation, adequate trend analysis, documentation, disposition and archival.

- Assessment and review of risk/benefit analysis in the context of evolving risk-based understanding.

Technology:

- Develop a centralized database that can integrate disparate data and information from different sources internally, third parties and physicians.

- Ensure the ability to draw PV information insights from case report forms (CRFs) on a "real-time" basis, which may have significant value on managing risks.

Approaching pharmacovigilance as an enterprise-wide business strategy is still not the norm but is quickly becoming so. Life sciences companies that embrace this shift will be able to meet near-term demands for drug safety assurances from a range of global stakeholders. Most approved products are subjected to risk mitigation plans of some sort. Simultaneously, life sciences companies are staking out a competitive advantage in the form of more and better data used intelligently to help evaluate and direct future clinical development and post-marketing evaluation of comparator products. The net impact will be that life sciences companies will be in a better position to deliver the higher quality, lower cost products the market requires and ultimately deliver better quality of life to patients.

Risk Management

The term "risk management" encompasses both risk assessment and risk minimization. Risk assessment consists of identifying and characterizing the nature, frequency, and severity of the risks associated with the use of the product. It is not enough to simply state that an adverse experience is associated with the use of a product. Pharmaceutical companies are expected to quantify that risk in different populations and try to determine risk factors that could explain why some individuals taking a product experience an adverse experience while others do not. Risk minimization involves minimizing a product's risk while preserving it's benefits. Risk management is a four-part iterative process which includes: (1) assessing a product's benefit-risk balance, (2) developing and implementing tools to minimize its risks while preserving its benefits, (3) evaluating tool effectiveness and reassessing the benefit-risk balance, and (4) making adjustments, as appropriate, to the risk minimization tools to further improve the benefit-risk balance. The basic activities of risk management are risk identification, risk evaluation, risk communication, and risk minimization. Although these activities take place throughout the life cycle of the product, the emphases of these activities change during each stage of development.

The world of pharmacovigilance is changing quickly and dramatically in response to a set of new guidelines and regulations developed over the past few years. The goal of these documents is to aid the industry in planning risk management activities throughout the drug development life cycle. Specifically, they define three types of activities: (1) pre-license efforts required to evaluate the safety of a product, (2) pharmacovigilance actions to be implemented in the early postmarketing period to monitor the products' safety profile, and (3) steps to minimize risk. As such, these guidelines and regulations describe a method for summarizing important safety issues and propose a structure for a risk management plan. The regulations and guidelines, which encourage pharmaceutical companies to make their pharmacovigilance activities more proactive, include five components:

- ICH (International Conference on Harmonisation) E2E guidance for Industry on Pharmacovigilance Planning, finalized in November 2004.

- Three FDA Guidance Documents on Good Risk Management Practices: (1) Premarketing Risk Assessment, (2) Development and Use of Risk Minimization Action Plans, and (3) Good Pharmacovigilance Practices and Pharmacoepidemiologic Assessment, published in March 2005.

- EMEA CHMP Guideline on Risk Management Systems for Medicinal Products for Human Use, published in November 2005. These guidelines have been updated in Volume 9A of the Rules Governing Medicinal Products in The European Union – Guidelines on Pharmacovigilance for Medicinal Products for Human Use.

The development of the ICH E2E document was based on four general principles. First, planning of pharmacovigilance activities should take place throughout the life cycle of the product. This can be accomplished by having the physicians who monitored product safety in the post-marketing environment to get involved earlier in the drug development process. Second, there should be a science-based approach to risk documentation.

Monitoring product safety is a difficult process. Rarely does one have all of the information necessary to determine if a rare adverse experience is associated with the administration of a product. Any study done to evaluate or characterize a safety concern should be based on sound epidemiologic principles, so that the newly acquired data are interpretable and contribute to our understanding of the safety profile of the product. Poorly-designed studies only produce disinformation, which can be more harmful than no information. Third, pharmacovigilance planning requires effective collaboration between regulators and the industry. Regulators and industry should agree on the issues discussed in a risk management plan. Fourth, the pharmacovigilance plan should be applicable across the three ICH regions which include Europe, Japan, and the United States. This is difficult to implement because different regulatory agencies have different concerns.

Content of a Risk Management Plan

Risk management plans are finalized during the latter part of clinical development. The most difficult part of preparing these plans is making the decision about which issues to address in the Safety Specification portion of the document, as well as how to address them. The complexity arises from the fact that, at this point, there is so much data – from pre-clinical studies, clinical pharmacology studies, clinical trials, the medical literature, and, in some cases, post-marketing experience also. The question, then, is which issues to consider risks – and whether they qualify as identified or potential risks. The EMEA defines an identified risk as an untoward occurrence for which there is adequate evidence of an association with the medicinal product of interest. Examples include:

- Adverse reaction adequately demonstrated in non-clinical studies and confirmed by clinical data.

- Adverse reaction observed in well-designed clinical trials or epidemiologic studies for which the magnitude of the difference, in relation to the comparator group (placebo or active substance, or unexposed group) on a parameter of interest suggests a causal association.

- Adverse reaction suggested by a number of well-documented spontaneous reports where causality is strongly supported by temporal relationship and biological plausibility, such as anaphylactic reaction or application site reactions, the challenge, however, is that while this definition and examples are helpful, they still leave room for personal interpretation. Making decisions about how to categorize issues is not always clear cut. Pre-clinical data, for example, may be difficult to interpret. We know, for instance, that what happens to animals, even at higher doses than given to humans, may or may not happen to humans. However, if an unusual adverse experience happens in an animal species, and a similar event happens in humans in clinical trials, it has to be considered an identified risk. What is the "magnitude of the difference" in clinical or epidemiologic studies that suggests a causal association? Statistical tests can be used to determine if there is a statistically significant difference between the numbers of reports in the two groups. Interpreting spontaneous reports for causality from the post-marketing environment can be difficult because of the factors that influence reporting, such as news media attention and legal cases. The number of well-documented spontaneous reports is helpful, as is biologic plausibility, but they are not the only criteria to use. Single events, such as the Stevens-Johnson Syndrome, also need to be considered. A potential risk is defined as an untoward occurrence for which there is some basis for suspicion of an association with the product of interest, but where this association has not been confirmed.

Examples include:

- Non-clinical safety concerns that have not been observed or resolved in clinical studies.

- Adverse events observed in clinical trials or epidemiologic studies for which the magnitude of the difference, compared with the comparator group (placebo or active substance, or unexposed group) on the parameter of interest raises a suspicion of, but is not large enough to suggest, a causal association.

- A signal arising from a spontaneous adverse reaction reporting system, or an event which is known to be associated with other products of the same class, or which could be expected to occur, based on the properties of the medicinal product. In summary, potential risks are those risks that may or may not be causally associated with the use of the product, but the data are insufficient to determine either way. The term "missing information" refers to data about the safety of a medicinal product which are not available at the time of submission of the EU Risk Management Plan, thereby representing a limitation of the safety data (i.e., too little data to predict the safety of the product in the market place). The missing information category can include populations that were not adequately evaluated in clinical trials, as well as outstanding safety questions that warrant further investigation to refine understanding of the benefit-risk profile during the post authorization period.

US Activities in Risk Management of Pharmaceutical Products

FDA evaluates the safety profiles of drugs available in the United States using a variety of tools and disciplines throughout the life cycle of the drugs. Under US regulations, manufacturers of approved drug and biological products are required to promptly report all adverse drug experience information obtained or otherwise received by the manufacturer from any source, foreign or domestic, including information derived from commercial marketing experience, post-marketing epidemiological/ surveillance studies, reports in the scientific literature and unpublished scientific papers. FDA also accepts reports directly from healthcare providers and consumers. Currently, the agency's adverse event database has over 3.5 million reports with increasing numbers reported annually. This system of post-marketing surveillance reporting the adverse event reports system or adverse event reporting system (AERS) and risk assessment programmes serves to identify adverse events that did not appear during the drug development process. The successful implementation of electronic submissions is a high priority for the center. Further improvements in this system include electronic submission of adverse drug reports that will result in more timely receipt and evaluation of adverse event reports at considerable cost savings both to FDA and to those submitting the reports. Data mining provides an important tool in facilitating signal detection of the more than three million reports in this database.

Risk Management Guidance

The Prescription Drug User Fee Act of 2003 (PDUFA III) specifically addressed risk management, noting that efficient risk management as one of FDA's five strategic goals, including both the new drug review process and oversight after approval. Acknowledging that it is impossible at the time of approval to know everything about a medicine's safety, PDUFA III mandated that there be increased surveillance of the safety of medicines during their first 2 years on the market (or first 3 years for drugs with potentially serious safety concerns identified at the time of approval). The FDA also agreed to develop regulatory strategies and guidance documents on risk management. Three guidance documents were developed with input from the public and industry. These guidelines, summarized below, were published as final documents in March 2005.

Guidance on Pre-Marketing Risk Assessment

This regulatory guidance focuses on approaches an industry might consider throughout all stages of the clinical development of products. Some key components of the guidance include:

1. Specific recommendations to industry for improving the assessment and reporting of safety during drug development trials;

2. Improving the assessment of important safety issues during registration trials and to provide best practices for analyzing and reporting data that are developed as a result of a careful pre-approval safety evaluation and;

3. Building on (but not superceding) a number of existing FDA and ICH (International Conference on Harmonisation of Technical Requirements.

Guidance on Development and Use of Risk Minimization Action Plans

This guidance provides a conceptual framework on the development, implementation and evaluation of risk minimization action plans for prescription drug and biological products. It focuses on: (1) initiating and designing plans called risk minimization action plans or RiskMAPs to minimize identified product risks, (2) selecting and developing tools to minimize those risks, (3) evaluating RiskMAPs and monitoring tools, (4) communicating with FDA about RiskMAPs, and (5) the recommended components of a RiskMAP submission to FDA.

A European Regulatory View

In the decade since the European regulatory systems were fully implemented in 1995, the concepts of risk management have developed and evolved in the light of growing knowledge and experience. The term 'risk management' may be broadly defined as the identification and implementation of strategies to reduce risk to individuals and populations, while a risk management plan in relation to a particular medicine has a specific interpretation set out in European guidance. The principles of risk management informed the '2001 review' of European Legislation, which was adopted in 2004 and was subsequently the subject of detailed guidelines. It is often said that regulation follows science; in the case of risk management, regulation has followed not only scientific and technical progress, but growing public expectations that the systems for monitoring the safety of medicines are optimally effective. Risk management in Europe faces particular challenges. The regulatory systems depend on the collective functioning of a network which now comprises 26 national agencies (2 in Germany), with the European Medicines Agency (EMEA) performing a supervisory and co-ordinating role. The withdrawal of cerivastatin in 2001 following spontaneous reports of cases of serious and fatal rhabdomyolysis represented a regulatory milestone. The extent of use of cerivastatin in Europe meant that a wide public debate ensued. This debate was reignited on an international scale in September 2004, when Merck withdrew rofecoxib, a selective cyclo-oxygenase 2 inhibitor widely used in the treatment of arthritic pain, because of clinical trial evidence of an increased risk of heart attack and stroke.

European Risk Management Plan

A European Guideline on Risk Management for Medicinal Products for Human Use, also published in November 2005, sets out in detail the situations when a risk management plan is required.

Part I consists of Safety Specification plan and A Pharmacovigilance plan, briefly **Safety Specification plan** is the starting point for proactive pharmacovigilance, the safety specification, summarises what is known and what is not known about the safety of the product. This encompasses the important identified risks and any important information and outstanding safety questions which warrant further investigation, in order to refine understanding of benefit risk during the post-authorisation period.

The purpose of the **pharmacovigilance plan** is not to replace but to complement procedures in place to detect safety signals. For medicines with important identified risks, important potential risks or important missing information, additional pharmacovigilance activities to address these concerns should be considered. The EMEA Guideline describes a range of study designs (e.g., active surveillance, comparative observational studies) and data sources. An inventory of European pharmaco-epidemiology centres and healthcare databases is to be created by EMEA to facilitate the implementation of pharmacovigilance plans.

Part II consists of an evaluation of the need for risk minimisation activities, and if there is need for additional (i.e., non-routine) activities and a Risk Minimization plan.

A risk minimisation plan is only required in circumstances where standard information provision via the medicine's summary of product characteristics, patient information leaflet and label is not considered adequate to address identified safety concerns. Where a risk minimisation plan is considered necessary, both routine and additional activities are to be included. Some safety concerns may have more than one risk minimisation activity, each of which should be evaluated for effectiveness.

Pharmaceutical risk management faces important challenges in addressing innovative therapies, public expectations of product safety and optimizing patient selection to better minimize adverse outcomes. Regulatory pharmacovigilence activities have a critical role in assuring product safety by means of proactively designing and implementing interventions to minimize a product's risks. Pharmacovigilence also provides a framework for evaluating these interventions in light of new knowledge that is acquired over time and revising interventions when appropriate.

REFERENCE

1. SARAH DAVIS, BRIDGET KING AND JUNE M. RAINE.

   Vigilance and Risk Management of Medicines, Medicines and Healthcare products Regulatory 6 Agency, London, UK.

2. David j. Graham, Syed R. Ahmad and Toni Piazza- HEPP Office of Drug Safety, Center for Drug Evaluation and Research, US Food and Drug Administration, Rockville, MD, USA

3. Klepper MJ. Integrated Safety Systems Inc, North Carolina 27709-3542, USA. m.klepper@issdrugsafety.com

4. Patrice Verpillat, Pharmacoepidemiologist, Section Leader Pharmacoepidemiology, Department of Special Projects, Corporate. Economics & Pricing Division, Lundbeck SAS, Paris, France. MONDHER TOUMI H. Lundbeck A/S, Copenhagen, Denmark.

5. Robert G. Sharrar, MD, MSc, September/October issue of American Pharmaceutical Outsourcing.

6. Jonca Bull, Acting Deputy Director, Office of Drug Safety, US Food and Drug Administration, Rockville, MD, USA

7. Atemnkeng et al. 2007; Bate et al. 2008; Onwujekwe et al. 2009.

8. WHO Collaborating Centre for International Drug Monitoring The Importance of Pharmacovigilance – Safety Monitoring of Medicinal Products. Geneva, Switzerland: World Health Organization; 2002.

9. Bobo R, Notte J. Safety reporting in clinical trials. Next Generation Pharmaceutical. Availablefrom:http://www.ngpharma.com/pastissue/article.asp?art=26377&issue=159.

10. Almenoff J, Tonning JM, Gould AL, et al. Perspectives on the use of data mining in pharmacovigilance. Drug Saf. 2005;28:981–1007. [PubMed].

11. Zhengwu Lu. Clinical Research Department, Abbott Vascular, Santa Clara, CA, USA. Information technology in pharmacovigilance: Benefits, challenges, and future directions from industry perspectives [PubMed].

12. Pharmacovigilance: A Practical Approach to Reshaping Patient Safety; Krishnan Rajagopalan.

13. ICH guidelines E2A, E2D and E6.

Chapter ... 15

GENOMICS
AND
DRUG RESEARCH

| *"If you want to understand function, study structure".* | **Francis Crick** |

INTRODUCTION

The genetics' landscape is marked with several milestone achievements, from the early advances that elucidated DNA structure to the more recent completion of international scientific research projects, the Human Genome Project [HGP] and HapMap project. These projects have enabled the availability of complete sequence of the human genome and the sequence variation data between individuals. Although intensive polymorphism maps have been generated only lately, speculation that these variations could be related to alterations in drug metabolism and efficacy had been rife for a long time. The recognition that such variations could be inherited and could predict the efficacy and toxicity of drugs in individuals, led to the coining of the term "Pharmacogenetics" by Vogel. With the advent of advanced high-throughput technologies, studies are no longer limited to single candidate gene analysis; rather the objective has shifted to gain deeper insights at the system level. The field of pharmacogenetics too has graduated to "-omics" with a long term goal of understanding drug action associated with the genome and it's products. Pharmacogenomics holds the promise of discovering new drug targets which will aid in drug discovery and development. With huge implications and applications, it is little wonder that pharmacogenomic studies have increased exponentially in a short span of time, leading to accumulation of information worldwide.

On the flip side, the sequence and structural information dispersed across different locations is futile until it is integrated and analyzed. In this era of information explosion led by advanced state-of-the-art technologies, a compelling need for inter-disciplinary approaches to translate the information into a better understanding of biological processes has been strongly felt. Computational biology has provided the much required relief by integrating informatics resources to bridge the gap between the information available and knowledge. Current bioinformatics resources, which provide a platform for data storage, retrieval and sharing along with analytical methods and algorithms, have thus become indispensable in pharmacogenomic studies. The development and expansion of essential bioinformatics resources and value-added databases will be instrumental in pioneering new frontiers in pharmacogenomic studies. This chapter provides an introduction to the various key tools needed to understand and model the genetic variations for drug response.

Understanding the GENE

The human genome, consisting of 23 pairs of chromosomes, is known to code for approximately 25,000-30,000 protein-coding genes. This coding region has been estimated to be roughly 2% of the entire genome, while the remaining genome comprises regulatory sequences, introns, non-coding RNA genes, pseudogenes and a large chunk of "junk" DNA. Nearly half a decade post-HGP, "junk" DNA still remains controversial, although recent studies have shown that this region might contain functional elements. Now that almost complete genome sequence has been made available, understanding the functional aspects of the sequence from the perspective of structure and expression patterns forms the immediate challenge.

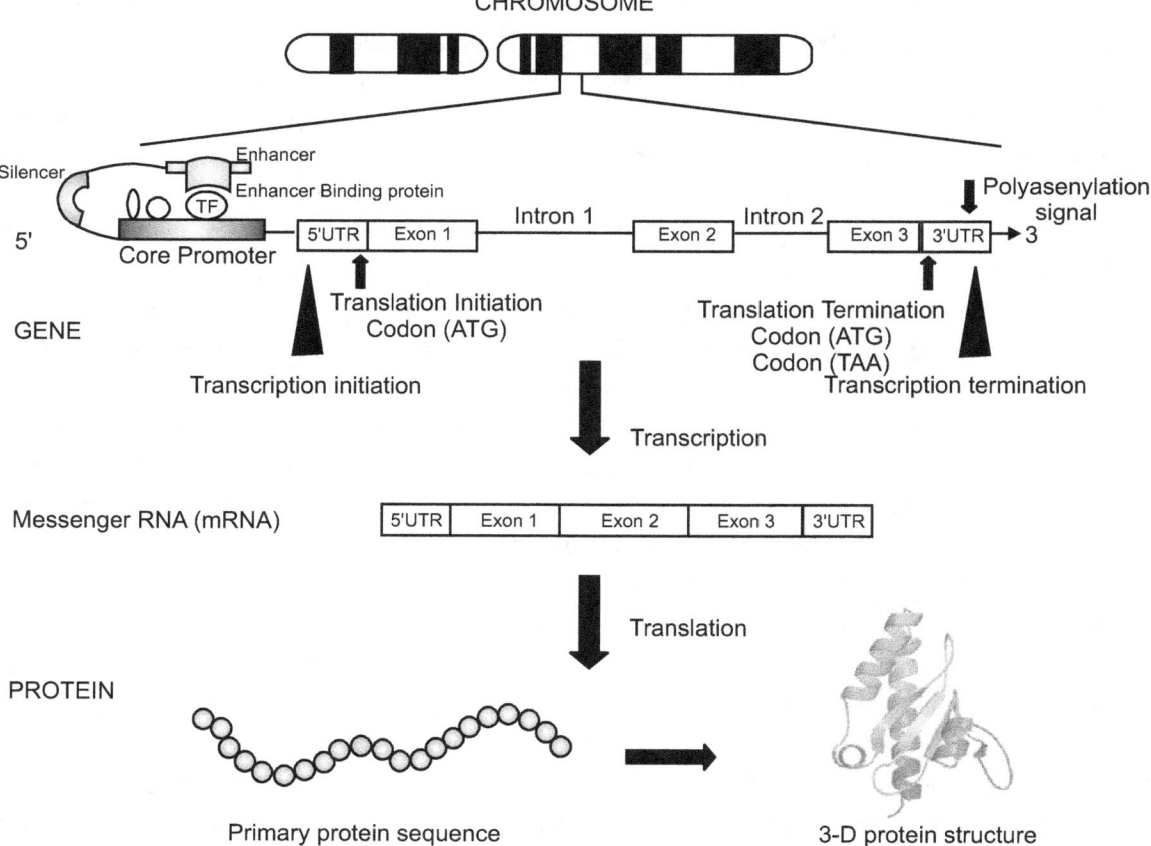

Fig. 15.1: Schematic Representation of a Hypothetical Eukaryotic Gene

The figure in the upper panel shows different regulatory and coding regions of a gene. The lower panel represents the flow of sequence information contained in a gene to functional protein molecules, which carry out the essential functions.

A protein coding gene comprises multiple exons, interrupted by non-coding introns which are sliced out from the mature RNA [Fig. 15.1]. The length of a gene varies greatly with the average size of roughly 3000 nucleotides; although the largest known human gene, dystrophin consists of 2.22 million nucleotides, and the smallest gene, insulin-like growth factor II is just 252 nucleotides long. Most of the genes are known to code for multiple protein isoforms through extensive alternative splicing. Another important feature is the regulatory sequences that appear within or near the genes and are known to control the gene expression. The 5' upstream region of the genes serves as the promoter region and includes transcription start sites [TSS], RNA polymerase and transcription factor [TF] binding sites. The eukaryotic promoters also consist of other regulatory regions such as enhancers and silencers that are generally present several hundred bases upstream or downstream of the gene or sometimes even within the gene. It has been proposed that the enhancer binding proteins can bind both to the DNA [enhancer region] as well as TFs [which bind to TF binding sites at the promoter], which enables the proximity of enhancers to promoters by looping of the intervening DNA strand. While the enhancer elements promote gene transcription, binding of TFs to silencer regions represses transcription of the gene. Other regulatory regions include the un-translated regions at either 5', 3' or both ends of the gene. The 5' UTR controls ribosomal binding and may facilitate attenuator control, while the 3' region has been shown to play an important role in mRNA stability. Sequence variations residing in any of these regions can be of great consequence for altering the expression and/or function of the gene. These variations include structural variants and single nucleotide polymorphisms [SNPs].

The structural variants include sequence repeats which are DNA stretches consisting of two or more nucleotides that are repeated throughout the genome either in tandem or interspersed fashion. Majority of human inter-genic sequences are composed of repetitive DNA. **Tandem repeats**, more commonly referred to as variable number tandem repeats [VNTRs], are present adjacent to each other and are classified as:

(a) **Microsatellites:** These are simple sequence repeat [SSRs], commonly found throughout the genome. The repeat units are generally 1-6 bp in length which might be repeated 10-100 times. These are highly variable among individuals in their repeat size.

(b) **Minisatellites:** Minisatellites have repeat units larger than microsatellites, varying from 10-60 bps and majority of them are found at the sub-telomeric regions of chromosomes. These have been extensively used for DNA fingerprinting as well as for genetic markers in linkage analysis and population studies.

Interspersed repeats mainly constitute the "junk" DNA and have been classified as DNA transposons and retrotransposons. The latter can be short interspersed repetitive elements [SINEs], long interspersed repetitive elements [LINEs] and long terminal repeats [LTRs]. Although functional consequences of these elements are not well understood, speculation that incorporation of LINEs and SINEs into novel genes to evolve new functionality has been put across.

Other structural variants include "indel" or insertion/deletion polymorphisms. These refer to insertions or deletions of one more nucleotides in the DNA sequence, and can sometimes even extend upto several kilobases. Insertion of large DNA chunks might occur through duplication of DNA sequences, which can insert as direct or inverted repeats. Large indels can lead to gene duplication or deletion. This phenomenon also gives rise to copy number variations [CNVs] which are large segments of DNA that vary in number of copies between individuals. CNVs have generated a lot of enthusiasm recently for their role in susceptibility to common diseases or in protection against them.

SNPs refer to a single base change in the sequence and are known to occur more often than the sequence repeats in the gene with a frequency of roughly 1 SNP/1.2kb. Depending on their location, SNPs can be been classified as:

     (a)   **Coding SNPs [cSNPs]** lie in coding regions of genes.

     (b)   **Regulatory SNPs** [rSNPs] lie in regulatory regions of genes such as promoters and UTRs.

     (c)   **Intronic SNPs** [iSNP] lie within the introns.

The functional role of the SNPs is determined by their position in the gene. Of late, keen interest has arisen in SNPs residing in non-coding regions, particularly regulatory regions, for the subtle changes caused by them in gene expression. However, the function of a SNP is more often than not dependent on the presence of neighbouring SNPs. The combination of alleles of SNPs present on the same chromosome that are inherited together is referred to as a haplotype. Each individual would then have two sets of haplotypes representing paternal and maternal set of alleles, which incorporate the recombination information of multiple susceptibility variants present within the gene. Studies have shown that while often single SNPs show moderate effects, haplotype based studies have proven to be more powerful in detecting associations.

Various experimental and/or statistical approaches have been devised to delineate the arrangement of multiple alleles on the chromosome:

(a) Use of Statistical and Analytical Tools:

     (i)   **Direct genotyping of pedigrees:** In a family-based study, the alleles present on same chromosome are transmitted together from parents to progeny as a haplotype, unless disrupted by a recombination event, which leads to formation of new haplotype. Thus, direct genotyping of pedigrees provides a convenient and powerful method to derive haplotype inferences. Several algorithms such as Genehunter, Merlin and Simwalk2 have been used for this purpose.

     (ii)   Population-based strategies rely on reconstruction of haplotypes from unphased genotype data of unrelated individuals. Several statistical software packages based on parsimony, maximum likelihood or Bayesian approaches have been devised for haplotype reconstruction. However, inaccuracies and uncertainties of these algorithms can lead to loss of power.

(b) Experimental approaches:

Novel methods have been devised to overcome the insufficiencies of statistical approaches, wherein experimental approaches such as allele-based long range PCRs and somatic hybrids are used to derive "molecular" haplotypes. Although these methods increase the accuracy and power of the study, they have proved to be expensive and time-consuming.

While haplotype studies are limited to chromosomal stretches encompassing one or more neighbouring genes, growing evidence indicates that susceptibility to diseases and drug response outcomes might be influenced by underlying genetic pathway architecture. The study of epistatic influences in pathway genes, which presents the potential to identify complex biological relationships, is gaining prominence. It can be envisaged that variants existing in genes lying upstream and/or downstream of particular candidate gene, which lead to putative functional alterations, might magnify its influence several fold.

Of late, studies have attempted to investigate gene interactions which might predict the outcome of drug response. Popular approaches undertaken by current studies include regression and dimensionality reduction methods. In a landmark paper, Arranz et al had demonstrated that synergistic effect of six polymorphisms of four neurotransmitter receptor related genes could predict response to antipsychotic clozapine with a predictive value of 76.7% (p=0.0001) and sensitivity of 95%. This was the first report to highlight the importance of predictive testing in pharmacogenomic setup.

Pharmacogenetics and Pharmacogenomics

Pharmacogenomics is emerging as an interdisciplinary area comprising numerous domains such as medicine, genomics, informatics, cell and molecular biology, statistics and pharmacology. Although the two terms, *Pharmacogenetics* and *Pharmacogenomics* are generally used interchangeably, the former refers to study of inter-individual genetic variability in candidate genes which plays a significant role in defining drug response and toxicity. The latter has broader implications as it is associated with the systemic identification of factors affecting drug response and toxicity; and involves the study of inter-individual variability in all the genes (genome), gene expression (transcriptome), and protein expression and activity (proteome), which might alter their function. Despite these definitions, there is no international consensus over the usage of the two terms; generally *"pharmacogenetics"* is used to define a single gene study while *"pharmacogenomics"* is used to depict a multigene study. For the sake of simplicity, we have also followed this practice.

Pharmacogenomic studies broadly cover two aspects of a drug's mechanism of action, namely drug kinetics (**pharmacokinetics**) and dynamics (**pharmacodynamics**). As the name suggests, pharmacokinetic studies entail the study of genes involved in drug absorption, metabolism, distribution and elimination, parameters which influence the ultimate bioavailability of the drug. Prominent among these are genes involved in drug metabolism and transport.

(a) Drug metabolizing enzymes (DMEs) have been classified as Phase1 and Phase II enzymes.

Phase I enzymes cause biotransformation of drugs either by oxidation, reduction, hydrolysis, cyclization or decyclization reactions, resulting in formation of polar metabolites.

Phase II enzymes are involved in conjugation reactions, and result in addition of functional groups.

(b) Drug transporter family comprises of transporters which play a key role in absorption, distribution and elimination of the drug in the body.

Pharmacodynamics is the study of the pharmacological effects of drugs, and entails the study of moieties that interact with the drug. Predominant among these are drug receptor families and other signaling molecules. Receptors for neurotransmitters, neuromodulators or hormones act as targets, where a drug can exert its effect by"

- mimicking the natural ligand (agonist),
- blocking the action of the receptor (antagonist),
- functioning opposite to the ligand action (inverse agonist),
- acting as partial agonists or antagonists.

Other than the receptors, drugs can target other moieties involved in cell-functioning and signaling such as enzymes, structural and carrier proteins, and ion channels.

The genetic variants present either at pharmacokinetic or -dynamic level can not only lead to altered drug efficacy and response outcome; but can also cause severe adverse drug reactions (ADRs). It should therefore be a necessity rather than an option to characterize these genetic variants and their impact on action of a drug. As research has graduated from studying single candidate genes to whole genome scans, pharmacogenomics is beginning to make its impact on therapeutics of complex disorders such as cancer, cardiovascular disorder, diabetes, asthma, epilepsy, and psychiatric disorders to name a few. The currently used conventional therapeutics only provide symptomatic treatment, and the major challenge encountered in clinical practice is therapeutic failure or adverse drug effects owing to variable response of patients. The possibility that few individuals might develop serious adverse effects often leads to complete removal of the drug from the market, even if the drug shows high efficacy. Pharmacogenomic testing for identification of individuals who might develop adverse reactions beforehand provides a ray of hope for increasing drug safety and re-introducing efficacious drugs in the market. Some of the pharmacogenomic tests that have been approved by FDA are listed in Table 15.1.

Table 15.1: Details of pharmaceutical drugs approved for pharmacogenetic tests by FDA

Drug (Generic name)	Drug action	Locus	Adverse Drug Reactions	Literature Citations
Abacavir	A nucleoside analog reverse transcriptase inhibitor (NRTI) used to treat HIV-I infection.	HLA-B*5701	Risk of hypersensitivity reactions	16
Azathioprine	An immunosuppressive agent used in the treatment of rheumatoid arthritis	TPMT (*2,*3A,*3C)	Increased risk for severe, life threatening myelosuppression or myelotoxicity.	17

Contd. ...

Drug (Generic name)	Drug action	Locus	Adverse Drug Reactions	Literature Citations
Carbamazepine	An anticonvulsant for the treatment of epilepsy	HLA-B*1502	Risk of developing Stevens-Johnson Syndrome/Toxic Epidermal Necrolysis (SJS/TEN).	18
Imatinib	A protein kinase inhibitor used for the treatment of newly diagnosed adult patients with Philadelphia chromosome positive chronic myeloid leukemia (CML).	BCR-ABL, KIT:D816V	Patients with KIT:D816V mutation were found to be resistant to imatinib treatment. The most frequently reported adverse reactions were edema, nausea, vomiting, muscle cramps, musculoskeletal pain, diarrhoea, rash, fatigue and abdominal pain	19
Dasatinib	A protein kinase inhibitor used for treatment of CML patients who are resistant or intolerant to other therapies, such as treatment with imatinib.	BCR-ABL 1 variants	Most common adverse reactions include low blood counts, fluid retention events, diarrhoea, headache, skin rash, nausea, hemorrhage, fatigue, and dyspnea.	20
Irinotecan	An antineoplastic enzyme inhibitor primarily used in the treatment of colorectal cancer	UGT1A1*28	Severe allergic reactions, black or bloody stools, pain, diarrhoea, fainting, severe or persistent dizziness, severe headache, unusual change in the amount of urine, vision or speech changes, vomiting etc.	21
Trastuzumab	A recombinant IgG1 kappa, humanized monoclonal antibody for treatment of HER2-positive metastatic breast cancer	ERBB2 variants	Fatigue, infection, neutropenia, anemia, myalgia, dyspnea, rash/desquamation, headache, diarrhoea, and nausea.	22
Warfarin	An anticoagulant for the treatment of retinal vascular occlusion, pulmonary embolism, cardiomyopathy, atrial fibrillation and flutter, cerebral embolism, transient cerebral ischaemia, arterial embolism and thrombosis.	VKORC1: G-1639A CYP2C9 (*2, *3, *5, *6, *9, *11)	Severe bleeding , hemorrhage, skin conditions such as hives, rash or itching, swelling and bruising, chest pain, nausea, diarrhoea, fatigue etc.	23

Contd....

Drug (Generic name)	Drug action	Locus	Adverse Drug Reactions	Literature Citations
Clozapine	A second generation antipsychotic for treatment of psychiatric conditions such as Schizophrenia and bipolar disorder.	HLA-DQB1	Agranulocytosis, seizures, myocarditis, and other adverse cardiovascular and respiratory effects, weight gain etc.	24
5-Fluorouracil	A pyrimidine analog, for cancer treatment.	DPYD-TYMS	Myelosuppression, mucositis, dermatitis, diarrhoea and cardiac toxicity	25

Such studies have helped in gaining some perspective regarding the old theory of "one drug fits all". In striking contrast, *"personalized medicine"* offers the advantage of evidence-based therapeutic approach, wherein the right choice of drug and dosage can be determined for each patient based on his genetic makeup. Rapid advances in science and technology have helped in covering a remarkable distance towards realization of this dream. It has been envisioned that high throughput technology will enable cost-effective *"personal genome"* determinations in the near future, which will be beneficial for diagnostics and personalized medicine. However, several ethical concerns still cloud this issue. Nevertheless, pharmacogenetic testing for minimization of adverse effects has already spread it's wings in clinical setting, as has been outlined earlier. It is just a matter of time before prospective pharmacogenetic tests become a necessity rather than an option. Interestingly, a recent study demonstrated that performing a prospective pharmacogenetic testing for a new drug after obtaining initial clinical data might prove to be a useful tool to check its efficacy before the final commitment to full drug development can be made.

Pharmacogenomics in new drug discovery and development:

The promise of pharmacogenomics has generated laudable enthusiasm among geneticists and clinicians likewise, as they gear up for taking the giant leap from bench to bedside. Further boost has been received from pharmaceutical companies with the recognition of pharmacogenomics-based approaches in the development and delivery of safe and effective therapeutics. The standard process of discovering new drug compounds with the motive of providing higher efficacy and minimal adverse effects as compared to the already existing symptomatic drugs has proved to be a challenging, high-risk activity owing to the huge costs, long procedures and tedious clinical trials coupled with high failure rates. This has generated a global initiative to develop a rational means for identifying new treatment strategies and optimizing drug therapy.

The drug discovery process includes pathway identification and target selection, chemical compound screening, preclinical and clinical studies and drug marketing. In the post-genome era, it is envisioned that pharmacogenomics will play an increasingly important role in each step of drug discovery. The annotation of human genome and functional pathways, identification of genetic variations and our increasing knowledge of the functional consequences of these variations provides concrete basis for prioritization of candidate drug targets. The key pathway players with invariable activity among populations will preferably serve as ideal candidates with reduced probability of variable response among individuals. Further, drug failure during clinical trials would be minimized by stratifying patients based on pharmacogenomic predictions of drug metabolizing efficiency, drug efficacy and dosage, and adverse effects. This can be of great consequence for successful drug discoveries, as a great number of potential compounds are rejected during clinical trials or withdrawn later due to low efficacy or adverse effects in a limited number of individuals. The application of pharmacogenomic approaches would ensure faster and more successful therapies for patient subgroups.

Bioinformatics infrastructure for pharmacogenomics study design

Bioinformatics has played a major role in the arrival of the "-omics" era, dominated by genomics, transcriptomics, proteomics, metabolomics etc; wherein the understanding of biological processes has graduated to system level. Current bioinformatics resources, which provide a platform for data storage, retrieval and sharing along with analytical methods and algorithms, have become indispensable for such studies. The various modules available with these web resources enable the following:

(a) Creation of databanks which allow data submission, storage, retrieval, and sharing of information for sequence, structure, expression and variations of genome and its products.

(b) Annotation of data.

(c) Prediction of secondary structure based on sequence information.

(d) Prediction of evolutionary properties derived from a phylogeny or sequence alignment.

(e) Prediction of function from information regarding comparative modeling of sequence and structure, gene expression, protein-protein interactions, pathways and experimental studies.

(f) Creation and curation of "interactomes" and pathways based on the gene functions and interactions.

(g) Target prediction and validation.

The availability of databases, browsers and servers and other comparative and analytical tools have simplified the otherwise cumbersome task of genome analysis. Although an astounding number of databases are available today, the next section of the chapter describes a few databases and web tools (Table 2) which are useful for pharmacogenomics researchers.

Table 15.2: List of weblinks for databases and analytical tools

Databases and analytical tools	Web links
Genome Browsers and Databases	
National Centre for Biotechnology Information (NCBI) Genome Browser	www.ncbi.nlm.nih.gov/
Ensembl Genome Browser	www.ensembl.org/
University of California Santa Cruz (UCSC) Genome Browser	genome.ucsc.edu/
DNA DataBank of Japan (DDBJ)	www.ddbj.nig.ac.jp/
Consensus Coding Sequence (CCDS) database	www.ncbi.nlm.nih.gov/CCDS/
Entrez Genomes	www.ncbi.nlm.nih.gov/sites/entrez?db=genome/
UniprotKB	www.uniprot.org/
Protein Data Bank (PDB)	www.pdb.org/pdb/home/home.do
Human reference protein database (HRPD)	www.hprd.org/
Protein family database (Pfam)	pfam.sanger.ac.uk/
Kegg pathway database	www.genome.jp/kegg/pathway.html
Reactome	www.reactome.org/
PubMed	www.ncbi.nlm.nih.gov/pubmed/
SNP database (dbSNP)	www.ncbi.nlm.nih.gov/projects/SNP/
HapMap database	hapmap.ncbi.nlm.nih.gov/
Human Mutation Database (HMD)	www.hgmd.cf.ac.uk/
Japanese SNP Database (JSNP)	snp.ims.u-tokyo.ac.jp/
Pharmacogenomics Knowledge Base (PharmGKB)	www.pharmgkb.org/
Gene SNPs	www.genome.utah.edu/genesnps/
Web Resources and Analytical Tools:	
Basic Local Alignment Search Tool (BLAST)	www.ncbi.nlm.nih.gov/BLAST/
CLUSTALW	www.ebi.ac.uk/clustalw/
WISE2	www.ebi.ac.uk/Wise2/

Blast2GO	www.blast2go.org/
Gene Finder	rulai.cshl.org/tools/genefinder/
Expression Profiler	www.ebi.ac.uk/expressionprofiler/
Gene Recognition and Analysis Internet Link (GrailEXP)	compbio.ornl.gov/grailexp/
GENSCAN	genes.mit.edu/GENSCAN.html
POLYVIEW	polyview.cchmc.org/
Interproscan	www.ebi.ac.uk/Tools/InterProScan/
PhyML	atgc.lirmm.fr/phyml/
Cn3D	www.ncbi.nlm.nih.gov/Structure/CN3D/cn3d.s html
RasMol	www.openrasmol.org/
Polydoms	polydoms.cchmc.org/
Functional Single Nucleotide Polymorphism (F-SNP)	compbio.cs.queensu.ca/F-SNP/
Fast-SNP	fastsnp.ibms.sinica.edu.tw/
Sorting Intolerant From Tolerant (SIFT)	sift.jcvi.org/
Large Scale SNP (LS-SNP)	modbase.compbio.ucsf.edu/LS-SNP/
SNPeffect	snpeffect.vib.be/
SNPs3D	www.snps3d.org/
Polymorphism Phenotyping (PolyPhen)	genetics.bwh.harvard.edu/pph/
Exon Spicing Enhancer Finder (ESEFinder)	rulai.cshl.edu/tools/ESE/
TFSEARCH	www.cbrc.jp/research/db/TFSEARCH
Consite	asp.ii.uib.no:8090/cgi-bin/CONSITE/consite/
O-Glycosylation Prediction Electronic Tool (OGPET)	ogpet.utep.edu/
Sulfinator	www.expasy.ch/tools/sulfinator/
KinasePhos	kinasephos.mbc.nctu.edu.tw/

Databases

Databases serve the very basic need of storing, sharing and retrieving data. The first semblance of a sequence database arose as early as 1960 to assemble the protein sequences, which came to be known as the Protein Information Resource (PIR). PIR also served as major DNA sequence repositories, till formation of official DNA sequence databases took place in 1980s. Three databanks were established: Genbank (now supported by National Centre for Biotechnology Information [NCBI]), European Molecular Biology Laboratory (EMBL) data library, and DNA DataBank of Japan (DDBJ), which exchange data on daily basis to maintain database homogeneity. Today, these databases are not just data storage facilities, but offer a myriad of modules for further predictions and analysis. The major genome browsers include NCBI, EMBL and University of California Santa Cruz (UCSC). These databases are not static, and provide the option for integration of data from subsequent projects and individual experiments. Although most of databanks store all the submitted information, they have also come up with "non-redundant" databanks where repetitions due to individual submissions have been removed to provide a single consensus representative sequence. The genome databanks are not only available for human genome, but efforts have also been made to characterize genomes of several other organisms ranging from microbes to chimpanzees. e.g.: Entrez (NCBI) has a whole genome collection for more than 1000 organisms.

Apart from the primary sequence databases, there are several other tools which continually add annotations to this data. With the availability of complete human genome sequence enabled by the HGP, the next step has been the prediction and functional annotation of genes. The gene prediction programmes are continually updated to scan the sequence for general properties of protein coding sequences (termed as content based and site based approaches), and search all available sequence databases for homology to known genes from other organisms (termed as comparative method). Majority of the genes have been annotated and gene maps have been made available by genome browsers. Furthermore, these browsers also provide information regarding the genome products- the transcriptome and the proteome. Transcriptome characterization has been made simpler with the advent of microarray technology, wherein the differential expression pattern of genes in tissues and organs has been studied for varied organisms. The microarray expression database supports data sharing and analysis and provides resources for data analysis of gene expression, significant gene finding, and other statistical components. The genome browsers also provide protein sequences and expression profile. Apart from these, specific protein databases include:

- **UniprotKB:** A protein knowledgebase which serves as a resource of protein sequences and functional information. Uniprot consists of Swissprot, a manually annotated and reviewed database; and TrEMBL which is automatically annotated.

- **Protein Data Bank (PDB)** is a repository for the 3-dimensional structural data of proteins as well as nucleic acids.

- **Human reference protein database (HRPD)** provides a centralized platform to visualize domain architecture, post-translational modifications, interaction networks and disease association for the human proteome.

- **Pfam:** Offers a collection of all protein families.

Apart from these, Expert Protein Analysis System (ExPASy) proteomics server maintained at the Swiss Institute of Bioinformatics [SIB] is involved in maintenance and curation of other databases and repositories such as Prosite (database of protein families and domains), NEWT (taxonomy browser and database); ENZYME (Enzyme nomenclature database), SwissVar (portal to human diseases and variant information in UniProtKB/Swiss-Prot), UniPathway (Metabolic pathways database) among others. Other databases include those for two-dimensional polyacrylamide gel based proteomics data such as World-2DPAGE Repository and SWISS-2DPAGE. These databases are linked through the ExPASy server to provide functional information.

An important requirement for any scientific endeavour is sharing and retrieval of experimental finding to replicate, validate and further build on the biological understanding. This is offered by literature databanks such as Pubmed, which is hosted by NCBI. Further, "interactome databases" such as KEGG PATHWAY and Reactome databases provide a knowledgebase for different biological pathways. Availability of such wealth of data has significantly eased the selection of critical genes for disease susceptibility and drug response studies. Databanks such as Online Mendelian Inheritance in Man (OMIM) and Orphanet provide comprehensive summary of the information available for human genes and genetic disorders. The SNP database (dbSNP) module of NCBI provides a platform that incorporates the information of SNPs, microsatellites, insertions and deletions from several sources. These include the variation data from HapMap project (maintained at HapMap database) as well as the mutations and polymorphisms submitted by independent research projects. Other SNP databases include Ensembl, Human Mutation Database (HMD), and Japanese SNP Database (JSNP). Of particular importance to pharmacogenomics study is Pharmacogenomics Knowledge Base (PharmGKB), which specializes in knowledge of the impact of human genetic variations on drug response. The database is involved in integration and curation of primary genotype and phenotype data, annotation of gene variants and gene-drug-disease relationships and provides summation of all important pharmacogenomic genes and drug pathways. The database information is also updated by thorough literature review. PharmGKB has become "one stop destination" of knowledge for pharmacogenetic researchers.

Web resources and analytical tools

Given the plethora of accumulating data and databanks, little wonder that the requirements of bioinformatic tools by analysts and curators is increasing by the day. Some of the standard tools hosted by different websites for nucleotide or protein analysis include those for search and alignment (e.g.: BLAST, CLUSTALW), genome annotation (e.g.: WISE2, Blast2GO), gene finding and expression profiling (e.g.: Gene Finder, Expression Profiler), structural analysis (e.g.: GrailEXP, Genescan, POLYVIEW), functional analysis (e.g.: Interproscan), comparative and phylogenetic analysis (e.g.: PHYML) and visualization tools for presentation (e.g.: Cn3D, RasMol) among others. The advent of additional modules and algorithms that predict the function of the SNPs is increasingly being appreciated as they lead to increased probability of hitting the causal/functional variant rather than an associated or linked variant. E.g.: Polydoms site uses information from both dbSNP and "Gene SNPs" to provide a graphic display of gene synonymous and nonsynonymous variations. F-SNP database provides integrated information about the functional effects of SNPs predicted at the transcriptional, splicing, translational, and post-translational levels, obtained from 16 different bioinformatics tools and databases. The other available tools include Fast-SNP, SIFT, LS-SNP, SNPeffect, SNPs3D, PolyPhen, ESEfinder, TFSEARCH, Consite, OGPET, Sulfinator and KinasePhos, some of which are used by F-SNP. Furthermore, HapMap project provides frequencies of over four million SNPs in four different populations from Africa, China, Utah, and Japan. Bioinformatic tools such as Tagger can use the Linkage Disequilibrium (LD) information provided by HapMap project to identify SNPs in high LD. The SNPs in tight linkage yield same information and usage of representative SNP per LD block (Tag SNPs) reduces the cost and information load. However, LD transferability between different populations might be a major limitation.

Although attempts have been made to constantly upgrade the resources and develop new tools with increased sensitivity and specificity, a major challenge faced by bioinformaticians is the lack of consistent information and analyses between different databases. For instance, the differences in annotation methods used by different Genome Browsers lead to discrepancy in the gene information available. More frequently, the number of SNPs displayed per gene differs between different databases. These discrepancies complicate analyses and necessitate consensus information through validation. The International Nucleotide Sequence Database collaboration was established by Genbank, EMBL and DDBJ to facilitate daily data exchange as the three databases serve as individual data submission points. A more recent collaborative consensus coding sequence (CCDS) project reflects another step taken in this direction. The project was undertaken with the aim of identifying a common protein-coding gene set for the human and mouse genomes.

The efforts undertaken have led to consistent representation of gene information across NCBI, Ensembl, and UCSC Genome Browsers which is essential to maintain a high standard of reliability and biological accuracy.

Conclusion

This chapter throws light on the accomplishments of pharmacogenomics in disease management, and draws attention to the initial milestones covered by the incessant efforts of researchers worldwide. Although these may seem miniscule given the need for broader implications and applications, pharmacogenetic testing has proved to be advantageous in clinical settings. Pharmacological and biotechnology companies have shown as much interest in promoting genetic tests as has been shown by physicians to improve the drug safety, efficacy and response outcomes. However, a chip in the block is the cost of these genetic tests, which can range up to a few hundred dollars. Nevertheless, with the advent of high throughput technology, the cost of sequencing has reduced drastically and it's just a matter of time before "$1000 genome" becomes a reality. In this scenario, bioinformatics promises to play a crucial role towards rendition of pharmacogenomics in clinical setting. The availability of databases and other web resources, search and analytical tools supplemented with user-friendly graphical interfaces and visualization tools have already set this process in motion. Currently, most of the clinical laboratories use commercial software in their quest for "sequence of clinical significance". With the ever-increasing plethora of data, pursuit of new tools and software which can handle high throughput data with increased sensitivity and specificity is the need of the hour. Perhaps more projects with open source format can enable the researchers from all over the world to help bridge the gap between information and knowledge, and realize the vision of "Personalized Medicine".

Definitions

Human Genome Project (HGP) was an international initiative undertaken in 1990 to sequence the entire human genome. The complete draft of the human genome sequence was completed in 2003.

The International HapMap Project was initiated with the objective to develop a haplotype map of the human genome (HapMap), and describe the common human genetic variation between individuals. The HapMap data describing the frequency of common polymorphisms in four populations comprising of individuals from Ibadan, Nigeria (YRI), Tokyo, Japan (JPT), Han Chinese individuals from Beijing, China (CHB), and United States residents of European ancestry (CEU).

Phenotype refers to the observable physical and biochemical characteristics of an organism, which are governed by both genetic makeup of the organism and environmental influences.

Genotype refers to the genetic constitution of an organism, which are inheritable traits and influence the phenotypic characteristics of the organism.

Food and Drug Administration (FDA) is a Government agency of the United States Department of Health and Human Services involved with diverse aspects of public health care. FDA is responsible for regulating and supervising the safety of food and dietary supplements, medication drugs and devices, vaccines, veterinary products, cosmetics and other sanitary requirements.

Gene has classically been defined as a unit of hereditary, consisting of a DNA segment that encodes for specific functional molecules (RNA and Protein) and determine particular traits of an organism.

Exons are gene regions which are transcribed into the gene transcript (RNA). These may be translated into proteins (coding sequence or CDS) or form un-translated regions (UTRs) which are involved in gene regulation.

Intron are non-coding regions interspersed between exons, and are spliced out from the primary mRNA transcript.

Epistasis refers to the synergistic effect of polygenic variants which can predict the disease or drug response phenotype.

Personalized medicine has been a long term goal of pharmacogenomic research, wherein individualizing drug therapy has been proposed according to the genetic makeup of individuals to achieve maximum drug efficacy and minimum adverse effects.

Personal Genome would facilitate an individual to have his complete genetic information for determining susceptibility to diseases or adverse drug effects. The individual genome sequencing has been estimated to cost approximately $1000 in near future.

REFERENCES

1. Somogy A. Evolution of pharmacogenomics. Proc. West. Pharmacol. Soc. 2008; 51:1-4.

2. Santangelo A.M., de Souza F.S., Franchini L.F.,et al. Ancient exaptation of a core-sine retroposon into a highly conserved mammalian neuronal enhancer of the proopiomelanocortin gene. PLoS *Genetics* 2007; 3:1813-1826.

3. Ionita-Laza I., Rogers A.J., Lange C.,et al. Genetic association analysis of copy-number variation (CNV) in human disease pathogenesis. Genomics 2009; 93:22-26.

4. Brasch-Andersen C., Christiansen L., Tan Q., et al. Possible gene dosage effect of glutathione-S-transferases on atopic asthma: Using real-time PCR for quantification of GSTM1 and GSTT1 gene copy numbers. Hum. Mutat. 2004; 24:208-214.

5. Faik I., de Carvalho E.G. and Kun J.F. Parasite-host interaction in malaria: genetic clues and copy number variation. Genome Med. 2009; 1:82.

6. Nakajima T., Kaur G., Mehra N. et al. HIV-1/AIDS susceptibility and copy number variation in CCL3L1, a gene encoding a natural ligand for HIV-1 co-receptor CCR5. Cytogenet. Genome Res. 2008; 123:156-160.

7. Knight J.C. Functional implications of genetic variation in non-coding DNA for disease susceptibility and gene regulation. Clin. Sci. 2003; 104:493–501.

8. Shifman S., Bronstein M., Sternfeld M., et al. A highly significant association between a COMT haplotype and schizophrenia. Am. J. Hum. Genet. 2002; 71:1296-1302.

9. Gupta M., Chauhan C., Bhatnagar P., et al. Genetic susceptibility to schizophrenia: role of dopaminergic pathway gene polymorphisms. Pharmacogenomics 2009; 10:277-291.

10. Crawford D.C. and Nickerson D.A. Definition and clinical importance of haplotypes. Annu. Rev. Med. 2005; 56:303–320.

11. Gillanders E.M., Pearson J.V., Sorant A.J.,et al The value of molecular haplotypes in a family-based linkage study. Am. J. Hum. Genet. 2006; 79:458-468.

12. Levenstien M.A., Ott J. and Gordon D. Are molecular haplotypes worth the time and expense? A cost-effective method for applying molecular haplotypes. PLoS Genet. 2006; 2:e127.

13. Briollais L., Wang Y., Rajendram I., et al. Methodological issues in detecting gene-gene interactions in breast cancer susceptibility: a population-based study in Ontario. BMC Med. 2007; 5:22.

14. Arranz M.J., Munro J., Birkett J., et alPharmacogenetic prediction of clozapine response. Lancet 2000; 355:1615-1616.

15. Meyer U.A. Pharmacogenetics and adverse drug reactions. Lancet 2000; 356:1667-1671.

16. Mallal S., Phillips E., Carosi G., et al HLA-B*5701 screening for hypersensitivity to abacavir. N. Engl. J. Med. 2008; 358:568-579.

17. Zhou S. Clinical pharmacogenomics of thiopurine S-methyltransferase. Curr. Clin. Pharmacol. 2006; 1:119-128.

18. Chung W.H., Hung S.I. and Chen Y.T. Human leukocyte antigens and drug hypersensitivity. Curr. Opin. Allergy Clin. Immunol. 2007; 7:317-323.

19. Kim D.H., Sriharsha L., Xu W., et al Clinical relevance of a pharmacogenetic approach using multiple candidate genes to predict response and resistance to imatinib therapy in chronic myeloid leukemia. Clin. Cancer Res. 2009; 15:4750-4758.

20. Keam S.J. Dasatinib: in chronic myeloid leukemia and Philadelphia chromosome-positive acute lymphoblastic leukemia. BioDrugs. 2008; 22:59-69.

21. Schulz C., Heinemann V., Schalhorn A., et al UGT1A1 gene polymorphism: impact on toxicity and efficacy of irinotecan-based regimens in metastatic colorectal cancer. World J. Gastroenterol. 2009; 15:5058-5066.

22. Kroese M., Zimmern R.L. and Pinder S.E. HER2 status in breast cancer--an example of pharmacogenetic testing. J. R. Soc. Med. 2007; 100:326-329.

23. Moyer T.P., O'Kane D.J., Baudhuin L.M., et al Warfarin sensitivity genotyping: a review of the literature and summary of patient experience. Mayo Clin. Proc. 2009; 84:1079-1094.

24. Dettling M., Schaub R.T., Mueller-Oerlinghausen B., et al Further evidence of human leukocyte antigen-encoded susceptibility to clozapine-induced agranulocytosis independent of ancestry.Pharmacogenetics 2001; 11:135-141.

25. Lazar A. and Jetter A. Pharmacogenetics in oncology: 5-fluorouracil and the dihydropyrimidine dehydrogenase. Dtsch. Med. Wochenschr. 2008; 133:1501-1504.

26. Roses A.D. Pharmacogenetics and drug development: the path to safer and more effective drugs. Nat. Rev. Genet. 2004; 5:645-656.

27. Burns DK. Developing pharmacogenetic evidence throughout clinical development. Clin. Pharmacol. Ther. 2010; 88:867-870.

28. Surendiran A, Pradhan SC, **Adithan** C. Role of pharmacogenomics in drug discovery and development. Indian J. Pharmacol. 2008; 40:137-43.

29. Mount D.W. 2004. *Bioinformatics: sequence and genome analysis.* 2nd Ed. Cold Spring Harbor Laboratory Press, Europe.

30. Baxevanis A.D. and Ouellette B.F.F. 2001. *Bioinformatics: a practical guide to the analysis of genes and proteins.* 2nd Ed. John Wiley & Sons, Inc. Publication.

31. Thorisson G.A., Smith A.V., Krishnan L. et al. The International HapMap Project web site. Genome Res. 2005; 15:1592-1593.

32. Pruitt K.D., Harrow J., Harte R.A et al The consensus coding sequence (CCDS) project: Identifying a common protein-coding gene set for the human and mouse genomes. Genome Res. 2009; 19:1316-1323.

Chapter ... 16

MEDICAL WRITING

> *"In science the credit goes to the man who convinces the world, not to the man to whom the idea first occurs".*
> **Sir Francis Darwin**

Scientific and biotechnological advances have enhanced and extended our understanding of health sciences and diseases. To implement and incorporate these advances in our daily practice, they have to be communicated to those who can use and benefit from them. Thus, the health care communicators, through medical writing, captures, collates, consolidates these information to the target audience in a logical, comprehensible and consistent manner.

Medical writing, therefore, is effectively communicating clinical and scientific information to a wide range of target audience who need to know and are benefited from the knowledge. The burgeoning information generated from research and scientific advancement has made medical writing a key specialty area. It requires a special profile of people who can amass, manage and communicate the data in a presentable format, so that the scientists can focus on research leading to more advances. As a result, medical writing has become a pivotal area for the past couple of decades, particularly in new drug development process.

PHARMACEUTICAL WRITING

With globalization and escalating regulatory requirements, the need for study data to be communicated effectively has become even more important. As drugs are becoming increasingly expensive, the pharmaceutical industry is forced to face public and private scrutiny. Moreover, timely dissemination of the knowledge for the researchers and academicians is essential for advancement of patient care.

Medical writing forms an integral part of the clinical research process. Protocol preparation is the first step of conducting a clinical trial which finally ends with reporting the trial in a specific required format (Clinical Study Report) for submission to the regulatory agencies. The publications based on the trials not only inform the external medical fraternity regarding the research but also serve to document the conduct of the trial.

The pharmaceutical writing can be broadly categorized as Regulatory Writing and Publication Writing.

Regulatory Writing:

Each country has a regulatory agency to govern the approval process for marketing new drugs for a specific disease or therapeutic indication. The agency requires evidence to approve the claims that are made by the drug companies. The documents which form a part of the regulatory submissions are known as regulatory documents.

Since the regulatory submission encompasses the complete research of a potential new drug, it is highly technical in nature. Usually, these documents are loaded with texts, graphs and tables and often supplemented with appended documents, which may be text, tables, images, graphs or listings. However, the structure and content of these documents are determined by type and nature of the documents. Among the various types of documents prepared by the regulatory medical writers, the most common documents are Investigator Brochures, Protocols, Case Record Forms and Clinical Study Reports.

All these are version-controlled documents, which means that they pass through several draft stages before they are finalized. The reason for these stages is that almost all the documents undergo multi-step and multi-disciplinary review. These reviews lead to incorporation of inputs given by different reviewers, resulting in number of subsequent drafts.

This chapter restricts it's discussion to the development of the three most important and essential clinical research documents, which subsequently form the essential and integral part of any regulatory submission dossier.

Protocol:

The first step of performing a clinical trial is to prepare a protocol. The protocol defines the aims and objectives of a trial including the minutest details of exactly how the trial will be conducted in a comprehensive manner. It includes inclusion-exclusion criteria, treatment of subjects, assessment of efficacy and safety parameters, statistical methods to be used to analyze data and also data handling and record keeping requirements.

Developing Protocol:

The protocol is generally prepared by the drug development team of the sponsor company. In the beginning, a Specific Protocol Summary (SPS) is prepared, which would generally contain the core scientific information of the trial. This is handed over to the medical writing team. The assigned writer develops the first draft based on the SPS and the information collated from the Investigator's Brochure and literature review. Similar to all regulatory documents, the draft undergoes subsequent multidisciplinary reviews, resulting in successive draft versions. Hence, numbering the versions of the drafts becomes very important to ensure the use of correct version.

ICH GCP does not provide any fixed template for protocol development, but defines the content of the protocol.

The content of the protocol should generally include the following topics. However, site-specific information may also be provided on separate protocol page(s), or addressed in a separate agreement.

The content of a generic protocol:

General Information

1. Protocol title, protocol identifying number, and date. Any amendment(s) should also bear the amendment number(s) and date(s).

2. Name and address of the sponsor and monitor (if other than the sponsor).

3. Name and title of the person(s) authorized to sign the protocol and the protocol amendment(s) for the sponsor.

4. Name, title, address, and telephone number(s) of the sponsor's medical expert (or dentist when appropriate) for the trial.

5. Name and title of the investigator(s) who is (are) responsible for conducting the trial, and the address(es) and telephone number(s) of the trial site(s).

6. Name, title, address, and telephone number(s) of the qualified physician (or dentist, if applicable), who is responsible for all trial-site related medical (or dental) decisions (if other than investigator).

7. Name(s) and address(es) of the clinical laboratory(ies) and other medical and/or technical department(s) and/or institutions involved in the trial.

Background Information

1. Name and description of the investigational product(s).

2. A summary of findings from non-clinical studies that potentially have clinical significance and from clinical trials those are relevant to the trial.

3. Summary of the known and potential risks and benefits, if any, to human subjects.

4. Description of and justification for the route of administration, dosage, dosage regimen, and treatment period(s).

5. A statement that the trial will be conducted in compliance with the protocol, GCP and the applicable regulatory requirement(s).

6. Description of the population to be studied.

7. References to literature and data that are relevant to the trial and that provide background for the trial.

Trial Objectives and Purpose

A detailed description of the objectives and the purpose of the trial.

Trial Design

The scientific integrity of the trial and the credibility of the data from the trial depend substantially on the trial design. A description of the trial design, should include:

1. A specific statement of the primary endpoints and the secondary endpoints, if any, to be measured during the trial.

2. A description of the type/design of trial to be conducted (e.g., double-blind, placebo-controlled, parallel design) and a schematic diagram of trial design, procedures and stages.

3. A description of the measures taken to minimize/avoid bias, including:

   (a) Randomization.

   (b) Blinding.

4. A description of the trial treatment(s), the dosage and dosage regimen of the investigational product(s). Also include a description of the dosage form, packaging, and labelling of the investigational product(s).

5. The expected duration of subject participation, and a description of the sequence and duration of all trial periods, including follow-up, if any.

6. A description of the "stopping rules" or "discontinuation criteria" for individual subjects, parts of trial and entire trial.

7. Accountability procedures for the investigational product(s), including the placebo(s) and comparator(s), if any.

8. Maintenance of trial treatment randomization codes and procedures for breaking codes.

9. The identification of any data which needs to be recorded directly on the CRFs (i.e., no prior written or electronic record of data), and has to be considered to be as source data.

Selection and Withdrawal of Subjects

1. Subject inclusion criteria.

2. Subject exclusion criteria.

3. Subject withdrawal criteria (i.e., terminating investigational product treatment/trial treatment) and procedures specifying:

   (a) When and how to withdraw subjects from the trial/ investigational product treatment.

   (b) The type and timing of the data to be collected for withdrawn subjects.

   (c) Whether and how subjects are to be replaced.

   (d) The follow-up for subjects withdrawn from investigational product treatment/trial treatment.

Treatment of Subjects

1. The treatment(s) to be administered, including the name(s) of all the product(s), the dose(s), the dosing schedule(s), the route/mode(s) of administration, and the treatment period(s), including the follow-up period(s) for subjects for each investigational product treatment/trial treatment group/arm of the trial.

2. Medication(s)/treatment(s) permitted (including rescue medication) and not permitted before and/or during the trial.

3. Procedures for monitoring subject compliance.

Assessment of Efficacy

1. Specification of the efficacy parameters.

2. Methods and timing for assessing, recording, and analysing of efficacy parameters.

Assessment of Safety

1. Specification of safety parameters.

2. The methods and timing for assessing, recording, and analysing safety parameters.

3. Procedures for eliciting reports and for recording and reporting adverse event and concurrent illnesses.

4. The type and duration of the follow-up of subjects after adverse events.

Statistics

1. A description of the statistical methods to be employed, including timing of any planned interim analysis(ses).

2. The number of subjects planned to be enrolled. In multicentre trials, the numbers of enrolled subjects projected for each trial site should be specified. Reason for choice of sample size, including reflections on (or calculations of) the power of the trial and clinical justification.

3. The level of significance to be used.

4. Criteria for the termination of the trial.

5. Procedure for accounting for missing, unused, and spurious data.

6. Procedures for reporting any deviation(s) from the original statistical plan (any deviation(s) from the original statistical plan should be described and justified in protocol and/or in the final report, as appropriate).

7. The selection of subjects to be included in the analyses (e.g., all randomized subjects, all dosed subjects, all eligible subjects, evaluable subjects).

Direct Access to Source Data/Documents

The sponsor should ensure that the investigator(s)/institution(s) will permit trial-related monitoring, audits, IRB/IEC review, and regulatory inspection(s), providing direct access to source data/documents which is specified in the protocol or other written agreement.

Quality Control and Quality Assurance Procedures

All the steps to be taken by the trial sponsor to ensure accuracy, consistency, completeness and reliability of collected data.

Ethics

Description of ethical considerations relating to the trial.

Data Handling and Record Keeping Procedures

Description of procedures to ensure ethical Data handling and record keeping with special mention about handling electronic data, if appropriate.

Financing and Insurance

Financing and insurance if not addressed in a separate agreement.

Publication Policy

Publication policy to be mentioned, if not addressed in a separate agreement.

Supplements

(**Note:** Since the protocol and the clinical trial/study report are closely related, further relevant information can be found in the ICH Guideline for Structure and Content of Clinical Study Reports.)

Case Record Forms (CRF):

The Case Record Form (CRF) is a data-collection tool, used to record data required by the protocol for analysis and subsequent reporting of the clinical trial. Although the study protocol is the blue print of a trial, the CRF forms the main day-to-day tool for recording the correct information at the correct time. The two essential uses of CRF are the collection and extraction of data.

Designing of CRF:

The CRF is completed by the investigator, reviewed by the monitor and extracted by the data manager. Therefore while designing, the ease of using the document by all these three profiles, have to be kept in mind. It has to be simple, clear, easy to follow and complete. The sequence should be logical and according to the flow of the study. The CRF design and layout should encourage or prompt instant cross checks and reviews. The questions in the CRFs should be clear, unambiguous and have minimal textual entries facilitating smooth data extraction. The CRF must comply with Good Clinical Practices and follow the guidelines on International Conference of Harmonization (ICH) and required regulatory specifications. However, the ICH and GCP guidelines do not provide any template for designing a CRF. Albeit, an ICH GCP guideline (section 8.2.2) mentions that it should be a part of the protocol, hinting that it should not be finalized until the CRF is completed.

Developing a CRF starts from creating a skeleton plan with the visits and assessments based on the Protocol. Based on this, a pagination plan is also prepared, which maps the number of pages required and content of each page. Following which, simple, clear, unambiguous questions are framed and fields are created for recording data. Protocol requirements are converted to list of instructions, which will eventually prompt the investigators to record the accurate information at correct timings as required by the protocol. Following this, the draft is reviewed by the multidisciplinary team comprising of but not limited to Medical Adviser, Investigator, Project Manager, Data Manager and Statistician. Once the review is complete, a team meeting is usually scheduled to discuss the suggested changes and their overall implications. After incorporation of all the changes, the final version is sent to the project manager for approval. Selection of printer, decision on the artwork, which usually entails the layout style, type and weight of the paper, organization of the CRF pages are decided simultaneously with the review process,. The final version of the CRFs should be ready by the distribution deadline.

Clinical Study Report (CSR):

The clinical study report as described in ICH E3 guideline is an "integrated" full report of an individual study of any therapeutic, prophylactic or diagnostic agent conducted in patients. These research reports are the formal documentation of research trials and are quite complex as they are based on a range of disciplines - clinical, pharmacological, statistical and regulatory.

The clinical and statistical descriptions and analyses of the trial data are integrated into the study report. The tables and figures are incorporated into the main text of the report, or at the end of the text. The appendices of the report contain protocol, sample case report forms, investigator-related information, information related to the test drugs/investigational products including active control/comparators, technical statistical documentation, related publications, patient data listings, and technical statistical details such as derivations, computations, analyses, and computer output, etc.

Most of the pharmaceutical companies generally maintain a template or several templates for developing CSRs to ensure uniformity and quality standard for reporting trials. A report template is a generic document which can be modified, as appropriate, for different regulatory requirements, phases of trial or the nature of the Investigational Product. An organization may have several templates for generating CSRs as Full CSR (for regulatory submission); Abbreviated CSR (for most of Phase 2 and Phase 3 studies which are not for regulatory submission); Synopsis CSR; CSR for exploratory Phase 1 studies; templates for Bioequivalence/ Bioavailability studies (for Abbreviated New Drug application). Some companies have a different template for Oncology studies. However, all these templates have to conform to E3 guidelines.

Content of the Clinical Study Report based on the ICH E3 Guidelines:

The structure of the report based on E3 guidelines divides the CSR into four main parts, namely; synopsis, main body of the report, supplementary section with tables, figures and graphs; and the appendices. The report contains a title page which gives each report a unique identity and provides the essential information on the trial and is subsequently followed by the 16 sections.

Although E3 guideline says that CSR is an integrated report containing clinical and statistical description, it is not generated by simply joining separate clinical and statistical reports. Apart from clinical and statistical description and interpretation of the efficacy and safety aspects of the drug in that particular trial, it should have enough information regarding the design and conduct of the study. Complete data generated from the trial should be provided in different levels in both the body of the text and appendices to allow replication of the critical analyses when the regulatory authorities wish to do so. The data is generally presented in three levels:

(i)   Overall summary figures and tables for important demographic, efficacy, and safety variables which are placed in the text to illustrate important points;

(ii) Other summary figures, tables, and listings for demographic, efficacy, and safety variables should be provided in the supplementary section in section 14 of the CSR;

(iii) Individual patient data for specified groups of patients in Appendix 16.2

(iv) All individual patient data in Appendix 16.4 (archival listings requested only in the United States).

The integrated full report of a study should not be derived by simply joining a separate clinical and statistical report. Although this guideline is mainly aimed at efficacy and safety trials, the basic principles and structure described can be applied to other kinds of trials, such as clinical pharmacology studies. For all regulatory submissions it is mandatory to follow the E3 guidelines. Most of the sponsor companies have their templates and SOPs based on this guideline.

A broad outline of a Clinical Study Report based on E 3 guidelines is discussed below.

Title Page:

Report Identity:

Each trial report should have a unique identification descriptor. The trial number is generally determined by an internal algorithm of the sponsor company and generally is an alpha numeric code. The title of the report is also very important. It should reflect the key aspects of the trial namely, design (e.g. blinded, randomized, controlled); therapeutic indication (e.g. hypertension, diabetes, asthma); Patient population (Pediatric/adult, inpatient/outpatient); Treatment, duration of the treatment. The title page thus should have a trial number and title giving the report a unique identification.

Key Dates:

All important dates should be indicated on the title page. The key dates include the following:

(i)   Trial initiated

(ii) Trial completed

(iii) Trial terminated

(iv) Report issued

Important Information:

The name and affiliation of the Principal Investigator, Sponsors name and contact number.

The title page should also declare that the trial had been conducted, recorded and reported according to the Good Clinical Practices guidelines and the Declaration of Helsinki.

Table of Content (TOC):

A complete list of the content of the report has to be provided including the sections, tables, figures and appendices. This is important as the TOC would help the reviewer to navigate through the document effortlessly.

Synopsis or Summary of the Report:

In this section, the whole report has to be summarized preferably within two to three pages. This document is a stand-alone document, as it intends to provide complete information about the trial to the reviewer, if he does not wish to go through the complete voluminous report and would do so if some critical information or issue comes across, which warrants complete review of the document. It should contain the key aspects of the report including primary objectives, study design, fundamental results and overall conclusions. It is a good idea to provide a textual description or a succinct table with the P value, denoting the statistical significance of the result.

Body of the Report (Section 1 to Section 15 as per E3 guideline):

Introduction

The introduction should contain concise rationale of the trial, placing the trial in the matrix of clinical development plan of the Investigational Product, and relating them with the critical features of the study (e.g., aims, target population, treatment, duration, primary endpoints). The key information about the drug has to be highlighted and it's intended therapeutic use has to be indicated. The best practice is to restrict the introduction within one paragraph, unless the situation is exceptional.

Objectives

The objectives have to be specifically defined and if appropriate, the primary and secondary objectives have to be distinguished. It gives a clear idea about the trial design and it's rationale, as the primary objectives drive the trial design and the secondary objectives propel collection of supportive data.

Methods

This is an elaborate and important section of the report giving detailed description and rationale for the methodology employed to conduct the trial according to the protocol, GCP and regulatory requirements.

Trial design

This section should give a clear structure and configuration of the study. The clinical trial design should include the following: Experimental treatments, target population, type and method of blinding, assignments of subjects to groups (kind of randomization) and overall configuration of the trial (e.g. parallel, crossover, sequential).

Description of the treatment period

The section should distinctively define the sequence and duration of the trial periods, such as baseline, active treatment, crossover washouts, treatment withdrawals and post treatment follow-ups. A graphical representation of the trial structure gives a clear picture of the structure of the trial.

Timing of Assessments

The timings of efficacy, safety, or other assessments have to be defined in this section. Generally a tabular or graphical presentation is preferred.

Description of Trial Population

The target population have to be defined (healthy or subjects with the medical condition) and the number of subjects intended for enrollment (sample size) has to be indicated [this should be referred to the section on power calculations].

Enrollment and withdrawal Criteria

The eligible characteristics of the subjects qualifying them for the trial and the characteristics of subjects disqualifying them from participating in the trial have to be listed in this section. The predetermined criteria causing elimination of the subjects after entry into the trial has to be defined. The possibilities include but are not restricted to noncompliance with treatment, individual choice, and adverse event. The steps taken to avoid impact on statistical analysis have to be indicated.

Concomitant Therapy

The allowance and dis-allowance of medicines and therapies other than the study drug, which were to be received concomitantly, have to be listed. Any issue pertinent to interactions with trial treatments or confounding results from the trial assessments should be discussed.

Trial Treatments

The specific treatments to which subjects were assigned, including active drugs or control treatments have to be described. Any circumstance pertinent to the trial structure (e.g. Cross over) or selection criteria (e.g., subjects previously responding, or not, to specific treatments) needs to be defined.

Treatment groups

The specific treatments to which subjects were assigned have to be defined, including active drug treatments, and other controls. The selected regimen of each trial arm, including the dose, timing and route of administration is to be defined. The rationale for dose and dose related interval selection has to be provided along with the information about dose-response pattern, pharmacokinetic profile, or blood level response of the trial treatments.

The procedures used for assigning subjects to specific treatments are to be described. If computer-generated randomization schedule was used, that should be described and the actual schedule has to be appended to the report. In case of a multi-centric study, the information has to be appended by the center.

Blinding Techniques

The type of blinding used and the procedures to ensure subject blinding to treatment in a single blind study and subject and investigator blinding in a double blind study are to be specified.

Material Identification

Source of treatments used in the trial, and specific lot or batch numbers of these treatments are to be listed. Any modification to treatments needed for blinding techniques (e.g., re-coating of tablets or grinding of tablets for capsule enclosure) are to be indicated.

Method Assessment

The methods to assess the results of efficacy, safety, pharmacokinetic or other criteria relevant to the trial objectives are to be clearly defined. A tabular and graphical display of trial design and assessments is preferable.

(i) Efficacy

The efficacy end-points and the methods of assessing these end-points have to be clearly defined. It is important as the primary endpoint determines the structure and configuration if the study and the secondary endpoints allow collection of supportive information.

(ii) Pharmacokinetics (or other assessment)

The pharmacokinetic or other assessments pertinent to this trial have to be specified.

(iii) Safety

This section should specify all the methods employed for assessing the safety of subjects participating in the trial. The methods used to capture the types and occurrences of adverse events have to be defined. Rating scales or other methods used for categorizing adverse events according to severity and relation to trial treatment have to be described. Specific safety tests which were performed to assess the safety parameters are also to be listed.

Statistical Consideration

Describe the analysis planned for trial assessments and specify the statistical test used for analyses. Issues regarding handling data from subjects who violated protocol specifications or withdrew prematurely from the trial or were otherwise deemed un-evaluable have to be explained and discussed. The level of significance, power of analyses, and predetermined sample size have to be defined.

Informed consent and Ethics Review board

The procedures for obtaining informed consent of subjects before enrolling in the study have to be described. The role of the Ethics Committee in approving protocol and its amendments are to be indicated. If any external committee (e.g., safety and data monitoring) monitored different aspects of the trial conduct have to be mentioned..

Quality assurance

All the steps taken by the trial sponsor to ensure accuracy, consistency, completeness and reliability of collected data have to enlisted.

Result:

The type and complexity of the protocol determines the format of presentation of the data in this section. This section is broadly divided into Demography, Efficacy, Pharmaceutics and Safety sections.

(i) Demography

This section should give an account of all subjects who entered the trial, clearly identifying the followings:

- number of subjects who completed any baseline period,
- number of subjects who were assigned to treatments,
- number of subjects who participated in each successive period of the trial's design,
- number of subjects who completed active treatment, and continued through any follow-up period.

The number of subjects, by treatment group, who withdrew from the trial, or who deviated from or violated the protocol also has to be indicated. Generally this information is well presented through flow chart or graphical display.

(ii) Efficacy

This section provides the overall grouping of efficacy results generated from the assessments stipulated in the protocol. The section contains sub-sections providing details on the primary and secondary assessments. The section is concluded by an overall evaluation of efficacy from the results of individual efficacy analyses. In case the result shows a subpopulation impact which warrants additional trial for clarification, that needs to be indicated.

(iii) Pharmacokinetics (or any other assessment)

If appropriate to the trial design, pharmacokinetics or any other assessments (e.g., microbiology) has to be presented in the similar pattern as efficacy.

(iv) Safety

The safety results have to be presented in sufficient detail to understand drug's safety profile as shown by the trial. Generally, this section contains tables of group summaries and figures of key trends in the main text. For individual data, the reviewers have to be referred to the individual data listing appended to the report. However, critical safety information, listings and narratives for individual subjects are to be inserted within the main text.

This section, like the efficacy section, is presented in different subgroups. The sub-sections entail details like the extent of exposure to trial treatment for subject groups, including placebo or other comparison agents; pattern and rate of occurrence of adverse events, supplemented by narrative description of supportive data and figures; clinical laboratory tests and overall safety evaluation. The sub-section on adverse events focuses on adverse events with high rates and severe levels, in relationship to treatments or associated with deaths, withdrawals or dose adjustments.

Discussion

Typically, results of a clinical study do not require extensive discussion or comparison with the scientific literature. But some studies with unusual result warrant a brief discussion on the unexpected observations and conflict with the established results. This section should contain pertinent references to substantiate the discussion.

Conclusion

The key findings of the trial are summarized. Ideally a conclusion has to be stated for each objective of the trial.

References

The bibliographic information of all the literature references should be given in accordance with the internationally accepted standards of the 1979 Vancouver Declaration on "Uniform Requirements for Manuscripts Submitted to Biomedical Journals" or the system used in "Chemical Abstracts."

Appendices (section 16 of CSR)

The appendices which forms the last section contains all study related documents required to support and substantiate the contents of the report. This section is grouped into 4 subsections, namely Study Information, Patient Data Listing, Case Report Form and Individual Patient Data Listings.

Publication Writing:

The goal of any scientific research is publication. External medical fraternity as well as the general public has the right to know the important and new medical information generated through research. Publications play a vital role in dissemination of this information. Unlike regulatory documents which are categorically for a restricted audience (regulatory agencies) who are essentially compulsory readers, publication documents are for a wider medical fraternity of healthcare practitioners who are voluntary readers. Therefore, a special effort has to be made for them to captivate their interest. The types of publication writing vary depending on their potential audiences. Publication writing includes, but is not limited to manuscripts for scientific journals, Review articles, posters for conferences and scientific congresses, Advertisement graphics in peer-reviewed journals, training material for sales promotions.

In this chapter, we will give an overview of Manuscripts, Review Papers and Posters which clearly dominate the workload for medical writers.

Manuscripts for Scientific Journals:

Journal manuscripts, which are essentially full articles on findings from a research study, play an important role in dissemination of scientific knowledge. It not only possesses the status of the first public dissemination of newly emerged information, but also the mainstay medium for public dissemination of research findings.

The IMRAD structure

The early structure of journal articles was descriptive, with chronological display of observations. This straightforward style of reporting was appropriate for the science prevalent at that time. As a matter of fact, the practice still prevails for a few scientific documents like Case Studies in Medicines. However, by the second half of 19th century, science began to evolve in a more sophisticated way. Methodology became very important for reproducibility of research. A separate section of methods followed by result, built on the background of Introduction gave way to highly structured IMRAD format.

       I = Introduction (Why was this research undertaken?)

       M = Methods (How was it conducted?)

       R = Results (What was found?)

       A = And (obviously not a section, but a mnemonic connector)

       D = Discussion (What do the findings mean? Why are they important?)

Abstract

The IMRAD structure of an article is preceded by an abstract, which is a summary of the article. It should mention each and every component of the study in 150 -250 words, depending the requirement of the journal. It should state the purpose of the study, basic procedures (selection of study subjects, methodology) main findings, statistical significance, the principal conclusion and implications. It is very important to remember that it is a stand-alone section hence should not contain any abbreviations. Key words (or short phrases) 3 to 10, should be listed covering all the aspects of the study. It is preferable to use terms listed as Medical subject headings (MESH) in Index Medicus (Medline).

Introduction

An introduction in an article is required in order to attract the readers and tell them what to expect. The introduction should provide sufficient information to allow the reader to understand the research and evaluate it's result. It should provide rationale for conducting the study and place the study in the already existing information matrix on the concerned subject. Introduction should be written in present tense because it essentially refers to the existing problem and established knowledge regarding the subject. It is also very important to maintain brevity, to make it crisp and not load with unnecessary information as that may disinterest the reader. Therefore, the author should avoid trivial and unnecessary facts. New information should be presented in a novel and intriguing manner. Pertinent references should be appropriately provided to orient the reader.

Methods

The method section is essential for describing how the research was conducted to ensure reproducibility of the study and give the result the required scientific merit. For a typical clinical research study, an author should provide the following information:

- What type of study was done? (study design)
- On whom the study was done? (subject)
- What was measured? (assessment parameters)
- How the data was analysed? (analysis)

Obviously, this section has to be written in the past-tense. It is ideal to use generic names instead of trade names as far as possible. The two main reasons being, the non-proprietary name is likely to be known all over the world while the proprietary names are familiar in the respective countries and also to avoid advertising, which may happen with the use of trade name. The analysis plan should be included and if needed the rationale for choosing the analytical methods should be discussed.

Result

This is the most important section of the paper. Following are the important features of this section, which should be borne in mind while writing the results of a study:

- The observations have to be summarized and important data have to be highlighted, unlike Clinical Study Report which warrants presentation of all observations.
- This section should contain only actuals and no opinions, unlike the Discussion section.
- The results should be presented in logical sequence in the text, tables and illustrations.
- There should be no hesitation in presenting any negative or unexpected result.

Discussion

The purpose of discussion is to show the relationships among the observed facts. This is the usually the toughest section to write. The discussion should ideally highlight the significance of the study. The essential features of a good discussion are:

- A possible explanation or significance of the result.
- Discuss how the results and interpretation agree or contrast with the already established knowledge.
- State the limitation of the study.
- Explore implications of findings for future research and clinical practice.

Review Paper

A review paper is not an original publication. The purpose of writing a review paper is to review the previously published literature and to put it in some kind of perspective. The subject is fairly general compared to that of research paper. Literature reviews are an essential part of preparation of a review article. They offer critical evaluation of the published papers and often provide important conclusions based on the literature review. They are usually lengthy, generally ranging from 10 to 50 printed pages.

The structure of a review paper is usually different from that of a research paper. Naturally, the Materials and Methods, Results, Discussion arrangement cannot readily be used for the review paper. Nevertheless, a review article may be prepared around the IMRAD structure. The Method section may describe how a literature has ben reviewed . However, unlike original research papers, there are no set organization for the review papers. Depending upon the subject matter, a review paper may have a prodigious Introduction and an extensive and argumentative Discussion. Since review papers are prepared for a wider audience, care must be taken to create an interest for the readers, as they decide to read, skim or skip the rest of the article depending on what they find in the Introduction. Conclusion is also an essential element of a review paper as it has to simplify and summarize a difficult subject to the satisfaction of a wide section of audience, appeasing both the experts and amateurs alike.

Types of Review papers

Before preparing a review article, it is essential to identify the intention of publishing the article. Sometimes it could be a critical evaluation of the management of a therapeutic indication, which would require authoritative and critical evaluation of published literature on the concerned subject. While others may intend to compile and annotate published papers on a particular subject and hence would be more concerned with bibliographic completeness and chronological organization of the papers. Though currently most review papers provide an understanding of a rapidly evolving field and for which only the recent papers are cataloged and evaluated.

Poster Preparation:

In recent years, poster presentation has become quite common in both national and international conferences as these conferences and meetings give a platform to share ideas and discuss new findings.

A scientific poster is a large document that can communicate your research at a scientific meeting and is composed of a short title, an introduction to the relevant issue, overview of the experimental approach and results accompanying some insightful discussion of aforementioned results. An ideal poster should be such that a reader can completely read it in 10 minutes.

The structure of a poster normally should follow the IMRAD format, although the graphic consideration and the need for simplicity should also be kept in mind. A well-designed poster has very little text and more of illustrations. The Introduction should present the problem succinctly, as the poster will fail if it does not have a clear statement of purpose at the beginning. The Method section is generally brief; a sentence or two should be sufficient. The Result is usually the major part of a well-designed poster. Most of the available space is used to illustrate Results. Discussion should be brief, may be even better to skip this section and keep a succinct, well-structured conclusion. Literature citation should be kept at the minimum.

Citation:

What's a citation?

A citation is a brief description of a published or non-published source of literature, used as references in a document. These references provide enough data to enable the reader or reviewer to quickly and easily find the source. These are generally alphanumeric expressions which are listed in the bibliographic reference section in the sequential order as used in the document. The necessity of citation in an intellectual piece of work is listed below:

- Give credit to author of an idea.

- Bring in expert witnesses to support argument.

- Show how the author's theory/idea fits into the web of already existing knowledge on that topic.

- Provide consistency and accuracy for readers/researchers.

What to include in citation?

In a citation, we need to provide knowledge to the reader to be able to locate the original source of document or source of information. The essential information provided in citing a reference is:

WHO?	Name of author(s)
WHEN?	Date of publication
WHAT?	Title
WHERE?	Publisher details (name, volume, location, edition, pages, etc);
	Journal (name, volume, page number(s); or internet address.

There are two elements to the referencing system; firstly an in-text citation giving basic publication details, and secondly an equivalent and matching entry in a reference list giving full details that are required for a reader to locate the original source.

Citation system

Broadly there are three forms of citation: footnotes (or endnotes), source lines, and bibliographies.

Footnotes and endnotes: Both cite the source of references. The footnotes are placed at the bottom of the page while the endnotes appear at the end of the document. The following are the main characteristics of the endnotes and foot notes.

- They are preceded by a number.

- The author's name is in natural order.

- The elements of the citation are separated by commas.

Source Lines: Source lines typically appear under charts, exhibits, tables, and other graphical items. The purpose is to acknowledge the source of the graphic or the data that was used to create it. A source line begins with the word *Source* and continues with the same information that would appear in a footnote or endnote.

Bibliography: A bibliography lists all of the references that were used to create a research paper. The bibliography appears at the end of the paper, after the endnotes, if any. Bibliographies have the following formatting conventions:

- The first author's name is inverted (last name first), and most elements are separated by periods.

- Entries have a special indentation style in which all lines but the first are indented.

- Entries are arranged alphabetically by the author's last name, or by the first word of the title, if no author is listed.

Citation style

Citation styles which are also called style manuals, give instructions and examples of how to create footnotes/ endnotes, in-text citations and bibliographies in research papers. Many of them also include advice on grammar and punctuation, research methods, and overall guidance on formatting the appearance of the final paper.

There are several types of these bibliographic formatting rules. The three main citation styles are the Chicago Manual of Style, the APA and the MLA Styles. However, the most commonly used citation style in Biomedical sciences, is the Vancouver style which is based on MLA style. This chapter limits it's discussion to the most important publication types in Vancouver style as it is the most predominantly used citation style in Biomedical literature. Nevertheless, if the reader wishes to consult the guidelines for other publication type, he/she may refer to Uniform Requirements for Manuscripts Submitted to Biomedical Journals: Sample References <http://www.nlm.nih.gov/bsd/uniform_requirements.html>

Vancouver style:

In-text Citing

A number is allocated to a source in the order in which it is cited in the text. If the source is referred to again, the same number is used. As a general rule, reference numbers should be placed inside the full stops and commas and inside colons and semicolons. However, this may vary according to the requirements of a particular journal.

Example:

There have been efforts to replace mouse inoculation testing with invitro tests, such as enzyme linked immunosorbent assays (57, 60) or polymerase chain reaction (20-22) but these remain experimental. Moir and Jessel maintain "that the sexes are interchangeable".

The author's name can also be integrated into the text.

Example:

American Diabetes Association diagnostic criteria for diabetes were also used based on FPG ≥7.0 mmol/l and/or 2-h glucose ≥11.1 mmol/l. Wiedmeyer.

Superscripts can also be used rather than brackets and more than one reference should be separated by commas.

Example:

The A1C test has recently been recommended for diagnosing diabetes, based on a detailed analysis of its attributes by an international expert committee.

BIBLIOGRAPHIC REFERENCES

References are listed in numerical order in the Reference List at the end of the paper.

Examples of citation of various types of document in the reference are listed below.

Journal Article:

- Journal titles are abbreviated. One has to refer to PubMed Journals Database

- for the correct acceptable abbreviation
  [<http://www.ncbi.nlm.nih.gov/entrez/query.fcgi?db=journals>]

- Only the first words of an article title and words that normally begin with a capital letter are capitalised.

- First 6 authors are listed; thereafter add a et al. after the sixth author.

- If the journal has continuous page numbering, one may omit month/issue number

Elements of a citation:

[Author's surname Initials, Author's surname Initials. Title of article. Title of Journal. (abbreviated). Year of publication Month Date; Volume Number(Issue number): Page numbers.]

Example:

Non-continuous pagination

Smithline HA, Mader TJ, Ali FM, Cocchi MN. Determining pretest probability of DVT: clinical intuition vs. validated scoring systems. N Engl J Med. 2003 Apr 4;21(2):161-2.

Continuous pagination

Gao SR, McGarry M, Ferrier TL, Pallante B, Gasparrini B, Fletcher JR, et al. Effect of cell confluence on production of cloned mice using an inbred embryonic stem cell line. Biol Reprod. 2003;68(2):595-603.

Conference Paper

Elements of a citation

Author's surname Initials. Title of the paper. In: Editor's surname Initials, editor. Title of the Conference; Date of conference; Place of publication: Publisher's name; Year of Publication. p. page numbers.

Anderson JC. Current status of chorion villus biopsy. In: Tudenhope D, Chenoweth J, editors. Proceedings of the 4th Congress of the Australian Perinatal Society; 1986: Brisbane, Queensland: Australian Perinatal Society; 1987. p. 190-6.

Journal article on the internet

Elements of a Citation

Author's surname Initials. Title of article. Abbreviated Title of Journal [serial on the Internet]. Year of publication Month day [cited Year Month Day];Volume Number(Issue number):[about number of pages or screens]. Available from: URL

Abood S. Quality improvement initiative in nursing homes: the ANA acts in an advisory role. Am J Nurs [serial on the Internet]. 2002 Jun [cited 2009Aug 12];102(6):[about 3 p.]. Available from: http://www.nursingworld.org/AJN/2002/june/Wawatch.htm.

Book

- Capitalize the first letter of the first word in the title. The rest of the title is in lower-case, with the exception of proper names (see example 3 below).

- Do not underline the title; do not use italics.

Elements of Citation:

Author/Editor/Compiler's surname Initials. Title of the book. # ed.[if not 1st] Place of publication: Publisher's name; Year of publication.

Carlson BM.Humanembryologyand development Biology. 3rd ed. St.Louis: Mosby;2004

Chapter in a book:

Elements of a Citation

Author's surname Initials. Title of chapter. In: Editor's surname Initials, editor. Title of the book. # ed.[if not 1st] Place of publication: Publisher's name; Year of publication. p. #. [page numbers of chapter]

- Abbreviated page numbers to p. (e.g., p. 14-26)

- Abbreviate numbers where appropriate eg p. 122-8.

Blaxter PS, Farnsworth TP. Social health and class inequalities. In: Carter C, Peel JR, editors. Equalities and inequalities in health. 2nd ed. London: Academic Press; 1976. p. 165-78.

Web site/homepage

Element of Citation

Author/Editor/Organisation's name. Title of the page [homepage on the Internet]. Place of publication.

Canadian Cancer Society [homepage on the Internet]. Toronto: The Society; 2006 [updated 2006 May 12; cited 2006 Oct 17]. Available from: http://www.cancer.ca/.

Importance of grammar in effective writing:

Any writing, scientific or nonscientific, begins with ideas which relate to one another. An author chooses words to express his/her ideas and chooses arrangement of words (syntax) to build relationships between ideas. To arrange these syntaxes into phrases, clauses and sentences, the author needs to obey the grammar and punctuation rules. However useful and critical an idea may be, it will have no impact if the writing is peppered with grammatical errors. Consequently, it will fail to effectively communicate to the target audience. The path to 'good writing' is to write well-formed sentences keeping the structure simple.

Ten Commandments of Good Writing:

1. Keep it simple.
2. Use Active voice.
3. Each pronoun should agree with their antecedent.
4. A sentence should not end with preposition.
5. Verbs have to agree with the subjects.
6. Don't use double negatives.
7. Don't split infinitives.
8. Clauses should be joined by a conjunction.
9. Don't use a long string of qualifiers in before a noun.
10. Use correct case (upper case or small case) and be consistent throughout.

How to get started on a writing assignment:

Writer's block is the one of the first issues which has to be tackled by the writer. It is very important to plan the structure of the document before getting started. The followings are few steps which would help a writer to get started on the project and manage the flow of the document.

1. The writer needs to focus his/her thoughts by writing the summary first, even for articles that don't require one. The process may start with outlining the draft with headings.

2. The first sentence of a paragraph usually sets the tone for that paragraph. It is better not to have unlinked ideas in the same paragraph.

3. A paragraph must consist of more than one sentence.

4. Try to make the ideas within each section flow together.

5. Don't put things in the wrong section or sub-section.

6. When appropriate, keep the order of ideas the same in different sections of the article.

7. Avoid contradiction or repetition in different sections of the article.

8. Aim for simplicity, as the target audience may not be technically as knowledgeable as the writer

Skills required to be a medical writer:

A medical writer, thus, should possess a right balance of scientific understanding and rhetorical skills for language. Besides professional qualifications, medical writers are expected to have a good understanding of basic statistics and strong computer skills. Good networking skills and ability to multi- task make a writer more competent and successful.

The fundamental purpose of medical writing is not simply presenting information and thought but it's effective communication to the target audience. It is very important for the target audience to perceive what the researchers want to convey. Therefore, the crux of good writing is writing a document keeping the target audience in mind, reaching their level of expectation and placing the piece of writing in context of their understanding.

INDEX

***